GOLDEN
EARRINGS

ALSO BY BELINDA ALEXANDRA

Tuscan Rose
White Gardenia

GOLDEN EARRINGS

A Novel

BELINDA ALEXANDRA

G

GALLERY BOOKS

New York   London   Toronto   Sydney   New Delhi

G

Gallery Books
An Imprint of Simon & Schuster, Inc.
1230 Avenue of the Americas
New York, NY 10020

Copyright © 2011 by Belinda Alexandra
Originally published in 2011 by HarperCollinsPublishers Australia Pty Limited.

First Gallery Books trade paperback edition August 2015

GALLERY BOOKS and colophon are registered trademarks of Simon & Schuster, Inc.

For information about special discounts for bulk purchases, please contact Simon & Schuster Special Sales at 1-866-506-1949 or business@simonandschuster.com.

The Simon and Schuster Speakers Bureau can bring authors to your live event. For more information or to book an event, contact the Simon & Schuster Speakers Bureau at 1-866-248-3049 or visit our website at www.simonspeakers.com.

Manufactured in the United States of America

10 9 8 7 6 5 4 3 2 1

ISBN 978-1-4767-9033-6
ISBN 978-1-4767-9035-0 (ebook)

For Selwa

Part I

ONE

Paloma
Paris, 1975

It was 24 November, the day after the funeral of Generalisimo Franco, the dictator of Spain, that I saw my first ghost. The morning started off ordinarily enough. I woke at six o'clock and stretched my arms and legs before slipping out of bed. It was still dark and I turned on the bedside lamp with its floral shade. By its mottled light, I pulled on my leotard and tights. My hairpins and headband were in the dresser drawer. I fixed my hair away from my face quickly and by habit, before guarding myself against the late autumn chill by wrapping my dressing gown around me and putting on my slippers.

The hallway was dark, but I didn't need the light to guide me along it towards the kitchen. I crept past Mamie's bedroom. My grandmother—whom I called 'Mamie' when we spoke French and 'Iaia' when we spoke Catalan—was a heavy sleeper and a herd of bulls wouldn't have disturbed her, but it was guilt that made me move quietly. Mamie said that no ballerina should even think of getting out of bed before nine o'clock, let alone practising before that time. But I was meeting Gaby at the café during her break in lectures, and I had classes to give in the afternoon. Despite the events of the previous summer, I could not give up my daily practise of barre and centre work, even if it meant rising early. I'd rather do without sleep and food than miss my routine of *pliés*, *tendus*, *ronds de jambe* and stretching. They were as essential to me as breathing.

I switched on the light above the stove, careful not to wake my cockatiel, Diaghilev, who was still quiet in his covered cage. The Australian parrot with the Russian name had been a present to me from Mamie for my eighteenth birthday and was a chatterer. As soon as the morning light entered the kitchen he would be whistling bars from Mozart's 'Alla Turca'. I turned on the tap and filled a saucepan with water. There was a copy of *El Diario*, the Spanish émigré newsletter, on the bench. The newsletter was directed at those refugees who had fled Spain for France in 1939, after the Civil War. Pictures of Franco from his youth to his old age were on the cover. The article said that the dictator, who had died two weeks shy of his eighty-third birthday, would be buried at a memorial commemorating the War Dead. The paragraph was crossed out in red pen. Next to it Mamie had written: 'The *Fascist* War Dead!' I could feel the vehemence in her scrawl. It was not her usual ladylike penmanship and, if there weren't only the two of us in the apartment, I would have thought someone else had written it.

I stood by the window while I waited for the coffee to brew. The wheaty smell of fresh bread drifted from the bakery across the street. I lifted the lace curtain and saw a queue of eager housewives waiting on the pavement outside. It was passion that made them early risers, like me. Their pursuit of the finest *pain frais* to feed their families enabled them to go without sleep. Dance affected me the same way. Nothing gave me more satisfaction than to unfold myself into a beautiful *arabesque* or execute a graceful *grand jeté,* even if I had to practise from morning until night seven days a week to do it.

A bittersweet aroma wafted around the kitchen, signalling that the coffee was ready. I let the curtain fall, noticing for the first time that its hem was frayed. I reached for a cup and saucer from the odd assortment of floral and plain designs in the cupboard. When I sat down to drink the honey-thick brew, my lip touched something rough on the china and I saw the cup was chipped. Mamie was fastidiously neat, but it was my mother who would never have tolerated things like chipped cups or frayed curtains. 'Beauty is always in the details, Paloma,' she used to say. But Mama wasn't here any more, and my grandmother and I muddled along in our chipped and frayed existence without her.

There were two entrances to my grandmother's ballet studio: one was directly from our kitchen; the second was next to the landing in the corridor outside. I took the key from the hook on the back of the kitchen door and entered the studio. Daybreak was starting to filter through the windows that overlooked the courtyard of our apartment building, so I didn't turn on the lights. Although the floor was swept and mopped daily, the closed air was choked with the scent of dust and mould that was common to old buildings in Paris.

I took my ballet slippers from the cupboard and sat on the floor to tie the ribbons. While I was tucking in the ends, I thought about Mamie's angry scribbling on the newsletter. When I was a child, I had often asked my grandmother about her Spanish past, but her lips would purse and the light would disappear from her eyes. 'Perhaps when you are older,' she would reply. I could see I was causing her pain and learned not to touch on the subject of her life before she came to Paris.

I left my dressing gown and bed slippers on the piano stool. Our accompanist, Madame Carré, would be in later to play Beethoven and Schubert for our students. But I liked to practise on my own in silence, following my body rather than the beat. From my *demi-pliés*, I moved to my *grand-pliés*, relishing the feeling of strength and flexibility in my legs. I cringed when a memory from last June's debacle at the ballet school tried to force its way into my thoughts. I closed my eyes and pushed the image of me standing in front of the noticeboard, bathed in sweat and with nausea rising in my stomach, out of my mind.

Years of training had taught me to focus on a single objective until I achieved it, and I was not going to give up on my dreams now.

After an hour at the barre, I was ready to do some centre practise. I positioned myself in front of the mirrored wall at the front of the studio and was about to commence a *tendu* combination when suddenly the daylight outside flickered. It was such a strange phenomenon that I lost my concentration. A thunderstorm so early in the morning? In November? I moved towards the window, perplexed. That was when I saw her, standing in the courtyard as if she was waiting for someone to arrive. I didn't realise that she was a ghost at first but I wondered—because of her black wavy hair and the proud way that she held her chin—whether she was Spanish. The woman wasn't anyone I recognised from Mamie's collection of former refugees who occasionally gathered in our apartment. My initial impression was that she was a mother coming to enquire about lessons for her child on her way to work.

I opened the window and called to her, '*Bonjour, Madame! Un moment, s'il vous plaît.*'

I grabbed my leg warmers and coat from the cupboard, and slipped some loose boots over my ballet shoes. Before I headed out into the corridor, I picked up a leaflet for our school that gave the times of the classes. It was only when I was halfway down the stairs that it occurred to me that the courtyard door should have still been locked. How had the woman got inside? We didn't have a concierge: my grandfather had never believed in them. He'd viewed anyone outside of the family as a potential spy.

I reached the ground floor and opened the door to the courtyard. The cold air bit my face and I shivered. I couldn't see the woman. Where had she gone? Then I felt someone watching me. I turned and saw her standing by the disused well. My breath caught in my throat. She emanated a quality that reminded me of the great *étoiles* of the Paris Ballet: majesty. Her face was a slightly offset oval, and her nose above her strong, red mouth was broad and flat. But her eyes . . . I had never seen such eyes. They were like two black shells shimmering under the sea. It was their depth that made me realise the woman was not of this world.

She moved slowly towards me, her arm extended from her cloak with the grace of a dancer. Her hand hovered near mine as if she wanted to give me something. Without thinking, I opened my palm. Two objects dropped into it. I glanced down and saw a pair of golden hooped earrings. I looked from my palm to the woman, but she had disappeared as suddenly as she had arrived, leaving only the fading echo of her footsteps and the earrings I held in my hand.

Two

Evelina

*M*y dearest sister,
 So the monster is finally dead! Let them give Franco's body all the honours they want, for his soul will rot in hell, along with those other devils Hitler and Mussolini! Now the leaders of Europe and America can pay homage to the man who took their help without repayment, and used their policies of non-intervention to destroy the legitimate government of Spain and murder thousands of people. Do they not realise how much Franco was hated? That he relied on repression to rule? Franco's death, while welcome, brings back too much darkness for me. Perhaps, in time, more light will illuminate what, for the present, I can't bear to see or remember. They say that now he is gone, a new Spain will emerge. But we have heard that promise before. Even here in my refuge in France, I never feel entirely safe. Or for you, far away in Australia.

 You asked how Paloma is faring. I fear that my granddaughter has had too many blows in her young life: the death of my darling Julieta, the disappointment in her father, the misfortune regarding her graduation from the ballet school. Today when I rose, Paloma was already dressed. She moved about the kitchen with a stunned expression on her face, dropping things, as if something had unnerved her. Although she copies Catherine Deneuve's bouffant hairstyle and accents her golden brown eyes with liner, she looked so young and vulnerable in her velvet coat and scarf that I almost wanted to sit her on my lap and feed her bread with tomato, as I did when she was a child. She was hurrying to meet her friend who is studying at the Sorbonne. When Paloma turned to say goodbye, I was tempted to ask her what had happened to make her so agitated, but I kept silent. She does not share everything with me these days. When she suffers a disappointment, she shrinks into her own world, avoiding contact with those who might force her to face reality. She still practises six or seven hours a day, and examines the post when it arrives as if all that happened last June might be reversed and she will still be offered a place with the Paris Opera Ballet. That damned Arielle Marineau. She always hated Julieta, and now that her rival is gone, she takes her revenge on the innocent daughter. Wouldn't be able to carry the load of a professional dancer—whoever heard of such nonsense? Paloma has undergone the most vigorous training since her childhood and is destined to be an étoile. Marineau wields too much power, and although it must have been obvious to the other examiners that Paloma is special, they are too terrified of upsetting the Opera's ballet mistress. That is the world of dance: beauty and treachery.

'Paloma,' I tell her, 'this is life. You make a plan and someone stops you. You must not give in to defeat. Find another way to your dream.' The Paris Opera is not the only ballet company—and she was made offers by the scouts from New York and London. But I am not sure that she even hears any of what I am saying. It is as if she thinks the only way to keep her mother's memory alive is to follow in her footsteps: Julieta excelled at the School of the Paris Opera Ballet, so she must too; Julieta became a première danseuse at nineteen and an étoile at twenty, so she must do the same, even though such rapid progression is rare. And so it goes. Paloma does not see that she is a different type of dancer to her mother. Julieta had superhuman physical strength—my poor darling even refused morphine until the very end. But Paloma . . . well, you have never had the experience of seeing her perform: this slender, quiet girl who comes to life on the stage, moving all with the beauty and delicacy of her performance. One's heart could break with it. But what can I do? The more I talk, the more she retreats. So now I say nothing. I simply protect her from anything that might upset her fragile equilibrium or stir up her already anxious mind. I am terrified that anything that causes her too much excitement will push her over the edge. I can only pray and hope that time will heal.

It grows late and my eyes are weaker than they used to be. I will stop here, but I promise to write again soon.

With kisses and love,
Evelina

THREE

Paloma

'*Mon Dieu*, Paloma!' cried Gaby, staring at me with her electric-blue eyes. 'A ghost?'

I glanced around the rue Mouffetard café, where we sat waiting for our coffee to arrive. The sudden influx of students from the Sorbonne hadn't disturbed the man next to us from his contemplation of his newspaper and I was glad to see Gaby's outburst hadn't either.

'Incredible!' she went on. 'It is fascinating!' Her face was lit up with curiosity.

I had been worried that Gaby's studies in law and political science might have turned her into a cynic, and had half-expected her to question my sanity when I related my account of the morning's otherworldly visitor. As for me, my hands were still shaking and I'd missed my stop on the Métro because I'd been replaying in my mind how the apparition had vanished so suddenly.

'Who could she be?' Gaby asked.

'I have no idea,' I replied.

'But what does it mean?' Gaby ran her hand through her chocolate-brown hair. 'When a ghost comes, it is supposed to have some unfinished business to conclude—or it has come to give a warning!'

I fingered the earrings in my jacket pocket. I had no doubt that the woman's spirit had meant to give them specifically to me. But why? I hadn't told Gaby about the earrings yet; how the laws of nature had been interrupted. I had made up my mind I would only show them to her if she believed my story about the ghost first.

Out of the corner of my eye, I saw the young, lithe waiter weaving his way between the tables with our coffees. We paused in our conversation as he put the cups down. After placing a serviette in front of each of us, he turned to go, but at that moment Gaby looked up. Always beautiful, she was especially ravishing today in her bell-bottomed pinstriped trousers and the floral mini-kimono she was wearing under her open coat. She was also fashionably braless and her small but shapely breasts jiggled along with her bangles each time she moved. The waiter was mesmerised.

'Would you care for anything else, *mesdemoiselles*?' he asked. 'Would a *baguette* or some soup tempt you? A *croque-monsieur* perhaps?' He addressed us both, out of politeness, but didn't even glance at me.

'Oh no, no,' said Gaby, flashing a vibrant smile. 'I'm watching my figure.'

The waiter stood there for a moment, opening and closing his mouth. Gaby's figure was obviously fascinating to him as well.

I leaned back in my chair. I was aching to show Gaby the earrings, but I had learned to be patient whenever a man interrupted our conversation. I often wished I could be like her—so carefree, so charming, so flirtatious. But I couldn't; where she was a complete extrovert, I was hopelessly trapped in my shell.

The waiter was doing his best to persuade Gaby to meet him after work, but I knew he wouldn't succeed. She was flirtatious but choosy, and he wasn't her type. She liked her men sporty. So while Gaby, in her usual charming way, flattered the waiter and at the same time quashed any hopes he entertained for an afternoon tryst, I looked at my hands and thought about why I was choosing to tell her about the ghost, rather than Mamie.

Making friends was not something I was good at, but I'd known Gaby since we'd met at Mamie's ballet school, before I was accepted into the School of the Paris Opera Ballet. Gaby had been a promising ballet student too, but then she hit puberty and her love of dance gave way to a keen interest in boys. Sometimes I believed that Gaby sincerely liked my company—she was an excellent listener with that talent of making everyone she talked to feel fascinating. At other times I'd find myself wondering if she only kept up her acquaintance with me in order to practise her Spanish, which she needed to realise her ambition of entering the French diplomatic service. She certainly wasn't my closest confidante: that was Mamie. But I knew if I told Mamie about the ghost she would think I'd gone insane with all the strain of the past year. And I had to tell someone.

I breathed in the heady air of the café—coffee, wine, garlic, bread and spicy cigarette smoke. These were the smells I associated with the Latin Quarter. I liked to walk around this part of the Left Bank, looking at the markets and bookstalls, and stopping at the record stores to listen to the Rolling Stones and Bryan Ferry. Although many of the streets had been tarred over after the student riots of 1968, the cobblestones of rue Mouffetard were still intact. That's why I always met Gaby at the café on the corner: the place was steeped in history.

The waiter tenderly dispatched to dream of what might have been, Gaby turned back to me. 'So tell me more about the ghost,' she said, taking a sip of her *espresso*.

I held her gaze for a moment, my hand near my pocket. Up until now, the ghost had been an interesting mystery, like a premonition come true or an eerily accurate astrological chart. Once I showed Gaby the earrings, the matter would escalate to a different level: we would both be forced to accept the reality of the apparition; or Gaby would think I was making the whole thing up.

I drew a breath and slipped my fingers into my jacket pocket. 'Well,' I said, 'there is more to this story—'

'*Bonjour!*'

Another interruption. This time it was Marcel, Gaby's latest boyfriend. I let the earrings drop back into my pocket.

'*Bonjour!*' Gaby replied, returning Marcel's kisses. I greeted him too, hoping he was just passing by. Despite the incongruity of their appearances—Gaby in her flamboyant clothes and Marcel in his Lacoste shirt and jacket—it seemed that wherever Gaby went these days, Marcel came too. I had been pleasantly surprised to find her waiting for me at the café alone.

'What's up?' asked Marcel, lighting a cigarette and signalling to a waitress to bring him coffee. He leaned back in his chair and my hope of having Gaby to myself faded.

'Paloma has seen a ghost,' said Gaby. 'In her courtyard.'

If Gaby had grabbed the butter knife and plunged it into my stomach, she could not have caused me more pain. This was something I had intended to confide only in her. *Our* secret.

'Ah,' said Marcel, blowing out a stream of smoke and flashing me a condescending smile. 'That's Paloma's Spanish blood. All Spaniards believe they are haunted by ghosts. A Spaniard without a ghost is like Paris without the Eiffel Tower: one can't exist without the other.'

I grimaced. I wanted to tell him that he didn't know what he was talking about. I was only half-Spanish—my father was . . . *is* . . . French. And my ghost was real. Not a figment of my imagination. Besides, the Eiffel Tower had been built in 1889, and Paris had existed long before then. But I said nothing because I didn't want to upset Gaby.

Despite the besotted way she looked at Marcel, Gaby must have realised he was being insulting. She changed the subject to current events in Spain.

'Everyone in the lecture this morning was talking about the implications of Franco's death. They predict Spain will declare a state of emergency, and that the students and workers will protest. Professor Audret thinks Republican supporters who have been imprisoned since the Civil War might be released as an appeasement to the people.'

Marcel smoothed his ash-blond hair. 'But Juan Carlos has been designated King. The monarchy has been restored and the dictatorship is over, as Franco promised. The Spanish people should be happy now.'

Gaby cast a glance at me. 'Perhaps they don't want a monarchy,' she replied. 'Perhaps they want what they had before the war: a democracy—like France.'

'Pfff,' said Marcel, taking another drag of his cigarette. 'The Spanish couldn't handle a democracy . . . that's why they had a war. They are not like the French. The Republicans lost the fight because they were divided.'

I held my tongue but inwardly I was fuming. I was used to this sort of condescension by the French. Marcel's family had a holiday apartment on the Costa Brava: all he knew of Spain was sun and cheap food and labour. I doubted he ever gave a thought to the police interrogations many suffered; the prisoners who were hung upside down by their feet. The Spanish government might tell the foreign press that political 'enemies' were treated humanely, but many of them were garrotted. If Mamie were with us, I knew what she would have told Marcel: 'The Republicans lost the war because the Germans and Italians helped Franco with planes and troops, while the British and French stood by and did nothing.' But I found Marcel impossible to engage in discussion. Any comment I made elicited that belittling smile of his, and I would rather remain silent than be subjected to it. For someone who was still living with his parents, he had an irritating habit of speaking as if he were a worldly expert on everything. But Gaby didn't see that. Or if she did, she ignored it.

After ordering and eating a salad *niçoise* with French fries, and smoking another cigarette, Marcel announced that he had an appointment with his supervisor.

Gaby glanced at her watch. 'I didn't realise the time,' she said, standing up. 'My next lecture starts in a quarter of an hour.'

Marcel paid for the food and coffees. '*Salut*, Paloma!' he said to me. 'Beware of any more ghosts.'

That smug smile again; I could have punched him.

Gaby kissed me on both cheeks. 'We'll meet again next week, *oui*?'

The moment to show her the earrings had passed. I doubted she would even ask about the ghost when we next met.

I watched Gaby and Marcel walk down the street arm in arm. Unlike Gaby, my experience with boys was nil. Contrary to popular belief, not all the male students at the Ballet School were homosexual, but with all of us pushed to extremes for limited places, nobody was thinking about anything except dance. When you checked out a male at dance school, the only question you were asking yourself was whether he was strong enough to lift you gracefully. I thought about the private lessons I had arranged with Mademoiselle Louvet in order to prepare myself for the next round of auditions. I simply had to get into the Opera Ballet. I was ruined for anything else. A normal life was no longer a possibility for me: I hadn't had the upbringing for one.

'Why the long face?'

I turned to see an elderly woman looking at me. Her hair was dyed flame red and her pencilled eyebrows stood out on her heavily powdered complexion. She had spoken with a Spanish accent but she wasn't anybody I knew.

The woman placed her hand on my arm. 'You're young! You're pretty! You should do something to make you happy. Did you ever think about dance lessons?'

I was too taken aback by the irony to respond as the woman thrust a leaflet into my hand. It was a flyer for a Spanish dance school in Montparnasse: Académie de Flamenco Carmen Rivas.

'Flamenco lessons?' I said.

'*Sí.*' The woman grinned. 'Come, you'll enjoy yourself. Make nice friends.' She gave me a little wave before heading off down the street.

I made my way towards the Métro station. Character dancing had not been my strength at ballet school, which had surprised my teachers because I was half-Spanish. Perhaps I'd been put off by Mamie's attitude towards flamenco. I remembered the look of disdain on her face when we had come across a group of street performers on rue de la Huchette. 'But you're Spanish!' I had said to her. 'I'm *Catalan*,' she'd corrected me. 'Flamenco is from Andalusia. Franco forced the image of bullfighting and flamenco dancers on the whole of Spain, but they are not Catalan traditions.'

I was about to toss the leaflet in the nearest street bin when the earrings in my pocket tingled, heating up my skin despite the two layers of clothing between them and my leg. The effect reminded me of when I put Diaghilev, my cockatiel, on my finger and scratched his head. His little feet would heat up with happiness like two hotplates. I looked at the flyer again. *Come, you'll enjoy yourself . . . make nice friends.* The beginners' class was on a night that I didn't teach at Mamie's school. I was a devotee of classical ballet, but with the Opera Ballet branching out into more modern choreography, maybe an interest in different forms of dance would look good on my résumé? I tucked the leaflet into my pocket. If I decided to go, I'd have to avoid telling Mamie.

On the way from the Métro stop to our apartment on rue Spontini, I stopped by the newsstand to pick up Mamie's journals. Micheline, the vendor, was sitting in her domed kiosk like a bird in a nest, absorbed in a copy of *L'Humanité* and surrounded by postcards, magazines and packets of cigarettes.

'*Bonjour!*' I said.

Micheline lifted her gaze from the newspaper and pushed her grey curls behind her ears. 'Ah, *bonjour*, Paloma,' she replied, standing up and smoothing down her crocheted vest. She placed Mamie's copies of *Le Monde* and *Libération* on the counter. 'I have something for you too today,' she said, reaching to the shelf behind her. She passed me a copy of *Paris Match* with Rudolf Nureyev on the cover. 'When do you start with the Ballet?' she asked innocently. 'I want to come and see your first performance. I'll tell everyone, "I've known her since she was a little girl, coming to pick up the newspapers for her grandmother. And here she is now, a star!"'

'Soon,' I told her. 'But remember, I only start with the *corps de ballet*. It will take a lot of work to become a *première danseuse*, let alone an étoile.'

I dismissed my qualms about the lie. I hadn't discussed my failed audition with anyone except Mamie. After my record at the Ballet School, everyone had expected me to breeze through graduation. That I would be accepted as a *quadrille* had been taken for granted by my teachers and fellow students. I hadn't told Mamie yet about my intention to audition again the following year. Mamie said that as long as Arielle Marineau was the ballet mistress at the Opera, I would not have a chance of being accepted. She had tried to convince me to accept the places I had been offered with companies in New York and London, promising to come with me if I did so, but for me there was only one ballet company. It was the Paris Opera Ballet or nothing.

'Whatever you do, it will be magnificent,' said Micheline, her broad mouth forming into a grin. 'Let me know as soon as you get the good news,' she went on, tying the newspapers together with string to make them easier to carry. 'I'll open a bottle of champagne.'

The sincerity of her good wishes touched my heart.

She handed me the package, then opened her mouth in alarm. 'Watch out! It's her again!' she said, nodding her chin in the direction of the street. 'Your stepmother.'

I turned to see Audrey—Hermès scarf around her neck, hair impeccably twisted into a roll—pulling up to the kerb in her Citroën. She had no reason to be in this area other than to pester me. Luckily she didn't appear to have spotted me yet.

'She's not my stepmother,' I told Micheline. 'She's just someone who married Papa.' I gave Micheline two quick kisses. 'I'd better go. I'll see you tomorrow.'

I calculated that if I walked quickly but steadily, I might avoid attracting Audrey's attention and reach the apartment before her. Once I was safely inside, Mamie was hardly going to insist that I open the door to 'that woman'. It used to be my father who launched these surprise attacks, but I hadn't seen him for months.

I was almost at the entrance to our building when I heard Audrey's heels clacking behind me. 'Paloma!' she called out.

I kept walking. How had she caught up with me? Had she *run*?

'Paloma!'

There was a huddle of pre-school children on the pavement, waiting to cross the road with their teachers. The last thing I wanted was a scene. But since it was impossible to avoid Audrey now, I decided my best defence was to be aggressive. I turned around.

'What are you doing here?' I asked. 'Are you following me?'

Audrey's forest-green eyes were unfazed. She waved her hand and I caught a whiff of the woody notes of her Rive Gauche perfume. '*Bien sûr*,' she said. 'Of course I am following you.' She looked at me with the same air of unruffled authority I imagined she used on the staff at her publicity company.

'Why?'

'Why?' she repeated, emitting a sharp laugh and shrugging her shoulders. 'Because you don't return your father's phone calls, because you don't answer his letters, because you refuse to see him. That's why. You are breaking his heart.'

I'm breaking *his* heart? I thought. What about the way he broke mine? Six months after my mother died, he remarried! A new wife. A new stepson. A new life! My mother's memory swept away as if their marriage—and her long, painful death—had never happened.

'Look,' said Audrey, reaching into her Louis Vuitton bag and pulling out a music cassette. 'He wanted to give you this.'

I shook my head. I felt a mounting outrage that I was still being drawn into this farce, despite having told my father that I wanted nothing more to do with him. I had an urge to grab the cassette and throw it in the gutter. Proud, self-confident Audrey in her peach satin suit must have loved my father a great deal to humiliate herself by approaching me. I had nothing but disdain for her. Six months! Had she been chasing after my father while the surgeons were removing my mother's tumour-ridden insides? But as suddenly as my anger flared, it dissipated. I felt drained. The appearance of the ghost had distracted me. I didn't have the energy to be furious any more. Tears pricked my eyes but I quickly blinked them away.

Audrey's face remained hard but something in her manner shifted. 'Go on, take it,' she said.

For a moment, it was as if we were two actresses in a play and Audrey was whispering my cue to me. It was typical of my father to make a recording when we could no longer share words. We had always communicated better through music. I took the cassette from her without looking at what was on it, and was about to shove it into my coat pocket when I remembered the earrings. I tossed it into my bag instead.

'Your father's fiftieth birthday is in January,' Audrey said, mistaking my acceptance of the cassette as a softening of my stance. 'I'm throwing a party for him. You know it would mean everything to him for you to be there.'

The nerve of her! Throwing a party? Did she think she was Mama? I stepped away from Audrey and put my hand on the entry door. 'He has friends,' I said over my shoulder. 'He has *you*. He doesn't need me.' I strode into the foyer and let the heavy door slam shut behind me.

'You're wrong,' Audrey called after me. 'He needs you more than anyone!'

I stood in the foyer a moment, trying to catch my breath. Why couldn't Audrey—and my father—leave me alone? *He needed me.* It was always about my father's needs first. Always! My mind flew back to the choking grief I had felt at my mother's funeral, while my father sat dry-eyed in the car next to me, talking about his upcoming concert in Berlin and humming the theme of Schumann's 'Piano Concerto in A Minor' under his breath. Was it because of Audrey that he had been so composed? Because he knew that he wouldn't be alone? I leaned against the staircase, shutting out the earlier memories of my father's deep, resonant voice; his promises to always protect his 'darling little girl'.

Our apartment could be reached from the foyer, or from a set of stairs at the rear of the courtyard. I decided to go through the courtyard, half-hopeful and half-afraid that the ghost would be waiting for me again. But there was no one—or nothing—there.

A wrought-iron chair stood amongst the pots of the herb garden. It was cold to touch, but I sat down on it anyway. The apartment building, with its iron balconies and mansard roofs, had been erected in the nineteenth century. I looked up at the stone walls and the dormer windows, built by workmen long before there were formal unions and compulsory safety equipment. A breeze tickled my cheek and I felt the flow of history pass through me. How many people had lived in this building over the past century? It must have been hundreds. I saw men leaning on fireplaces; women chatting in parlours; maids opening windows to air rooms; children and dogs tumbling along corridors in games of hide-and-seek. Yet, with all that record of life, I had seen no ghosts here except for today: that one Spanish spectre. Everyone else's presence had vanished. It occurred to me that in one hundred years' time, if the human race hadn't perished from an atomic war, another woman might look up at the windows and feel no trace of me.

The sound of something scraping jolted me from my thoughts. I turned, but it was only Mamie's friend Conchita coming through from the foyer with her mail.

'Ah, *hola*!' she said, when she saw me.

As usual, she was looking chic in a two-piece blouson dress and matching salmon-pink shoes. She was nearly seventy years of age, and had the knack of giving the appearance of wealth while not having a cent to her name. She'd replaced the missing diamonds in her wedding jewellery with white paste so her rings still sparkled with brilliant effect, and she remained impeccably groomed by giving the girls at the beauty salon deportment lessons in exchange for her weekly hair and nail appointments.

'Conchita's never accepted her change in circumstances,' my mother had once explained to me. 'And Mamie hasn't the heart to break her fragile grip on reality. Conchita's always been taken care of; she has no idea how to look after herself.' It was Mamie who organised the twice-weekly deliveries to Conchita's apartment from the grocer and baker. 'Otherwise, I'm afraid she uses the meagre life insurance payments her husband left her to buy more hats instead of feeding herself,' my mother had said.

Mamie owned three of the apartments in our building. Owning property in Paris's sixteenth arrondissement should have made us wealthy, but we only appeared so on paper. The apartment that I shared with Mamie was mainly taken up by the ballet studio, so our living area was only forty square metres; and the apartment on the ground floor was given rent-free to Conchita. The other apartment, a three-bedroom place where I used to live with my father and mother, was let out to an American businessman and his family, but the rent from it went into my grandmother's fund for supporting elderly Spaniards who had never been able to re-build their lives after coming to Paris when the Civil War ended. The building had never had a concierge. Having been betrayed by that Parisian icon during the Second World War, my grandfather and the owners of the other apartments, a Jewish family, had agreed not to have one. 'It's better to bear the inconvenience or be robbed than to be betrayed,' my grandfather used to say when visitors complained about having to call from a telephone booth if the front door was locked.

'Would you like to come in for a cup of rosemary and lemon tisane?' Conchita asked me.

I had an hour before my first afternoon class. I'd intended to write down the events of the morning so that they would remain real to me. But I hadn't visited Conchita for a while, and I knew she was lonely. Although she wasn't as affectionate with me as Mamie, I'd grown up with her. She'd played dress ups with me when my parents were away on tour and had taught me how to put on make-up properly.

'Of course,' I said, taking her spindly arm.

Like its inhabitant, Conchita's tiny ground-floor abode exuded a kind of standoffish elegance with its encaustic tiled floors, chandeliers and lace curtains. It was morbid too. On top of her radio cabinet, Conchita kept two framed pictures: the first was of her French husband, Pierre, embracing their rosy-cheeked baby sons; the second was a newspaper clipping detailing a fatal car accident. With these two pictures, Conchita told the story of the events that had punctuated her life in France. When the few people who ever entered the apartment—the doctor, the occasional salesman, a delivery boy—saw the pictures, they knew what questions not to ask.

There was no photograph of Conchita's eldest son, Feliu, nor of his Spanish father. I had seen Feliu a few times over the years. He drove trucks through Europe for a French transport company and when he was in Paris he sometimes visited Mamie, but never his mother. He was friendly enough to me, but always gave me the impression that he was something like a sparrow: happy to visit, but as eager to flit away.

'Why doesn't Feliu see his mother when he comes?' I asked Mamie after one of these visits. 'It must hurt her.'

'It's complicated,' said Mamie. 'He left home at fourteen, and he and Conchita have never been close. But he always leaves me some money to help with her expenses, so he still has a sense of duty towards her.'

I guessed the root of the rift had something to do with the Civil War, and therefore it was never likely to be revealed to me.

While the water for the tisane was boiling, Conchita turned on the radio. The announcer was translating a statement that Richard Nixon had given in honour of Franco. 'A loyal friend and ally of the United States,' the former American president had called him. 'A true leader.'

Conchita listened with tears in her eyes. 'He was not as bad a man as your grandmother thinks, Paloma,' she muttered. 'Franco wanted to make Spain great.'

I sat back in the upholstered chair and wondered how Conchita and my grandmother had remained friends when their views of Franco were so polarised. But they never seemed to discuss politics, and Conchita didn't attend Mamie's gatherings of émigrés.

Conchita and I drank the tisane together and kept our conversation to the weather and the new *chocolatier* that was opening near place Victor Hugo. I promised that I would be first in line outside its Art Nouveau windows to buy her favourite coated almonds.

'Ah,' said Conchita, clapping her hands with delight. 'You are always so good to me.'

When it was time for me to go, she accompanied me to the front door. I bent to kiss her and the leaflet for the Spanish dance school dropped onto the tiles.

'What's this?' she asked, picking it up. Her eyes narrowed. 'Flamenco lessons?' She gave me a sharp look, which took me by surprise.

'I'm thinking of taking lessons to improve my character dancing,' I explained. 'And it might be fun.'

Conchita's back stiffened. I wondered if she had the same objections that Mamie did to a 'low-brow' art that had been forced on the Catalans.

I shrugged awkwardly. 'I know it's not Catalan,' I said, 'but it could be good for my repertoire. It's very expressive. Please don't tell Mamie. She doesn't seem to like it. I guess because it's not from her part of Spain.'

Conchita cleared her throat. 'Yes, of course,' she said, pursing her lips as if she was trying to contain what she really wanted to say. 'Ballerinas need inspiration from other forms of dance. I understand. It's not the culture you are looking for, but the style.'

She opened the door for me and I stepped out into the corridor. As I turned towards the stairway, I heard her say in a small voice from behind the door, 'It's not because she's Catalan that your grandmother hates flamenco.'

FOUR

Celestina
Barcelona, 1909

You who judge me: come! Let me tell you a story. Let me take you to a part of Barcelona not glorified by intellectuals for Gaudí's revolutionary architecture, for its impressive paintings and sculptures, for its elegant Modernista style; the 'Pearl of the Mediterranean', the 'Paris of the South'. No, this place is far from the passeig de Gràcia with its shops selling gold-embossed inkpots and mother-of-pearl hair combs. You will not find tree-lined boulevards here, nor cafés serving vanilla wafers with their fine filtered coffee. Follow me along las Ramblas where the street vendors peddle everything from parakeets to corn cobs, where the prostitutes lean on lampposts and stare indolently at the passers-by, and the cabarets play music all night. Here now, let me lead you through these streets that grow narrower and grimmer. Hold your handkerchief to your nose lest the stink—of rancid garlic and urine trapped in the hot, humid air—assaults your nostrils.

A woman opens a door and shouts something to another in the sing-song inflection of Catalan. Her friend answers with the inflated expressiveness of an Andalusian dialect. A third woman, taking threadbare shirts from a clothes line, adds her nasal Majorcan tone to the conversation. We turn a corner and see a beggar worrying at his sores with a stick in the hope of eliciting more money; and we evade the dogs feeding on the refuse thrown in the street. Walk with me across this square that is nothing more than mud and give no thought to your precious shoes. Let us come to a stop before a tenement building that was built to accommodate twenty people, but whose landlord has been subdividing the apartments into smaller and smaller units as rents have risen sharply over the last few years. This building now houses sixty wretched souls, who share one working toilet. Disease has visited this place many times: cholera; tuberculosis; meningitis. An outbreak of typhoid took a much-loved mother's life just last year. Turn your eyes to the empty lot next to it, piled with shards of rubble. Another tenement building once stood here, like the one we are looking at, with cracked walls and stained windows. But its foundations collapsed in the winter rains, crushing all those inside.

Here, let me take you up the narrow, worn stairs of the building and show you an apartment on the top floor, where a family is sleeping. It is five o'clock in the morning and summer light is beginning to penetrate the broken slats of the shutters. The heat-laden air is pungent with the smells of rust and mould, but the apartment's occupants have become so used to the odours that they no longer notice. The apartment consists of a kitchenette and one room that serves as both bedroom and eating area. In this room, on a narrow iron bed, lies a prematurely grey-haired man. On his left, with his back turned to him, is his eighteen-year-old son. Tucked under his right arm is his ten-year-old boy. In a corner of the room, where most of the paint has peeled away from the walls and a stain darkens the ceiling, stands a cot bed with a girl lying in it. The girl is eight years old and too big for the bed; she has to twist herself like a piece of rope to fit in it, but there is nowhere else for her to sleep—the rats prevent her from stretching out on the floor. Look at her, curled up tightly, not only to fit into the tiny bed but also to curb the hunger pangs she suffers each night when she goes to sleep. Her arms and legs are raw with flea bites, made worse by the heat. Her greasy hair has not seen soap and water for weeks. Can you find no pity in your heart for such a child? Look at her carefully before you judge. For that young girl is me.

'Celestina!'

I opened my eyes at my father's call, although I'd already been awake for an hour. The hunger pangs in the pit of my stomach gnawed at me like rats. But one look at Papá's haggard face and all desire to complain left me. He had given me his share of bread the night before, and it hurt me to think he would go to work with worse pains than I suffered.

I stood up and Papá lifted me out of the cot. While he sat on the bed to put on his workboots, I struck the floor gently with the soles of my feet, responding to a rhythm no one else could hear. Papá said I had danced before I could walk, that it was in my blood. My mother had always danced too.

Anastasio was at the dresser, crouching so he could see himself in the speckled mirror. I watched him contorting his face to shave. Although I was young, I understood from the way women turned when he passed by on the street that my eldest brother was handsome. My father said that Anastasio had inherited his good looks from our mother. She, on the other hand, had always insisted that he was the spitting image of Papá when he was a youth. I glanced from Anastasio to Papá and tried to discern in that beloved wrinkled face Anastasio's chiselled features and dark broody eyes. Papá was only forty-two years of age, but the troubles that had plagued him since he left his village in Andalusia twelve years earlier had aged him. He'd come to Barcelona with my mother and Anastasio after a peasant uprising, but had only found more of the same poverty and suffering he'd tried to leave behind.

'Dancing! Dancing! Always dancing, Celestina!'

My brother Ramón grabbed me in a headlock. His fingers caught in the tangles in my hair and I yelped.

'Be gentle!' scolded Anastasio, turning from the mirror. 'She's little.'

'Of course,' said Ramón, pinching my cheeks. 'I only have one sister.'

This was true. Those who had been born in the years between Anastasio and himself had all died in infancy.

Ramón was not handsome like Anastasio. He had a head the shape of an egg and his body was round like a stuffed artichoke. But what he lacked in looks, Ramón made up for in personality. He charmed the street vendors into giving us their spoiling fruit and vegetables, and had even managed to convince our avaricious landlord to give us a week's grace on our rent during the strike at the factory. Whenever Ramón had a big win, like the time a shopkeeper had given him an entire box of almonds, he was always generous in sharing it, even with the sickly Fernández children who lived in the apartment next to us.

'Come on, or we'll be late,' said Papá, opening the door to the corridor. We filed out in order of age, then Ramón picked me up in his arms. Although I could walk perfectly well and Ramón was only a few inches taller than me, he liked to carry me about.

'Put her down, Ramón,' said Anastasio, taking both our hands. 'She's not a doll.'

A few streets away, on our way to the markets on las Ramblas, we came across workmen clearing up broken glass and twisted metal outside a bicycle shop. The air was putrid with the stench of burnt rubber. There was a gaping hole in the blackened wall of the building and the inside of the store looked to have been reduced to ash. Policemen were in attendance, searching through the rubble and questioning witnesses.

'Another bomb,' muttered Papá.

The explosion had been close enough to our building that we should have heard it, but we'd become so used to the blasts lately that none of us had woken up. We were no longer surprised by the sight of a bicycle pump embedded in the wall of the shop opposite, or the saddle that had melted into a lamppost and now resembled a wilting flower. A few years earlier, the city had suffered a series of fatal bombings in revenge for the execution of four anarchists. But those attacks had been directed against the wealthy and the authorities. These latest bombings seemed to have no political purpose. They occurred in the streets of the poorest neighbourhoods in the early hours of the morning, as if those responsible were trying not to hurt anybody.

Something shiny in the gutter caught my eye. I recognised the brass dome as a bicycle bell, still in one piece and barely even scratched. Ramón noticed it too and bent to pick it up out of curiosity. A policeman spotted him and shouted, 'Get lost, you little thief!'

Ramón straightened, red with mortification at the accusation. Charmer? Yes. Salesman? Yes. Talented persuader? Yes. But thief? Never!

Anastasio's lips drew into a thin line and he clenched his fists, ready to defend his brother's honour. But Papá grabbed his shoulder. 'Come, or we will be late,' he said. He spoke with measured calm, but the look he gave the policeman was as sharp as a knife.

The plane trees that lined las Ramblas were in their full summer leafiness. Housewives and housemaids were bustling about the Boqueria Market. That cornucopia of fruit and vegetables, meat, seafood and sweets was Ramón's favourite place in the world. Many of the vendors knew him by name and were happy to give him a little something—some olives in winter, some overripe fruits in summer—in exchange for the fanciful stories he told with such aplomb. I could never forget the day he returned with a piece of *tortell*: a round pastry stuffed with marzipan and topped with glazed fruit. We shared it between us, and the sweet sensation on my tongue was so blissful I was sure I had died and gone to heaven. Inspired by Ramón's acquisitions I'd followed him into the market the following day. But the sight of boiled goats' heads hanging from hooks and other animals' organs laid out on cabbage leaves horrified me. I was sure I could see the kids' hearts beating still. I screamed when one of the butchers touched me with his icy finger and fled back out onto las Ramblas. The market became associated with the stench of death and I never wanted to return there.

My idea of paradise was the place we were headed now: the flower market, on the opposite side of the street to the Boqueria. I loved to spend my day there amongst the rainbow of colours and alluring scents, the blooms bursting from buckets and cascading from pots: trailing geraniums, fragrant roses, waxy begonias, vivid marigolds. My favourites were the blood-red clusters of carnations, like dancing girls swishing their skirts. The beauty, charm and exotic fragrances of the flower market were the exact opposite of the world in which I usually existed.

'*Buenos días!*' called out Teresa when she saw us. She lifted a bucket of gardenias onto her stall table and the sweet, summery scent of the flowers wafted through the air.

Big-boned Teresa was a widow who looked after me and Ramón when Papá and Anastasio were at the textiles factory, a responsibility for which she refused to accept payment. She had met my father at a meeting of the Radical Party, where she was a leader of one of the women's groups: Damas Rojas. The other group was Damas Radicales, which was more conservative in its politics. Teresa owned her own stall at the market and wore tiny pearl earrings, both of which made her fabulously wealthy in my eyes. In reality, however, she was only a little better off than we were. Teresa was originally from Madrid, which was why she spoke in Spanish to us instead of the Catalan she used with her customers. She had come to Barcelona with her husband, who had intended to fulfil a lifelong dream of working on a ship. But before he could realise his ambition, he cut his finger on a piece of wire and died a week later of an infection.

Teresa placed her man-sized hands on her hips and shared her theory on the latest bombing. 'It's the Radical leaders inspiring the workers to revolution.' She cast a reproachful look at my father. 'You know that these strikes, negotiations and do-gooder social legislation are getting you nowhere. The factory owners show some mock resistance, then send you all home with a few more *céntimos*. The only way for real change is to create an entirely new system.'

'You might be right,' agreed Papá wearily. 'The economy has recovered since the loss of the colonies, but our wages have stayed the same. Yet costs go up and up.'

Delfina, the flower vendor at the next stall, looked over her bluebells and winked at Anastasio. He nodded courteously to her but his mind was on other things.

'You know what I think?' he said to Teresa. 'I think the factory owners are setting off the bombs themselves to discredit the labour movement. Every time one goes off it's an excuse for the police to arrest and torture the union leaders and scare off the workers.'

The market clock struck six. Papá and Anastasio still had a way to walk to the factory, so they hurriedly kissed us goodbye. Before they left, Teresa reached into a basket and gave them each a long sandwich wrapped in newspaper. The salty smell of ancho-vies tickled my nostrils.

'Teresa, you shouldn't . . .' began Papá. He'd just paid the rent on our apartment and there was no money for 'extras'.

Teresa raised her hand to stop him. 'I had a very good day yesterday, and I'm sick of seeing the two of you get scrawnier and scrawnier,' she said.

My father cast a glance at me and Ramón. He would never eat if we were going without.

'Don't worry,' Teresa told him. 'I have something for them too.'

After Papá and Anastasio had departed, Ramón and I ate the olive oil and garlic sandwiches Teresa had prepared for us and then helped her set up the flower table. As we were finishing, Laieta came by on her way home from work. She was the daughter of a friend of Teresa's who had died three years before. I didn't understand what it was that twenty-year-old Laieta did for a living, or that she'd been forced to take up her current trade when she was laid off from the sweatshop where she had worked. I simply thought her glamorous in her narrow ankle-length skirt, her wavy hair swept up on top of her head and her hat cocked jauntily to one side. Her sweet, powdery perfume was as exotic to me as the Arab markets down by the port.

Laieta greeted Teresa with kisses, then she turned to us.

'I have a gift for you, my little ones,' she said, reaching into her bag and taking out a tin. She handed it to me. 'A friend of mine gave it to me last night.'

I prised open the container and a sweet aroma wafted out. Although I had devoured my sandwich, I was still hungry and my stomach rumbled with anticipation when I saw the tiny nut cookies inside. Ramón grabbed the tin from me and offered the cookies to Teresa and Laieta first, who both refused, before handing it back to me.

'Mmm,' I said, biting one of the cookies and relishing the feeling of it crumbling in my mouth. It was almost as marvellous as the *tortell* had been. 'What are they called?'

'*Pets de monja*,' replied Laieta, stifling a laugh. 'Nun's farts.'

'Why are they called that?' Ramón asked, taking one of the cookies and sniffing it.

Laieta shrugged. 'I think it's because of the popping sound they make when they are baking . . . but it could be because they are small and discreet.'

Teresa laughed so much her breasts and hips shook. 'Why do you assume nun's farts would be small and discreet?' she said, wiping the tears from her eyes. 'Those religious bitches are full of gas.'

She hated the Church, which she saw as a corrupt bastion of repression for the poor.

Laieta grinned and leaned towards Teresa. 'Speaking of explosions—that bicycle shop was an unlikely target for the bomb that went off last night. Personally, I think the clergy are setting them off so the municipal council will close the rationalist schools, which they claim don't teach respect for authority.'

'Well, whoever is setting the bombs off for whatever reason, it's turning Barcelona into the Wild West,' replied Teresa.

Laieta's bracelets tinkled when she reached up and adjusted her hat. 'They hired some big shot from Scotland Yard to find the perpetrators, but all he's been able to conclude is that a tourist is still safer in Barcelona than in London or Paris.'

'How did you find that out?' Teresa asked, tugging a brown petal from one of the roses. 'About the detective from Scotland Yard?'

Laieta gave a wry smile. 'I have connections, you know.'

Teresa turned to me and Ramón. 'Run along for a bit, you two,' she said. 'I don't need you right at this moment.'

It was obvious that she wanted to talk to Laieta about things they didn't want us to hear, but Ramón and I didn't mind. It gave us a chance to visit our favourite place in the market: the wall where posters were pasted for upcoming entertainments. Ramón always gravitated towards the ones advertising bullfights.

'*Olé!*' he cried, swishing an imaginary cape. He did a good job of demonstrating the difficult butterfly stance that was nearly always depicted in the advertisements.

I applauded him and threw him a pretend rose.

'When I grow up, I'm going to be a famous bullfighter,' he announced, puffing out his chest. 'Then I'm going to buy us a grand villa on passeig de Gràcia and Papá and Anastasio will never have to work again.'

'With maids and servants and crisp white sheets,' I cried, clapping my hands together. 'And lilies in every room.'

Neither Ramón nor I had ever seen a bullfight and we couldn't imagine the gore of the bullring, or the cruel way the noble animal was put to death. Nor did we know that *toreros* and their horses were often disembowelled or trampled to death.

We were innocent children with no sense of bloodlust. We only knew the handsome matadors in their 'suits-of-lights' from their posters. They were like film stars to us—poor gypsies and peasant boys plucked from poverty and launched into a world of impossible riches: villas, luxury cars and beautiful women. For us, such fantasies were an escape from the reality that Ramón would join Papá and Anastasio in the factory soon; and that I would follow suit a couple of years later.

While Ramón fantasised about being a matador, it was another poster that captured my imagination. My eye was drawn to the picture of the alluring woman with her arms poised above her head. She wore a yellow dress with a ruffled skirt like petals, and her long dark hair spilled over her shoulders and back, pinned with a red carnation behind her ear. Her gaze was towards her bare feet, and the fierceness of her downcast eyes suggested a strength and defiance that stirred something deep in me. I stamped the balls of my feet and raised my hands above my head.

'And when I grow up,' I told Ramón, 'I will be a famous flamenco dancer.'

A shadow passed over me, causing a chill to run up my spine. Ramón's face froze. We both turned to see a woman wearing a crimson scarf staring at us. I knew immediately from her swarthy skin and the basket of herbs she carried by her side that she was a gypsy.

'You must never make a wish in front of a Romani,' whispered Ramón, his face as pale as a corpse's, 'lest they grant it in some perverse way.'

I knew of that superstition but I wasn't afraid. I was intrigued by the woman's face, her knotted brow and the mole in the crease of her nostril. There were gypsies all over Spain, pure-blooded and those who had intermarried with Spaniards. My mother herself was said to have descended from a line of *gitanos*.

I held the gypsy woman's gaze and made my wish again, silently this time but with all my heart.

*　　*　　*

When Ramón and I returned to Teresa's stall, Laieta had gone but Amadeu was there, in the wheelchair his neighbours had made for him using bicycle tyres and a wicker chair. As a young man, Amadeu had been sent off to 'fight for the colonies' in Cuba and had returned without his legs. It was from him that we learned about the horror of life as a conscript with the Spanish army: minimal rations and no pay. 'Those of us who didn't die in battle or perish from malaria simply died of starvation,' he'd told us.

'The officers treated poor men like Amadeu with the same contempt in battle that their rich families do in civilian life,' Teresa had explained. 'They robbed them, and insulted them by giving them "uniforms" that were nothing more than straw hats, rotted rope sandals and pyjamas! The Great Spanish Army, indeed!'

'I sacrificed my legs for their sugar, and they can't even give me a pension,' I'd heard Amadeu tell Teresa. 'What pride I had left after losing my manliness was taken away by having to beg. When our poor families saw us off at the dock, they were fare-welling most of us forever.'

I liked Amadeu—he always had a smile and a kind word for us, despite his difficulties—but his stories also produced a kind of morbidity in me. Now Anastasio was eighteen years old, he would soon be called up for compulsory military service. Most likely it would involve nothing more than being stationed with a garrison for a couple of years of training. But I dreaded the thought that he, too, could be sent away.

Ramón and I sat under the flower table and listened to Ama-deu and Teresa talk about the latest bombing. I realised from the crumbs in Amadeu's lap that Teresa had made a sandwich for him too. She had adopted us all: Ramón and me, Laieta and Amadeu. She was like a vagabond woman feeding the pigeons in the town square.

To show his gratitude for the food and clothing Teresa managed to find for him, Amadeu came by each day to read the radical newspaper *El Progreso* to her. For while Teresa was intelligent by nature, she had only the rudiments of an education and reading a political newspaper was beyond her. Amadeu was not far into the news before the morning rush began. Housemaids rubbed elbows with restaurant owners; the wives of doctors and lawyers came in droves, determined that their new homes in l'Eixample be as elegant as those of the old ruling elite.

Amongst the influx were two figures whom every flower vendor watched as keenly as a cat watches mice: the Montella family's housekeeper and lady's maid. The housekeeper wore a brown dress with a white collar and cuffs. Her grey hair was tucked under a mob-cap and her expression was grim. The lady's maid was younger and was dressed in a lace blouse and striped skirt, with a lace mantilla on her head. Their mistress adored flowers and they only ever bought the best quality ones, especially if it was to make an arrangement for a special occasion. The Montella family owned several factories in Barcelona, including the one where Papá and Anastasio worked. They had stakes in the profitable iron-ore mines in Morocco, and were inferior in fortune only to the Güell family and the Marqués of Comillas.

That day, the housekeeper and lady's maid had another servant with them: a young woman in the blue uniform and white pinafore of a nursemaid. She was pushing a pram with a cream chassis and a navy-blue hood; the Montella family crest of a gold mastiff was embossed on the side. Holding on to the brass handle of the pram, and guided by the nurse, was a girl a year or two older than myself. She wore a white cotton piqué dress, high button shoes and a bow in her hair—clothes I could only imagine wearing in my dreams.

The lady's maid fixed her eyes on the lilies Teresa had on display and headed straight for our stall. The other women followed her. The lady's maid nodded to the housekeeper.

BELINDA ALEXANDRA

'Your lilies aren't as good as last week,' the housekeeper barked at Teresa. 'Yet, outrageously, you want the same price!'

Senyora Montella sent her lady's maid to buy flowers because of her polished taste, and the housekeeper because of her ability to drive a hard bargain. Teresa knew the game.

'Indeed they aren't as good,' she agreed. 'They are *better*!'

Ramón and I peered out from under the table. Watching the housekeeper and Teresa haggle was not unlike watching a couple dancing the fandango. The dance was a courtship ritual full of quarrelling: boy sees girl; girl rejects boy; girl pursues boy, and then flees. The housekeeper offered a third of Teresa's asking price for the lilies. Teresa folded her arms and said she would not accept less than three-quarters. After some more bargaining gymnastics, they settled on half of the original price and moved on to bargaining over some roses.

While the women were negotiating, Ramón and I sneaked a look at the baby in the pram. Her face was as pretty as a wide open aster flower. She had translucent skin, quite unlike the sickly complexions of the babies born in our neighbourhood, and her watchful eyes were honey-coloured. Although she looked to be only about six months old, she was already crowned with luxuriant locks of chestnut hair.

The little girl holding onto the pram saw us admiring the baby and smiled. She took my hand. 'That's my sister,' she said.

'What's her name?' I asked.

The nursemaid, whose attention had been on the negotiations, heard my question. She glanced down and saw me and Ramón under the table. Her face twisted with disgust when she noticed the girl was holding my hand. She tugged the pram back and grabbed the girl, wiping her hand furiously with a cloth as though it was coated in something filthy. 'Margarida!' she hissed. 'I told you not to touch . . . beggar children!'

It was just as well Teresa didn't hear her. Customers or not, she would have chased them away. The nursemaid's words were humiliating, but Ramón and I were used to rebuffs. Anastasio often said the Catalans looked down on the rest of Spain as if their language and culture were somehow better than everyone else's. Behind their backs, he called them '*señoritingos*': spoiled little rich kids.

Teresa and the women concluded their transaction: they had squeezed her on the lilies but had also bought three bouquets of fine roses and several posies at her best price. She wrapped the flowers and placed them in the women's baskets. As the Montella party turned to go, something urged me to ask the baby's name again.

'Your sister . . . what's she called?' I shouted out to Margarida.

The nursemaid sent me a scathing look. But Margarida wrestled against her grip and beamed at me. 'Her name is Evelina,' she called out. 'Little baby Evelina.'

Evelina. It sounded like a name full of light; a name that would belong to someone bursting with hope and life. I watched the party disappear amongst the forest of flowers, as fascinated as if I had seen a court of magical beings. I recalled baby Evelina in the lace dressings of her pram. What a wonderful life she must be destined for! She was a fairy princess.

Neither baby Evelina nor I had any inkling of the hell that was about to break out around us—or that our lives would one day be tragically entwined.

FIVE

Paloma

The day after I saw the woman in the courtyard, I went to the Bibliothèque Sainte-Geneviève to find out more about ghosts. I had been intending to visit the library since I had turned eighteen and was allowed to access the materials. It was a kind of pilgrimage to honour my grandfather, who used to visit the library once a week to look up information on an eclectic range of topics. Reserved by nature, he would suddenly come to life if someone needed to know the length of the Ganges River, or which civilisation had used aluminium first, or that a pregnant goldfish was called a 'twit' in English. It was from him that I learned that female watermelons were bigger, sweeter and had fewer seeds than their male counterparts, and that my left lung was smaller than my right lung to make room for my heart.

'Don't let the French convince you that they are the inventors of chocolate desserts,' he would tell me. 'Sweetened chocolate was introduced to Europe by the Spanish in the 1500s.'

A piano tuner and restorer by profession, my grandfather was precise in every way. While others might be content to skip over an unfamiliar word in the newspaper as long as the context made sense, my grandfather would refer to his *Dictionnaire Larousse* and then to his *el Fabra*, switching between the French and the Catalan until he was convinced that he had absorbed the word's exact meaning. I was only ever allowed to use the Catalan 'Avi' to address my grandfather, never the French equivalent, 'Papi'. He claimed that if I called him Papi, it would erode his soul.

When I stepped inside the entrance vestibule of the Bibliothèque Sainte-Geneviève and gazed at its Arcadian murals and philosophers' busts, I remembered how Avi had always advised me that knowledge was the best way to dispel fear. *Turn on a light and the darkness disappears* was his favourite saying. And I was afraid. The night before, I'd put the earrings in a Russian ebony box that had belonged to my mother, and slipped the box into the top drawer of my dresser, alongside the cassette from my father, which I didn't want to acknowledge either. I'd hoped that when I opened the drawer in the morning light, they might both have disappeared. Of course, that hadn't happened.

I searched the library's card catalogue, filled in my request slip and waited twenty minutes for my books to arrive. I found a seat in the grand reading room, which was crowded with students and scholars, journalists and members of the public, and took a moment to admire the fluted cast-iron columns and vaulted plaster ceiling with its cast-iron semicircular trusses. I remembered Avi telling me that the library's designer, Henri Labrouste, had been groundbreaking in using a material normally reserved for utilitarian buildings like factories and train stations and applying it to a classical-style building. The effect was breathtaking.

I turned on my reading lamp and looked at the books in front of me. I had selected Sir Arthur Conan Doyle's two-volume set *The History of Spiritualism*, a collection of writings by Helena Petrovna Blavatsky, and a book on the supernatural and paranormal by a contemporary French psychic, Mireille Fourest. The last book seemed the most concise, so I decided to start with that. In her introduction, Fourest claimed that *Ghosts are spirits bound to the physical plane by an unfilled desire or a troubled memory*. That was an explanation given in every ghost story I had ever read, and even Gaby had mentioned it, but I wrote it down in my notebook anyway.

The chapter on the temperament of ghosts was more interesting: *A ghost is not a divine visitor like an angel or spiritual guide. A ghost retains the same personality the deceased person had when alive. If the person was angry, their ghost will be angry; if they were kind, their ghost will be kind; a mischievous person will leave behind a mischievous ghost. That is why the ghosts of children are frequently naughty.*

I made a note of that too—*same personality as when they were alive*—before leaning back in my chair and staring at the pattern of leaves and flowers on the ceiling. I tried to conjure up an image of the ghost's face: those strong, exotic features; her penetrating eyes. She hadn't given me much clue to her personality, but whatever she had been in her earthly life, she must have had some sort of powerful influence on others.

I returned to the book. *Often ghosts are loved ones returning to us to give us messages of comfort or encouragement . . .* I skipped over that point because I had never seen the woman before. She was nobody that I knew; let alone a loved one.

I skimmed through the chapter on how to tell if I had special psychic powers, assuming that if I had, I would be seeing around me the ghosts of all the exiles, artists, romantics and political activists who had sat in this same room through the years since 1850 when the library was built. I turned to the chapter titled 'Dangers'.

Beware of trying to communicate with a ghost yourself if you have no experience in these matters, Fourest warned. *Some ghosts are demonic and will possess you if you attempt to make any contact with them.*

I glanced at my watch and saw that the morning had passed faster than I had expected. I had just enough time to get back to the studio to help with Mamie's afternoon class. I carried my books to the returns desk.

The bespectacled librarian took the books from me. 'Ah, spiritualism and the paranormal,' he said, looking at the spines. 'Well, to each his own taste. My favourite stories are those where the supernatural occurrences turn out to have logical explanations, like "Sherlock Holmes and the Adventure of the Speckled Band" or that play by Patrick Hamilton, *Gas Light*.'

As I made my way back down the stairs to the first floor, I thought about what the librarian had said. I would love for there to be a logical explanation for my ghost, I thought, walking out into the sunshine. Unfortunately, the only 'logical' explanations I could come up with for the physical presence of the earrings weren't very comforting: I was either suffering hallucinations or I had gone completely mad.

While waiting at the Métro station, I reviewed the notes I had made in the library:

Troubled or unfulfilled
Kind or mischievous
Beware: could be evil and demonic

'All right,' I said, closing my eyes and picturing the spirit again: her waves of black hair, her chin held erect. 'Which kind of ghost are you?'

Six

Celestina

After she had finished her work at the market, Teresa would take me and Ramón to the Casa del Pueblo while we waited for Papá and Anastasio to finish at the factory and come to collect us. It was a type of communal workers' house set up by the Radical Party, with meeting halls, classrooms, a library and a café. Teresa would buy food at the cooperative, and we would spend the rest of the afternoon watching a theatrical production, or squashed up together on one of the wooden benches in the instruction rooms, struggling with the rudiments of reading and writing taught in the free classes. Despite the lack of concentration caused by our malnourished bellies, the three of us did our best to improve ourselves. *Celestina Sánchez* I would write over and over again in large, uneven letters.

When our mother was alive and making a little money in a sweatshop, Papá had sent Ramón to one of the municipal-subsidised schools offered by the clergy. But after my brother returned home one day with a black eye because he hadn't answered a mathematical problem quickly enough, my father withdrew him. After that, Papá joined the Radical Party and that was how he had met Teresa.

There was never anything between Papá and Teresa but friendship based on shared suffering. But it was obvious that my father respected the flower seller. 'Do everything Teresa tells you,' Papá advised me. 'She has a sense of direction.'

Despite my father's admiration for Teresa and his enthusiasm for the Radical Party's proposed reforms, he didn't entirely give up on the idea of God. Crucifixes still hung above our beds. Rather, he saw the difference between the worship of a divine being and the behaviour of the Spanish clergy. He shared Teresa's disgust that the convents and monasteries of Barcelona were amongst the wealthiest in the world, prospering on stocks and investments while the poor perished around them.

'The true evil that afflicts humanity stems from religion,' Teresa said. 'Have you noticed that in Barcelona a workman never greets a priest on the street? They never even exchange a glance. It's because the convents and the monasteries are the ruin of us. They pay no rates so everyone else in the district has to make up the difference. They pay no taxes on their orphan labour so all the laundresses and embroiderers are put out of work.'

Our life continued along the humdrum routine of the flower market, the Casa del Pueblo, then home and bed, until one day in July when everything changed forever.

Papá and Anastasio did not return from the factory at their usual time. Teresa was due to lead a meeting of Damas Rojas in the communal room and had no choice but to take me and Ramón with her.

The women moved the wooden chairs into a circle when they saw Teresa arrive. I recognised a number of them as regulars at the Casa del Pueblo. There were a few intellectuals, teachers from the rationalist schools, but most of the women were semiliterate factory workers with furrowed brows and twisted, arthritic fingers. There was Juana, who worked at a chocolate factory and whose clothing always smelled of peanuts and cocoa; and Pilar, a fishmonger whose greasy hair and clothes reeked like the port when the tide was out. Núria from the slaughterhouse was there too, stinking like a graveyard, her fingernails and shoes stained with blood. Ramón and I always did our best to avoid sitting next to her in the reading classes. Although they couldn't vote, the women of Damas Rojas were determined to see change. They were formidable in mob action, putting themselves in the front line at strikes. They counted on the fact that the police were less likely to open fire on women who reminded them of their mothers. Usually they were right, but not always.

Teresa began the discussion. 'We've been waiting for change for years. Maura's reforms are deadlocked in the Cortes. Nothing has come of the promises for representative government. Nearly half the men and a third of the women in textile factories in Barcelona and the Ter Valley have been locked out. It's time to take matters into our own hands.'

Her remark brought a profusion of voices, either murmuring agreement or crying out in protest. Although I couldn't understand most of the discussion in the hot, crowded room, it was clear that there was tension in the air.

A woman with a baby in her arms rose to her feet. 'There is nothing we can do! We are too poor. Spain can't compete with the United States in the cotton market—that's why they are closing the factories. How can people who can't rub two *céntimos* together take matters into their own hands?'

Paquita, a willowy woman who worked as a teacher at La Escuela Moderna, responded. 'On the contrary, Spain is a wealthy country—but the money is in the hands of a few. If the money was shared around equitably, instead of the majority of Spaniards living in poverty, then a domestic market might be created. If that were to be the case, what happens internationally wouldn't affect Spain so drastically.'

'That's very noble,' said Teresa, pacing the floor. 'But it's not realistic, Paquita. How are we going to convince the rich to share their wealth without force? The only way is to take that wealth for ourselves—in a revolution.'

'Revolution is going too far,' Carme, another teacher, replied. 'We need to strike across the board in *all* industries and in *all* cities. If the textile-industry workers alone strike, the factory owners will simply bring in scab labour. But if the whole country unites and strikes, we will bring them to their knees.'

'Easy for *you* to say, Carme,' the woman with the baby scoffed. 'You don't have children. The workers can't afford to strike. As it is, we don't eat some days. Our family needs five *pesetas* a day to exist on, but even with both my husband and I working from morning to night, the most we ever make is four.' The woman fell silent for a moment, and took a breath before continuing. 'I lost my poor little Ignacio because we couldn't afford medicine.'

'It will take more than a strike to save us,' a male voice said.

All eyes in the room turned to the doorway, where Papá was standing with Anastasio. My father was pale-faced, stricken. It was the same look that he had worn the night my mother died.

'They are calling up the reservists for Morocco,' he said.

Cries of horror rang through the room. For several months, skirmishes between Spanish troops in Morocco and Riffian tribes had been intensifying. Spain had an international mandate in Morocco, and there was a fear that the French, who also had interests in the Rif, would take over the protectorate if Spain's army proved incapable of maintaining order. It was only later that I came to understand the politics. What I saw that day, from the way my father grasped Anastasio around the shoulders, was that he was afraid that not only reservists would be sent to Morocco but conscripts too.

My mind shifted to Amadeu, who had lost his legs in Cuba and now had no choice but to beg. I remembered his words, *When our poor families saw us off at the dock, they were farewelling most of us forever*, and felt something I didn't understand bearing down on me: a premonition of doom.

My terror was echoed by the women around me. The state of the soldiers who had returned from the wars in Cuba and the Philippines was imprinted on many of their memories.

'They are going to take our husbands again!' cried Juana. 'But Antoni has already served. Our youngest child is less than a year old.'

The woman with the baby pursed her lips before asking, 'Like last time? With no means for a wife and children to live on while their men are away?'

'And without compensation for disability,' said Teresa through gritted teeth. 'Like poor Amadeu.'

'And what about our sons?' screamed another woman. 'My twins have just turned eighteen. They've been called up for military training.'

'It's only the reservists for now,' said Anastasio gravely. 'They say it's only for police action. But from the numbers that are being called up, it seems they are expecting heavy fighting. I suspect it's a matter of time before the rest of us are called.'

'But if you can pay, they won't take your sons,' Papá added. 'You can get them exempted from military training.' For all he had suffered in his life, it was the first time my father had sounded so bitter.

'How much must you pay?' asked a woman with wiry hair that stuck out in all directions. 'I'll sell myself if it will save my sons.'

'Fifteen hundred *pesetas*,' Papá replied.

The room fell into a shocked silence. It was more money than any of these women would make in three years; for some, more than they would make in their entire working lives. Many of the women had several sons. Even if they could, by some miracle, obtain fifteen hundred *pesetas*, which son would they choose to save?

'Who can pay that?' said the woman with the wiry hair, a bewildered look in her eyes. 'Who can pay that sort of money?'

'The rich, of course,' said Teresa, folding her arms. 'If you are of the *bourgeoisie* you can dip into your savings or take out a loan. But to the rich, fifteen hundred *pesetas* is nothing. It's like a sneeze to them. La senyora Montella would spend more than that a year on flowers.'

'Our men are going to be sacrificed,' said Juana, so quietly that we had to strain to hear her, 'so the wives of the iron magnates can decorate their tables with flowers?'

A heavy veil seemed to fall on the room, as if the women were facing the futility of their existence. There they were, struggling to make a living, struggling to feed their families, struggling to improve themselves by learning to read and write, even struggling to make society better and fairer. But it was all futile. In the end, when our lives were weighed against those of the rich, ours were valued at nothing.

Immediately after the decree recalling reservists to active duty was published in the official *Gaceta*, the Third Mixed Brigade in Catalonia was mobilised. Protests against the war broke out in Madrid when the First Mixed Brigade, which was stationed in that city, was called up next.

Although the press was censored, rumours about the situation in Morocco were rife: the Spanish army had deliberately taunted the local tribes into battle so that the officers could receive combat pay; the Spanish soldiers were being routed by the Rif guerrillas; the government, which had been reluctant until now to fight in Morocco, was being forced to send troops by the Jesuits, who had vested interests in the country's mines. The last rumour served to further inflame the anti-clerical sentiments of the worker population.

'We should be turning our rifles on the clergy not the Rifs,' Teresa told the women of Damas Rojas. 'The Rifs are as oppressed as we are. Spain has no right to be plundering their lands.'

'Why don't they send the priests to fight instead?' senyora Fernández, our neighbour, suggested. 'They have no families and are of no earthly use to us.'

For a few hopeful days, it seemed only the reservists would be called, but then Anastasio received his notice to report to the

Barcelona barracks. To my surprise, my fiery brother took the news stoically, as if injustices were his lot in life. It was Papá who worked himself into a fury.

'You must go to France,' he told Anastasio. 'I spoke with a man who will take you out of Spain tonight.'

'No!' said Anastasio, jumping to his feet. 'If I flee, they will put you in gaol. Then what will happen to Ramón and Celestina? They will be out on the street. Say no more of this plan . . . to anyone!'

After Anastasio's refusal to desert, Papá seemed to age even faster. The worry lines around his eyes deepened and he walked about with his shoulders hunched. Anastasio wavered from isolating himself to embracing Ramón and me so robustly that it hurt. 'You'll take care of Celestina, won't you, little brother?' he asked Ramón the day he had to report to the barracks. 'You'll always watch out for her?'

Ramón nodded solemnly, although his face wore the same lost look that Papá's did.

I thought of Anastasio's handsome features and his strong physique. 'He'll be all right,' I told myself. But inside I was crumbling.

When I went to the flower markets, I looked for the gypsy woman with the crimson scarf. I wanted to make a wish for Anastasio to come home safely, no matter how perversely she granted my desire. But I couldn't find her.

The date set for Anastasio's embarkation was 18 July, a Sunday. The afternoon was hot and the air in the apartment was stifling. Trickles of sweat poured down my neck although I had just washed. Teresa came to our apartment with a new dress for me.

'You must look nice for your brother,' she told me. 'It will lift his spirits.'

Although the dress was made from a lesser grade of cotton, it had pretty bishop sleeves and roses appliquéd on the skirt. I was so used to my old patched frock that when I put it on I felt like a princess.

The battalion Anastasio was to travel with to Morocco was due to march down las Ramblas at half past four in the afternoon. The atmosphere on the street was sultry, the air laden with the oppressive humidity that heralded a thunderstorm. Las Ramblas was already crowded when we got there, not only with the families of the reservists and the few unlucky conscripts, but with promenaders out for their Sunday afternoon stroll. So many bodies pressed together created a curious scent that was a mix of lavender water and rose soap, perspiration and horse manure.

We took our place in the crowd.

'Here they come!' somebody called out.

We turned to see the soldiers marching down the boulevard, escorted by a police guard. People began to call out to their husbands, sons and fathers. A young boy broke away and ran in front of the battalion. His father saw him and hoisted him onto his shoulders while his wife took her husband's rifle and marched along beside him. One of the policemen stepped forwards to pull the soldier back into line, but another policeman restrained him. 'It's only by the grace of God that we aren't being sent with them,' I overheard him say. 'Let them have a moment longer.'

More women and children stepped out to walk with the soldiers. I spotted Anastasio. I grabbed Ramón's arm and we leaped towards him, followed by Teresa and Papá. Anastasio's face broke into a smile at the sight of us. He lifted me onto his shoulders while Teresa took his gun, and Ramón linked arms with him. Papá walked beside him, his arm around his waist.

The orderly formation had turned into a throng of soldiers and their families moving towards the harbour. The men seemed resigned to their fate, but the women cast angry glances at those left in the crowd, watching the parade. The spectators seemed unnerved by the sight of mothers, wives and sisters wielding rifles.

When we reached the port, there were more police and soldiers waiting to supervise the embarkation. The Governor of Barcelona and the Captain General were there too, but it was the sight of the black-hulled steamer, the *Cataluña*, with its three masts and funnel looming above us that drove home to the crowd the reason why the men were being sent to Morocco. The steamer belonged to the Marqués of Comillas, and was the same vessel that had taken those ill-fated soldiers to Cuba eleven years earlier.

'Let the Marqués send his sons,' one woman muttered. 'Let Güell go.'

'Don't the Montellas have a son?' another asked. 'Why isn't he being sent?'

The military authorities at the port ordered the civilians and the soldiers to separate. Wives and mothers broke down weeping.

Anastasio embraced Papá, Teresa and Ramón before lowering me from his shoulders. I held onto his waist.

'If you don't let me go, Celestina, how will I come back?' he asked, stroking my cheek.

I looked into my brother's eyes. He seemed even more beautiful than usual. Reluctantly, I loosened my grip and let him move away, but as I did so I felt something in my heart break.

Unnerved by the crowd, the military authorities ushered the soldiers onto the gangway. The men boarded the ship and lined up on the deck, under the canopies. Standing near the gangway, dressed in their Sunday finery and handing out cigarettes and religious medals, were Barcelona's society women. These were the women who had saved their sons from military duty with the payment of fifteen hundred *pesetas*. In the crowd behind them, I spotted senyora Montella's housekeeper and lady's maid.

'She couldn't even be bothered coming herself,' I heard Teresa mutter beside me.

One of the women, dressed in a hat resplendent with ostrich feathers, stepped towards Anastasio. 'Bless you, young man, for fighting for our country,' she said, handing him a medal.

Anastasio grabbed it from her then threw it in the water. Other soldiers did the same.

I felt something move beside me. I turned to see Teresa, her face crimson, her body seeming several inches taller. It was as if she had caught on fire. She stormed towards the woman with the hat, grabbed the tray of medals and tossed them into the woman's face. The woman staggered backwards, lost her footing and fell on her backside.

'The rich pay with their money and our poor men pay with their blood!' Teresa screamed, looming over the woman, who burst into tears.

The society women around her cowered away from Teresa. She sneered at them before turning to the families of the reservists and conscripts. 'If the rich don't go, no one should go!' she shouted.

Her protest was met with a stony silence. It seemed that she was all alone in her outrage. Then another woman's voice rose from the crowd. 'That's right: all or none! If we are truly fighting for Spain, then all must go. Rich and poor alike!'

My father stepped up beside me and raised his fist. 'All or none!' he shouted.

Ramón and I joined in with him, repeating the sentiment until we were hoarse. Other voices, rough and fierce, rose from the crowd. Something like an electric current ran through the gathering and within seconds the entire mob was chanting in unison: 'All or none! All or none!' Together, we began to move forwards.

Unnerved by the multitude surging towards the boat like a swarm of bees, the Captain General ordered that the gangway be raised. Steam rose from the funnel as the *Cataluña* prepared to move away from the port.

'All or none!' shouted the crowd, rushing towards the departing boat. 'Throw away your guns!'

I caught a glimpse of Anastasio clutching the railing and watching the chaos on the dock as the ship headed out to sea. He cupped his hands to his mouth and bellowed, 'Ramón, look after your sister!' He shouted something else, but his voice was drowned out by the roars of the crowd as it pushed against the policemen.

The Captain General ordered his men to fire. They raised their guns and shot volleys into the air. The sound was deafening. A bullet ricocheted off a post and whistled past my ear. Women screamed, and the crowd flew into a panic. Some of the police rushed forwards, beating protesters to the ground before arresting them. A policeman made a lunge for Teresa, but my father grabbed her and pushed her behind him. She was sucked up into the writhing crowd and carried away.

The soldiers fired into the air again. 'Disperse!' the Captain General shouted. 'Or the next shots will not be above your heads!'

His warning had mothers gathering their children and rushing back in the direction of las Ramblas. Papá took hold of me and Ramón and we ran until we were out of breath.

We stopped for a moment on a corner. My legs were unsteady beneath me and Ramón's teeth were chattering despite the heat. Several people who had also escaped from the port gathered around us and we exchanged glances. The authorities had fired on us and terrorised us, but there was an inferno in our blood. We had seen the alarm we could evoke in our enemies when we acted as one. Perhaps we were not as powerless as we had thought.

SEVEN

Paloma

Mamie's ballet studio might not produce dancers of the standard of the School of the Paris Opera Ballet, but it turned out highly competent ones. The students at l'École de Danse Evelina Olivero gracefully executed their *glissades* and their *jetés* and passed their examinations with honours. Many had gone on to careers in film and modelling, and one was even a television star. Mamie took pride in the fact that her school's dancers were recognisable by their graceful deportment and, as in the case of Gaby, their self-confidence. A good number of Mamie's students stayed in touch with her long after their ballet studies were behind them, sending her greeting cards and pictures of their children.

Helping Mamie with her class of fourteen- to sixteen-year-olds a week after I'd seen the ghost, I couldn't help pondering how differently these girls experienced ballet from the way I did. The dissimilarities had always been there, but they were becoming more apparent to me, perhaps because I was not training at the Ballet School any more. Mamie's students were all different heights and sizes, whereas at the ballet school anybody taller than 175 centimetres or developing curvy hips or a full bust was out. You couldn't even contemplate a place in the *corps de ballet* unless you were slender, had a long neck and small head, and a perfect limb-to-torso ratio. I had started at the school when I was eight years of age, and my fellow students and I had approached puberty with trepidation. For us, it wasn't a time for blossoming, discovering love or rebelling against our teachers and parents. Instead, we existed with the dread that after all our training and the sacrifice of our childhoods, our bodies would ultimately betray us. As our ballet teachers warned us: 'Nothing must spoil a perfect line.' By 'nothing', they meant breasts, hips or a bottom. Mamie saw things differently. She revelled in her students' womanly blooming. If the pink tights and leotard of the school uniform didn't flatter a student's new shape, she would discreetly recommend that 'a pretty chiffon skirt' would be most becoming.

When the class was over, I watched her students skipping out the door and down the stairs, or stopping a while in the corridor to chat. One of the older girls blew kisses to Mamie before she left.

'Which film are you and Gaby going to see tonight?' Mamie asked me.

I remembered that seeing a film was my alibi for going to the flamenco class, which started that night, and quickly thought of something Mamie would be unlikely to go and see herself.

'*The Towering Inferno*,' I said. Although I wasn't a fan of disaster movies, it starred Paul Newman and Steve McQueen and was the type of film that Gaby would want to see.

'Just you and Gaby?' Mamie asked.

I nodded. 'Yes.'

'But Gaby . . . she seems to know lots of nice young men.'

I rolled my eyes. Although the outing with Gaby was fictional, even the thought of going out with Marcel and any friend of his made me cringe. At the same time, I thought it was very

'French' of Mamie to suggest I double-date with Gaby. Most of the Spanish émigrés never let their daughters out of their sights, and no young man could visit their homes unless he came with the serious intention of marriage.

'Well, you'd better have something to eat before you go,' said Mamie, turning off the lights in the studio and heading towards the kitchen.

I hated to eat before dance classes; even a piece of bread gave me a stitch. I wondered if it would be the same with flamenco.

'Not too much, Mamie. Gaby and I might get something to eat after the film.'

'I hope so,' Mamie replied, taking bowls from the cupboard. 'You could do with a bit more weight.'

She warmed up the bean soup she had made earlier and sliced up some bread.

'You might not believe this, Paloma,' she said, placing our bowls on the table and sitting down, 'but I used to be painfully shy too.'

I knew Mamie meant well but her comment irritated me. She always spoke to me as if I were some sort of fragile flower. She had no idea of the nerves of steel I'd had to develop to make it to the final level at the Ballet School; the incredible physical and psychological endurance I'd had to maintain. As delicate as the dancers looked, it was only a mask. The ballet world was not a place for the weak. Not one of Mamie's students would have lasted a term in that microcosm of Darwinian theory.

I decided the best way to handle Mamie's concern was with a dose of humour. 'You, shy?' I said, smiling. 'How did you overcome it?'

She didn't take my comment as it was intended, and looked thoughtful for a moment. 'I was much shyer than you,' she said. 'Until I met your grandfather, I hardly spoke a word. The merest greeting from a stranger would send me into a fluster. My mother was the opposite, of course. She was a social butterfly. She loved conversation and she loved parties. I would watch from behind a column or potted plant as the elegant guests arrived for her soirées: the women draped in silk and lace, the men in smartly cut suits. But even though my mother had the most exquisite dresses made for me, and everyone admired my prettiness, I would run away as soon as I could and hide in the kitchen, where I'd watch the cooks preparing giant platters of food, until somebody came and found me and compelled me to join the party.'

I had stopped eating, my spoon halfway to my mouth. *Mamie was talking about Spain.* She had never mentioned her mother before . . . or anything about elegant soirées. I was intrigued.

Anybody seeing the way we lived would have assumed Mamie and I were close. And we were: I loved her dearly and she loved me. But listening to her now, I realised how little I knew about her life, and I certainly didn't tell her everything about mine—the appearance of the ghost for one. It seemed we often skirted around issues, each unwilling to cause pain to the other—or to herself. We rarely talked about Mama, although she was always on my mind and would have certainly been on Mamie's too.

'If you were so shy, Mamie, how come you took up ballet?'

Mamie's eyes rested on my face. 'Unlike you and Julieta,' she said, 'I didn't begin to dance ballet until I was seventeen. I had studied Spanish classical dance since I was a child, but you cannot imagine what a scandal it was in my day to expose one's legs as ballerinas did. The Mother Superior at the school I attended simply would not have allowed it. Then, on my sixteenth birthday, my parents took me to the Liceu to see the ballet. I was moved by the dancers' elegance, their sensitivity to the music. I watched them leap high into the air and land as softly as feathers. I fell in love with their precision, their fragile yet powerful physical beauty. Afterwards I was in raptures. The ballet had opened a space between heaven and earth and had transported me closer to the angels. Night after night I dreamed that I was floating in the air, dressed in delicate white tulle. It took me a year to convince my parents to let me have lessons.' Mamie sighed and fidgeted with her hands. 'Pare,' she said, using the Catalan word to refer to her father, 'only consented in the hope that it would bring me out of my shyness and stop me from scaring off suitors. "I don't need another old maid in the house," he said.' Mamie laughed, sounding girlish. 'When I became quite good at ballet, Mama, who took my side in most things, suggested to Pare that if I were allowed to dance for her guests, rather than being forced to speak to them, I could show them a world of emotion. But of course, performing was unthinkable for a girl from a good family. "That," Pare used to say, "is for whores and gypsies."'

I studied my grandmother, chic in her headscarf and saffron caftan, and tried to see the young woman she was describing. Physically, it wasn't difficult. Mamie was still beautiful, although not one feature on her face could be called 'classical'. She had enormous honey-coloured eyes, which she enhanced with false lashes, her nose was largish and her mouth was broad. And yet together, all of her features, along with her pale porcelain skin, created a face that was best described as 'arresting'. When I looked at her, I couldn't help thinking of a big open flower. I wondered what she was like as a young woman, when Avi had fallen in love with her. Then it occurred to me that I'd never asked her, and she had not been able to bring any photographs with her when she had escaped.

'So your father was strict?' I asked. 'What was your maiden name?'

A tremor seemed to run through Mamie, but she collected herself and changed the subject. 'What time do you have to go?' she asked, glancing at the clock. 'There will be traffic this time of night.'

Although I was looking forward to the flamenco class, I didn't want to leave. I wanted to hear more about Spain. But years of ballet training had instilled in me a military-like punctuality and a respect for my dance teachers that precluded turning up late for class. Reluctantly, I went to my room and pulled on a pair of jeans over my leotard. I'd already packed a bag with my skirt and character shoes in it. It was lucky for me that large bags were in fashion and so Mamie didn't pay attention to my oversized one when she helped me slip on my coat.

'Mamie,' I said, looking at her, 'now that I'm older, I hope you will tell me more about Spain. I don't have Mama any more, and Papa . . . well, he has a new family now. You're all I've got, and yet I know so little about your life . . .'

I stopped because Mamie's back had stiffened and her mouth had clamped into a thin line. It was the same reaction I'd received whenever I'd asked about her past before. So why had she started talking to me tonight about how she came to dance ballet? Maybe she was thinking the same thing I had been.

I sat down to tug on my boots. I didn't want to cause Mamie pain, but could everything about her life in Spain have been painful? Surely, suffering alone could not have produced such a gracious and generous woman? From her description, it sounded as if Mamie had come from a wealthy family. They must have had quite a nice life before the war.

'Yes, all right,' she said, so suddenly that it gave me a start. 'It is your heritage and I shouldn't allow Franco to take that away from you. God knows, he got everything else. But I will only talk to you on one condition: that you do not ask me any questions. You must allow me to tell you only what I can bear to tell you. Is that understood?'

I nodded, understanding that Mamie was setting a boundary; a safeguard against going to places that were too painful for her. That was all right with me. I'd rather know something than nothing at all.

Mamie walked with me to the door. 'Enjoy your evening,' she said.

I kissed her and she gave me a long look. 'I was once a Montella,' she said. 'But it's been a long time since that was my name.'

I embraced her again before heading down the stairs. When I reached the door of the building, it occurred to me how strangely she had worded her sentence. *I was once a Montella.* As if 'Montella' was something you were, rather than what you were called.

Mamie's 1967 Mercedes Benz was parked in the street. I sighed and put my key into the lock. If the flamenco class had been earlier, I could have taken the Métro to Montparnasse, but it wasn't safe to travel that way alone after dark. It wasn't that I minded driving; it was the behaviour of the other drivers that made me ill at ease.

No sooner had I turned off rue Spontini than I had a car beeping behind me. I was well aware that French men hated women drivers. Most of them, having forbidden their wives from picking up the car keys, could not comprehend that a woman my age needed to display such independence, let alone doing it in a conspicuous aubergine Mercedes. With its roomy beige interior and velour seats, the car was superior to the Renaults most of these men who shook their fists at me or cut me off were driving. The car horn sounded again, more loudly this time. I did my best to ignore it and thought instead about what Mamie had told me that evening. So her father had been strict and, although he had allowed her to learn ballet, she had been forbidden from performing in public. Perhaps that was why Mamie had never stood in the way of my or Mama's ambitions.

The driver behind me opened his window and shouted at me to move over. But we were in a narrow one-way street and I couldn't drive any faster without the risk of scraping the car or running over a pedestrian. The street widened at one point and the driver slammed his foot on the accelerator and swerved to overtake me, knocking over a restaurant sign and a flower planter on the way.

'Out of the way, bitch!' he screamed, cutting in front of me.

'*Crétin!*' I imagined myself shouting back. In reality, I said nothing. Perhaps Mamie was right: I *was* too timid.

* * *

The first thing that struck me as I made my way up the worn stairs to the studio of the Académie de Flamenco Carmen Rivas was the noise. I could hear someone clapping out a rhythm and dozens of feet pounding the floor.

'I can't hear you!' a woman's voice called out. '*Planta!*'

You must be kidding, I thought. From day one in ballet, we were taught the importance of moving as noiselessly as possible. Flamenco, it seemed, was the opposite.

The studio space was small, with a scuffed wooden floor and red velvet curtains at the windows. There was a raised stage at the front of the room and a woman with curly dark hair was standing on it, watching a group of women in black leotards and flared skirts stamping on the floor. It was obviously an advanced class and they were performing together. I was struck by the way their arm and head movements and the positioning of their bodies were all different. Even their facial expressions seemed individual. It was nothing like a ballet class.

The elderly Spanish lady who had given me the leaflet was sitting at a table at the front door. She smiled when she recognised me. 'I had a feeling you'd come,' she said. She noted down my name and took the fee for the class. 'You can change there,' she said, indicating a screen.

I went behind the screen and slipped out of my jeans and into my skirt. I was putting on my dance shoes when the advanced class finished up and the teacher, who introduced herself as Carmen Rivas, the director of the academy, called the beginners' class to the floor.

'Welcome to our special world of flamenco,' Carmen said in her strong Spanish accent. There were deep wrinkles around her eyes and mouth, but her body looked as well-toned and supple as a healthy thirty-year-old's. 'You are about to enter a world of fierce passion,' she promised us, flashing a mesmerising smile. 'Flamenco incorporates three types of expression: *cante*, *baile* and *guitarra*—the song, the dance and the guitar. There is some controversy as to its origins: the gypsies claim it is theirs, while the Andalusians argue it rose from their culture. In my opinion, it is a beautiful intermarriage of the two worlds. The gypsies could not have given birth to flamenco without Spain, and the spirit of flamenco would have lain dormant in the Andalusian soil if the gypsies had not breathed life into it.' Carmen paused a moment to look into each of our faces. 'I am going to teach you some steps, but how you interpret them, how you express them when you dance, must be totally your own. There is nothing that flamenco aficionados appreciate more than the internal force of your spirit combining with the spirit of the dance and the music: what we call *duende*.'

The seven other women on the floor were as mixed in body shape and size as the students I'd just seen in Mamie's adolescents' class. They were all different ages too. One woman looked to be in her sixties. The closest one in age to me was in her early twenties: blonde with a ski-slope nose, like the singer from ABBA. I wondered what they each did when they weren't dancing, and what had attracted them to flamenco.

After some warm-up exercises, including rotating our wrists and ankles, Carmen began the class by demonstrating a step where we had to swing our leg back from the knee and strike the floor with the ball of our foot, then snap down our heel.

'*Planta*! Heel! Change weight! *Planta*! Heel! Change weight!' she called, bringing the class into rhythm.

I picked up the step easily. My classmates had more trouble, but nobody seemed worried about it. They looked at each other and laughed.

Carmen gave them encouragement. 'Don't worry if you don't get it at first; it takes a little while,' she said. 'But soon dancing flamenco will be as natural to you as walking . . . or even as breathing . . . you'll see. The main thing is to not take yourselves too seriously.'

In terms of my experience of dance lessons, Carmen might as well have been speaking a foreign language. In ballet school, the teachers were much less sympathetic. If you couldn't pick up at least the basics of a routine after one or two tries, you were out.

'Now I'm going to talk about posture,' Carmen announced. 'In flamenco, this is the most important element of all, even more important than the steps. When you think of flamenco I don't want you to think elegant or dainty. There are two words that you must hold in your mind: majestic and powerful.' She drew in a breath and raised her arms in the air. 'From the navel down, you are firmly planted into the earth. But from the navel up'—she stretched her arms higher and arched her back—'you are reaching to the sky. This is the true flamenco dancer: her feet are always planted firmly in the earth but she is striving for heaven at the same time.'

She was about to teach us another step when her attention was drawn towards the door. We all turned to see a young man with a guitar case entering the room and heading towards the stage. He was tall with long, glossy black hair. The lustre of it was like a thoroughbred's mane and I had an urge to touch it when he passed by me.

Carmen clapped her hands. 'I have a special treat for my beginners' class tonight,' she said. 'My nephew has returned from Spain and is studying at the Conservatoire de Paris. He will be accompanying us for the lesson.'

The young man put his guitar case down near a stool and turned to us. He had a striking face: luminous dark eyes framed by thick eyebrows, broad cheekbones and a full-lipped mouth. His open-necked shirt revealed a muscular chest, and around his neck he wore a silver chain with a pewter bat pendant.

'Good evening, ladies. My name is Jaime,' he said. 'And it will be an honour to accompany you.' He spoke French perfectly, and with a lighter accent than his aunt's.

The collective sigh of female desire that swept through the room was almost palpable. The blonde woman grinned and winked at me.

I had been surrounded by examples of male physical beauty at the Ballet School, but there was something especially intriguing about Jaime. When he sat down on the stool and adjusted his guitar, he looked around the room as if trying to take in everyone. The expression on his face was intense, as though he were reading the dancers' minds. Our eyes met, and he tilted his head and gazed at me curiously. I quickly turned away.

He tuned his guitar then began a *tangos*, his hands moving smoothly over the strings. Carmen clapped out the rhythm, putting the emphasis on the first and fourth beat. Most of the class fell in and out of rhythm, but I hit the *compás* perfectly each time. I held my posture as Carmen had instructed and lifted my chin in the air. A shadow briefly passed in front of my eyes and I blinked as some unformed image sprang to mind. The movement . . . the music . . . I had felt this way before. But how could I have? Flamenco was foreign to everything I had been doing in my life. Still, the sense of *déjà vu* was there. It was as if something had temporarily possessed me. Was that what Carmen had meant by *duende*?

I sensed Jaime's eyes on me. I assumed my sinewy arms and legs made me stand out as a trained dancer, or the fact that I could respond to the music so well. Jaime finished the piece and Carmen added another step to our routine. We were working on that when Jaime stopped playing, leaving Carmen to clap out the accompaniment. He jumped to the floor and came to stand behind me, gripping my raised arms and bending them slightly. He turned my face to his with his hand. 'You are a ballerina, yes? But when you think of flamenco,' he whispered, 'you must think of fire, not of air.'

He let go of me and returned to playing his guitar. I joined with the others in practising the new step. It was easy to think of fire now: my skin burned where he had touched me.

When the class was over, we applauded to thank Carmen and Jaime, and to congratulate each other.

'Well, ladies,' Carmen said, smiling proudly, 'you have taken your first step on what will be a wonderful, wonderful journey.'

The class broke up and Carmen moved to speak with Jaime. I sat down on the bench at the back of the room to take off my shoes. The blonde woman who had danced beside me sat down too and nudged me in the ribs. 'I think *you've* started a *wonderful, wonderful journey*,' she said, nodding her head in Jaime's direction. 'He couldn't take his eyes off you the whole lesson.'

'Not for the reasons you're thinking,' I told her. 'It must be obvious to him that I've been dancing for years.'

The woman's face twitched and her smile faded. I realised I'd alienated another potential friend with my serious attitude. 'But if you put *tu* in the middle of his name, you've almost got *Je t'aime*—I love you,' I said quickly. The joke didn't really make sense, but it was my attempt to soften my abruptness.

'You're right,' the woman said and giggled. She stood and picked up her handbag. 'I'll see you next week,' she said, and gave me a beaming smile, which I did my best to return, silently berating myself for my awkwardness.

I noticed Carmen heading towards me, Jaime in tow.

'I hope you enjoyed the class,' she said. 'It's obvious that you have danced before. I think the beginners' class is too easy for you, but you aren't quite ready for the advanced level yet. Why don't you come for private lessons? You'll learn more that way, and I think it would be a great pleasure to teach you.'

I had enjoyed the class much more than I had expected. It had stirred something in my heart: perhaps the Spanish part of my blood that I was so unfamiliar with. I nodded my agreement. I preferred private tuition anyway, and I wasn't too worried about the cost. There wasn't anything I spent my money on besides dance: lessons, tickets, workshops, shoes.

'Good!' Carmen said, clapping her hands. 'Now all we have to do is work out a time. I have other students that I must sort out first . . . Can I telephone you early next week?'

Jaime picked up a notepad and pen and handed it to me so I could write down my telephone number. Although I could feel his gaze on me, I avoided his eyes.

'If I'm not at home and my grandmother answers the telephone,' I said, writing down my number, 'do you mind not mentioning that you are calling about flamenco lessons?'

Carmen raised her eyebrows quizzically.

'She's Catalan,' I explained. 'She doesn't . . . appreciate flamenco.'

'But if she's Catalan, she should know that the most famous flamenco dancer of modern times came from Barcelona,' replied Carmen. 'She is considered the mother of modern flamenco.'

'Really?' I asked, wondering if Mamie knew that or not. Perhaps I should be honest with her about taking flamenco lessons; it might appeal to her Catalonian pride.

'Her family was originally from Andalusia, but she was born in Barcelona,' added Jaime, placing his pleasingly shaped hands on his hips. 'It was the city that made her famous. She was taught by gypsies.'

'What was her name?' I asked, focusing on his chin to avoid his intense eyes.

'La Rusa.'

'La Rusa?' I repeated, surprised. 'The Russian? Why, if she was Spanish?'

'It was her stage name,' Carmen explained. 'Many flamenco singers and dancers had names like that: la Argentina, la Serneta, la Chunga. Either because that was the town they came from, or in honour of a relative or the person who made them famous.'

'Is she still alive?' I asked.

Jaime shook his head. 'No, la Rusa died in the 1950s. In Paris, in fact.'

'She committed suicide,' added Carmen. 'She'd led a tragic life.'

'Suicide? How sad.'

'Well, suicide was how it was reported, but there's always been controversy about that,' Jaime said, rubbing his chin. 'There are many who are convinced she was murdered.'

After warming up during the class, my skin suddenly felt cold. I was getting uncomfortable tingles down my spine.

'Who do they think killed her?' I asked.

Jaime frowned. 'No one knows for sure—or if they do, they aren't telling. Let's just say she had a reputation for being ruthless . . . and that she'd made a lot of enemies during the Civil War.'

EIGHT

Evelina

*D*earest Margarida,
   The inevitable has happened: Paloma has asked me to talk to her about Spain. For so long I have been able to avoid reliving the past. Julieta did not possess the same desire to understand her heritage. But Paloma, one step removed from the upheaval and missing her mother, is naturally curious. What shall I tell her? What can I say that doesn't rip at my heart? If I try to remember Mama and Pare and the beautiful house on the passeig de Gràcia where we spent so many happy years, all I can think about is how they were torn from us. And how can I talk about Barcelona without remembering our dearest brother? For many years, I could not bear to recall his kind eyes, his open face, his deep belief that the human race could evolve with compassion and reason. He loved the world so much that he wanted to change it—but he paid the price for such dreams. When I think of him, all I can see is that terrible day when you and I burned all that was precious to him: his papers, his party badge, his photographs . . . Oh, Xavier! Our darling Xavier! Forgive us! And then, of course, if I think of Barcelona I remember that whore . . . the one who betrayed him . . .

NINE

Celestina

After that day at the port, civil order in Barcelona began to break down. Workers and their families took part in nightly demonstrations against the war. They marched to the residence of the Marqués of Comillas to shout, 'Down with the war! Long live Spain and death to Comillas!' The protests ended with the police firing into the air and arresting the leaders.

Every evening, no matter how tired he was after work, Papá stayed late at the Casa del Pueblo's café to learn the latest news. Newspaper reports cabled from Madrid informed the people gathered there what was happening before the Barcelona newspapers could print it: that the reservists, seasick and with inadequate military training, were being marched off the transport ships and straight into battle. They were being routed.

To stop the flow of news from Madrid to Barcelona, Governor Ossorio ordered the cable lines cut. The Radicals called on Prime Minister Maura to reopen the Cortes, Spain's parliament, which he had closed to avoid debate on the war. The street demonstrations grew in mass, forcing the merchants to close their stores early. Workers were told to prepare for a general strike. Governor Ossorio prohibited groups from meeting on thoroughfares and warned that demonstrators could be shot. His proclamation further inflamed the workers. The editor of *El Poble Català* observed that all the valves had been closed and the steam was rising: *Does Ossorio truly believe that there won't be an explosion?*

The following Sunday, the Civil Guard made its presence felt on the streets, and sand was spread over the boulevards—a measure to prevent the horses of the mounted guards from slipping when they galloped in pursuit. Such a precaution was only adopted when serious trouble was expected. Unlike the previous Sunday, when Anastasio's battalion had marched down las Ramblas, the theatres and cafés were deserted.

Believing he had done all that was necessary to deter unrest, Governor Ossorio retired to his summer home on Mount Tibidabo, which overlooked Barcelona, with instructions that he was not to be disturbed until the following morning. Several hours before that, however, strike leaders had started gathering on street corners and in front of factories to alert workers that the general strike had begun.

'Celestina!'

I felt my father's hand on my shoulder, shaking me awake. I opened my eyes: it was still dark. The only light in the room came from a bulb above the door. Surely it couldn't be five o'clock already?

'Celestina,' Papá repeated, lifting me out of the cot. 'I must take you to Teresa earlier this morning.'

I yawned and tried to concentrate on what Papá was saying about us not seeing him for a few days, but everything was still blurry. I noticed Ramón standing by the door, dressed and with his shoes on.

'Here,' Papá said, sitting me on his bed and slipping on my sandals. But it was hopeless. My eyelids drooped again and my head lolled. The last thing I remember was Papá hoisting me over his shoulder.

When I awoke a few hours later, Teresa was leaning over me. 'Come on,' she said, sitting me up and holding a spoonful of bread soup near my lips. 'Quickly, eat this. Ramón has already had his. I need you both to be alert today and to listen to everything I say.'

She was wearing a white bow pinned to her sleeve. I didn't know the meaning of the bow, but I understood that something in our lives had changed.

'Aren't we going to the flower market this morning?' I asked.

Teresa shook her head. 'No. I will not be selling flowers today.'

Out on the street women with shopping baskets laden with bread and fruit hurried home from the market. They sensed trouble was brewing. Some factory workers strolled to work as if it were any other Monday, until other workers stopped them. 'Join us in protest against the war,' they said.

A few streets away, Juana, Paquita and some other women from Damas Rojas, also wearing white bows, were waiting for us. Laieta was there too. She told Teresa that Governor Ossorio, to promote himself as an able administrator, had cracked down on prostitutes and gamblers.

'Can't work in a factory. Can't work in a brothel. I'm screwed from all sides,' she said wryly.

We started walking in the direction of the port; from the women's conversation, I gathered we were heading towards a garment sweatshop owned by the Montella family.

'The workers there have been frightened out of striking,' Teresa explained to the women. 'But they take a break at eight o'clock. We will talk to them then, and explain how important this is.'

As we drew closer to the factory, more women joined us, spilling out of homes and shops. Some brought their children with them.

We arrived shortly at a building that looked similar to the tenement building where we lived, except waiting outside it was a carriage drawn by two white horses. The Montella family's crest was engraved on the carriage doors, and a driver in elegant black livery sat on the box.

'It looks as if Montella himself is here today,' noted Laieta. 'I've heard he likes to check up on the management of his sweat-shops.'

'It's his wife's carriage,' said Paquita. 'He gets around in a motor car. I didn't think she'd ever set foot in this place.'

I remembered baby Evelina. Would she be here today with her sister, Margarida?

Teresa expressed her surprise that no security guard was in attendance at the factory door. 'They usually have them to stop workers stealing things,' she muttered.

'You'd think today of all days there would be a guard,' Juana noted. 'But it's to our advantage that there isn't one. We won't have to wait until the break to speak to the workers.'

We piled into the factory after Teresa and Juana. There were gas lamps on the walls, but they hadn't been lit and the filtered daylight through the windows was barely enough to illuminate the interior. It was hotter inside the factory than it was out on the street. Many of the female machinists and cutters had stripped down to their camisoles and underskirts. The source of the heat was the pressing machines, worked by two men. The fabric dust burned my nostrils and I sneezed. It made me sad to remember that my mother had once worked in a place like this one.

'*Hola!*' Teresa cried out.

At first no one heard her above the din of the machines. She called out again. This time one of the machinists noticed her and took her foot off the pedal. Other workers looked up. When they saw the delegation of women and children, they stopped what they were doing.

'Come, join us!' Teresa urged them. 'If we don't all go out together, nothing will ever change.'

A couple of the women swept the pieces of fabric off their tables and stood up to join us. But most stayed at their places.

One young woman, perhaps only fourteen years of age, spoke up. 'Senyora, the foreman tells us he will hire prostitutes in our place if we walk out. I have no parents and six siblings to feed.'

'He can't replace all of us, Jimena,' one of the women who had joined us told her. 'And he'd be stuck to find any prostitute who can sew on buttons as quickly and as perfectly as you do.'

The sound of footsteps coming down the stairs caught our attention. We turned to see two men and a woman and child looking at us from the first-floor landing. The woman was more a vision than a human being. She wore an elegant gown of cream silk and white lace with a pink satin taffeta belt. On her head was a hat of black satin decorated with roses, buds and foliage. The hobble skirt of her dress just touched her black satin boots, which were embroidered with rosettes. The woman must have been around thirty years of age, but she did not look anything like the other thirty-year-old women in the factory. Her skin was soft and white, without a wrinkle or blemish. Next to her was a young boy of about ten years of age. He had the same honey-coloured eyes and chestnut hair as Evelina, and I guessed in an instant that he was her older brother. While his mother's eyes darted around the room like those of a frightened animal, the boy looked directly at me. I had the impression from the way his mouth twitched at the corners that he was trying not to smile. His eyes seemed gentle, and his stare captivated me for reasons I didn't understand. I remembered one of the women at the port saying, 'Don't the Montellas have a son?' She couldn't have been talking about this boy. He was too young to go to war.

The older of the two men eased himself past the woman and child and stepped onto the floor. 'I knew there was trouble when I heard the machines stop,' he said, eyeing Teresa up and down. 'What's going on here?'

Although his unruly hair was oiled down and he wore a suit, something told me that he was the foreman of the sweatshop.

The other man was too elegantly dressed, and I assumed he must be senyor Montella, the owner. He had a pug nose, like an Englishman; and the touches of grey in his hair and moustache, as well as the slight heaviness of his build, made me think he was in his early forties. But unlike Papá, his skin was still smooth except for some wrinkles around his eyes. It was the complexion of a man who went into the sun for leisure, not for work.

If Teresa was aware that she was being watched by one of her best customers, she didn't show it. 'If you don't let these workers join the strike, the men will come and smash your windows,' she warned senyor Montella and the foreman.

Senyor Montella moved onto the factory floor, guiding his wife behind him. 'Quickly, Rosita,' he said, nodding towards the waiting carriage. 'Take Xavier and go straight home. It is not a day to be out visiting.'

'But la senyora de Sagarra is expecting us,' his wife protested. 'And she's been so sick.'

'She has her nurse and her maids. She will understand,' senyor Montella assured her.

His wife took her son's hand and slid past us like a person trying to avoid a herd of predators. The boy, Xavier, wasn't afraid, however. He didn't take his eyes off me, as if he were puzzled by something. What fascinated him so?

'I don't know what you are hoping to achieve,' senyor Montella said to the women of Damas Rojas once his wife's carriage had departed. 'Without the iron mines in Spanish Morocco, our economy will collapse. There won't be jobs for anyone. Then what will you do?'

'If that is true,' said Juana, facing him squarely, 'then why aren't the twenty-year-old rich boys going to war instead of poor young fathers and husbands?'

Senyor Montella lifted his chin. 'That,' he said, tugging at his shirt cuffs, 'is simply the workings of the economic system in which we live. Those who can pay reap the benefits.'

The women of Damas Rojas scoffed and catcalled at such outrageous arrogance.

'You see,' said Teresa, turning to her supporters. 'These are the words of a devout Catholic!'

One of the older machinists who had been listening rose from her seat. The movement was so regal, so calm and dignified, that everyone in the room fell quiet. All eyes were on the grey-haired woman, who said nothing as she packed away her fabric and wrapped her shawl over her shoulders. She then walked slowly across the factory floor to join the women of Damas Rojas. The rest of the workers followed her. It was only when the factory was cleared that the woman lifted her eyes to her employer.

'If that's the economy we exist in, senyor Montella, then it must be changed. I can accept that the rich can buy better shoes and clothes and live in nice homes. But I cannot accept that one human's life is worth more than another's simply because he has money.'

By nine o'clock that morning, the strike had closed factories all over the suburbs of Barcelona. Two hundred and fifty workers at the Hispano-Suiza automobile works had walked out on their jobs and had persuaded the workers in more than a dozen other plants to join them. The movement now headed towards the centre of the city.

Ramón and I marched with the women of Damas Rojas and their supporters towards the passeig de Gràcia, where many of the shops were still open. The wide, tree-lined boulevard was a striking contrast to the place where we lived. Even the air smelled different, free of the disease that plagued the atmosphere of the barri Xinès. Everywhere we saw boys on bicycles, women being chauffeured in motor cars, men with bowler hats and walking canes, as if it were any normal day.

Our group ran to the shops and banged on the doors. 'Close now for our brothers in Morocco!' we shouted. The shopkeepers hurriedly locked their doors and pulled down their grilles as if they had been only awaiting our command.

I had never seen such luxury. Apart from the bookshops, *chocolatiers*, delicatessens and shops selling porcelain and silverware, there was a shop devoted entirely to silver spice and tobacco boxes. The store next to it was full of strange stick-like devices with numbered dials on them. 'They are telephones,' Paquita explained to me. 'So people in one part of the city can speak to those in another.' I was amazed.

The protest might have remained a peaceful one-day strike if not for the trams, which were still running. Mariano de Foronda, the director of Barcelona's tram system and a close friend of King Alfonso, was a known opponent of the labour movement. The rumour was that he was driving around the city in his motor car, threatening the tram drivers if they stopped work.

Teresa and the women hurled abuse at the drivers when the trams passed us. 'You are traitors to the cause!' they shouted.

'We are just obeying orders!' the drivers replied.

We met some more women from Damas Rojas and Damas Radicales. They were carrying a banner that read 'Down With the War!'

'The workers from Poble Nou are here,' Pilar, the fishmonger, told Teresa. 'They say trams have been attacked by workers in that district and now Governor Ossorio has put armed security guards on them. But that won't stop us!'

'Be careful,' warned Juana. 'The authorities might be deliberately trying to provoke violence. That way they can declare martial law and bring in the army.'

Pilar shrugged. 'We've been asked to walk in front of the workers with our sign so the guards and police won't shoot.'

I looked around the crowd and wondered where my father was right now. Things were beginning to sound dangerous.

The women and workers started to organise themselves into a formation, but before they had a chance to finish, a tram appeared around the corner. People picked up stones to throw at it. A side window shattered. The security guard on board, a young man not much older than Anastasio, aimed his gun at the workers, who were ripping up the track ahead of the tram. He fired. Luckily for them, he was a poor shot. But his action enraged the crowd, which included onlookers and their children.

Before we knew what was happening, Ramón and I were caught in a crush of people pressing towards the tram, which had come to a stop before the ruined track. The driver, guard and passengers alighted in a panic as the crowd threw its weight against the side of the vehicle, heaving against it until it toppled on its side. The workers and women cheered. A young man ran out of a nearby building with a lit torch in his hand. He threw it into the tram and the wooden seats quickly caught fire, eliciting more whoops and cheers from the onlookers.

Later in the day, Teresa took me and Ramón to the Casa del Pueblo, which was abuzz with activity.

'What's the latest?' Teresa asked Núria, who was handing out food packages.

'A short while ago some workers attacked a tram, with guns they had stolen from a police station. They forced the driver and passengers to get off, then released the brakes and sent the tram careening down the street. The Civil Guard arrived and fired on the workers, who opened fire in return. Now, two tram drivers and three of our own are dead. Many others were wounded. A little girl was killed in the crossfire.'

The news about the child who had been killed upset Teresa. 'That's it for the day,' she said, urging Ramón and me back out onto the street. 'We are heading home. I promised your father I'd look after you, and that I will.'

We stayed inside Teresa's stifling apartment that afternoon, while women from Damas Rojas came and went with messages regarding the progress of the day. Teresa jumped from her chair and raised both her fists in the air when Carme arrived with the news that the trams had been brought to a standstill.

'I hope that arrogant de Foronda is satisfied now,' she said. 'What did he achieve? Burned-out trams and ripped-up tracks!'

A young boy brought us a note from Papá to let us know that he was unharmed. *Teresa, we've been told that workers in*

Madrid are impressed by how quickly we've crippled the city's industry and commerce, and that they are now planning to strike themselves, he wrote.

His message brought light to Teresa's eyes. 'If the whole country unites against the war, they will have to stop it,' she said. 'If we act as one, we can change things.'

Although there had been a bloody exchange of fire between police and protesters outside the army headquarters on passeig de Colom the previous evening, Tuesday morning started quietly. Women hung out the washing and children played in the streets. There was no wheeled traffic and no newspapers. There weren't even communiqués posted on public buildings by the Captain General ordering workers to report to their factories and places of employment.

Teresa opened her flower stall at the markets until nine o'clock, joking with the other vendors that the Montella servants had wisely not shown their faces. Laieta brought the news that Governor Ossorio had resigned.

'What?' exclaimed Teresa, keeling over with laughter. 'Is he that great a coward? What governor leaves his post when his city is in the midst of a battle? Who have they got to replace him?'

'General Santiago has stepped in.'

'No!' Teresa laughed again. 'I've heard he is incompetent.'

'He is as long as he has men from Barcelona in his command. Did you hear what happened at the docks yesterday evening?'

Teresa shook her head.

'That bastard General Brandeis ordered his dragoons to fire on the dock workers and their wives. But the people hoisted themselves onto crates and trolleys and shouted, "Don't shoot, our brothers, we are fighting for you! We are fighting for your lives!"'

Teresa's jaw dropped. 'What happened?'

'The soldiers refused to fire. How could they do otherwise? They may as well be shooting their own families.'

Teresa put her hands to her mouth in delighted amazement.

Laieta smiled. 'Now the workers all over the town are doing the same thing. They cheer and applaud the soldiers who are sent to attack them and the men won't fire.'

Despite our elated mood after Laieta's news, the streets around Teresa's apartment looked different on our way home from the market. The residents were ripping up the cobblestones to build barricades, and adding sewer covers, bed frames, lampposts and anything else they could get their hands on to reinforce them. Where there were electrical lines, they were being cut. It looked as though people were preparing for a full-scale battle.

'What's going on?' Teresa asked one of the women.

'We've been told something big is going to happen this afternoon, and to ready ourselves against mounted charges.'

Teresa glanced at the men wielding weapons and practising their aim. I could see she was torn between her promise to protect us and her longing to be part of the action. We were about to move on when a boy on a bicycle came to a halt in front of us.

'Are you Teresa Flores García?' he asked. Teresa nodded and the boy handed her a slip of paper. 'It's instructions from your friends at the Casa del Pueblo.'

The boy rode off and Teresa opened the paper. Ramón and I stared over her shoulder, anxious to know what information it contained. I couldn't read the words; all I could see was that it was a list along with a map. Ramón, who was more advanced in reading than I was, muttered the names: 'Sant Antoni, Sant Pau del Camp . . .'

Teresa looked at us, then turned to the workers at the barricade. 'It has begun!' she cried. 'The Revolution!'

The people stopped what they were doing and stared at her. She waved the paper in the air so they could see it.

'They are burning the churches!' she said, her eyes shining. 'This afternoon!'

TEN

Paloma

The day after my first flamenco lesson, I returned to the Bibliothèque Sainte-Geneviève, intending to continue my research on the supernatural. It was coming up to examination time at the Paris universities, and the library was even more crowded than it had been on my previous visit. The atmosphere had transformed from scholarly zeal to exhaustion and edginess. I noticed one student leaning against the staircase, who appeared to have fallen asleep standing up. I was glad to see that he shook himself awake after a few seconds and picked up his books before his knees relaxed and he toppled to the floor. If I had gone to a regular school, I could have been one of the students swotting here now. What would I have studied? Art, or the history of music, perhaps? I couldn't even imagine it. It seemed to me that from the moment I had opened my eyes and taken my first gasp of air, I had lived and breathed ballet. Hadn't my mother been dancing the part of Giselle when she first realised she was pregnant? Hadn't she been listening to the waltz from *Sleeping Beauty* when she went into labour?

While I waited for the librarian to retrieve the books by Sir Arthur Conan Doyle and Helena Petrovna Blavatsky, I found myself thinking about Jaime. I wondered whether he had been born in Spain or France. I guessed Spain because of his slight Spanish accent. Which region was he from? Then I wondered why I was wondering about him, and stopped myself. I thought about what he'd told me about la Rusa instead. What had she done during the Civil War that had made her so hated that somebody might have killed her all those years later? It occurred to me that Mamie might know, but I had to stick to my promise of not asking her questions about the past.

I collected my books, but before sitting down with them, I searched the card catalogue to see if the library's collection included anything on flamenco dancers. I found a book titled *The Encyclopaedia of Flamenco* that I thought could be a good start. The wait for the book, however, was longer than it had been for the other materials. When the librarian finally placed the encyclopaedia on the pick-up shelf, I couldn't find a free seat at one of the desks to read it. So I balanced it on the edge of a desk and leafed through the pages on the great flamenco guitarists and singers until I reached the section on dancers. Carmen had been right about the stage names. La Joselito had taken her name from a bullfighter who had been trampled to death in 1920; Antonia Mercé was la Argentina because she was born in Buenos Aires; la Mejorana was named after an herb. Flamenco aficionados, it seemed, were not averse to designating names in reference to dancers' physical disabilities, or those of their parents: La Sordita was deaf; and la Niña del Ciego was 'the daughter of the blind one'. The gypsies had a particularly warped humour, or maybe it was superstition, because the contemporary dancer la Chunga's name meant 'the unattractive one', even though in the photograph the encyclopaedia showed of her she was bewitchingly beautiful.

Then I found what I was looking for:

La Rusa was born in the slum area of Barcelona known as the barri Xinès to Andalusian parents in 1901. Out of her pov-

*erty she rose to become one of the most famous flamenco danc-
ers of her time. Despite her newly gained wealth and prestige,
she sided with the Republicans in Barcelona during the Civil
War (1936–39), perhaps in memory of her father, who had been
a member of the Radical Party during the strikes of 1909. Her
loyalty to the masses turned out to be a decision for which she
paid dearly when she was forced to live in exile. She died in 1952
in Paris.*

That was all. There was nothing about la Rusa's real name,
or why she had taken her unusual stage name. There was nothing about where she had lived in Paris. But one thing puzzled
me above all else: if she had fought on the side of the Republicans against Franco during the Civil War, why would anyone in
the Spanish émigré community have wanted to kill her? Most
of them had been Republican supporters too. Then I remembered Mamie once telling me that Franco was supposed to have
arranged the assassinations of several high-profile exiles, especially if they had continued to speak out against his regime. Was
that what had happened to la Rusa?

The snippets of incomplete information made my curiosity
grow. I returned the book along with those on the supernatural,
and went back to the catalogue to see if I could find another
book that might have more information about la Rusa. The clock
on the wall caught my attention. It was already half past twelve.
I was cutting it fine to get back in time for Mamie's afternoon
class. If there was anything my grandmother hated, it was a lack
of punctuality—especially in front of her students.

I found two other books on the history of flamenco and filled
in the request slips quickly. The notice at the desk said there was
a waiting time of thirty minutes for books, but those I had requested didn't arrive until three-quarters of an hour later. I had
fifteen minutes to get to the Métro station if I wanted to make
Mamie's class on time.

I didn't even bother taking the books into the reading room,
but crouched down against a wall and balanced them on my lap.

I browsed through the first book, which explained flamenco in general terms. *It is an art that has been taken over by show business, but it wasn't always the gaudy tourist spectacle that it has become today.* Interesting, but I would have to save reading that for later. I swapped the book for the next one. It had a long chapter at the front about the history and origins of flamenco, but at the back there was a section on the artists of the past and present. It didn't list the dancers in any logical order, however, and I had to scan the copy to see if it contained anything about la Rusa.

'Mademoiselle, you cannot stay here.' I looked up to see the security guard frowning at me. 'You must place yourself at a reading desk to use the library's books.'

I only had five minutes left to skim through the book, but I could see from the guard's expression that pressing the point was not going to get me anywhere. One of the students in the reading room stood up and left his seat. I quickly took it, cringing inwardly when I found it so warm.

I checked the page titled 'The Women of Flamenco'. *Zapateado—the drumming sound made with the feet—was originally performed only by male dancers. The women used mostly their hands, arms and shoulders. That was changed by dancers such as la Rusa . . .* I flipped over to the next page and my heart skipped a beat when I saw the woman in the black-and-white photograph: the mane of jet-black hair; the arched brows framing panther-like eyes; the broad nose and the full lips. The lips were black in the photograph, but I knew they were blood-red in real life. I swallowed and tried to breathe. My pulse was hammering in my head. I read the caption: *La Rusa—Celestina Sánchez, 1932.*

The room around me turned white as my blood drained to my feet. I was staring at the face of my ghost. It was la Rusa who had given me the golden earrings. It was la Rusa who had come to see me.

ELEVEN

Celestina

The first religious building we saw set alight was the Royal Monastery of Sant Mateu, which housed an order of cloistered Hieronymite nuns. Although numerous churches, monasteries, convents and religious schools were scheduled to be burned that afternoon, Teresa and the women from Damas Rojas were keen to attend the torching of Sant Mateu because the laundries they owned had put many of the local women out of work.

The workers agreed that attacks were to be on the clergy's property only; no lives were to be taken. It was therefore necessary to clear the buildings before setting them alight. Although the nuns of Sant Mateu had been warned in advance that their building was on the list to be destroyed, they refused to leave.

The crowd cheered and chanted when groups of youths brought ladders to scale the building while men and women worked together to force open the doors. A man in a well-cut suit and sporting a cane instructed the rest of us to build a bonfire from the materials that the youths, who had now entered the convent, were throwing down to us. We worked quickly to build a stack from the chairs, books and bedding. We had no idea that the papers being thrown down to us were stocks worth over a million *pesetas*.

'The convents have enjoyed their wealth at your expense,' the stranger said. 'We are to burn everything—jewels, cash, statues. All of it. There is to be no looting.'

No sooner had he spoken than a gold chain with a large medallion dropped near my feet. I threw it on the unlit pile, but another woman, who obviously understood its worth better than I did, grabbed it when she thought no one was looking and slipped it into her pocket.

'They are escaping out the back,' a cry from a window alerted us.

Teresa called to Ramón and grabbed my arm and we ran together with the others to a street at the rear of the convent. The nuns were fleeing through the laundries at the back of the building, but their escape was blocked by the neighbourhood women, who were throwing stones and jeering at them.

'Now you will be as poor as we are,' screamed one of the women. 'May you know what it is like to have no food in your belly!'

One of the nuns screamed back, 'You are fools! That wealth is the dowries of nuns for over four hundred years, and all those stocks you are throwing on the bonfire are the property of private citizens!'

The women paid no attention and continued to jeer.

One nun saw a gap in the crowd and made a break for it. Some of the others raced after her, with the local women on their heels. The nuns banged on the door of a house of a leading factory owner. A servant opened the door, but Teresa shouted, 'Let them in and we will torch your building too!' The door slammed shut.

For a moment, the nuns were confused that their neighbours should turn on them this way. Then they began to scatter in all directions. The women were about to pursue them when a young girl cried out that smoke was beginning to rise from the convent.

Teresa called to the women. 'Let them go. We've scared them enough. Long live the Revolution!'

The atmosphere that evening was eerie. From the roof of Teresa's building, we saw fires burning all over the city and we could hear the blasts of cannons and shooting as the guards and police attacked barricades. It was a still, hot night and the smell from the drains was rank. I rested my head against Ramón's shoulder, resisting falling asleep in case we suddenly had to flee the building. I had participated in the burning of a convent that afternoon and yet I still prayed to God to keep Papá, who we had heard was fighting in the Clot-Sant Martí area, safe.

Paquita arrived with some bean stew for us. Ramón and I were so famished that we wolfed down the hearty mix. Paquita leaned against Teresa, exhausted.

'A Franciscan father was killed in Sant Gervasi today,' she said. 'He was trying to run away with cash and someone shot him.'

Teresa shrugged. 'Barcelona will be better off without those hypocrites.'

Paquita lifted her eyebrow. 'I am against the clergy because their manner of education perpetuates ignorance and misery. But you, Teresa, you seem to truly hate them.'

Teresa stared at her hands. 'They've given me good reason,' she said. 'My father died when I was five years old, and my mother had to place me and my sister in an orphanage so she could work. I think she believed the nuns were good women and would take care of us.'

Paquita and Teresa exchanged a glance. 'I'm guessing that they didn't,' said Paquita.

'Good women!' cried Teresa. 'They spoke of God's divine love and at the same time forced sick children to eat their own vomit. I saw a boy beaten near to death for using his left hand.'

Despite the heat, I shivered and snuggled closer to Ramón, who put his arm around me.

'I can't bear to hear those stories,' said Paquita, shaking her head. 'There are far too many of them. But there are decent nuns and priests too. That's why they spared the hospital for incurably ill children at Les Corts.'

We sat on the roof for another hour before Teresa decided it was time for us to go to sleep. She tucked us into her bed before accompanying Paquita to the door.

'Decent nuns? Decent priests? I've never seen such a thing!' I heard her tell Paquita. Teresa always spoke in a passionate manner, but the sound of her voice shocked me: it was the howl of a wounded animal.

Paquita, also taken aback, put her hand on Teresa's shoulder. 'What happened to you?'

There was a long silence before Teresa found the courage to speak. 'My sister always stood up for me. "We will break that will of yours," the nuns used to tell her . . .' Teresa's voice faltered. 'And they did . . . They used to make her sleep in the damp cellar and turned a blind eye to the priest who went there to molest her.'

'Oh God!' said Paquita, putting her arm around Teresa's shoulders.

'She died as a result of one of his sick beatings,' said Teresa, turning her face to Paquita. 'She was seven years old!'

I pressed closer to Ramón. Molested? I didn't understand the word. But I could see from the way Teresa's shoulders shook as she gave way to tears that something terrible had happened. Perhaps that was why Anastasio had refused to desert. If Papá had been put in gaol, maybe Ramón and I would have been sent to an orphanage too. We had been poor and hungry all our lives, but our parents were always kind. We had never been mistreated by them.

Teresa's story stayed with me the next day when we went with her to meet some of the women from Damas Rojas at the plaça del Pedró. Housewives and factory workers had gathered there to exchange news of the rebellion. Suddenly an excited woman started screaming that her sister, a nun at a nearby convent, had been tortured by her fellow nuns for being attractive. The crowd followed the woman to the convent in question. Some of them entered it and a while later reappeared dragging caskets with mummified remains in them. I reeled back in horror at the sight of the desiccated faces and sunken torsos. The corpses' mouths were stretched wide open, as if they were screaming.

'They were buried alive,' whispered Ramón.

'Look, their feet and hands are tied,' observed one woman. 'They've been martyred.'

The women took the caskets to plaça del Pedró and put them on display. Juana made a sign for them: 'Martyred Nuns'.

'Why are they permitted to bury their dead inside the convents when the city's health laws forbid it?' Juana asked the gathered spectators. 'It's due to their unhygienic practises that the rest of us suffer typhoid and cholera.'

Typhoid? I thought of my mother, buried in a pauper's grave. Had she died because of these nuns? Rage boiled in my blood. My reaction was reflected in the crowd as several women cried out that they had lost children to those diseases.

'We'll take these corpses to City Hall,' said Juana. 'And demand they stop the practise of cloistered orders burying their dead in their walls.'

Her announcement brought enthusiastic shouts from the spectators. Some youths picked up the caskets and headed for City Hall, most of the crowd following to make their demands. A few women, however, dragged some corpses to the barricades on the corner of carrer del Carme and carrer d'en Roig. We later learned that men from the barricades had dumped the cadavers on the doorsteps of the houses of the Güell, Comillas and Montella families. One of the bodies had ended up propped up in front of a church with a cigarette in its mouth, like a prostitute; while a simple-minded coalman danced with another. He was later arrested and executed for his profane act.

The following evening, my father returned for us. He looked weary and exhausted.

'General Santiago has only been biding his time,' he told Teresa. 'He knows the troops here in Barcelona can't be trusted. He's brought in new troops—a lot of them—from Valencia and Zaragoza. These soldiers will not shoot above our heads.'

'Yes, they will,' said Teresa. 'Whether the troops are from Barcelona or Zaragoza, we are fighting for them all.'

Papá shook his head grimly. 'The reports we heard about the rest of the country striking along with us . . . they weren't true. They were lies perpetrated by the Strike Committee to keep us fighting. Nobody else has stopped work in protest, not even in Madrid.'

Teresa flinched. 'I don't understand,' she said.

'While communications with Barcelona have been cut off, the Minister for the Interior has been doing a good propaganda job in convincing the rest of the country that we are not waging an anti-war movement but a Catalan separatist uprising. They are against us, not for us!'

'So there will be no Revolution?' asked Teresa, her voice cracking. 'Because we are outnumbered?'

'It is futile to continue,' said Papá.

Teresa was as pale as a ghost. 'So what now?'

Papá clenched his fists. 'What there will be now are arrests and executions.'

Our meal together that evening was grim. There wasn't much fresh food available in the barri Xinès, so Teresa made us chickpeas and rice. We ate together in silence. Afterwards, Ramón and I returned with Papá to our own apartment. It seemed strange to be there without Anastasio. Papá lay down on the bed and Ramón and I nestled on either side of him. Ramón fell asleep immediately, but Papá remained awake and listened to my story about the dead nuns with bound feet.

'We don't know that they were tortured,' said Papá, trying to comfort me. 'It might be some sort of Hieronymite ritual. Maybe the nuns bind the feet and hands of the dead so they fit in the coffins.'

'Nobody thought of that,' I said.

Papá stroked my hair. After a while, he sat up and slipped out of the bed. He took a knife from the cupboard and kneeled to loosen a floorboard. After lifting it, he placed his hand into the space and pulled out a box. When he opened the lid, I caught a glimpse of something shiny inside. He took out two golden hooped earrings and lifted them for me to see.

'Do you remember these?' he asked. 'They were your mother's.'

'Yes, I remember them,' I said. I saw my mother before me, as she had been when she was well: her dark skin and flashing eyes; her mane of rich black hair. She was dancing, her feet connecting with the ground as if she and the earth were one.

'She didn't want to take them to the grave,' Papá said. 'She insisted that they be left for you. Do you remember the legend she told you about them?'

I nodded. 'They must never be sold,' I said, repeating the exact words my mother had said. 'If they are stolen, the thief will die a terrible death.'

Father put the earrings back in the box and returned them to their hiding place. 'Now you know where they are,' he whispered, fixing the floorboard back. 'You mustn't tell anybody.'

I gave him my promise.

Truthfully, the powers my mother had told me that the earrings possessed frightened me and I didn't like to think too much about them. But what was more upsetting was the pinch of sadness in my heart. Why was my father showing me where the earrings were now? Did he have some premonition that something would happen to him?

* * *

The following morning, we rose at five o'clock as usual. It could have been any ordinary morning, except that Anastasio wasn't with us and the defeat we had always felt in our hearts now lay heavily upon us. The last of our hopes that anything might change for the better left us when we saw officers of the Civil Guard holding workers at gunpoint, ordering them to dismantle the barricades. In some of the outer suburbs, the fighting continued, but without the support of the rest of the country the hope of a revolution was futile. The number of troops being brought in far outweighed the strikers. All the workers could do now was go back to their daily lives and wait for the repercussions that would surely follow their acts of protest.

When we arrived at the market, Teresa was putting on display the few carnations and geraniums that she had on hand.

'Paquita's been arrested,' she told my father.

'You'd better lie low,' Papá warned her. 'Although it might be because she worked at the Ferrer School. You know the government and clergy have been dying to get their hands on them for years.'

'And you?' Teresa asked, looking at my father with a worried expression on her face. 'You are going back to the factory?'

Papá nodded. He was about to leave when Juana arrived. Her complexion was wan. She turned even greener when she saw Papá.

'What is it?' Teresa asked her. 'Has someone else been arrested?'

Juana shook her head. 'I've heard the most terrible rumour,' she said. 'When the troops arrived in Morocco after that incident at the port, they took ten men off the ship who had thrown their religious medals into the water and shot them as a warning to the others.'

Papá reeled back. His fingers gripped Teresa's stand, as if he were trying to steady himself. A sick feeling rose in my stomach. Juana's husband had thrown his medal into the water, but so had a lot of the men. It was Anastasio who did it first: the other men had followed his example. Was it possible that Anastasio had been executed?

'If those hypocritical bitches hadn't been at the port that day, none of this would have happened!' sobbed Juana. 'They were the ones that set everyone off with their two-faced blessings.'

A look that frightened me fell over Papá's face. His pupils dilated like those of a crazy man.

Teresa grabbed his shoulders. 'José, it's only a rumour! And we've heard nothing but lies all week. We risked our lives believing the whole country was behind us. *Estupideces*! This is probably another trick to get us back onto the streets! Why would they be shooting soldiers they have just transported over to Morocco? It sounds like they need everyone they can get!'

Teresa's logic calmed Papá. He stood up and straightened his clothes. If no other blow had come to my father that day, then perhaps he would have gone quietly to his work at the factory and normal life would have resumed. But then Laieta arrived with more bad news.

'That bloody Santiago,' she said. 'He is thumbing his nose at us. He's going to march the Saboya Infantry to the wharf today and ship them off to Morocco, as he did Anastasio's battalion.'

Papá didn't go back to the factory that day. Instead, we joined the crowd of spectators who watched in silence as the Saboya Infantry was marched down las Ramblas with a guard of troops and mounted policemen. We had risked our lives and gone hungry to show our opposition to the war. Who would take up our cause now? Did we have anyone to represent us in the Cortes? The Radical leaders and Republicans had not been prepared to lead us to revolution; they had been more concerned with protecting their own political ambitions. The only action available to us—to strike and to rebel—had failed. The footsteps of the marching soldiers stamped out the obvious: we were the downtrodden and always would be.

Ramón hoisted me onto a parked cart so I could see better. I turned to my father, and cringed when I noticed that the mad look had returned to his eyes.

Despite the overwhelming numbers of the police escort, he cupped his hands to his mouth and shouted out to the soldiers: 'You are allowing yourselves to be led off to the slaughterhouse!'

No one in the crowd said anything. No one seconded his cry. But Papá wasn't to be stopped. He shoved his way past the spectators and into the midst of the battalion.

'Refuse!' he shouted. 'You are going to your deaths!'

The soldiers marched on, impervious to my father's entreaties. He grabbed one man's shoulder. 'Young man, is your life not as precious as anybody else's?'

The soldier's face remained blank as he shoved Papá away with the butt of his rifle. I had the sense that the soldier's action was not so much out of anger but for Papá's own safety. The guards had been ordered to arrest any dissenters.

Teresa pushed through the crowd, trying to reach Papá. 'José! José!' she called.

Ramón tried to get through too, but the crowd was packed together. I knew that I had to reach Papá. I had to bring him back.

I jumped off the cart and struggled between the sea of legs, my size to my advantage, and out into the parade. A soldier bumped into me and I fell backwards.

'Papá!'

I saw him running ahead of me. 'Don't go! Don't go!' he was shouting to the soldiers.

A policeman grabbed him and flung him into a crowd of women spectators. The women tried to hold on to him but he wrestled himself free.

I struggled to my feet. 'Papá! Papá!' My legs were trembling beneath me although I had gained some ground.

But before I could reach him, Papá grabbed the reins of a horse carrying a guard. The horse whinnied and pranced backwards with fear. The guard pulled out his revolver and pointed it at Papá.

'*Vete, cerdo*! Let go, scumbag!'

'Papá!' I tried to scream, but there was no air left in my lungs.

'You're a pack of murderers!' my father shouted at the guard. 'Nothing but a cheap bunch of murderers!'

The guard tried to kick my father away, but he held on to the reins. The horse reared. A shot rang through the air. Suddenly the spectators were screaming and reeling backwards.

I saw my father clutch his neck and fall to his knees. I ran towards him. When I reached him, he was lying on his back. Blood was spurting from his neck. I pressed my hand to the wound and tried to stem the bleeding, but I could feel the blood pumping out.

A crowd gathered around. The gun had not been fired by the mounted guard but by an officer a few yards away. I remembered Papá's words: *He's brought in new troops—a lot of them—from Valencia and Zaragoza. These soldiers will not shoot above our heads.*

Papá looked into my eyes. He tried to say something but the words wouldn't come. His eyes glazed over and I knew that he was gone.

Part II

Part II

TWELVE

Paloma

Saturday was our busiest day for classes at Mamie's ballet school, so in the evening we'd usually eat a simple meal of chicory leaf salad and saffron rice with pine nuts and bell peppers. 'Our pick-me-up-gently meal' Mamie called it. Afterwards we would sit on the sofa in the living room, massaging each other's feet and watching *Numéro 1*, the Maritie and Gilbert Carpentier variety show, on television. The week that I had started flamenco lessons at the Académie de Flamenco, Mamie seemed perturbed. She sat with her arms folded and pursed her lips. I had an uneasy feeling that she might have found out that I was up to something behind her back. Had she run into Gaby and discovered that we didn't go and see a film together? I did my best to look innocent, dangling my tired legs over the side of the sofa and playing with my hair. Joe Dassin was singing his hit '*L'été indien*' against a backdrop of shimmering lights. I was humming along with him when Mamie rose and turned off the television. I sat up with a start. But Mamie wasn't about to remonstrate with me for learning flamenco. She had something else on her mind.

'I want to tell you about my family,' she said, her frown lines deepening. 'The Montellas.'

She stared at me, studying my reaction. There it was again: 'the Montellas'. What was so significant about the family? I placed my hands in my lap, letting her know that she had my attention. Mamie cleared her throat.

'Your grandfather once made me promise never to tell you this . . .' She hesitated and fidgeted with her hands. I knew that talking about the past was difficult for her; she had kept her silence for so long. But I didn't want her to stop now she had built up the courage.

'Go on,' I prompted her.

Mamie sucked in a breath. 'My brother, Xavier, was thirty-nine when he was executed by Franco's forces,' she said with measured calm, as if she had been rehearsing this opening for some time. 'He had been betrayed by someone he loved; someone for whom he had sacrificed himself but who turned on him like a wild animal one foolishly believes has been tamed. Your grandfather and I had to flee Spain, along with my sister, Margarida.'

Mamie paused for a moment, to see if her words were making sense. I found it hard to meet her gaze. I was battling with a sense of shame at my own self-absorption. Why had I always assumed that Mamie was an only child, like myself and my mother? It had never occurred to me that she might have had siblings. I realised it was because I'd only ever seen Mamie in relation to myself, as my grandmother. Not as a person who might have once had parents, brothers and sisters, and youthful ambitions of her own.

'But that is the end of the story,' Mamie said, coming to sit beside me. 'And I must tell you it from the beginning. But before I can do that, there is something else I have to tell you; something that might come as a bit of shock.'

My jaw clenched. I dreaded what I might hear. But hadn't I asked for this? Hadn't I been the one to beg for stories about Spain? There was nothing for me to do but nod for Mamie to continue.

Mamie rubbed her hands and glanced at the wedding ring she still wore on her finger. 'Conchita isn't a friend of the family,' she said. 'She was once my sister-in-law: Xavier's wife.'

I felt as though I'd been struck by a hammer. I tried to comprehend what Mamie had just said. I saw Conchita as I held her in my head: a beautifully groomed, eccentric old lady who gave me sweets and whom Mamie looked after. Now I found the image shaken up. So the Spanish husband who was never spoken about had been Mamie's brother? That made reticent Feliu Mamie's nephew—and my cousin! I thought of him in his brown leather bomber jacket, sitting quietly with Mamie over a cup of coffee and never staying more than half an hour. Questions ran around in my head, but then I remembered I wasn't allowed to ask them. Instead I made sure I had the facts right.

'So Conchita was your brother's wife?' I asked. 'She was Conchita Montella by marriage, and you were Evelina Montella before you married Avi?'

Mamie nodded and touched my knee, as if she was trying to soothe me. 'So you might understand better, I'm going to tell you a story,' she said. 'It's about something that seemed ordinary the day it happened, but soon came to carry great significance. I think it will help you understand the Montellas and our place in Catalan society.'

It was 1927: the fourth year of the rule of General Primo de Rivera. He was the dictator who had overthrown the Cortes, Spain's parliament, and made Spain prosperous again, lining the pockets of the 'good families' of Barcelona, including my own, the Montellas. It was November, and these families had gathered in the Old Cemetery for the Feast of All Souls. The section of the cemetery where our procession was headed had not been part of the architect's original plan for an egalitarian burial ground that was to be symmetrically laid out, divided by broad, tree-lined avenues, like a well-planned city. We passed under an arched portico and into an empire of neo-gothic and neo-classical mausolea and crypts with monuments that had been created by famous sculptors. It was where the rich of Barcelona buried their dead.

I cast my eye over the gathering. It was the same collection of faces that I saw everywhere: at church, at the opera, at any significant social event. These were the elite who had controlled the Catalan economy for almost two centuries. They kept their wealth intact through intermarriage and the custom of a single heir, so family fortunes were never diluted. It seemed everyone there that day was only a step or two removed from a Güell, a López or a Girona. Even the tombs bore the names of the families who still influenced Barcelona: the Nadals; the Serras; the Formigueras. Except my family, of course: the Montellas. We were the *nous rics*, the 'newly rich'—something Pare hoped to correct by marrying me off to a son of an established family whose declining fortune might cause him to find me attractive not only for my youthful charms but also my substantial dowry.

The gathering separated, with each family heading in the direction of their mausoleum. I linked arms with my mother and we followed Pare to the part of the cemetery where the Montella family's tomb had been built. It was as grand as any other in the section, fashioned from Carrara marble and covered in carvings of beautiful doves, but so far it contained only two coffins. It had been commissioned by my grandfather, Ignaci Montella, who had made his fortune in Puerto Rico. He now lay at peace there with his wife, Elvira, who had died young and left my father an only child.

While Pare strolled ahead, enjoying the parklike atmosphere of the cemetery, my mother and I took a detour to look at our favourite sculpture. It was a reproduction of Federico Fabiani's famous statue of a winged angel lifting the soul of a young woman heavenwards. There were many beautiful sculptures in the cemetery, but this one held a special attraction for me: it was somehow comforting and I didn't fear death when I gazed at it.

But what did I know of death? I was only eighteen and had no inkling of the carnage that was to come.

'Excuse me, senyora Montella. May I take a picture of you with your daughter?'

We turned to see the society writer from *Diario de Barcelona* smiling at us from beneath his hooked moustache. Before my mother had a chance to answer, he signalled to his photographer, but my mother raised her hand to cover my face.

'That is out of the question,' she told the reporter firmly. 'My daughter isn't out in society yet.'

At my age, I should have already made my debut. But Pare said I needed to learn to 'talk without stuttering and stammering' before he would give my mother permission to bring me out. That was why he had finally agreed to Olga. My ballet teacher had arrived at our house the week before in a cloud of Guerlain's Shalimar perfume and with a Fabergé pendant dangling from her swan-like throat. She had been a dancer in St. Petersburg and had fled the city during the Revolution, escaping on a steamer bound for Sweden. Olga had already filled my head with such romantic stories that even if she didn't build my confidence, she would at least make my life infinitely more interesting. Her presence inspired terror and adoration in people: a combination Pare had hoped would shock me out of my silence. Whether it would or not I didn't know, or care. I was simply happy to be studying ballet at last.

The reporter and his photographer mumbled their apologies and scurried away, and Mama and I continued on to the family tomb. When Pare heard us approaching, he turned around and lifted his eyebrows as if to ask where Xavier and Margarida were. I shrugged in reply. I hadn't seen them since the entrance gate. They were twins and from childhood had often disappeared together for private conversations or shared adventures.

Pare had just lit the candles in the doorway of the mausoleum when donya Elisa de Figueroa, Xavier's mother-in-law, came to greet us, along with donya Esperanza de Figueroa, the ninety-year-old matriarch of the de Figueroa family, and donya Josefa Manzano, whose husband owned a shipping company.

'Where is Xavier?' asked donya Josefa. 'I must congratulate him. He played so beautifully at my soirée the other evening. I knew that he was talented, but his touch . . . well, it is simply sublime. He plays as well as any pianist I have heard in Paris or Vienna.'

'He showed a talent for music from a young age,' my mother said, lowering her eyes humbly but smiling at the compliment.

'Hah!' said donya Esperanza, waving her bejewelled hand. 'It is more than a talent. It is a gift!'

'He paints beautifully too,' added donya Elisa. 'It's a pity that such a talent is wasted on a man. If he had been a daughter, donya Rosita, you could have married him off into royalty without so much as a curtsey.'

The women laughed together. It was what Margarida would have called the 'society lady' laugh: a bit too forced and a bit too shrill.

'Xavier won't have much time for those pursuits any more, I'm afraid,' said Pare, walking down the steps of the mausoleum to greet the women. 'We are going to invest in banking. I'll need his help in the business more than ever next year.'

Donya Josefa nodded her approval at my father's policy of diversification. Out of the women, she was the one who best understood the business world because she had helped her husband build his company from the ground up. I had heard her say to Xavier once: 'If your father hadn't taken Ignaci Montella's fortune and invested it in textiles, iron ore mines and machinery, the whole lot would have disappeared when Spain lost the colonies.'

'Yes, I suppose he will have less time for artistic pursuits,' said donya Esperanza, with a wink at my mother. 'Newlyweds are usually kept very busy . . . and we are so hoping for the patter of little feet before long.'

'Here comes the beautiful bride with her father now,' said Pare, nodding in the direction of the path.

We all turned to see Conchita making her way towards us with don Carles de Figueroa. The late morning sun glinting off her glossy black hair and her porcelain skin made it easy to see why many considered her the most beautiful woman in Barcelona. She was stylish too. While the other society wives of her age were still being dressed by the houses of Vionnet and Patou, she had discovered the couturière Coco Chanel. Conchita was looking impossibly chic in her *poverty de luxe* wool jersey dress.

'So simple, so elegant . . . so French,' said donya Josefa, admiring the tailoring of the dress.

Don Carles and Pare stepped away from the gathering and were soon involved in a lively discussion.

'What are they talking about?' asked donya Josefa.

'The demands of the workers, unfortunately,' said my mother.

Donya Esperanza shook her head. 'I will never forget that terrible time in 1909, and those heathens who burned the churches.'

Donya Elisa put her hand on her heart. 'I was terrified of the mobs shouting "All or None!" in the streets. It was ludicrous! If we had sent our sons to Cuba, who would have been left to run the factories and create jobs? The country would have collapsed.'

My mother flinched, recalling a bad memory. 'I never made it to the wharf that day the trouble started. Evelina was only a baby and she had come down with a terrible fever. I sent my maid and housekeeper instead to give those brave young men our support . . . but they threw the medals into the water and horribly abused my servants.'

'Yes, I remember,' said donya Esperanza. 'Poor Maria Parreño was pushed over by one of their brutish women. It gave her such a shock.'

'It irks me what they write in their "workers'" newspapers about our husbands and families,' said my mother. 'It's as if we are monsters. But when a man in one of our factories was badly hurt, Leopold and Xavier were the first to line up to offer their blood for a transfusion. Besides, who do they think is funding the construction of the Sagrada Família, the parks, charitable schools and other public works?'

'They don't understand,' said donya Elisa. 'If we gave them all our money, it would be gone on gambling, drink and whores in a week. They don't know how to handle wealth any more than they know how to eat properly with a knife and fork. They don't understand the responsibility we bear . . . and I guarantee that if we gave it to them, they wouldn't want it.'

'The Socialists say that the workers should run the factories,' said donya Josefa. 'Tell me, is Russia better off now that the workers run the factories and riffraff has taken over the palace?'

Donya Esperanza laughed. 'Well, as my dear late husband used to say: "Even the cats want shoes nowadays!"'

Conchita, who had no head for politics, stifled a yawn and leaned towards me. 'What do you think of la senyoreta Dalmau's dress?' she asked, nodding her head in the direction of the Dalmau family's tomb, where the youngest daughter of the family was standing on the steps with her brother. Senyoreta Dalmau was wearing a printed knit dress. It seemed perfectly respectable to me.

'You'd think with the amount of money her family has, she'd dress better,' Conchita said. 'That olive colour and those big flowers make her look like a sofa.'

I cringed at my sister-in-law's nastiness. Conchita didn't seem so beautiful when she gossiped about others. I knew that when we were out of earshot, she and her sisters probably said the same things about Margarida. While my mother still had control over what I wore, she had lost the battle with my sister, who preferred English tweed to anything offered by Parisian designers. 'But, Mama, you are always saying that clothes are a woman's armour,' Margarida would tell our mother with a sly smile. 'Why then should I not wear sturdy fabric rather than something that will tear in the tiniest of breezes?'

At 180 centimetres, Margarida was never going to be a petite beauty, so she'd developed a style all of her own. And even though she was something of a tomboy, her bronze-gold hair and vivacious eyes gave her a certain allure.

Seeing that she didn't have an enthusiastic audience for her commentary on clothes, Conchita changed tack. 'Where is Xavier? I haven't seen him since we arrived.'

'I'll go find him,' I told her, glad to have a reason to get away.

It took me a while to discover that Xavier and Margarida weren't visiting the crypts of the other families. My search was delayed by having to stop and greet the people who waved to me as I passed. I inwardly cringed each time one of the mothers glanced from me to her son, sizing me up as a potential daughter-in-law.

'Such an attractive, graceful girl,' I heard senyora Almirall say to senyora Calvet. 'But so shy. You only have to greet Evelina Montella for her to turn as red as a tomato. Perhaps she would have learned to talk more if she had a less garrulous sister.'

I rushed back through the portico into the interior section of the cemetery to get away from my social obligations. While it was true that Margarida, who was full of spirited self-confidence, could hold a conversation as easily with a street sweeper as she could a member of the nobility, she wasn't the reason I was shy. No one knew the reason I was so timid, not even me. And Margarida was the only person I could confide in. If I had told my mother that being in a crowded room made my heart pound so hard I couldn't breathe, she would have worried and that would have made everything worse. Margarida, on the other hand, simply told me to imagine that everyone around me was a chimpanzee. Although it didn't make things easier, at least it made me laugh.

The interior of the cemetery, where I found myself, consisted of blocks of niches, several rows high, in which coffins were placed. There were tombs in the middle of the space and a few monuments. It was mainly middle-class families who buried their dead here; although some of the older Barcelona aristo-crats, who had died before the new section had been built or had considered it too showy for their tastes, were interred here too. I shivered when I remembered what Margarida had once told me: that if the families of the deceased couldn't keep up the rental payments on a niche, then the remains of their loved one were tossed in the paupers' pit.

'That's heartless!' I'd exclaimed. 'The dead should rest in peace!'

'That's the reality for most people in Spain,' Margarida had replied. 'Open your eyes, Evelina. Not everyone lives as we do.'

Some of the families were using ladders to climb to the upper niches so that they could place flowers inside. I passed a young woman dressed in black and kneeling before a niche. She was sobbing pitifully, and her grief was so palpable it brought tears to my eyes too. Then I saw a picture of a child at the front of the niche and I understood.

My mind skipped back to the procession that I'd been part of that morning with the other 'good families' of Barcelona. With our expensive clothes and quality educations, we should have been living life to the fullest and deepest levels. Why was it, then, that these people, with less money and more problems, seemed more real?

Was I starting to think like Margarida? For a Spanish woman, even for a Catalan, Margarida had progressive ideas about soci-ety. I remembered the time a maid had found a copy of *La condi-ción social de la mujer en España* by Margarita Nelken, the feminist and freethinker, under Margarida's bed. Margarida did not advocate free love, as other feminists did, but she did believe in freedom of the spirit and the right of women to fulfil their talents and abilities without the censure of men. But in our house-hold, literature that espoused equality of any kind—between rich and poor, master and slave, man and woman, human and beast—was comparable to indulging in pornography. It wasn't that Pare was cruel; it was just that he was so completely *paternal*. He truly did believe that his family and his workers alike had no choice but to obey him.

'What is it that you object to about Nelken?' Margarida had demanded of Pare. 'That she is a highly educated woman—*or that she is a Jew?*'

If I had spoken to Pare like that, he would most certainly have slapped me. But Margarida's absolute sureness of herself had exasperated my parents to the point that even my strict father had no idea how to discipline her. She had been expelled for rebellious behaviour from every exclusive school she had attended. The option in the past had been to send daughters like Margarida to a convent, but even my parents weren't 'Catholic' enough for that. Then one wise nun at a school Margarida was attending advised my parents: 'I think your daughter is simply *too* bright. She's bored here. Find a way to direct her energies and you will end up with a daughter of whom you can be proud.'

'Margarida inherited your keen intellect, that's the problem,' Mama often told Pare. Indeed, while Pare was perturbed by a daughter who defied feminine norms, there was no equal in his eyes to Margarida when it came to intellect and an understanding of politics. She grasped the details of his business dealings, and read stocks and figures with ease. I once heard Pare lament to my mother that it was a pity that his daughter had such a head for sums while his son had been born with a gift for the fine arts. 'It should have been the other way round,' he'd said. 'They must have swapped talents in the womb.'

'You shouldn't indulge Margarida so much,' my mother scolded him. 'I sometimes think that you want her to remain a spinster so you can keep her to yourself.'

While being so tall did not enhance her marriage prospects, Margarida's spinsterhood was largely of her own making. Her vitality drew many men to her, but she could always tell when someone was lying and wasn't afraid to tell them so. It was a quality that Spanish men did not like at all. Except Xavier, of course, but Xavier was her brother.

I couldn't find Xavier and Margarida anywhere in the cemetery and retraced my steps to the entrance. That was when I saw them. They were standing in the paupers' cemetery, flower bouquets held between their clasped hands, their heads bowed as if in prayer.

I did not like that section of the cemetery and usually avoided it. There were no sculptures of angels or white doves here, only a pit in which coffins were placed on top of each other with no markings or monuments except the lone Celtic cross that had to suffice for everyone buried there. If you were buried in the paupers' cemetery, as most of the workers in Barcelona were, you were lost to oblivion. Your relatives might remember you, until they ended up in the paupers' pit too.

I inched forwards. Xavier and Margarida had their backs to me. They looked so absorbed in their contemplation that I was loath to disturb them. They seemed to share such harmony of mind that I often thought no one could ever understand them as well as they understood each other. I approached quietly.

When I was close to them, I overheard Xavier say to Margarida, 'I've never forgotten her face, you know: that hungry girl who came with the others to the factory the day of the general strike. I often wonder what happened to her . . . Did she end up in this pit like so many of the other starving and diseased children of Barcelona? Thrown on the heap like a piece of rubbish?'

Margarida pressed her cheek to Xavier's and whispered something I couldn't hear. Together they stepped forwards and placed their white chrysanthemums at the base of the cross. Goosebumps rose on my skin and I was left with an uneasy feeling in my stomach.

Xavier stepped back from the cross and straightened. He turned around when he saw me from the corner of his eye and the serious expression on his face melted. 'Ah!' he said. 'The fair Evelina has come to collect us.' He took Margarida's arm. 'Come, dear sister,' he said. 'For now we must join those whose lifetime ambition it is to die the richest person in the cemetery.'

He was smiling, but there was a tinge of hardness in his voice that I had not heard before. An anxious feeling gripped my heart, as if I was experiencing a premonition of the sinister future.

Mamie's voice trailed off, the crypts and statues of the cemetery faded from my mind and I found myself back on the sofa in the living room. Until Mamie's story, I had never considered how the rich and poor of a city could be so definitely divided, even after death. But I sensed there was something else Mamie wanted me to understand. I looked at her questioningly.

'I want you to appreciate the tightness of the circle that we "good families" moved in,' she said. 'We Catalans had a system of a sole heir, which meant Xavier would inherit three-quarters of the Montellas' considerable fortune on my parents' death. The remaining quarter was to be divided between me and Margarida, as our dowries. If there had been a younger brother, he also would have inherited part of that quarter, with the expectation that he would use it to forge his own career. Xavier was seen as a young man who had every advantage: he was the eldest son, good-looking, charming, and he had married into another elite family. Conchita's dowry had consisted of a considerable amount of cash and properties. You must understand the tremendous responsibility that lay on Xavier's shoulders—and the burden. It wasn't a role someone could give up on a whim. We were rich enough that Margarida's "eccentric" behaviour might be tolerated, but an *heir* who flouted tradition or broke with society . . . there could be serious consequences.'

I waited for Mamie to say more, but her eyes started to droop and I realised that the storytelling had come to an end for the night. I made some camomile tea, and we drank it in the kitchen, each of us lost in a thoughtful silence.

But when I climbed into bed, I couldn't sleep. I lay with the bedside lamp on, staring at the ceiling. I committed each of the details of Mamie's story to memory. So her family had been wealthy before the Civil War. I had always put her regal bearing down to her ballet training, but now I understood its origins better. I reflected on Margarida and Xavier. I found something very appealing about my great-aunt and uncle and was saddened by the thought that I would never meet them. Xavier had been a talented pianist, like my father.

I suddenly remembered the cassette tape Audrey had given me. I climbed out of bed and took it from the drawer, hoping my father hadn't done anything as disturbing as recording a voice message on it. I put the tape in my cassette player and was relieved to hear only music. My father was playing a piece I recognised but could not name. I looked at the label on the cassette: 'El Corpus Christi en Sevilla' by Isaac Albéniz. I thought it a touch ironic, given Mamie's story that evening, that the piece was by a Spanish composer whose music Xavier might have played.

I climbed back into bed and shut out of my mind whatever message my father was trying to send me. Instead, I imagined it was Xavier playing for me. The piece's mood changed dramatically from sombre to flamboyant to quiet to *fortissimo*. It was a long piece that required both strength and flexibility of the hands. As I listened, I pondered on how Mamie had said nothing of Margarida's fate. Had she been killed in the war too, or was she a refugee somewhere, like Mamie? Perhaps she had remained in Spain, hiding from Franco? Possible scenarios danced around and around in my head in time to the staccato phrases of Albéniz's music. I sighed and turned off the light. I had to wait for the answer until such time as Mamie was ready to tell me.

THIRTEEN

Celestina

After Papá's death, Teresa took Ramón and me to live with her. I'd just had time to retrieve the golden earrings and secrete them in my pocket before the landlord locked up the apartment we had shared with Papá and Anastasio, and sold off our meagre belongings to make up for the unpaid rent. In the crackdown that was imposed on Barcelona after the uprising, he wasn't taking any chances of being seen to be sympathetic to rioters. '*Delatad!*' was a catchword promoted by the right-wing newspapers. It meant 'turn them in!' People were using it as an excuse to denounce neighbours, and even relatives, against whom they held grudges. Citizens were being arrested on the flimsiest of charges, such as having sold matches and oil to the rebels or having given rioters directions to convents.

I watched Teresa take three plates from the cupboard and place them on the kitchen table. 'How will Anastasio find us when he comes home?' I asked her.

Although I had seen Papá die and had witnessed his cheap coffin being lowered into the paupers' pit at the Old Cemetery,

I still believed that the events of the past few weeks had not been real. I expected that at any moment there would be a knock at the door and we would open it to find Papá and Anastasio standing there waiting to take us home, as they had collected us every day after work from the Casa del Pueblo.

We hadn't received any letters from Anastasio, but that was to be expected. The mail from Morocco was slow, and Anastasio was only semiliterate so he would have to wait until someone was able to write on his behalf; not something likely to happen quickly in a war.

'Juana is going to write to her husband,' Teresa said. 'He is with Anastasio in Morocco. She will let him know that you are with me.'

Teresa's own position was precarious. As a leader of Damas Rojas, and one who had participated in the burning of the convents, she could be arrested at any time. One morning, when they thought I was still sleeping, I heard Teresa tell Ramón: 'If anything happens to me, go with your sister to Juana in la Barceloneta. Now memorise the address.'

Papá's death meant that Teresa now had two more to feed. To lessen the burden, Ramón and I tried to help her sell more flowers at the markets. One day, when we were minding the stall while Teresa was running errands, Ramón came up with an ingenious idea.

'Celestina, go around the market and see what prices everyone else is selling their geraniums and lavender for,' he instructed me.

I had no idea what he was up to, but I did as he told me. When I returned with the information, Ramón lowered our prices for the same flowers and upped the asking price for the roses. He was a cunning salesman. The other vendors looked on in amazement as Ramón attracted housewives and housemaids to our stall in droves, firstly catching their attention by whistling a song about a bird flitting amongst the blooms, then reeling them in with our lowered prices for standard flowers before overcharging them on the golden roses.

'Look at the colour of these roses, senyora,' Ramón would say, tilting his head and shrugging his shoulders in a charming manner. 'Have you ever seen anything so beautiful? Now smell them. The scent is a heavenly mix of exotic spices and honey, is it not? Now touch the petals. They are as delicate as a baby's eyelids . . .'

I was amused to see the way Ramón fooled the rich women. I hated wealthy people: I was sure they had been the cause of Papá's death. I thought of the sweatshop owner, Montella, I had seen on the first day of the general strike, and his fancily dressed wife. I no longer cared that they were the parents of pretty baby Evelina. I vowed to myself that one day, when I was older, I would find a way to avenge Papá against people like them.

Before the morning was over, Ramón and I had sold all of Teresa's flowers. We sat under the table and grinned at each other. Wouldn't Teresa be pleased when she saw the day's earnings!

When Teresa returned and we told her what we had done, she raised her eyebrows and glanced sheepishly at the other flower vendors, who were not impressed by Ramón's undercutting tactics. She pursed her lips, trying to suppress a smile.

'You shouldn't have left them alone at the stall!' Delfina scolded Teresa. Her reprimand was supported by grumbling from the other flower sellers.

Teresa burst out laughing. 'Can I help it if they are smarter than all of you?'

One night, after we had been with Teresa for a while, I dreamed that I was in a place where colossal limestone mountains rose from the sea. Between the mountains were valleys with torrential rivers running through them. I turned and saw that Anastasio was waving to me from a forested slope. He opened his mouth and spoke to me. But I couldn't understand what he was saying.

When I awoke I had a strange sensation in my heart. I wasn't sure if the place I had seen in my dream was a figment of my imagination or if my soul had mysteriously left my body and I'd truly been with Anastasio at the Rif.

The next day, Juana came to see Teresa at the market. I could tell by their grim looks that their conversation was serious. They talked for a long while and, when Juana finally left, Teresa returned to the stall pale and shaken. She made several mistakes in her calculations, which she had never done before. In the evening, when Ramón and I were lying in our bed together, I asked him what he thought Juana and Teresa had been talking about. I jumped when he punched the mattress.

'What's wrong?' I asked.

'Juana gave a letter to Teresa,' he said. 'I saw her slip it into her pocket. I bet it was from Antoni. I thought she would read it to us at dinner, but she didn't. Why? It must contain bad news about Anastasio!'

The idea that anything bad could have happened to Anastasio was unthinkable. There must have been some other explanation of why Teresa wouldn't share the contents of the letter.

'Do you know where she put the letter?' I asked him.

He nodded. 'I watched her read it in her bedroom through the crack in the door. I couldn't see her face, but I saw her hide it in the top drawer of her dresser.'

The next few days were agonising as Ramón and I waited for an opportunity to sneak into Teresa's room and read the letter. We had to wait until Wednesday, when, as usual, she left us at home while she went to the secret food cooperative set up by Damas Rojas away from the Casa del Pueblo. Sometimes Teresa used the cooperative as an opportunity to catch up on news about the crackdown, but most of the time she didn't linger there too long because of the danger. We watched from the window as she disappeared down the street with a wicker basket under her arm. Ramón and I ran to her room, but to our dismay the top drawer of the dresser was locked.

'We'd better find the key,' said Ramón, feeling behind the dresser.

'What if she took it with her?' I asked.

Ramón stared at me. 'Even two orphans like us couldn't have such bad luck,' he said, before continuing his search.

We'd have to find the key quickly; the food cooperative was not far away. I searched around the room, trying to think where it could be. The only furniture besides the dresser was a four-poster bed with a sagging mattress, a washbasin with a metal jug, and a footstool. Something urged me to look behind the curtains. I couldn't believe it when I saw a key lying on the windowsill.

'This must be it,' I told Ramón.

He tried the key in the lock and it turned. The drawer slid open when he pulled it, and I waited in torment as he took out the mud-stained letter. He was right: it was from Antoni.

'Read it aloud!' I begged him.

Ramón's forehead wrinkled as he read Antoni's description of how difficult life was for the Spanish soldiers in Morocco: how they were never sure where the enemy was until it was too late; how the natives were skilled guerrilla fighters who could survive on local food sources without having to lug around supplies, and who slept in trees, forgoing the need to set up camps. *Neither artillery, cavalry nor bayonet charges work against them. And these are the only strategies our officers know . . .*

Ramón stopped for a moment, then began to read again:

I did eventually manage to find out information about Anastasio Sánchez, as you requested. Although this report has come to me through multiple sources, like a series of Chinese whispers, and despite the fact that his family has not been given official news, it does sound plausible to me. The young conscript died only a few days after his arrival in Melilla. He was sent as part of an exercise to a mountain where the natives were firing on troops as they tried to advance. With no knowledge or accurate map of the region, their officers led the men straight into an ambush. Sánchez was among the few survivors rescued, but he lasted only a day in the camp hospital before succumbing to his wounds. The priest who administered the last rites to the young man said that he died with the names of his brother and sister on his lips. That, my dearest, is all that I can tell you . . .

Time seemed to come to a standstill. I could feel the blood rushing in my ears. My gaze moved from the letter to Ramón's face. He reread that part of the correspondence again, desperately, as if he had missed something, as if there must be some mistake.

We heard a noise and turned to see Teresa in the doorway. She saw the letter in Ramón's hand and the expression on our faces and dropped her basket. Dried beans and onions spilled onto the floor. I expected her to scold us for snooping around her room but she burst into tears, rushed towards us and gathered us in her arms.

'I didn't know how to tell you,' she said. 'You have already borne too much!'

Ramón and I exchanged glances. The awful truth could not be denied: our beloved brother was dead. We had no family left. It was just the two of us now.

FOURTEEN

Evelina

*D*earest Margarida,
    After decades of silence, the past is like a new shoot determinedly making its way through cracked and ruined soil towards the light. I do not know what tree this shoot will become, or what fruit it will bear for me and Paloma—sweet-tasting and nutritious, or bitter and toxic? Yet I know that now I have commenced my story, I must continue. I have raised the dead and I cannot leave them vulnerable and without closure.

    At first, I thought that I could tell Paloma everything and yet somehow not mention you. I discovered that this is impossible, my dear sister, for not only are you Xavier's twin but you are part of my soul too. For while the Spanish émigrés here are in a state of great excitement about Juan Carlos beginning the process of transforming Spain into a constitutional monarchy, who would trust him? We have seen them all, haven't we— monarchies, republics, benevolent dictators and monsters! No, Margarida, I will not reveal your whereabouts, not even to Paloma whom I love and trust.

There have been many times when I have missed you so much that I have longed to flee this place and be with you but my daughter and granddaughter needed me. One day I know that we will meet again . . . and then, dear sister, what a reunion we will have!

FIFTEEN

Celestina

After we had learned of Anastasio's death, I often woke in the night to find that Ramón was not beside me. I would sit up, my heart racing and my head pounding with terror. Surely Ramón would not leave me too! It was only when I spotted him through the open window, sitting on a neighbour's roof, bathed in the eerie light of the moon, that I could calm myself.

I kept my mother's golden earrings in my pocket always, like a talisman, but I cringed whenever I touched them. The legend about the earrings frightened me, but with everyone except Ramón gone, they were all I had left of my family. Sometimes I wondered if I was doomed to lose everyone I loved, and whether it was perhaps better for me not to love anyone.

One morning in early September, when the sun stayed behind the clouds and the temperature reached a high long before midday, my worst nightmares were realised. Ramón and I were helping Teresa display the day's flowers on her stall at the market, the oppressive humidity causing sweat to sting our eyes and drip down our backs.

'Here,' said Teresa, pointing her plant mister at us.

Ramón and I closed our eyes and spread out our arms, and Teresa spritzed us from head to foot as lovingly as she would her most precious blooms. The relief was magic. Ramón and I giggled. It was the first time we had laughed in a long time. Teresa laughed too, and then suddenly stopped. The usual bustle and shouts of the flower market fell silent along with her.

I opened my eyes and turned to where Teresa was looking. Two policemen were making their way through the stalls towards us. A sickening sensation stirred in my stomach. It wasn't as if we hadn't seen policemen—plenty of them—on the streets since the week of the uprising, but there was something menacing about these two. Each flower vendor breathed a sigh of relief when the policemen passed them by. They came to a stop in front of our stall and fixed their gazes on Teresa. My feet shuffled, as if my body was telling me to run, but where was I supposed to go? Teresa stayed rooted to the spot, her hands clasped in front of her.

'Teresa Flores García?' one of the policeman asked. He was tall with sallow skin and eyes the colour of mushrooms.

Teresa nodded.

'Show us your papers.'

She reached inside her blouse and produced her papers, passing them to the policeman. He unfolded the documents and studied them before handing them to his colleague, who did not return them to Teresa.

'By order of the Minister of the Interior you are to accompany us to the police station to answer some questions,' the first policeman said.

Teresa was baffled. 'Am I being arrested?' she asked. 'Or am I being taken in to tell tales about someone else? If that's the case, I have nothing to declare.'

'I am sure you are right,' answered the policeman, a condescending smile on his face. 'But you must come just the same.'

Teresa's mouth twitched but she quickly composed herself. She called to Delfina and asked if she could watch her stall for the day. Delfina nodded. Teresa then took Ramón's and my hands in hers; I could feel her trembling.

When we arrived at the police station, we found others there who had received the same summons: Carme and Pilar from Damas Rojas, along with several teachers from rationalist schools, and other people who looked like shopkeepers and accountants. There were only three other children, all about Ramón's age.

'Núria denounced us,' Pilar told Teresa, 'in order to save her own skin.'

We waited in the hot sun in the courtyard of the police station for several hours. No one was questioned. When we asked for water, a policeman came out with a single cup to be shared between all of us.

Finally, in the mid-afternoon, a sergeant from the Civil Guard arrived. He smoothed his handlebar moustache and stood before us with his feet apart. His hooded eyes revealed no emotion when he read out in a Madrid accent a brief statement from the Governor of the Province of Barcelona: '*By virtue of the power conferred on me by the Law of Public Order, I deem that you and your kin are to be banished from the city of Barcelona, never to return within a radius of 245 kilometres. May God preserve you for many years!*'

A stunned silence was soon followed by cries of protest.

'You can't exile us without a trial!' one of the teachers said, running his hand through his hair. 'We have a right to prove our innocence!'

'I wasn't even in Barcelona to be burning any churches!' a woman said. 'I was in Málaga, visiting my parents!'

The sergeant shrugged. 'In the light of recent events, all constitutional guarantees have been suspended,' he answered matter-of-factly. He sounded like a shopkeeper telling customers his store was closed for the day, rather than an official who had just condemned over fifty people to be exiled from their homes. 'A unit of the Civil Guard will be arriving shortly to escort you to the train station. From there you will be transported to Alcañiz.'

His statement caused more cries of protest and despair. One of the older women fainted.

'Where is Alcañiz?' Pilar asked the man next to her.

A young woman turned to the sergeant. 'I've left my children in the care of a neighbour,' she said. 'I must go back to fetch them.'

'That won't be possible,' he answered. 'Your train for Alcañiz departs within the hour.'

People screamed. The teacher who had protested the lack of justice lunged towards the sergeant, but was pushed back by the tall policeman who had arrested Teresa.

'My elderly mother is sitting in the kitchen, expecting me to come and feed her at any moment!' the teacher screamed. 'I am her only child. What is going to happen to her?'

'The notice said that our kin were banished too,' shouted Carme. 'You should allow these people to go back and collect their families!'

The gathering cried out their agreement. Their desperation sent chills through me. The scope of what people were being forced to leave behind was terrifying: children who had not accompanied their parents to the police station; elderly relatives; animals; businesses; homes; and more.

'We should at least be allowed to take our money from the bank,' a man in a pinstriped suit said. 'How are we going to feed ourselves?'

Their protests fell on deaf ears. Several people began to weep.

Ramón and I looked towards Teresa. 'It's all right, it's all right,' she said, gathering us into her arms and putting on a brave face. 'We're together, that's the main thing. One flower market is the same as another. In some ways it's a blessing to not own too much.'

The unit of the Civil Guard arrived and the shell-shocked group was herded into single file. The woman who had left her children with her neighbour could barely stand. 'My husband is in Morocco,' she wept. 'What's going to become of my babies?' Carme gave her arm to help her.

The sergeant who had made the announcement checked off people's names against the papers that had been confiscated when they were arrested. When we came before him, he looked me and Ramón up and down. 'How old are they?' he asked Teresa.

'The boy is ten and the girl is eight,' Teresa replied.

The sergeant opened his notebook and studied something in it for a long time. When he looked up again, he smiled. For one optimistic moment I thought there had been some mistake and he was going to let us go.

'Ah, Teresa Flores García,' he said, half laughing. 'A leading figure in Damas Rojas.' The look in his eyes changed from apathy to one of ill intent. 'Now, what are we going to do with you?' he said, fixing his eyes on me. Suddenly he grabbed my arm and yanked me to the side. 'She can't go. She's too young,' he said.

Several people gasped. 'What?' screamed Teresa.

'Children her age are to be placed in orphanages,' the sergeant said.

Teresa staggered backwards. Her face turned grey and she struggled for breath. Chills ran through me as I remembered the story Teresa had told Paquita about what had happened to her sister in an orphanage. Everything around me turned white.

'You can't be serious!' Carme said, stepping forwards. 'There is nothing in the order that states that!'

'No,' said the sergeant. 'I am the one who has decided the journey will be too arduous for this child. Look how skinny she is.'

'Not an orphanage,' said Teresa, barely able to get the words out. 'If she can't come with me then I have a friend who will take her.'

The sergeant lifted his eyebrows. 'Oh, and what is this friend's name?'

Despite the panic that must have been muddling Teresa's thoughts, she realised that he was trying to trick her into revealing Juana's name.

'Maria,' she said, looking pointedly at me. I knew she was hoping that I would understand that she meant Juana. 'You remember the address, don't you?'

In the confusion, Teresa must have forgotten that she had given Juana's address to Ramón, not to me. All I could remember was that Juana lived somewhere called la Barceloneta.

'Well, she can't go to your friend anyway,' the sergeant said. 'She must go to a Church orphanage!'

Teresa cried out and made a grab for him. One of the Civil Guard lunged forwards and knocked her to the ground with the butt of his rifle. I had a flashback to the death of Papá and ran towards her. Ramón grabbed me and held me close to him. I could feel his heart beating furiously against mine.

The sergeant chuckled. 'What are you afraid of, Teresa Flores García?' he asked. 'That I might send her to one of the convents you burned down? I'm sure the nuns there would be very happy to see her!'

Ramón and I clung to each other when two of the guards tried to pry us apart. But they were much stronger than us, and eventually one guard restrained Ramón while the other dragged me backwards.

'Ramón! Ramón!' I screamed, kicking my legs frantically.

'I'll find you, Celestina!' Ramón cried out to me as he and the others were led away. 'I'll come back one day, Celestina! I will find you!'

I watched in horror as Ramón and Teresa, along with the others, were marched at gunpoint down the street. I kept my eyes on them until they disappeared around the corner. Each turned to give me one last, desperate look before disappearing from sight.

After that, I was left to sit alone, dazed and with a parched throat, in the courtyard for another hour. Although the weather was hot, I shivered violently.

The sergeant reappeared with a young policeman in tow. 'The girl should have been sent with her mother,' the younger man was saying. I realised that he was talking about me and had assumed Teresa was my mother.

'The girl should have been sent with her mother,' repeated the sergeant, mimicking the policeman's Catalan accent. 'The whole reason I am in Barcelona is because you milksops were too soft on the rioters! Now get her to the priest. He can decide where to send her.'

The policeman's face turned dark. 'Come,' he said, directing me out the gate.

When we were a few blocks away from the station, he turned to me. 'Listen, do you really know where your mother's friend lives?'

I nodded although I didn't know Juana's exact address.

'Do you need me to take you there?' he asked.

I looked into his kind eyes. He reminded me of Anastasio, although he wasn't quite as handsome. I should have trusted him: he probably could have found Juana in la Barceloneta for me. But after what I had been through, I didn't trust anybody in a uniform.

'It's not far,' I told him. 'I can find her myself.'

He nodded and grimaced. 'That bastard! I know he forgot you the moment we walked out of the gate.' He gave me a gentle shove with his hand. 'All right? Are you sure you know where it is?'

'It's not far,' I reassured him.

The policeman watched me to the end of the street. When I turned the corner, I ran for my life. I didn't think about where I was going, I only wanted to get away from the police station as quickly as possible. When my legs tired, I hid in a doorway or under a cart until I got my breath back and I was ready to move again.

On one street, a unit of the Civil Guard marched by so I jumped into a courtyard garden. 'Go away! Get lost!' a woman yelled at me from a window. I scrambled out of the garden and continued down the street. Barcelona was full of homeless children. No one would have thought to help an eight-year-old girl any more than they would have taken in a stray cat.

I stopped on a corner. Could finding la Barceloneta be so difficult, I wondered. Wasn't it near the port somewhere? I hurried down a street, past an Arab plying dusty Tabriz rugs, and a spice merchant whose multicoloured trays of saffron, oregano and Indian pepper tickled my nostrils. I must be heading in the right direction, I thought. But then the streets grew wider, and I started passing construction sites where magnificent apartment buildings were being erected. The large rooms and curved façades were very different from the cramped and dismal tenement buildings of the barri Xinès. With their stone, ceramic, wrought-iron and stained-glass embellishments, the buildings looked more like palaces for fairytale princesses and knights than anywhere real people might live.

I ran on, turning this way and that, becoming disoriented when I didn't seem to be catching any glimpses of the sea. The houses became fewer, and I found myself in a field where a herd of goats and a lone cow were wandering around. What was this place? On the other side of the field was a structure that seemed to rise out of the earth, towering over everything around it. 'Oh!' was all I managed to say.

I continued towards the structure and saw from the piles of cement sand, and the workers moving to and fro on scaffolding, that the building was in the process of construction. Although it was still a shell, it was hauntingly, disturbingly beautiful. Gothic spires pointed towards the sky; the clouds moving past them made me dizzy. The structure seemed to be crumbling even as it was being built: like a gingerbread house melting in the sun. There was a brick wall around the building site, and an assortment of people milling around it. Elegant women in kimono-shaped coats over tailored dress suits posed for men with cameras on tripods; artists sat at easels sketching the building's progress; I overheard scholars and students debating its artistic, cultural and religious merits.

'Gaudí is a crazed madman and they have put him in charge of this monument to the Divine?' a man in a bowler hat complained to his wife as he helped her into their motor car. 'What the hell are those things there? They look like mushrooms!'

I looked at where the man was pointing. Indeed, while parts of the church resembled traditional Gothic structures, other parts did look like shapes found in nature, particularly vegetables.

In amongst the well-heeled tourists there were beggars. The sight of their missing limbs and the scars on their faces sent shivers through me. They looked like veterans of Cuba, like Amadeu. I thought of Anastasio and tears filled my eyes.

Two policemen stood near the gate to the construction site, waving through carts and trucks that carried supplies to the workers. I drew back, frightened.

A young boy wearing a slotted apron filled with postcards and a satchel over his shoulder approached the tourists. 'The Sagrada Família! The Cathedral of the Poor! Buy a postcard now!' he called out.

The Sagrada Família? I had never heard of it. But I had fallen under the spell of its grandeur and its monstrosity.

'Excuse me,' I said to the boy. 'Where is la Barceloneta?'

He pointed south and then looked at my blistered feet. 'You've a long way to go.'

I thanked him and he moved on. It would soon be dark. Trucks and carts began to pour out of the Sagrada Família site, while the workers put away their tools for the day and disappeared into their makeshift cottages. The beggars built fires and shared around what food and drink they had managed to scrounge. I stood on the outskirts of this activity, evening falling around me. After I had rested a little, I decided that I had no choice but to go in the direction the boy had pointed.

Not long before she died my mother had warned me against wandering alone at night. 'It is not the atmosphere for you, Celestina,' she'd said. 'Night-time is for ghouls and ghosts, thieves and murderers. Not little girls.' But what choice did I have?

I had only travelled a short way when I began to understand that the city by night was not the same place it was during the day. The buildings became confusing mazes of grey stone; trailing vines turned into tentacles reaching out for me; façades that were probably beautiful when the sun shone on them now cast sinister shadows all around me. The shops, which might have given me a better clue as to where I was, had their shutters down. I panicked. Rushing this way and that, my heart pounding in my chest, I found myself back in the hub of the city again. But those who populated it during the day—the housewives, the shopkeepers, the nuns and schoolchildren—had transformed into people of the night. I cringed at the sight of the pale-skinned women with their rouged cheeks lounging in the doorways. Their belladonna eyes searched the street where men strolled or drove past slowly in cars. Some of the men wore their hats pulled low, but others, more brazen, winked and jeered.

'You! What are you doing here? Go away!'

I turned to see two girls, maybe just a couple of years older than I was, staring at me. They had rouge painted on their cheeks. One of them wore a floppy hat; the other had her hair piled up on her head and held with a comb. Their skin was smooth, but all the muscles in their necks were stretched taut. They looked even unhealthier than I did.

The girl in the floppy hat stepped towards me. 'Get lost! This is our territory!'

I had no idea what she was talking about, but she smelled like rotting flesh, like Núria had. I ran under an archway, and passed a group of gypsies sitting on a blanket and playing cards. A woman in a beaded headdress sat near them, offering to tell the fortunes of the passers-by. She looked at me in surprise when I rushed past. She called out to me but I didn't stop. I felt remote from everything around me. All wanted to do was cry.

After a few more turns I found myself on a street that I thought might be las Ramblas. Crowds were moving along it, and piano music and the fruity smell of wine wafted from the cafés and bars. A smoky bitterness hung in the air. Perhaps I should have asked someone for help—one of the surly doormen; the scrawny-necked woman selling tickets to a show—but I was too frightened of all these strangers. I continued on my way, knowing that if I could only find the flower market, I could wait there until morning and maybe Delfina or another of the flower sellers could help me. But I took a wrong turn, and found myself in an alleyway that stank of urine and spoiling seafood. The only illumination was a streak of light from an upper-storey apartment window.

'Look, it's a little girl!'

I peered into the darkness and saw the figures of two men crouched on the ground. They were smoking something from pipes that smelled sweet and sickly, not like normal tobacco. One of the men rose and walked towards me. The light from the window flashed over his face for a moment. His features were thin and sunken, as I imagined a ghoul would look.

'Do you want to make some money?' he asked. 'I could help you. Lots of the tourists here like little girls.'

I stepped back. The man made a grab for me.

'Leave her alone!' a hoarse female voice growled.

Everything seemed to stand still. All I could hear was the laboured sound of my breath and the faint hum of a motor car cruising down las Ramblas.

The man backed away as if he were being directed by an unseen force. 'All right, all right,' he said, crouching down and picking up his pipe again.

I turned to look at the shadowy figure of my rescuer. She clicked her tongue and said, 'Come.' I followed her out of the alleyway and back onto las Ramblas. When I saw the woman's face in the bright lights from the nightclub signs, I thought I might be suffering a hallucination. The mole in the crease of her nostril and the piercing eyes were familiar. She was the gypsy I had seen at the flower market with Ramón, the one who had overheard my wish to become a famous flamenco dancer.

'Are you lost?' she asked.

I nodded.

'Where are your parents?'

'Dead.'

'And the rest of your family?'

'They took my brother and Teresa to Alcañiz.'

The woman stared into my eyes for a long time, as if something was puzzling her. Her own eyes were bright but her skin was leathery. It was impossible to tell her age. She could have been forty. She could have been seventy. But something about her seemed ancient.

'You're a *paya* but you have the gypsy magic,' she said.

She extended her hand and I took it, relishing the warmth of her rough skin. I'm not sure why I trusted her. Perhaps it was because she spoke with an Andalusian accent, like Papá. I did not understand that in going with the woman, I was stepping from one world to another—and that when a gypsy took a child from the street, the child would belong to them forever.

Sixteen

Paloma

Carmen gave private lessons at her apartment in Montparnasse, not at her dance studio, where another teacher took the group classes on Wednesday nights. My feelings were a mix of anticipation and nervousness as I parked Mamie's car near rue Raymond Losserand and walked to the quiet street where Carmen's apartment was situated. I hoped that I would have the chance to ask her about la Rusa after the lesson. There must be people in the flamenco community in Paris who had known her. Perhaps if I had a chance to speak to one of them, I would understand why she had given the golden earrings to me.

I knew I was in the right place from the sound of flamenco guitar coming from inside the building. I pressed the bell for the ground-floor apartment and a few moments later Carmen appeared in a red flamenco dress with a shawl over her shoulders.

'*Hola*, señorita Batton,' she said with a smile, before ushering me through the chilly foyer and into the warmth of her apartment.

I was struck at the sight of the crimson walls and the mosaic coffee table. The apartment, while small even by Paris standards, was a vision of Moorish splendour. The floor was covered in Fez rugs, and a lattice screen separated the kitchen from the living area. The decor, along with the maidenhair ferns in ceramic pots and the smell of rosewater, made me feel as if I had stepped from a Parisian street into a casbah. There was a framed poster of the Alhambra Palace above the sideboard, and I deduced that the family must have originally come from Granada in southern Spain. They were Andalusians, as la Rusa's family had been.

'Come this way,' said Carmen, holding aside a beaded curtain. She led me into her studio, which was the converted main bedroom of the apartment. Through the French doors I could see a small garden lit by hanging lanterns. The trees were winter bare but the cobalt blue garden chairs made the space look inviting. Jaime was already in the studio, tuning his guitar. The intense look on his face made him especially handsome. I remembered the stir his appearance had caused amongst the ladies in the flamenco class.

The telephone rang and Carmen excused herself to answer it. Jaime looked up and flicked back a lock of hair that had fallen over his forehead. He had eyes the colour of dark chocolate, I noticed, with very bright whites: inquisitive eyes that didn't miss much.

'*Hola! Cómo estás?*' he greeted me.

'*Molt bé*,' I replied.

He looked surprised and I realised that instead of replying to his 'how are you?' in Spanish, I'd answered him in Catalan. Replying to a Spaniard in Catalan was exactly the kind of thing an uppity Catalan might do to make a point of difference. I blushed and tried to hide my embarrassment by sitting down on a chair and slipping on my flamenco shoes.

'Too many languages,' I said, attempting to smooth over the awkwardness of the moment. 'I speak some English as well. Sometimes I go to speak one language and another one comes out instead.'

Jaime put his fingers to the front of his head. 'The Broca's area.'

'What?'

'It's in the frontal lobe of your brain. The area responsible for language and motor movements of the mouth.'

'Oh, that's fascinating.' Without knowing why—perhaps to compensate for my rudeness—I launched into an explanation of my history of language learning. 'I spoke Catalan and French as a child, so I don't often get them mixed up although they have many similar words. I didn't really learn Spanish until I was a teenager. That's why I sometimes get it mixed up with the others . . . it's quite similar to Catalan and French. I guess it's because they're all Latin languages.'

I felt as though my frontal lobe and my motor mouth were running out of control. Why couldn't I stop talking? I remembered Mamie telling me how socially awkward she was at my age—was it a family curse? I decided the best thing to do was to change the subject.

'So, how do you know so much about the brain?' I asked.

'My father is a doctor,' he replied.

'Is your family in Paris too?'

'Some of them, but my parents and sisters are still in Granada. I live here with my aunt.'

I liked his voice: it was deep and clear.

'You speak French very well,' I told him.

He looked startled. 'I came here when I was thirteen,' he said, with a tinge of irony. 'I hope that I do!'

Just shut up, Paloma! I screamed at myself inwardly. I thought of the blonde woman at the first flamenco lesson: why was it when people were friendly to me, I found a way of putting them off?

But if Jaime was offended, he didn't show it. He adjusted his guitar and played a few chords before looking at me and smiling. 'The good thing about music is you don't need words. It is a language everyone understands.'

Carmen returned. 'Indeed it is,' she said, brushing down her dress. 'So let's get started, señorita Batton.'

I was relieved. At least I wasn't such an imbecile when I danced.

Carmen stood opposite me and lifted her skirt to show her feet. 'Now, I'm not going to go into all the ins and outs of who developed flamenco—the gypsies, the Andalusians, the Moors, the Latin Americans, or all of them—but the style I'm going to teach you is based on classical Spanish dance. I think it will complement the lovely elegance and poise your ballet training has given you.'

We began by repeating the steps I had learned in the beginners' class, then Carmen gradually made the footwork more complicated by adding variations. At first I imitated each pattern to the sound of Carmen's counting, but when she thought I was ready, she nodded to Jaime. He started playing slowly, and gradually increased the speed until it reached a point where I could no longer dance evenly.

'Your timing and rhythm are excellent,' Carmen said. 'Now I want to see what you can do with your arms. You may have heard that traditionally there were dancers known as "upper-body dancers" and others who were known for their footwork. It was rare for a dancer to do both superbly well. The exception, of course, was la Rusa. That's why she was a legend. She was an all-round dancer of the highest level. A genius!'

The mention of la Rusa sent a shiver down my spine. I could almost imagine that she was in the room with me.

Carmen took me through a series of exercises where I held my hands in front of my chest and rotated them, following my middle finger for several turns and then my little finger.

'Now watch this,' she said, nodding to Jaime.

He began an upbeat, playful piece and Carmen moved around using the footwork patterns she had shown me. Then she added her arms, twirling them and twisting them around her body and above her head. I watched with amazement. In ballet, the strength and grace of the arms were important: they formed part of a ballerina's 'line' and lent a graceful frame to the body and steps. But Carmen's arms were something else. They were expressive and musical and seemed to be performing a dance of their own, separate from the rest of her body, moving in different time to her feet. The only other time I had seen anyone use their arms so evocatively was the time Mama took me to see Yvette Chauviré perform in *The Dying Swan*.

When Carmen finished her dance, I applauded. It always gave me a thrill to watch a wonderful dancer, no matter what the style.

'It must have taken years to learn to do that!' I exclaimed.

Carmen shrugged. 'In my day, we didn't have lessons. We learned to dance by watching our mothers and aunties. I started to learn as soon as I could walk. Now everything is so much more professional, with the emphasis on technique. When I was growing up, most flamenco guitarists in Spain couldn't even read lyrics let alone music. Jaime is the only musician in my family who is knowledgeable about musical terms.'

We returned to the lesson, and to finish Carmen showed me some arm exercises to practise at home. I was pleased to see Jaime put his guitar away. It meant that there wasn't another student after me.

I was about to ask Carmen about la Rusa when she said, 'I hope you will stay for dinner, señorita Batton?'

Her invitation took me by surprise, but the aroma wafting from the kitchen did smell very good. Someone else must be here, cooking.

'Yes, thank you,' I replied. 'But please call me Paloma.'

'Paloma. A dove,' said Carmen with a smile. 'It's a lovely name. It suits you well.'

When we stepped into the living room, I was surprised to see two people sitting on the sofa. One of them was the elderly lady with the red hair who helped at the dance academy. The man next to her looked slightly younger in age.

'This is my mother, Vicenta, whom you have already met, and my uncle, Ernesto,' Carmen said, indicating the pair.

After we had exchanged greetings, a pretty woman in her late thirties with long curly hair and a big nose and lips appeared from behind the kitchen screen. She was carrying a stack of dishes, which she put down on a round table in the corner of the room.

'And this is my daughter, Isabel,' said Carmen.

'*Hola!*' Isabel said, smiling broadly.

Ernesto stood to give me his place on the sofa. He squinted at me through his black-rimmed glasses. 'Ah, Jaime has got himself a pretty girl,' he said.

I was too embarrassed to look at Jaime, but at the same time I was flattered that Ernesto thought I might be his grand-nephew's girlfriend. I was expecting Carmen—or Jaime—to correct him, but before anyone could say anything the doorbell rang and Carmen went to answer it. She returned a moment later with a handsome couple in their forties, accompanied by two small boys in hooded coats.

'And this is my sister, Mercedes, and her husband, Félix,' said Carmen. 'And their sons, Ricardo and Víctor.'

The room was so full of people that it began to feel like a crowded elevator.

'Dinner is ready. Please come to the table,' called Isabel.

Although there were enough chairs, I wasn't sure how we were all going to fit around the small table, but somehow we did. I felt a thrill of excitement when Jaime deliberately sat next to me but did my best to act nonchalant.

'Now,' Carmen announced to the gathering, 'our guest tonight is of Catalan descent, so I am going to explain each of these dishes to her.'

Her tone gave the impression that she was about to embark on the telling of an exotic fairytale and the gathering fell respectfully silent. Instead, she lifted the lid off a large casserole pot to reveal a dish of tomatoes, lima beans and artichokes.

'People from Barcelona, like your grandmother, Paloma, live

by the sea and have much in common with their Mediterranean neighbours,' Carmen said. 'But we Granadians, we are influenced by the Arabs. We like our spices.' She picked up a spoon and indicated for me to pass her my plate, which I did. 'Let me present to you . . . *cazuela de habas*!'

A sigh of anticipation rose from the gathering. Carmen passed my plate back to me and, rather than continuing to serve everyone else, urged me to try the dish. Aware that all eyes were on me, I scooped up a forkful. A blend of garlic, mint and cumin burst on my tongue. But there were other more subtle flavours too.

'I can taste saffron,' I said. The deduction brought nods of approval from the gathering. 'And peppercorns?' More murmurs of assent. 'And . . .' Everyone leaned forward, waiting to hear what I would say next. 'White wine,' I declared. 'I definitely detect a touch of white wine.'

'*Muy bien!*' said Mercedes. 'She knows her food.'

'The white wine is my special touch,' said Isabel, lifting her chin proudly. 'Not everyone adds that.'

'Ah,' said Ernesto, his neat moustache twitching with his smile, 'Paloma shows us that there is hope for the Catalans yet!'

Dinner progressed the same way as various dishes were presented to me: a delicious almond soup; cod fish soaked in orange; and Sacromonte omelette, which I regretted accepting after Félix divulged that it contained veal calf testicles. 'Arabs eat everything,' he said.

I noticed Jaime passed on the *manitas de cerdo*, which was made from stewed pigs' trotters. 'It's not for me,' he explained. 'Pigs are as intelligent as dogs and have the same emotions. As I won't eat dogs, I won't eat pigs either.'

'Jaime is becoming an American!' declared Ernesto.

His comment brought giggles from Mercedes and Isabel. Jaime glanced at me and shrugged his shoulders. 'I don't know why he always says that. I've never been to America, although I would like to go.'

'I feel the same way about rabbit,' I confided in him. 'I had a pet one when I was a child. Whenever they served *lapin à la cocotte* at ballet school, I could never bring myself to eat it.'

He smiled, and I felt the regard grow between us. I had assumed, because of his good looks, that he would be arrogant and aloof. Instead, I discovered that he emanated a warmth I never found in French men. The feeling of amiability was increased by the fact that we kept bumping elbows while we ate. At first it was awkward, but then we found it funnier the more it happened. At one point I knocked Jaime when he had his fork in his mouth and he pretended that he'd broken a tooth. His pantomime made everybody laugh, and me the most of all. I wasn't used to people being so lively at the dinner table. In Paris, you were supposed to talk quietly when eating or not at all.

'*Excusez-moi*; *perdó*; *perdón*; *pardon me*,' I told him in French, Catalan, Spanish and English. He laughed. Having been so mortally embarrassed by my slip-up earlier in the evening, I was surprised at myself for being able to make light of it now.

After the main meal's dishes had been cleared away, Vicenta brought out the desserts she had made. Ballet training had made me a light eater and I was already too full. But I didn't want to insult her so I tried one of her honey-coated pastries.

'This is delicious,' I told her. 'I don't know how you all stay so slim.'

'Because,' said Carmen, standing up from the table and clapping her hands, 'after dinner, we dance!'

I thought she must be joking, but after everyone had helped tidy the table, Jaime and Félix moved the furniture against the walls. Ernesto began to play a folk song on a *bandurria*, a Spanish instrument similar to a mandolin. After he had played a few songs, Jaime picked up his guitar. I watched in amazement as Vicenta stood up and danced. She performed complicated footwork and danced so vigorously that I realised I had more to learn about flamenco than I had ever imagined. After her performance, the others took a turn at dancing, including Ricardo and Víctor.

Carmen signalled to me once everyone else had performed. 'Come on. Try what you've learned.'

Even though I was with people who had been dancing flamenco all their lives, for some reason I didn't feel as competitive as I usually did. I wasn't driven by the need to outshine everyone; I was content to simply perform my percussive steps with pleasure—and Jaime's family were even generous enough to shout '*Olé!*' for me.

The evening didn't end until long after midnight, when Mercedes remembered that Ricardo and Víctor had school the next day.

'I'll walk you to your car,' Jaime offered to me.

The night air was freezing after the warmth of Carmen's apartment, but the sky was clear.

'So are you still in ballet school or are you with a company?' Jaime asked.

I was caught off guard by his question. My muscles tensed. After the light-hearted evening I'd just spent, I'd forgotten what a 'non-person' I had become. I wasn't a student any longer, and I wasn't part of the *corps de ballet*.

'I'm teaching and taking extra lessons while I'm waiting for the next audition for the Paris Opera Ballet,' I told him.

Jaime gave a low whistle. 'The Opera Ballet! Well, that explains your high level of skill.'

It was flattering that he was impressed, but I would have felt better if I had been able to tell him that I was a *quadrille* and that we were rehearsing for *La Sylphide*.

'And you?' I asked, keen to turn the conversation away from me. 'You are at the Conservatoire?'

Jaime nodded. 'I'm majoring in composition and classical guitar. But I've been away for several months—I had to return to Spain to do my compulsory military training.'

'What was that like?'

He shrugged. 'It's not my style to hold a gun, but if I hadn't returned for it, I would have been labelled a deserter. That would have made it difficult for me to travel to Spain as frequently as I do to see my parents and sisters.'

We reached the car and I realised that I hadn't had a chance to ask him about la Rusa.

'Listen,' I said, 'I'm very interested to learn more about la Rusa. She sounds like a formidable dancer. Are you acquainted with anyone who knew her?'

Jaime looked thoughtful for a moment. 'Yes, in fact I do know someone,' he said. 'If you are free on Friday night, I can take you to meet him. He's playing at a flamenco club in Montmartre.'

I didn't know which part of what Jaime had said made me more excited: the idea of meeting someone who had known la Rusa; or that I would be seeing him again on Friday night.

'I'll come,' I said. 'That would be great!'

We gave each other the standard Spanish and French parting of a kiss on both cheeks, but I was sure Jaime lingered a bit longer than usual. I felt drunk from the warmth that emanated from his skin.

He opened the car door for me and I climbed inside. I had to let the engine run for a few minutes before the heater would work. When the car was warmed up, he shut the door and I gave him one last wave before pulling away from the kerb. As I drove towards the sixteenth arrondissement, I contemplated the evening that had passed. I used to think that Gaby had the closest family I had ever known, but her family had nothing on Jaime's. I had never experienced such exuberant energy at a dinner before. Although they were hardly poor, they didn't seem to have a lot materially and yet they made so much of what they did have. Carmen's apartment was tiny, but she had decorated it beautifully. Nobody was working in a prestigious profession (over dinner I had discovered Isabel was a waitress, Félix was a mechanic and Mercedes was a stay-at-home mother) and yet they appreciated the food on their table as if they were eating at La Coupole. It seemed to me they knew how to make the most of their lives—whatever circumstance they found themselves facing—and put their full energy into it.

I couldn't help comparing them to my own family—or lack of it. My mother had been an only child, and my father's brother had moved to New York when he'd finished university. We used to see Mamie and Avi every day, but my father's parents only visited us at Christmas and other special occasions despite living just outside Paris. I'd had no idea that I had a Spanish cousin until Mamie had told me Conchita had been married to her brother.

I didn't know why I did it, but instead of heading home I turned in the direction of avenue de l'Observatoire, in the fifth arrondissement, where my father now lived with Audrey and her son, Pierre. Although I had never been there, the address was imprinted in my memory from all the times I had seen it on the back of the letters my father had sent me after his marriage to Audrey, even though I hadn't opened or kept one of those missives.

As I drove, I thought about my childhood. Being the offspring of highly accomplished parents, I had often been treated like an adult. I remembered lunches at Maxim's and other haute-cuisine restaurants where I'd eaten things like quail with truffle sauce and cream of mussel soup—dishes any other child my age would have found unpalatable. Then it dawned on me how little I'd seen of my father after I'd started at the Ballet School. My mother had retired from performing after it was confirmed she was pregnant with me, and she'd made a point of being home during the school terms instead of touring with my father as she had done previously. My mother had been an object of fascination to me: a dark beauty whom I would have loved to emulate. But I'd inherited my father's blond hair and his golden brown eyes. I'd adored watching my mother dress for the evening, putting on her silk gloves and perfume. Yet, despite my closeness to her, it was my father whom I'd most intensely missed when he wasn't around. I remembered our reunions at airports and train stations when he returned from a tour. Mama always had to hold on to me to stop me from rushing down stairs dangerously or pushing other people out of the way. I remembered how my father laughed and embraced me when I finally got the chance to fling myself into his arms. 'Ah, Paloma,' he used to chuckle, 'there is never anyone who welcomes me anywhere as unreservedly as you do!'

Tears filled my eyes, and I blinked a few times so I could concentrate on driving. I was angry at my father but I still missed him, even now. He sent me cassette tapes and he tried to see me, but there was nothing he could do to change what had happened. He had been with another woman when my mother—and I—had needed him most!

I turned into the avenue de l'Observatoire and pulled up outside the neoclassical apartment building where he lived. I looked up to the second floor and was surprised to see the lights were still ablaze. I wondered what my father was doing up in the small hours of the morning. My eyes took in the building's elegant wrought-iron balconies and lion's-head cornices. The memory of a trip my father had taken me on to Vienna when I was seven years old came flooding back to me. He was scheduled to perform a series of Christmas concerts in the city. Mama was helping my grandmother nurse Avi through a severe bout of influenza so she hadn't come with us. My father and I checked into the prestigious Grand Hotel Wien, where the organisers had booked a room for us. But when the bellboy brought our bags and offered to make a reservation for us at the hotel's restaurant, my father declined. 'We already have arrangements,' he explained. After the bellboy left, my father turned to me. 'Come on,' he said. 'Let's see the real Vienna.'

We caught a taxi to Bandgasse, where my father showed me the tiny apartment he'd stayed in as a student a few years after the war. We ate soup and dumplings in a café he used to frequent with his friends.

'Vienna had a special atmosphere then,' he'd explained. 'The Soviet Union, America, Britain and France were occupying the city. It was said that Vienna was full of spies. But I didn't pay too much attention to that; my head was too full of the beautiful music.'

The next day, my father eschewed the limousine the hotel had offered him and hired an old Volkswagen to show me around the city. We explored Stephansplatz, the Schönbrunn Palace, and ate sachertorte in a traditional coffee house. My father was already a famous concert pianist by then and people recognised him in the street. But he didn't mind; he simply returned their curious glances with a self-deprecating nod.

I realised that the trip had given me my most vivid memory of my father.

I glanced again at the apartment building. Papa had always had an innate sense of style, but he had never been concerned with status. Whether something cost two francs or a thousand made no difference to him. 'It's the feeling an object gives you that matters,' he always said. But the avenue de l'Observatoire, near the jardin du Luxembourg, was where you lived if you had money and you wanted people to know it. And the second floor, with its full-length balcony, was the most prestigious position in the building. When had my father become such a snob?

I sighed. How could I know the answer to that? I didn't know anything about my father any more: not what he was doing up so late; not what pieces he was working on for his next performance; not even what he ate for breakfast these days. My father was a stranger to me now.

Resisting the tears that were filling my eyes again, I restarted the engine and headed for home.

SEVENTEEN

Celestina

The old gypsy woman listened to my stories about the death of my mother, father and Anastasio and the exile of Ramón and Teresa on our way to the gypsy camp in barri del Somorrostro. I also told her about Juana and how I had been trying to find her.

The camp was by the beach. We passed a group of men sitting around a fire drinking something that smelled like burned matches. The youngest of them, a man of about forty, stood up when he saw us. He rounded his muscular shoulders and fixed his eyes on me for a moment before turning to the woman. 'Francisca, why do you bring this *paya* to the camp?' he asked, his eyebrows raised in alarm.

'She was in danger. I saved her.'

'Good,' said the man, grimacing and revealing a row of gleaming teeth. 'Now take her back to her family and ask for a reward.'

Francisca shook her head. 'She has no family,' she replied. 'She belongs to me now.'

The man wiped his hand over his jaw. 'The townspeople already think we are child thieves,' he said. 'If the police learn we have a *paya* child in the camp, they will crawl all over the place looking for others.'

Francisca raised her hand to calm him. 'There's nothing to fear. The guardian spirits told me to take her. For what purpose, I will discern tomorrow. For now, she needs rest.'

Ignoring the man's exasperated expression and the murmurings of the others, Francisca directed me through the camp. It was a shanty town of dwellings fashioned from whatever the occupants had been able to scavenge—plywood, corrugated metal, pieces of canvas and rope. One even had an old fishing boat for a roof.

Francisca's shack was located on a mound slightly above the other dwellings. The hinges creaked when she pulled open the door, which looked as if it was made from a tabletop. She pushed me inside and lit a lamp, which she then rested on an upturned crate. Despite the poverty of the camp, the interior of Francisca's shack was a magical wash of colour. Magenta Jarapa rugs on the walls made the space cosy, while the makeshift furniture had been painted sky blue. Next to a small stove was a lopsided cupboard with dishes and pots arranged on it. Francisca pulled aside a curtain that divided the space and directed me towards a bed with a crocheted blanket.

'Lie down and rest,' she said.

I took off my shoes and laid my head on the lace pillow.

Francisca moved towards the cupboard, then returned with a glass of muddy-coloured liquid. She indicated that I should drink it. I gagged because it tasted like seaweed and sewer water. A few seconds later, my vision blurred and I felt drowsy. My eyes stayed open just long enough for me to notice the rabbits' feet dangling from the bedpost near my head.

'For protection,' Francisca whispered. 'Now go to sleep.'

The series of shocks I had suffered left me ill for some time, but Francisca was a patient nurse. She was the gypsies' *chovihani* and *patrinyengri*: their healer and medicine woman. 'You are safer with me, little one,' she said. 'The authorities might take your friend Juana as well, and the police don't come to the barri del Somorrostro if they can avoid it.'

After a few weeks of rest, I started to feel stronger and joined Francisca to search for herbs and mushrooms. Perhaps it was my mother's Romani ancestry, or perhaps a desire to belong somewhere after having lost my family, but I took to my gypsy life as naturally as a fish lives in water. Francisca and I were welcomed into any shack we chose to visit: the families always invited us in and shared their meals with us.

At first, the lice-ridden gypsy children were wary of me, but soon I was allowed to join in their games on the coal-blackened sand. We would run towards the waves, shouting with joy, and then flee when they rolled into shore. We often found debris that had been dumped by the factories, and which the waves deposited on the beach. Once we discovered a broken conveyor belt and took turns dragging each other around the beach on it.

The company of other children soothed some of the loss I felt over Ramón, although I still cried if I thought too much about my family. Ramón had promised to come back for me one day. Until then, I would have to make the best of my new life: after all, I was being well looked after. The gypsy women busied themselves adjusting old clothes to fit me or brushing my knotty hair.

Only Diego, the leader of the clan who had objected to my presence, continued to eye me with a look of mistrust. 'And what did the guardians tell you the role of this little *paya* will be?' he asked Francisca after I had been with the clan for few months. 'Will she weave baskets like Ángela? Or tell fortunes like Micaela?' Although Diego himself was lazy, he didn't like anyone in his clan to be idle. Even the youngest children were given chores to do each day.

Francisca looked him straight in the eye, something none of the other gypsy women dared to do. 'This one is a dancer. I will take her to Manuel and give her lessons.'

Diego's face twitched. Because of Francisca's privileged position, he had to bow to her wishes and that seemed to make him dislike me even more. At the same time, Francisca's statement sent a quiver of excitement through me. My feet tingled and my fingers involuntarily opened and closed like the petals of a flower. Francisca noticed, and smiled. Diego frowned.

'She'll never be one of us,' he said. 'So teach her to dance and then send her to town to take money from ignorant tourists who don't know any better. They'll think a little girl dancing flamenco is cute.'

The tourists and townspeople were the gypsies' favourite prey. It didn't take me long to understand that the Romani saw non-gypsies, *payos*, as inferior and unclean: they were not clever enough to live by their wits and were slaves to their jobs. Because of that, the gypsies had no qualms about separating them from their precious *pesetas* or belongings. One day, at the water fountain with some of the women from the encampment, I learned that their 'psychic' abilities were nothing but con tricks.

'This is what I do to the *payos*,' said Micaela, a young woman of sixteen who already had four children. She fixed her eyes on a point in front of her and murmured as if in a trance: 'You are a good person, I can see. You do a lot for other people. But they don't always treat you well.'

Aurora laughed, smoothing her shock of salt-and-pepper hair with a bony hand. 'Ha! That's the way. Hook them in by telling them what they want to hear. They will search their memories until they find a match. Then you'll have their trust.'

The women egged each other on to share their deceptions.

'I always tell the men that the "petite woman" is their soul mate,' giggled Estrella, a middle-aged woman with a downy moustache. 'The chances are good that he will relate what I'm saying to someone he knows!'

'The ones whose mothers have recently died are the best,' added Micaela. 'They can't pay enough to communicate with their mamas.'

These fortune tellers, who went out daily from our camp and returned with legs of ham and bags of olives, were scammers and cheats. But Francisca was different. She told people about their past, not only their future, and she was concerned whether a person was on their soul's true path.

'Your mother had the spirit of flamenco in her,' she told me. 'And that's how I know you will be a dancer. She couldn't use the gift in her short life and she passed it on to you.'

Sometimes, if I awoke at night, I would hear Francisca walking around the shack and speaking out loud to her divine guides. She believed that everything—animate or inanimate—had a spirit. If she broke something, she prayed over the object as the glue dried as sincerely as she would pray over a child with a fever or a man with a broken limb. When she pushed her wheelbarrow of healing potions around the camp, she spoke to it as a cart driver might coax an old horse. Before commencing a healing, she whispered to the herbs she intended to use, revering them for their magical qualities as much as for their medicinal ones.

Most of her patients became well, unless it was a baby with typhoid fever or dysentery. In those cases, Francisca prayed for the soul's safe journey to the Otherworld. So when she told me that I was destined to be a dancer, I believed her. That was why I trusted her enough to show her the golden earrings.

'I *knew* you had gypsy magic,' she said, handling the earrings with reverence. 'But you must not walk around with these in your pocket. That is why you attracted such grave danger. We must find a place to hide them.'

That night, she woke me at midnight and led me out of the camp to a park by the beach. The sea air tugged at my clothes and made my hair flap against my ears. Francisca dug a hole next to a palm tree. I pictured my beautiful mother as I handed them to her. She wrapped her headscarf around them and placed the bundle deep in the earth. As she filled the hole, I watched the sandy soil trickle over the package as solemnly as if I were attending the burial of my family.

'Remember this park and this tree, little one,' Francisca told me. 'The earrings will speak to you when it's time for you to collect them.'

*　　*　　*

Three days after we had buried the golden earrings, I commenced my dance training. The 'studio' where I learned was not a building with a sprung floor, four walls and a mirror. It was the beach. My first lessons were sitting with Francisca and listening to the undulations of the sea.

'Breathe in time with the waves,' she told me. 'For their rhythm reflects your life force perfectly.'

Other times, she would clap out syncopated beats and make clicking noises with her tongue, which I was to follow. One day, the frenzy of her sounds overtook me. I leaped up and, without thinking, began to dig my heels and feet into the sand in time with her clapping.

'How you can move!' she exclaimed, pleasure in her eyes.

A few days later, she took me to meet Manuel. Although he had been the husband of Francisca's youngest, and now deceased, sister, I had never seen him before. I learned that was because he played guitar in the bars of the barri Xinès all night and slept during the day.

'When my sister was alive he used to make more money,' Francisca explained to me on our way to Manuel's shack. 'All his sisters are dancers, but their husbands won't let them out of the camp because they are so jealous. I know Diego has suggested to Manuel that he should take you to amuse tourists instead. But I have other plans.'

The waves had been large earlier in the morning, and Manuel's shack was flooded. We found him sitting on his bed and playing his guitar while shoes, water containers and various other objects bobbed on a muddy tide around him.

'Manuel!' cried Francisca when she saw the mess. 'Why don't you move to higher ground or dig a drainage trench?'

Manuel shrugged and held up his battered guitar. 'As long as this is with me, the other things don't matter.'

He took us to a part of the camp where the buildings were better constructed. Next to a mud-brick dwelling, three women in brightly coloured dresses and their children were sitting under a canopy of thatched reeds. Manuel introduced us to his sisters—Pastora, Juanita and Blanca.

'They will teach her how to dance,' he told Francisca. 'And if they can't do it, nobody can.'

I was not given a dance lesson in any traditional sense. Nobody broke down steps for me into components, or explained to me the difference between *baile grande* and *baile chico*. Rather I was told to sit and watch Manuel's sisters dance.

The first to demonstrate her talent was his youngest sister, Blanca. Manuel strummed his guitar while Pastora and Juanita accompanied him with hand clapping. Blanca pushed back her thick hair and made a few artistic turns with the train of her dress. At first the expression on her face was serious, but gradually a smile tickled her lips and her steps became lighter and lighter until she gave the impression that she was floating. She stopped abruptly, one foot arched in front of her, looking back over her shoulder. Manuel also ceased playing. The women, however, continued their clapping. Blanca narrowed her gaze and started moving her feet again. Her footwork became progressively faster, until she was kicking up sprays of sand and her sisters struggled to keep their *palmas* up to her speed. Then, without any signal to each other, Blanca and her sisters ended in unison.

I gasped with awe, but no one paid me any attention. They were not dancing for my sake.

Next, Juanita, who had golden eyes like a cat, stood up and danced with lively steps and rapid arm movements. She was followed by Pastora, whose chunky arms and rolls of stomach fat did not detract from the gracefulness of her turns or her intricate hand movements. Out of the three sisters, she had the strongest presence and made me think of an ancient tree deeply rooted to the earth.

Francisca was the last to dance and, when she did, time seemed to stop still. If her age gave her less agility or vitality than the younger women it didn't show in her performance. The lines on her face and the streaks of grey in her hair merely heightened the effect of her dance. As her movements became more and more frenzied, the veins on her forehead stood out and the grooves around her mouth deepened. She aged before our eyes, but in doing so became more beautiful and dignified. Although I was still a child and I had no words to express what I was seeing, I innately understood from her performance that flamenco was not about outer beauty, nor was it an art that aimed to please or entertain.

That night, I lay in bed and stared into the darkness, reliving the day. Flamenco was not dancing, it was a religious rite. Even thinking about it made the blood throb under my skin.

My sessions of watching Manuel's sisters dance continued for several months. Nobody explained to me the technique of *pitos*, the snapping of fingers, nor showed me how to execute a *llamada*. I had to learn these for myself by observing. I drank it all in with eager eyes. Whenever I was free from chores, I ran to the water's edge and imitated all I had seen—the gently arched backs of the women, their arms held in graceful curves, the proud tilt of their chins. I pilfered their moves and imitated their soulful expressions. I yearned to be one of them.

Each time I went with Francisca to these dance gatherings, I willed that my turn to take part would finally come. When it did, it would turn out to be an event that I would remember for the rest of my life.

Blanca had finished a lively *baile chico*, when Manuel commenced playing music for a *soleá* and nodded to me to stand up. My heart beat wildly when I realised that my chance to impress him and the others had arrived. I was sure that the reason he had chosen a serious dance for my premiere performance was because of his high expectations of me. I marked the rhythm with my own soft clapping and began slow steps, twisting my skirt around me. I cast my eyes down as I had seen the other women do when the music was tragic. Juanita had told me that I had beautiful hands so to make sure that I used them. I curled my fingers into arabesques for effect, and pinched my face into what I believed was an eloquent expression. I was pushing myself to the limit to impress the others, when Manuel abruptly stopped playing. I wondered what was wrong. He sucked in a breath and frowned.

'In flamenco,' he said, gritting his teeth, 'the dancer does not move to the music. The guitarist plays to the dancer. How can I follow you when you send me no true feelings? I get absolutely nothing from you! In all this time, you haven't learned anything!'

The blood rushed to my face. The last thing I had expected was to be humiliated in front of the other dancers. Hot tears burned my eyes and my feet twitched as if they were readying themselves to run away.

But Francisca touched my shoulder and whispered, 'Follow the sea and the music will follow you. Always respect the elements and they will help you.'

Manuel commenced playing again, his eyes fixed on me. This time, I pictured the waves and breathed in time with them. I imagined the sharp shells on the beach digging into my feet and felt the gritty sand between my toes. The cool water rippled around my legs, stinging the grazes on my shins. Suddenly my mother rose from the waves, her hair dripping down her back and her moist skin glimmering in the sun. I cried out when I saw her, overwhelmed by my longing. My mother moved about me, lifting her hands to her waist then above her head. I danced with her. With my torso, I told her of my sadness that I was growing up without her. With my arms, I related to her how Papá had died and how I mourned for the losses of Anastasio, Teresa and Ramón. With my eyes, I expressed how I had become lost and how I had come to live with the gypsies. My feet became leaden with loneliness and despair. I struggled to breathe, as if I were drowning in all the loneliness and hunger I had known. I lost all consciousness that I was being watched by others. I did not feel like a performer—it seemed to me that I had become a conductor for some supernatural power that could join the living with the dead.

I reached out to touch my mother but she vanished into the air. Shocked by her sudden departure, I stopped in my tracks. I realised then that Manuel was no longer playing. I turned to see that tears were pouring down his face. The sound of weeping assailed my ears: the sisters were hysterical. Juanita and Pastora clung to each other, rocking backwards and forwards. Blanca was on her knees, tearing at her hair so furiously that spots of blood stained her blouse. Francisca stared at her hands, bereft. She lifted her eyes to me and I felt her breath flow over me, like the afternoon breeze skimming the sea.

'The dark angel,' she said quietly. 'You have the demon.'

Manuel dried his face and turned to Francisca. 'You were right. Her ancestors are with her. Before us stands a great *bailaora*. Diego told me to take her to the restaurants on the waterfront to amuse the tourists. But never have I seen the dark angel in a child as young as this. I will not take her to those places until she can resist bending her gift for the entertainment of those who do not understand.'

I learned flamenco from Manuel and his sisters until I was ten years old and Manuel felt I was ready to dance in public. Late one evening, he came by Francisca's shack to take me with him to the barri Xinès, where I had been born. But the girl who walked those streets in bare feet and with a patched skirt was not the same one who had left the district. I was darker and dirtier, and older in a way that had nothing to do with age. I could certainly pass for a gypsy now. I thought of Ramón and wondered if he would recognise me.

Manuel came to a stop outside the café where we were to perform that evening. I looked at the arched doorway with a grave sense of destiny. Inside, the place was noisy and reeked of wine and vomit. The only women there wore flowers in their hair and low necklines. The 'aficionados' Manuel held in such high regard turned out to be factory workers, gangsters and bohemians. I peered into the darkness, looking for Ramón, as I always did whenever I left the camp. But there was nobody there who resembled him.

When the café owner laid eyes on me, he glanced towards the door nervously. 'If you attract the Civil Guard here, I will lose all my customers,' he said to Manuel, pressing his palm to his wrinkled forehead. 'How old is this girl? She is too young to be working so late and in a bar.'

Manuel shrugged and patted the man's shoulder. 'What this girl will earn will pay off not only the Civil Guard but the Governor as well. People will flock to your café to see her dance.'

The café owner stared at my dirty face and feet and shook his head. 'You will pay the fine, Manuel.'

Manuel grinned. 'Where is Sancho?'

The owner jerked his head in the direction of the bar where a man was sitting with a stoic look of resignation on his face. He was tall and lean with the dark, weathered skin of a gypsy.

'All right, listen,' Manuel said, turning to me and indicating a stool in the corner of the room. 'You sit there and don't move. I'm going to accompany Sancho first, and then you will dance.'

I watched Manuel and Sancho greet each other. They took up their places near the bar: Manuel sitting on a stool and Sancho next to him, also sitting, with his hand on Manuel's shoulder. Sancho began to sing and the crowd fell silent. His voice was raspy and the veins in his neck stood out as he sang his lament about the suffering of his people and the curse of being born a gypsy:

Do not pick flowers for me
Or walk slowly behind my coffin
Do not bury me in the cemetery
Because I am already dead

Every so often someone in the audience would shout out '*ay*' to give him encouragement or to sympathise.

When Manuel had said he was going to accompany Sancho before it was my turn to dance, I had thought that he meant for three or four songs. But Sancho wailed his grievances without a break for two hours. With each new song, his voice became hoarser and he grasped Manuel's shoulder more desperately, as if he were trying to draw strength from him. Beads of sweat dotted his brow and patches of wetness stained his shirt. But the rougher his voice became, the more the audience appreciated his singing. '*Olé, Sancho!*' they shouted to him.

Sancho's voice was painful to listen to—and yet somehow irresistible at the same time. His hard eyes glowed, and I wondered if it was reflected light or whether he was being possessed by the 'demon'. I thought of the Sagrada Família and how its newly built walls had already appeared to be crumbling that day I'd seen it while lost. Then I thought of how the wrinkles on Francisca's face enhanced her beauty. Was there some sort of magnificence in destruction?

> *This poor bundle is my father*
> *Who perished in the mines*
> *Where we were forced to work*
> *Because of our blood*

Sancho's voice cracked on the last line of the song. The audience was sobbing. One of the prostitutes collapsed to her knees in a faint and had to be revived with a splash of cold water.

Sancho sat down without a word. Manuel glanced at me. How could I dance after such a performance? I was relieved when the café owner brought Manuel a glass of wine and he slowly sipped it. The café patrons returned to their conversations and noise filled the space again. It was another hour before Manuel approached me, and by then my eyes were drooping with sleep.

'Just dance as you do in the camp,' was all Manuel said.

There was no stage in the crowded bar, so he placed me in the gap between the tables that the waiters were using as a corridor to deliver drinks to the patrons. One waiter tripped on me when he hurried past with a tray of glasses. A prostitute and her lover sitting nearby burst into laughter.

'Whose child is this?' the whore screeched, arching her thinly pencilled eyebrows. 'She should be home in bed!'

Manuel adjusted his guitar and began to play. A few people stopped talking to listen to him, but no one even glanced at me. I hesitated; there were butterflies in my stomach. Then I remembered that this wasn't a performance. How to summon the demon again? I thought of the sea and calmed my breathing. I tried to conjure up my mother, but nothing happened.

'Come on!' a sailor shouted. 'Give us a dance, sweetie!'

Manuel frowned at me then turned back to his guitar. Pins and needles prickled my feet. I gave a start when I saw Anastasio standing before me. A mountain rose up behind him and he began to climb it. I wanted to follow him, but I could only take tiny steps. My feet slipped on the loose stones. I lifted my arms, begging for his help. 'Come! Come!' he called to me, but I couldn't follow. I threw back my head and cried, but no sound came out. Then Anastasio was beside me again, weaving around me in circles. He told me how he had felt his heart break when the *Cataluña* had pulled away from the dock and his family became nothing more than tiny dots in the distance. He told me that his last thoughts before dying were of Ramón and me, and his fear about what would become of us. I asked Anastasio if he knew what had happened to Ramón and Teresa, but before he could answer me a sinister shadow engulfed him and he vanished.

I desperately searched around for Anastasio before realising the music had stopped and everyone in the bar was staring at me. Then anarchy broke out. The reaction was like a wave rushing towards the beach. Everyone was shouting, screaming or singing at once. People reached out to touch me. I was overwhelmed, and retreated. A woman swished her skirt around her ankles, in what

I guessed was an imitation of me. Something hit me in the knee and tinkled to the floor. People were throwing me money: notes and coins. Although the patrons of the bar were poor, they emptied their pockets in honour of my performance.

Manuel squeezed his way through the crowd towards me. 'Don't pick up the coins,' he said. 'Only the notes. The coins are an insult.'

I did as he told me, but regretted it as there were more coins than notes. Had I picked them up, there probably would have been enough for bread for the whole clan. Manuel took my arm and guided me towards the door. I followed him, but could not take my eyes off the coins we were leaving behind. I had been hungry all week and I was tired of always longing for food.

Outside, the pale light of sunrise was falling across the street. 'Why only the notes and not the coins as well?' I asked Manuel.

'Why do you worry about money?' he asked me, lifting his chin proudly. 'Only *payos* worry about those sorts of things. What you gave those people can't be bought.'

Manuel didn't care about money, but Diego certainly did. As clan leader he took my share of the earnings, and Francisca and I still went hungry.

After that first public performance, I accompanied Manuel every night to barri Xinès. But the 'dark angel' did not come to me every time on demand. Its presence became more fleeting, and sometimes it did not appear at all, leaving me with only the steps I had learned and Manuel's music. The tourists in the restaurants along the wharf didn't know any better, but the aficionados could tell. The game of cat and mouse I played with the demon only increased my desire to experience my communion with it again.

'It showed itself to you so that you would believe in its presence,' Francisca told me. 'But now you have to earn it.'

Early one morning, when I returned to the camp after a night of performing in bars, I found Francisca lying on her bed, clutching her lower back in pain.

'What is it?' I grabbed her hand. It was swollen like a sponge full of water.

She looked at me with compassion in her deep eyes. 'Do not panic, little one. All is well.'

Not panic? Her fingers were like ice. Her eyes were puffy.

Francisca took a breath and rallied herself. 'Look,' she said, sitting up. 'The fire is still burning. Why don't you make some liquorice tea?'

I did as Francisca asked, taking the dried liquorice from among the tins of herbs she kept in her cupboard and boiling the water. I handed her a cup, and sat on the end of her bed. We drank the tea in silence, breathing in its strong aromatic fragrance. Colour came back to Francisca's cheeks. Perhaps she would be all right, after all.

'You rest now,' I told her, pulling her blanket around her shoulders and propping her feet on a cushion. I stroked her forehead until she fell asleep.

Afterwards, I stepped outside and stared at the sea, trying to calm the terror that was seizing me. I had come to love Francisca deeply, and because of that I harboured a fear that my love would doom her, as it had the rest of my family.

EIGHTEEN

Paloma

When I returned home from my flamenco lesson and dinner with Jaime's family, I was surprised to find Mamie still up. She was sitting at the kitchen table with only the stove light on. Diaghilev's cage was uncovered but he was asleep, with his head tucked behind him, so Mamie must have been quiet for some time. If she had moved at all, Diaghilev, a light sleeper, would have been awake and playing with his toys. I'd forgotten to telephone to say I would be late when Carmen asked me to stay for dinner; and when I had remembered, it was too late to call. Mamie was usually in bed by ten-thirty.

'I'm sorry,' I said. 'I didn't want to wake you up by ringing. Gaby and I got talking.'

Mamie gave me such a puzzled look that I thought she must have telephoned Gaby's parents and discovered that I wasn't with Gaby at all. What was I going to say?

'I don't worry so much if you have the car,' Mamie replied. 'But please call anyway.'

'I will next time. I'm sorry.'

I filled the kettle and lit the stove to make camomile tea. I was too restless for sleep. Thoughts about Jaime, his family, la Rusa and the visit to my father's apartment were making my head whirl. I placed the teapot and cups on the table, then strained some of the infusion into Mamie's cup. When she lifted the rim to her lips, I noticed her fingers were stained with ink.

'Have you been writing letters?' I asked.

She glanced at me, lost in a dream, before she realised that I was speaking to her. 'Talking about letters,' she said, ignoring my question and reaching towards the bench, 'this came for you today. It's from the Ballet School.'

I took the letter and the opener she handed me. My fingers trembled as I slit the envelope and read the contents.

'My request to re-audition through the school has been accepted,' I told Mamie. 'They have also approved me having private lessons with Mademoiselle Louvet.'

I glanced at Mamie, expecting her to repeat her speech about how I should be auditioning for other companies as well, not 'putting all my eggs in one basket'.

Instead Mamie surprised me by saying, 'Normally you would have to re-audition externally so it shows how highly they think of you. I want to you to concentrate fully on your preparation for the examination. I can manage the weekday classes on my own.'

'Mamie, are you sure you're all right?'

She stared at her hands and sighed. 'I've been thinking about your grandfather,' she said. 'I want to tell you about him—and also more about Xavier. Are you too tired?'

I shook my head. I was in the mood to hear another story: I needed some distraction. My anticipation regarding the audition was now another thing I had to think about.

Mamie took a sip of tea and then began. 'You see, Cemetery was not the only place where class mattered. There were other locations in Barcelona where society was rigidly stratified . . .'

* * *

'*Grand-plié, relevé . . . coupé fondu, développé, relevé . . . tombé, chassé, grand rond de jambe en l'air . . .*' Olga commanded in her Russian-accented French.

I was standing in front of the grand mirror in the ballroom of our house on the passeig de Gràcia, wearing a chiffon tunic with a long flounced skirt and tulle underlay, and following the instructions while Margarida accompanied me on the piano. Years of classical Spanish dance training had given me strong feet and ankles and a sense of balance, but the ballet positions and degree of turnout Olga demanded of me were not easy. I worked with determination to please her. If Olga remained indifferent after our daily lesson, I was deeply wounded and would spend the day locked away in my room. But if she praised me, I scampered around the house like a kitten.

Olga, with her arched eyebrows and satin-smooth skin, had achieved what my parents had hoped she would: she had broken my habit of stuttering and staring at my feet when people spoke to me. But she had achieved it by instilling in me the fear of disapproval; specifically, her disapproval. I was still nervous around people only now I was too terrified to show it.

Olga watched me perform a series of *piqué passé* turns across the room. She blew a stream of cigarette smoke between her blood-red lips and her eyes narrowed like a cat's. If her expression had stayed that way, it would have meant another day spent in my room, but fortunately she smiled.

'*Maladets*! Well done, Evelina,' she said. 'You are showing progress.'

The great clock in the hall struck the hour, indicating it was time for Olga to leave.

'Ah,' she said, sweeping her hand through the air before bringing it to rest on her heart. 'I have no time for stories today, Evelina. I must hurry. I have to give a lesson to the nieces of the Marqués de Comillas. I promised him when I saw him at the Liceu.'

Margarida turned from the piano and grinned. She enjoyed making fun of Olga: mimicking the ballerina's regal walk behind her back, holding her nose in the air and pointing her toes in front of her. I shook my head and looked away, not seeing what was so amusing. I worshipped the woman, which was how she managed to maintain such a hold on me.

I curtseyed to Olga, every muscle in my legs burning. I was disappointed that I wasn't going to hear one of her stories about her life in Russia while I did my stretches. But her words of encouragement would set me working even harder in the next few days. I would do anything to hear 'well done' pass her lips again.

After Olga had been shown out of the house by the maid, Margarida turned to me. 'Your teacher is a con artist!' she said. 'She speaks to you as if she is doing you some favour by teaching you rather than turning up for the money. I don't believe a word of her stories! Really, how many men could have shot themselves after being rejected by her? And if so many of the male sex desire her, how come she is living by herself?'

'Her great love was executed by the revolutionaries when he tried to help her out of Russia,' I explained. 'He was a prince. She could never love again . . .'

'*Bah!*' scoffed Margarida. 'Have we met *any* Russian refugees who weren't once princes or princesses?'

I shrugged and continued with my stretches. I valued Margarida's opinion on most things, but not regarding Olga. Without my ballet teacher's stories, my life would have been drearily boring.

Realising that I was ignoring her, Margarida opened the French doors and strode out onto the balcony. Now that Xavier had become a father and didn't spend as much time with her, Margarida was restless. The scent of roses from the pots outside wafted into the room. The ballroom was one of my favourite spaces in the house; I loved everything about it: the ornate walnut piano, the chandeliers, the decorative wrought iron that wound around the windows and fireplaces like overgrown brambles. But I only liked the room when it was empty and peaceful like this, not when it was full of people.

Margarida returned from the balcony and shut the doors behind her. 'Speaking about the Liceu,' she said, 'you are making your debut there in two weeks. Mama hasn't told you because she's afraid you will clam up again. But she and Conchita have been conspiring with the dressmaker to create you a suitable dress.'

'I'm not dancing at the Liceu,' I said. 'Pare would never consent to that.'

Margarida laughed so much she nearly choked. 'Not your dance debut, Evelina,' she said, wiping her eyes. 'Your *social* debut. Mama did the same thing for me—little good that it did. She is having a very grown-up dress made for you, and you will wear some of the jewels allotted to you in your dowry. When everyone sees you sitting like that in the box, they will understand that Mama and Pare are giving their permission for their sons to court you.'

I couldn't be sure whether Margarida was teasing me or not. When I was younger, she had told me that babies were made by a man leaping on a woman the way male pigeons climbed on top of their females. When I'd asked Mama if that were true, she had blushed and told me Margarida had a vivid imagination. Margarida and I got along very well, but without Xavier's company my sister was becoming obnoxious. I hoped that she was somewhat perturbed by the potential loss of me as well. As was the custom, Xavier and Conchita had been given an apartment on the third floor of our house, but if I married, I would have to live with my husband's family. The idea of being separated from Margarida and the rest of my family didn't appeal to me either.

'Look at this,' Margarida said, unpinning her hair.

I waited for the full mane to drop as she undid the roll, but it remained where it was. She smoothed her locks with her fingers.

'You've cut your hair!' I cried.

She chuckled. 'It's called a bob. It's the latest fashion!'

'Mama is going to kill you!'

Margarida gave me a wry look. I had to admit that she appeared fetching with her hair that way.

'She won't see it,' Margarida assured me, arranging her short hair back into a roll. 'I'll keep it pinned up at home.'

I admired her daring. I would never have the courage to do such a thing. I was bound by some invisible force to always do what I was told. Besides, thanks to Margarida's rebellious behaviour, my parents were twice as strict with me as they might otherwise have been.

While Margarida settled into Victor Hugo's *Les Misérables* in the library, I decided to pay a visit to my nephew, Feliu, who had been born two months previously. He was the image of Xavier, with a perfectly shaped head and tender eyes. I was making my way towards the stairs, when I heard my father talking in the drawing room with Conchita's father, don Carles.

'Surely you can't see murder as a solution to our issues?' my father was saying.

The word 'murder' stopped me in my tracks. Pare was strict, conservative and religious. But don Carles, while all those things on the surface, was of the extreme right-wing persuasion—a fact we were only understanding now that our families were on intimate terms.

'I don't condemn the business owners who resort to it,' don Carles replied, with a calmness that chilled me. 'What choice are they left with but to hire assassins to get rid of those troublesome union leaders? How many innocent civilians have been killed by those scoundrels' bombs? And what about the gangs roaming the streets of Barcelona? If the working class abandon their children, then what else can we do but deal with the problem? We must think of our own wives and children first.'

'And how do you propose we deal with the abandoned street children?' Xavier asked.

I was surprised to hear my brother's voice. I had assumed he was upstairs with Conchita and Feliu.

I pictured don Carles fixing his steely eyes on Xavier and rubbing his black, bushy brows as he replied: 'You cull them like you would any other pest species. It is they who grow up into revolutionaries and anarchists.'

I almost cried out in disgust. How could anyone who claimed to be religious propose such a thing? I imagined Xavier was similarly shocked. He and Margarida battled frequently with Pare over his conservatism, but my father's views were not as extreme as those of don Carles.

Xavier replied with measured courtesy, but I detected the undertone of disdain. 'Perhaps we might have fewer anarchists if we had a different political system—one that was fairer. The workers resort to revolutionary activity because they have no other hope of equality.'

Pare coughed. 'Equality, Xavier? Now, I wouldn't go so far as don Carles . . . but some people are born to rule while others are not. Women, for instance, were made by God to exist in the home. You were too young in 1909 to remember what Barcelona became when the working classes burned the churches and schools.'

'You see,' interjected don Carles. 'You give them schools to improve themselves and what do they do? They burn them down!'

Xavier hesitated a moment before responding. 'Actually, I've not forgotten 1909 at all. It's the reason I feel as I do. The purpose of religious education is to keep the poor in their place. That's why the government was so keen to execute Ferrer after the Tragic Week: his schools had a different objective. It's easy to control people when they are illiterate.'

'The government was too lenient in light of the damage caused,' said don Carles. 'They only singled out for execution one representative for each crime committed—one for destroying property, one for profaning the clergy, one for inciting a rebellion . . .'

'They threw hundreds of people into gaol under terrible conditions,' Xavier protested. 'Many of them died of diseases or from the torture they suffered before their cases were ever tried. Others were sent into exile, where they faced destitution, starvation and the hostility of the locals.'

'If you are going to refer to that flower seller again, Xavier,' Pare said, 'I feel no remorse about her. She wasn't a simple working woman, she was a leader of Damas Rojas. She led the burning of convents, for goodness sake!'

'She came to the dress factory on the day of the general strike,' said Xavier, paying no attention to Pare's objection. 'She had two small children with her. Do you ever wonder what might have happened to those children after she was taken away? I do. I remember looking into the girl's face. Her expression of hunger has haunted me ever since.'

'*Bah*, you are too soft,' said don Carles, finally showing his temper. 'And softness will not help this city. The future will be tough and we will need leaders who aren't afraid to make unpopular decisions. You must put aside your artistic dalliances and face reality.'

A maid entered the room from the other door to the drawing room, the one that connected it to the music room, and brought the conversation to a stop. She told Xavier there was a gentleman on the telephone for him. Xavier excused himself, and I heard him exit the room and make his way towards the study.

'I should be getting along,' don Carles told my father.

There was the sound of fabric rustling as the men rose from their chairs. I slipped behind a statue as the door opened and Pare and don Carles emerged. A maid appeared with don Carles's hat and coat.

'With all the foreign influences in the city these days, and the jazz clubs, young people seem to be entertaining strange ideas about a second republic,' Pare told don Carles. 'But experience always wins out in the end.'

My father was famous for his self-assuredness; many would even go so far as to call him 'smug'. But on this occasion, he was clenching and opening his fists behind his back as if he was uncertain of something. I had the impression that he was trying to defend Xavier.

At the door, the men shook each other's hands. But there was an unmistakable chill in don Carles's manner.

'Your son isn't some sort of libertine, free to say and do as he pleases,' he told Pare before departing. 'It is one thing to have opinions, don Leopold. It is quite another to voice them. I suggest that you speak to him.'

From the grave tone of don Carles's voice, it was clear that he was not giving Pare a piece of advice: he was making a threat.

I felt compelled to warn Xavier about what don Carles had said. When Pare returned to the drawing room, I ran to the study and entered it just as Xavier was putting down the telephone. He turned when he heard me shut the door. The frown on his face softened and he smiled.

'Xavier . . . be careful . . . don Carles is very angry.'

My brother nodded and waved his hand. 'He's only saying what most people think. God almighty, they go on about their churches being burned—and this, the country of the Inquisition! How many innocent people did the Church burn at the stake?'

I couldn't get what don Carles had said about culling the street urchins out of my mind. 'Do you really think that's what people feel about the children on the street? I mean . . . Mama does a lot of charity work in the Church orphanages.'

Xavier's shoulders relaxed. He stepped towards me and clasped my hand. 'The rich families of Barcelona have the power to end the starvation and suffering in the city and yet we do nothing but perpetuate it,' he said. 'How can we go to Mass every week and mouth prayers about God's love for all humanity? I can't stand being such a hypocrite!'

I looked into my brother's eyes and saw how troubled he was. He had always hated injustice, but now I saw a deep unhappiness in his face that hadn't been there before he'd married.

'What worries don Carles,' continued Xavier, 'is that the way the Montella businesses are succeeding, we are eventually going to overtake the Güell and the López dynasties to become the most powerful family in Barcelona, and one day I am going to be head of the family. I promise you, Evelina, Barcelona will be a very different place then.'

Margarida had spoken the truth when she'd said that I would be making my social debut at the Liceu. Now, instead of being left alone to practise my ballet steps, I was called up for fittings in Conchita and Xavier's apartment, where my sister-in-law and mother were busy arguing over dress styles.

'No, not that one,' said Conchita of a pattern for a silk charmeuse evening dress with gold metallic thread. 'It will make her look too young.'

'But I don't want Evelina to appear too old either,' Mama protested.

My mother was always elegantly dressed, but I was pleased Conchita had been given a say in the dress. She looked stunning in everything she wore, and was also able to tell at a glance whether a style would suit another person or not.

'This one,' she said, holding up a pattern for a silk dress with gold lamé across the bust and around the hem. The dress was exotic and sleek. A flurry of excitement ran through me. I imagined myself climbing the steps of the Liceu looking like an Egyptian goddess.

'*You* could wear that,' Mama told Conchita. 'But Evelina is too shy. She needs something plainer.'

My spirits dropped. The exotic dress dissolved into a more conservative one: sleeveless, with a high V-neck and ruffled skirt. The kind of dress one found in a catalogue.

'If you give her something beautiful and different to wear, she'll feel less shy,' argued Conchita.

'Senyores!' pleaded the dressmaker, senyoreta Garrós. 'You have only given me a short amount of time to have this dress ready. You must decide on the pattern today.'

While Mama and Conchita debated over my dress, I looked around the apartment. The rooms used to be filled entirely with eighteenth-century furniture and Sèvres porcelain, but Conchita had introduced some Modernista pieces, including a mahogany screen and the chairs with swan-motif upholstery and slender, bone-like legs that she and my mother were sitting on. With Conchita's sense of panache, she and Xavier should have had much in common, but they did not have similar tastes at all. Conchita hated Gaudí's architecture while Xavier revered it; she had insisted on walking out of a Stravinsky concert when Xavier had wanted to stay; and they no longer attended avant-garde art exhibitions together as they used to when they were engaged.

'She likes fashion, not art,' Margarida had said to me. 'You watch, in another few years all that Modernista furniture will be replaced by whatever happens to be in mode then.'

But whatever aesthetic conflicts they had, when Xavier walked into the room that morning carrying Feliu, Conchita could not have looked more enamoured of her husband and child.

'Ah,' she said, holding out her arms and taking Feliu into her lap. 'My little boy.' She turned her cheek so Xavier could kiss her. 'Can you stay with us a while?' she asked him. 'Or do you have to rush off somewhere? We are deciding on Evelina's dress for opening night. And as your mother and I have such differing opinions, a male adjudicator would be helpful.'

'I'm afraid Pare and I have a luncheon with the mayor today, but I can stay for a cup of coffee,' Xavier said, sitting down next to his wife.

With Conchita's dark beauty and even features, and Xavier's tanned skin and perfect teeth, it was easy to see why they were considered Barcelona's most attractive couple.

'Why don't you let Evelina decide on the dress?' Xavier suggested. 'After all, she's the one who has to wear it.'

Conchita pinched his arm as if he had made an absurd suggestion. Xavier gave his opinion on some of the patterns the dressmaker showed him, while Conchita made cooing sounds to Feliu.

A maid entered and announced that Conchita's mother had arrived for a visit. We all stood up as donya Elisa strode into the room. 'Ah, Feliu!' she said, paying no mind to us and heading straight towards her grandson. None of us was offended; we all took it as a given that Feliu should command everyone's attention.

Mama instructed the maid to bring us more tea, which she served in black and white ceramic cups.

'Don't keep him too long,' Conchita pleaded with her mother as she handed Feliu over to her. 'I can't bear to not have him with me. Even when the wet nurse takes him, I have to sit with her. You can never be sure that another woman will do everything correctly.'

Donya Elisa looked at her daughter in surprise. 'But, darling, you have to be a bit tougher with boys or you'll make Feliu a sissy.'

Mama patted Conchita's arm. 'We are all like that with our firstborn children, but you will calm down as the others come along. You will see that children can manage without us much better than we think.'

Conchita blinked at my mother. 'But I have borne a male heir,' she said. 'I don't see the need for *other* children.'

Mama and Xavier exchanged a glance.

'Of course, giving birth makes you think you could never go through that again,' said donya Elisa, brushing down her dress. 'But you will want more children. They bring such joy into your life.'

A strange look passed over Conchita's face. She pursed her lips.

Mama glanced doubtfully at Xavier again. The thin lines of a frown were scarring his forehead and his fingers thrummed on his knee, but if Conchita's attitude troubled him, he shrugged it off.

'It's because Feliu looks so much like me that she thinks that way,' he said with a laugh. 'If he resembled her, she'd want a dozen more children.'

Donya Elisa, Mama and senyoreta Garrós chuckled. Xavier had saved the moment. Donya Elisa flashed him a grateful smile, but Conchita wouldn't look at him. She and Xavier may have appeared like a perfect couple, but something was clearly wrong.

The Gran Teatre del Liceu in Barcelona was not simply an opera house, it was an institution. Like many of the great opera houses of the time, the seating was in a horseshoe shape around the stage and tiered into five balconies. A family's status in Barcelona society was reflected by where that family sat in the Liceu. The *planta noble* was reached by a grand marble staircase from the lobby and was the most prestigious tier on which to have a box. From there, the staircases became less decorative and narrower, up to the fourth floor where the boxes were owned by families of lesser importance and the seats by the middle-class families. The uppermost tier contained no boxes and could not be reached from the internal staircases but had to be accessed via an unadorned entrance in the side street. It was there that the students and factory workers sat. Many of them came simply to listen, as not every seat on the top floor afforded a view of the stage. While donya Esperanza referred to people who sat in the uppermost floors as 'riffraff', they were probably the only ones—along with Xavier—who came to the opera to appreciate the performance. Everyone else was there to bolster their egos, reaffirm their alliances with Barcelona's other powerful families, show off new evening dresses or catch up on gossip.

On the opening night of *Turandot*, we entered our box to find donya Esperanza already sitting there. 'As Conchita isn't coming tonight, I decided to keep Xavier company,' she said. 'As a representative of the de Figueroa family.'

Having recently had a baby, no one expected Conchita to appear at the opera until she had regained her figure. And, as matriarch of the de Figueroa family, donya Esperanza should really have been chaperoning Conchita's younger sisters. But donya Esperanza's age and standing in society put her beyond convention, so no one bothered arguing with her. And, of course, our box had a better view of the boxes opposite than the one owned by the de Figueroa family did. Donya Esperanza might have been in her nineties but there was nothing she enjoyed more than a chance to spy on others and to gossip.

I took my place next to her in the lower corner of the box. 'That's a beautiful gown, by the way,' she said. 'It suits your complexion perfectly. You look radiant.'

After all the disputes regarding what I should wear, we had finally found a design on which we had all agreed: a gold lace gown over a beige silk underdress with a bias-cut skirt. The capped sleeves and the pink rose at the centre of the neckline lent the dress the sense of feminine modesty my mother had been aiming for, while the fabric and cut gave the gown the glamour Conchita had championed. I was happy simply to be dressed like a young woman instead of an overgrown girl. Mama had lent me a gold peridot and pearl necklace from her collection.

I straightened my skirt and noticed Francesc Cerdà stealing a look at me from his family's box on the opposite side of the tier. The expression of surprise on his face was so palpable it gave the impression that he had never seen me before, when in fact he had gone to the same Jesuit school as Xavier and we had often seen each other at social occasions or in church. His interest in me pleased Mama. She nudged Pare so hard he jumped. The opera was Pare's chance to catch up on sleep, and he'd perfected the art of resting his chin on his palm so that he gave the appearance of listening when, in fact, he was not.

Mama's pleasure at my being noticed by the Cerdà family heir was well justified. They came from a long line of nobility. Francesc's father was a *marqués*: a title Francesc, as the eldest son, would inherit one day.

Margarida leaned forwards from her seat behind me and whispered in my ear, 'Ah, Francesc Cerdà! Very good-looking, rich and athletic—but as silly as a sole's shoe.'

I turned around and scowled at her, but when she grinned back at me it was difficult not to laugh. Francesc was a blond, blue-eyed Catalan, and Xavier had said that whenever he stayed at the Cerdàs' holiday home in S'Agaró, Francesc always seemed to be running around in a pair of shorts, pummelling a punching bag or performing somersaults. But it was also known that Francesc wasn't the brightest male in the family, and his father, who was savvy, had manoeuvred Francesc's youthful uncles into positions of management in the Cerdà properties so that Francesc would be nothing more than a figurehead, signing whatever documents were placed in front of him.

'Still,' whispered Margarida, 'it would be fun to be a *marquesa*.'

I stifled a giggle. Despite the dress, the occasion and my age, I wasn't taking things too seriously. Marriage was far from my mind. I had no intention of giving up my ballet lessons just yet.

'Who is that young man next to Francesc Cerdà?' asked donya Esperanza.

'Don't you recognise him?' asked Margarida. 'That's Gaspar Olivero.'

I leaned forwards to see who they were talking about. Alongside Francesc sat another young man, maybe two or three years younger. He had reddish-brown hair, alert eyes and a sweet smile.

'Oh,' said Mama, 'I didn't expect to see him with the Cerdà family. Don't the Oliveros live in Zaragoza now?'

'Yes, terrible business,' said donya Esperanza. 'Fancy being born into such wealth only to have your irresponsible parents whittle it away on extravagant living. It was a scandal for the Marqués to have his sister fall so low. There were creditors' notices in the newspaper and auctions . . . The shame!'

If there was one thing the 'good families' of Barcelona despised more than poor people, it was those who had been born rich but had been foolish enough to lose their fortune. I shifted in my seat; I didn't like the way donya Esperanza spoke about

Gaspar Olivero, as he seemed so kind and gentle. The way he looked around him with interest reminded me of a squirrel.

'Well, it's generous of the Marqués and Marquesa to take the young man into their care,' Mama said, trying to give the conversation a positive direction. Perhaps she was worried that I'd be turned off Francesc if I thought his cousin's family was irresponsible.

'Gaspar is studying law,' Xavier said. 'And he's brilliant at it. He'll be all right. He doesn't need his family's money.'

'And he's an accomplished pianist and artist too,' added Margarida. 'He accompanies the star acts at a prestigious theatre on las Ramblas, and some of his drawings are being exhibited in Josep Dalmau's gallery, where Salvador Dalí is shown. He's quite a genius!'

I studied Gaspar Olivero again. How could anyone have such a range of gifts—and have developed each of them to such a high level? I was intrigued.

At that moment, Gaspar turned in my direction. He saw me and smiled. One corner of his mouth lifted slightly higher than the other, which I found charming. Without thinking, I smiled back. I can't describe what happened at that moment. I had not spoken a word to him, but suddenly I felt as if my heart was rising up in my chest. It seemed to float out of the top of my head and drift towards Gaspar Olivero! I quickly looked away.

'Who is Salvador Dalí?' asked donya Esperanza. 'I don't believe I'm acquainted with the Dalí family.'

Mama shot Xavier and Margarida a chastising look. 'It is commendable that Gaspar is trying to make his way in the world rather than relying on the charity of his uncle and aunt,' she said. 'I'm sure that he will marry a respectable girl and be happy.'

We all knew, without Mama saying it, that by 'respectable' she meant middle class. In Mama's eyes, there were 'good' girls from rich families, 'respectable' ones from middle-class families, and 'unfortunate' ones from poor families.

'Oh, but the shame of it all,' said donya Esperanza, unwilling to let go of the grimmer aspects of the Oliveros' situation. 'They had to sell their box at the Liceu. It had been in the family since 1850.'

'I know,' said Xavier, a touch of sarcasm in his voice. 'We are sitting in it!'

The uncomfortable silence brought on by Xavier's statement was relieved by the general silence that followed the dimming of the lights and the commencement of the performance. I was intrigued by the story of *Turandot*—which was about a princess who challenged her suitors to answer three riddles or forfeit their lives—and by Puccini's beautiful music. But donya Esperanza, who had little enthusiasm for opera, wanted to talk. I wouldn't have minded so much if she didn't have such a fascination with the morbid.

'You know, I was here that night in 1893 when that anarchist dropped his bombs into the audience,' she whispered to me. 'It was terrible. Twenty-two people were killed and many others badly injured. There were legs, arms and heads everywhere. Blood and bone splattered onto the stage. They say that a lady's hand, with a diamond ring on every finger, fell into the first violinist's lap . . .'

Donya Esperanza had told me that story many times before and, as a result, I couldn't look down into the stalls without imagining that horrific scene. I thought that if I didn't add to the conversation, she might move on. But she had another story, one I hadn't heard before, to top that one. 'And that section over there, that's where Enriqueta Martí used to sit. Who knew, as she sat there in all her finery, that she was a serial killer?'

I shouldn't have reacted but, without thinking, I turned to donya Esperanza, aghast.

'Oh, yes,' she said, her eyes widening with the thrill of having an audience on whom to inflict her gory tale. 'She used to murder street urchins. Then she would cut them up and boil their bodies to make beauty creams for the high society of Barcelona!'

This last story was too much for Mama who leaned over towards us. 'Donya Esperanza, please . . . Evelina is sensitive. You'll give her nightmares.'

'But it's true,' protested donya Esperanza, neither offended nor chastised. 'Martí found her clients for her potions *here*.'

Mama shook her head. 'I've heard that too, but I can't think of one person who would have bought such an atrocious concoction! The very idea of harming children! I am sure it was a rumour sent around by the Communists to make the workers hate us even more.'

'Well, *somebody* was buying it,' said donya Esperanza, bemused by Mama's scepticism. 'It was in the police reports. I've always had a suspicion that one of Martí's clients was . . .'

Thankfully, before donya Esperanza could implicate anybody who would—rightly or wrongly—be held in my mind forever after as a villain of the most heinous kind, the music for the opera swelled in volume.

The act came to an end shortly afterwards and it was time for the interval. The boxes on the prestigious levels of the Liceu opened onto wide passageways that were designed for promenading. My mother linked arms with me and 'promenaded' me swiftly in the direction of the Cerdà family's box. Margarida and Xavier accompanied us, while Pare stopped to chat with don Bartomeu Manzano, donya Josefa's husband.

A blond woman of statuesque proportions was heading in our direction on the arm of a distinguished-looking gentleman. The woman's champagne silk dress shimmered like the chandeliers that lit the passageway and she had crystal blue eyes like a doll's. They were the kind of looks that would normally turn heads—and people's heads were turning, but, strangely, in the opposite direction to her. While people nodded greetings to the man, they ignored the woman.

As she and I passed one another, we caught each other's eye. The woman stopped, as if about to engage me in conversation, but I felt a tug on my arm and turned to see Mama shake her head. She gave a shake of her head and moved me forward. The blond woman's face fell. I was surprised at my mother's behaviour. Mama had a strong sense of propriety but she was never rude to anyone. What had the beautiful woman done to deserve being so severely snubbed?

When Mama stopped for a moment to chat with donya Elisa and Conchita's sisters, Margarida sidled up to me. 'That was the heir to the de Artigas fortune and his second wife. They live in Paris. She's an American,' she said.

'Why were people so rude to her? Even Mama! Surely not because she's a foreigner?'

My sister shrugged. 'They snub her because she's not from our circle. She's the daughter of an American shopkeeper who happened to capture the heart of a very rich man.'

'So she doesn't come from a wealthy family,' I said, still not comprehending the reason for the cold-shouldering. 'It doesn't mean she's not a decent person. After all, she's el senyor de Artigas's wife, not his mistress.'

'Ah,' said Margarida, raising her finger. 'You are not thinking like the group, Evelina. And that can be fatal. You see, she's not from our circle but *she has married a man from our circle*. What does that mean? It means there is one less matrimonial prospect for a daughter of one of Barcelona's good families.'

Xavier, who was listening in on our conversation, added, 'It's the same reason why the English get so put out about people marrying "above their station".'

'Well,' I said, 'she's much more beautiful than any of the women in our circle, except for Conchita, of course. No wonder el senyor de Artigas married her.'

Xavier smiled. 'Our Evelina of the romantic heart, whatever are we going to do with you?'

'Olga has been filling your head with romantic notions,' Margarida chided me. 'Don't think there aren't other debutantes trying to elbow their way into the Cerdà family. Maria Dalmau, for one. You are friends, yes? Well, let's see what happens when

Francesc Cerdà shows more interest in you because you are prettier.'

I noticed Mama glance from donya Elisa to the clock. We were going to have to make haste if we were to see the Cerdà family before the next act. Luckily for us, Francesc Cerdà's mother must have had the same idea. I turned to see her hurrying towards us.

'Donya Rosita, this is very late notice,' the Marquesa said to my mother. 'But we are having supper after the opera at our home. It will only be a few people. We would like you and your family to join us if you are free this evening. My mother is too elderly to come to the opera now, so we try to give her some entertainment at home. My nephew, Gaspar, will play the piano for us. Perhaps Xavier would also honour us with a piece or two?'

Normally, for such a spontaneous change of plans, Mama would have consulted Pare before making a decision. But as Pare was nowhere to be seen, Mama told the Marquesa that we would be delighted to come.

The final act of *Turandot* was so full of tragedy and triumph that even donya Esperanza stayed quiet for the aria 'Nessun Dorma'. But time dragged for me. For reasons I couldn't fathom, I was dying to meet Gaspar Olivero. I was glad when the curtain came down and I heard Mama say to Pare that we had better start making our farewells as we were going to the Cerdà family's supper. It took us forever to leave the Liceu: the society reporters wanted to photograph me in my new dress; donya Josefa stopped us to remind Mama about a charity lunch; and senyor Dalmau asked Pare what he thought about the performance and Pare had to make something up. It was a relief when our driver pulled up in the Hispano-Suiza and we all piled inside.

The Cerdàs' house on the passeig de Gràcia was one of the grandest in Barcelona. Behind its magnificent stone façade was an entrance hall with a domed ceiling, lacquered columns and marble sculptures of goddesses by Josep Clarà. As was the fashion in many aristocratic houses, each room had a different colour scheme and style. As the butler led us to the drawing room, we passed through a medieval-style library with burgundy walls, gargoyles, and a suit of armour in the corner. From there we were directed into a Far East-themed hallway featuring an oriental rug runner, embroidered silk curtains and a chest of black lacquered wood with a dragon carved on it. By the time we reached the inner reception area and stopped a moment to admire the classical columns and fountain that conjured up images of Ancient Greece, it felt as though we had made a journey through civilisation in the span of five minutes.

'You might live here one day,' Margarida whispered to me.

She was joking but her words sent a chill through me. I was at home with my family in our tranquil and elegant house with its smooth parquetry floors and the clean lines of the Homar and Busquets furniture. The Cerdàs' house was a palace, but I couldn't see myself being comfortable in it. And who was Francesc? What did I know about him? How should I decide whether or not I wanted to spend the rest of my life with him? The pulse in my temple began to throb. I stumbled on the hem of my dress but luckily Xavier caught me.

We were ushered into the drawing room, where the curtains, blinds and tablecloths were all the same lavender damask. Cerdà ancestors stared down at us from their gilded frames. The Marqués and Marquesa, the only occupants of the room besides an elderly lady in a wheelchair whom I took to be the Marquesa's mother, rose to welcome us. They were both statuesque and fair-skinned, more like Nordic gods than Spaniards.

'You are the first to arrive,' said the Marqués. 'The others have been held up.'

As we already knew each other, there was no need for introductions, but pleasantries about the opera and enquiries into each other's health had to be exchanged. Fortunately, my mother answered on my behalf. I felt my old anxiety about being around people I didn't know well returning. My hands and feet had turned cold.

But then the Marquesa turned and addressed me directly. 'I've been admiring your dress all evening, Evelina,' she said. 'Did you have it made here or is it from Paris?'

My larynx tightened and I found it hard to breathe. I opened my mouth but I seemed to have lost my tongue. 'Tha-a-ak you,' I stuttered.

The Marquesa raised her eyebrows in astonishment, not sure if she had heard me correctly. Mother paled. Pare stared at me, horrified. All Olga's good work had flown out the door.

'She was cold in the car,' said quick-thinking Xavier, putting his arm around me. 'I'm afraid she's caught a bit of a chill.'

My brother spoke with such ease and confidence; I would have given anything to be like him.

'Ah, yes,' said the Marquesa, nodding sympathetically. 'I was the same at her age, always cold. It's this time of year. A warm evening can suddenly turn chilly. We didn't have the fire lit tonight because once this room fills up, it can get stuffy. Perhaps Evelina would like a cup of tea?'

'Oh, that's not necessary,' said Mama.

'It is no trouble at all,' insisted the Marqués, ringing for a maid.

The Marqués and Marquesa were being kind, which made me all the more embarrassed. I hated being the centre of attention. My one comfort was that Gaspar Olivero wasn't in the room to witness me making a fool of myself.

The tea arrived, and at the same time we heard the sound of voices coming through the reception room. The butler opened the door and announced the arrival of the other guests. Thankfully, their appearance took the attention away from me. Because the Marquesa had said that the evening would be a small, informal affair I was surprised to see that the Dalmau and López families had been invited, along with other significant members of Barcelona's elite. Suddenly the room was crowded with people. Francesc arrived but there was no sign of Gaspar.

My head began to throb again and I had trouble breathing. I tried to imagine everyone as a chimpanzee, but my panic had already taken hold and I couldn't laugh it off. It was bad enough to have an anxiety attack in my own home, where I could escape to some familiar room until I felt more comfortable. But what to do when I was in someone else's house? I looked to Xavier, but he was involved in lively conversation with the Marqués. Margarida had somehow ended up across the other side of the room talking to Francesc. I wouldn't have been able to reach her without encountering a whole lot of other people.

I put down my teacup and inched my way to the back of the room, trying to find some clear space. I noticed a door, slightly ajar, and thought that if I could escape the crowd for a while, I would calm down enough to get through supper. I slipped through the doorway and found myself in a room that was decorated more tastefully than the others we had seen. The carved cherry-wood furniture was upholstered in a soft apple-green and the curtains were a pale gold yellow. It was as though I had stepped into a forest. A long dining table had been set with silver cutlery and Art Deco plates and glassware. There was also a grand Bösendorfer piano in the corner. I gathered this was where we would be eating supper. On one wall there was a marquetry panel depicting nymphs dancing the *sardana* in a glade. In an effort to calm my racing mind, I tried to guess the types of woods that had been used. Walnut? Olive? Jacaranda? Xavier would know. I sank into an armchair in the corner of the room and rested my aching forehead in my palm.

'Your brother tells me that you are studying ballet?'

I gave a start. The voice had come from the other side of the room. I lifted my eyes to see Gaspar Olivero leaning against the fireplace and studying me.

It took me a moment to answer. I had been so flustered I hadn't noticed that anyone else was in the room.

'Yes,' I said. 'You know my brother well?'

'I'm Gaspar Olivero,' he said, walking towards me. 'Xavier and I have been friends for years but you probably don't remember me. The last time we met, you were still a girl. Your brother and I shared the same first piano teacher: Enrique Granados.'

The face that I had spied from the opera box was as sweet up close as it had been from afar. I wondered how it was that I didn't remember such a character-filled countenance, but I was so shy as a child I was probably looking at my feet when we were introduced. There was something reassuring in Gaspar's manner. I relaxed for the first time since we had entered the Cerdà mansion.

'I've heard that you are a wonderful pianist too,' I told him.

Gaspar picked up one of the dining chairs from the table and sat down next to me. 'Well, if that's true then I have my parents to thank for it,' he said, looking at me with his bright eyes. 'They never forced me to take up music . . . they *inspired* me to do it. From the earliest time I can remember there were always musicians in the house. Music is as much a part of me as my heart or lungs.'

I liked how he spoke about his parents—with deep gratitude, not resentment. The way donya Esperanza had referred to them, she had implied that Gaspar should be ashamed of them. But I didn't get the impression that was what he felt.

'Why are you here and not in the other room?' I asked him.

He grinned. His teeth overlapped slightly at the front, making his face all the more appealing. 'The opera was so sublime, I needed a few moments to take it all in . . . to relive it. Francesc is a wonderful fellow, but he talked non-stop all the way in the car.'

Gaspar didn't ask me why I had snuck away from the gathering. Had he guessed?

'But let's talk about your dancing,' he said, clasping his hands on his knee. 'I'm a great admirer of Diaghilev's ballets. Did you see the Ballet Russes at the Liceu?'

I shook my head. 'I would have liked to. But it wasn't in my father's taste. He doesn't like modern things much.'

'So you will dance with a more classically oriented company? The Paris Opera Ballet?'

'No,' I said, laughing, although I was flattered by his suggestion. 'My father would never let me dance in public.'

Gaspar looked amazed. 'But *you* would like to?'

His question caught me off guard. I never thought about what I would like to do. I couldn't see the use of dwelling on the impossible.

'Yes, I would like to,' I confided in him, surprised at my sudden boldness. 'I'm not so nervous when I dance.'

He nodded understandingly. I realised how comfortable I was with him. Despite the surprise he had given me, I hadn't stuttered once. I could speak to him as easily as I could to Xavier or Margarida. I was about to tell him about Olga when Xavier came through the door.

'There you are, Evelina! Mama was wondering where you had disappeared to,' he said.

Gaspar stood up and shook hands with my brother. 'I was going over the performance tonight in my head when your charming sister wandered into the room.'

'She doesn't like crowds,' Xavier said, looking at me affectionately.

'I can't blame her,' said Gaspar. 'I'm not crazy for them myself.' Then, as if to save me further embarrassment, he changed the subject. 'What did you think of the tenor tonight?' he asked Xavier. 'As good as Miguel Fleta?'

'His voice was rich and lyrical,' Xavier agreed.

'They say he will be the new Caruso.'

I would have been content to listen to Xavier and Gaspar talk about the opera all night, but it wasn't to be. Three maids moved into the room, switching on the lights and setting the food out on the table. A moment later, the concertina doors were folded aside and the Marquesa entered with her guests behind her, like Moses leading his people through the Red Sea.

I was placed between Xavier and Mama with Francesc opposite. When I looked at senyora Dalmau and Maria, they were sending daggers with their eyes at me. Margarida had been right.

'I didn't recognise you this evening, Evelina,' Francesc said. 'I think the last time I saw you, you were only a little girl.'

Unlike Gaspar, the last time Francesc had seen me was at Mass the previous week, but obviously it had taken the gown for him to notice me.

'I find coming home after the opera much more pleasant than going to the Hotel España or the Ritz, don't you?' the Marquesa asked me.

This time I was able to answer her calmly. 'It was very kind of you and the Marqués to invite us,' I said in my most ladylike manner.

'The pleasure is ours, I assure you,' the Marquesa replied, nodding to her husband.

If she had not been surrounded by people, I think Mama would have grabbed my face and kissed me.

Something shiny on Francesc's collar caught my eye. He saw me looking at it. 'Ah, so you have noticed my pin,' he said. 'I'm a toxophilite.'

I had never heard the term. It sounded like the member of an ancient tribe.

When Francesc saw my confusion, he laughed. 'I'm an archery enthusiast,' he explained. 'I won last week's championship.'

He then began to elaborate on the mechanics of a bow: how it was a simple but marvellous piece of engineering. He was so passionate about the subject, I found myself quite interested. Margarida was wrong to have said that Francesc was stupid. As I listened to him talk about archery before moving on to football and the Tour de France, I realised he was simply a person who did not concern himself with complicated or controversial subjects. Nevertheless, when the main course was served, I found myself looking in the direction of Gaspar. Although he was a relation of the Cerdà family, he had been placed at the lower end of the table. It was not meanness on the part of the Marquesa, but the way things were done. Another person might have been humiliated—Gaspar's family had once been one of the wealthiest in Barcelona—but the conversation taking place around his end of the table was more animated than the artificial laughter emanating from our end. The normally stern-looking senyor Homar was laughing heartily, and even sour-faced senyora Casas was managing a smile.

There was a lull in the conversation at our end of the table, long enough to hear senyor Homar say, 'I'm looking forward to hearing Gaspar and Xavier play for us this evening.'

'Even when Gaspar was a child,' the Marqués said, addressing the guests, 'he never rushed into playing a piece before he was ready. He worked at his scales and technical exercises until he felt he was prepared to tackle the piece. I think that patience has rewarded him well and made him the virtuoso that he is.'

'Ah, but feeling is the soul of a musician,' said senyor Dalmau. 'Without it, one is merely a mechanic.'

'What you say is true,' Gaspar replied. 'But what is also true is that the greatest music is intellectual as well as sentimental. If you look at Beethoven's Sonatas, for instance, you will see that the composer put a lot of thought into the structure of the motifs and the movements. Beethoven's music is truly divine, and yet it is also well planned. For me, he is the perfect proof that art requires discipline and thought; that it doesn't drop out of the sky from heaven in perfect formation.'

An awed hush fell over the gathering. Gaspar had everyone's attention, whether they were interested in music or not. It wasn't only what he said, but the way he said it. When he spoke, his eyes were alive with passion. I noticed that Xavier was watching him intently.

'I agree with you entirely,' he told Gaspar. 'There is this idea that art is somehow supposed to reflect life. But it doesn't at all, does it? Life is chaos. It is art that gives meaning and order to life.'

'Well said!' replied Gaspar, raising his wine goblet to Xavier.

Francesc leaned towards me. 'I don't know how you feel, but this is all going straight over my head.'

'Well,' said the Marqués, standing up. 'As we appear to have finished supper, perhaps this discussion is the perfect lead-in to hearing these gentlemen play.'

Xavier was the first to take his place at the piano. He treated us to the hauntingly beautiful 'Clair de Lune' by Debussy. As I watched my brother play, I was filled with love for him. There was so much beauty in him—and so much conflict too. It was more apparent when he moved on to Tchaikovsky's 'Symphony No 6, *Pathétique*', which he had been memorising and perfecting for over a year. The piece was filled with sorrow, hope, happiness, grief and a sense of foreboding. I saw every one of those emotions pass over Xavier's face as he played.

When Xavier finished the symphony, the gathering applauded him.

'So beautiful, so moving,' said the Marquesa to my mother.

Because Xavier had been asked to play at the last moment, he limited his performance to the two pieces. 'Now,' he said, standing up and making a flourish with his hand towards the piano stool. 'I would like to invite my good friend, and a true virtuoso, Gaspar Olivero to play for us.'

Gaspar had chosen music by Spanish composers for the evening and commenced with a composition by the teacher he had shared with Xavier: 'The Maiden and the Nightingale' by Granados. It was a romantic, moving piece and it made me think of the sad fate the composer had suffered. During the Great War, he had been travelling across the English Channel on board the *Sussex* when it was torpedoed by a German submarine. Granados had been able to reach a lifeboat, but when he searched around for his wife, he spotted her flailing in the sea. He dived in to save her but they both drowned.

My mind returned to the present, and I became aware of the intense expression on Gaspar's face and the way the piano seemed to be a continuation of his arms. 'Music is as much a part of me as my heart or lungs,' he had said. I saw the difference between him and Xavier. Although they were both superior musicians, Xavier was a man divided while Gaspar was a man complete. Xavier had to compartmentalise his life: his role as an heir in the Barcelona elite; his role as a husband and father; his music and art. But Gaspar put all of himself into his playing: all his emotions, intellect and personality. His spontaneity was evident in the music, along with his goodwill, his cheerfulness and even his sense of law and order. It was wonderful to hear it. Then I realised that while people pitied Gaspar because his parents had misspent his inheritance, perhaps in reality they had given him something far superior. Xavier was wealthy, but he did not have Gaspar's freedom.

Gaspar continued to thrill the gathering with pieces by Albéniz and Rodrigo. When he finished, the applause was enthusiastic. He returned to the table while the servants brought out fruit and cheese.

'Gaspar, that was marvellous,' said Xavier, his eyes shining with admiration. 'Maestro Granados would have been proud!'

'Well, I take my hat off to you,' senyor Dalmau told Gaspar. 'You have proved what you said earlier about technique and emotion. You certainly have both.'

It intrigued me to watch how Gaspar, who had been seated at the end of the table, had turned things around to become the centre of attention for the night. Then he said something prophetic, although I didn't realise it until much later.

'I'm glad you see that my emphasis on technique does not exclude emotion,' he said, touching his heart. 'For I am a deeply sentimental person. There are certain pieces I never play because I have some terrible association with them. I had been working on Brahms's "Concerto No 1" when I learned of Granados's death. I was fourteen years old at the time and I have never touched that piece since. I dread that something extreme may happen one day that will cut me off from music forever.'

The evening ended, and the Marqués and his wife, along with Francesc, saw the guests off at the door.

'Do you like tennis, Evelina?' Francesc asked me. 'Perhaps you and Xavier would like to play doubles with me and my sister, Penélope, when she returns from finishing school this summer?'

I had never played tennis in my life, but I knew Mama would be upset if I declined the invitation. 'Thank you,' I told him. 'I would like to if you will teach me how to play.'

'It would be my pleasure,' he said, grinning from ear to ear.

Mama and Pare were still talking with the Marquesa, and Margarida and Xavier were admiring the house's façade, so I waited on the steps for them.

'I hope that I will have the chance to see you dance one day, Evelina.'

A thrill of delight ran through me. I knew who was speaking and turned to face Gaspar.

'And I hope to hear you play again soon,' I told him.

He smiled. 'Why don't you ever come with Xavier and Margarida to the club where I play? Some of the best musicians and dancers from around the world perform there. I see your brother and sister there all the time, but never you.'

A pang of jealousy at Xavier's and Margarida's independence jabbed me. 'My brother and sister seem to do what they like,' I said. 'But I'm not even allowed out of the house without Mama or a servant.'

'Well, now you are in society things might be different,' Gaspar said, looking at me hopefully. 'Surely your parents won't mind if you come with your brother and sister as chaperones? Truly, you should see some of the dancers.'

I was sure that my cheeks must have been as bright as sunrise. I laughed and turned to see Mama glaring at me. What had I done to earn such displeasure? I had thought she would be happy because I hadn't stuttered most of the night.

Our car pulled up and the driver opened the door. Pare waved to us all to get inside.

'I'd better go,' I told Gaspar.

I was about to climb into the car when Mama gripped my arm, her fingers pressing into my flesh. She had never been so fierce with me before. 'Evelina,' she said under her breath, 'being out in society is not all fun and games and pretty dresses. You have responsibilities towards your family and your peers.'

I stared at her, not understanding her meaning.

She paused and then said, 'It is important that you behave as a young lady of your position should behave.' With a quick glance in Gaspar's direction, she added, 'And that you do not put ideas into the heads of young men who have absolutely no chance of ever attaining you.'

Mamie ended her story with a whimsical smile. I couldn't believe she was going to leave me hanging there! The man Mamie had described was not the Avi I had known. While there were certain similarities—his attention to detail, his knowledge of a wide variety of topics, his enjoyment of sketching scenes and objects in his notebooks, and his kind manner—my Avi had been an introverted man whose love for pianos was limited to restoring and tuning them. I had rarely heard him play anything beyond a few phrases of this and that to check that all the parts of the instrument were working properly.

'What happened to Avi's music?' I asked. 'Was it the Civil War?'

Mamie shook her head. 'It was not the war in Spain that killed Gaspar's music. If anything, he endured that uprooting better than any of us. If it had not been for his sangfroid in those circumstances, I would not have survived. No, the loss of Gaspar's music happened here. You already know that during the German occupation he was interned in a concentration camp. Hitler was friends with Franco, and the Nazis persecuted the Spanish Republicans who had fled to France. Gaspar had sent me and Julieta out of Paris to protect us, but he stayed here to assist with a line of safe houses that were smuggling Jews and other people at risk out of the country—ironically, many of them into Spain. Being a Catalan who spoke perfect French, he'd been able to hide his identity. But he was betrayed by our concierge and sent to a camp with other Spanish refugees from Paris. The story of the incident I am about to share with you didn't come from Gaspar: he never spoke of it. It was told to me by Curro Verger, who was interned with him. The superintendent of the camp, a sadistic man, learned that Gaspar was a virtuoso and had a particular liking for Liszt's music. The superintendent had Gaspar brought before the assembly of prisoners onto a stage where a piano had been placed. He held a pistol to Gaspar's head and ordered him to play Liszt's "Transcendental Étude No 4 in D Minor" by sight while he turned the pages. He said that for every mistake Gaspar made, one of the Spanish prisoners would be shot, starting with the women.'

I held my breath and closed my eyes, trying to imagine what my grandfather must have felt in that situation. I knew from Papa that that *étude* was a notoriously difficult piece, even when you were not half-starved and exhausted out of your mind. A nauseating fear gripped my stomach. Papa had told me that every concert pianist dreaded a lapse of memory during a performance, but the truth was that even the best of them lapsed sometimes, even after months of practise and memorisation. They usually picked up the music again and carried on with nothing but their wounded pride to deal with. None would ever have faced the consequences that Avi faced that day, even if he had the sheet music in front of him.

I opened my eyes again, but it was a while before either Mamie or I could speak.

'According to Curro, Gaspar did not make any mistakes,' Mamie said eventually. 'His lifelong attention to detail and technique as well as his familiarity with Liszt paid off. But the superintendent had the other prisoners shot anyway, except for Curro and Gaspar. After that day, your grandfather was never again able to approach the piano as a musician.'

'Oh,' I said, feeling nauseated. In some ways I was glad to be learning more of my Spanish heritage and my loved ones, but in other ways it disturbed me. Poor Avi! I never knew what he had suffered. If I had, I would have found some way to comfort him. Now it was too late.

'I wanted to tell you about your grandfather tonight,' said Mamie, brushing a tear from her cheek. 'I wanted to tell you who he had once been. You know I loved him dearly, but the man the Germans returned to me was a ghost of the man I had known in Barcelona. For the Nazis had not only taken away Gaspar's music, they had destroyed his faith in humankind. He no longer believed in people's ability to progress to higher ideals. Unlike Xavier, who held on to that foolish notion until the end.'

NINETEEN

Celestina

By 1919, the *cafés cantantes*, where I danced and Manuel played for audiences that appreciated gypsy flamenco, had almost disappeared from Barcelona. The public had new enticements—cinemas, jazz clubs and ballroom dancing. Manuel would have been content to play only for private fiestas, but I couldn't dance enough. I didn't care where I performed or for whom as long as I was dancing. I was eighteen years old and for the past ten years I had lived and breathed flamenco. It consumed me. My fingers clicked of their own accord. My feet glided when I walked.

Manuel wanted to follow the other gypsy artists who had returned to Seville and take me with him, but Diego objected. The clan leader had a gambling habit, and losing the income I earned would cause Diego to miss out on his cock and dog fights.

'Take her to that place on the waterfront,' he told Manuel. 'I hear the Americans tip well. Our little *paya* isn't exactly pretty, but she has a certain charm.'

Manuel and I found ourselves auditioning for variety shows in dusty theatres alongside actors, comedians in top hats and jugglers dressed as clowns. The first booking we obtained was to perform after the Saturday evening film in a cinema in carrer del Carme. We were shouted off the stage after three minutes.

'You were meant to leave the audience on a high note!' the furious manager screamed at us. 'Not make them want to throw themselves off a cliff!'

I realised that we were going to have to adapt our style if I was to keep Diego flush with money. I gathered discarded flowers at the market and, disguising myself as a flower seller, snuck into theatres and cabarets so I could see the new flamenco acts. A great shift had indeed transpired: the beauty of the dancers and their costumes had become more important than talent, and none of the singers performed in the Andalusian dialect any more. Instead everyone sang in good Castilian Spanish. Flamenco was being absorbed into classical Spanish dance with its soft balletic postures and footwork. I didn't tell Manuel, but hardly any of the new dancers were accompanied by a guitarists. Most of them performed to piano music. I absorbed everything—as I had when Manuel's sisters had shown me their flamenco—from la Argentina's Spanish folk dances to Raquel Meller's crimped hairstyle. I realised that I had the best of both worlds: I was Andalusian with a gypsy upbringing and I intended to make the most of it.

The young woman I was at eighteen was not the same innocent child I had been at eight. I was a survivor with a survivor's instinct for self-preservation. I forgot about the 'dark angel' when the theatre managers paid us with dinner as well as wages. If they wanted me to flounce around and swish my skirt, I would.

When I started dancing with a pair of castanets I had 'acquired' from a performer who had left her dressing room unlocked, Manuel thought things had gone too far.

'Stop prancing around with those "clackers" in your hands. After all Francisca has taught you . . . You have no principles.'

I shrugged. I might not have had principles but, having gorged myself every night for the past month on noodle and rice dishes, I did have breasts and hips for the first time.

But while I grew stronger, Francisca grew weaker. Her attacks of vomiting and nausea were becoming worse. She no longer had the energy to go to the flower market to tell fortunes and spent her days sitting on the beach and contemplating the sea.

Manuel's sister, Pastora, helped Francisca prepare the healing potions she needed. Francisca had been training Pastora since she was a child to take over as the clan's *chovihani* when the time came. However, after blood appeared in Francisca's urine, I kept back some of the money I earned—risking a black eye or a split earlobe from Diego for my deception—so I could buy modern medicine, which I slipped into Francisca's tea. Francisca had told me that she was taking on the magical harm that was coming to the clan for having lost the *tacho Romano drom,* the true gypsy path, but the doctor I consulted with a list of her symptoms informed me that her kidneys were failing.

When Francisca started having trouble breathing and would no longer eat, Diego ordered that she be moved out of her shack and under a canopy, in keeping with the gypsy ritual that the dying should not pass away in their habitual place lest their spirit remain there. Gypsies from all over Spain came to pay their respects to Francisca. During that time, I did not dance. I busied myself finding places for the visitors to sleep.

One evening, when Francisca's breath started to rattle, Pastora and I sent the visitors away so that we could wash Francisca and prepare her for the journey to the Otherworld. We would not be allowed to touch her after death. I gave her my flamenco dress to wear because it was the best outfit I owned.

Francisca turned to Pastora. 'If the gypsies do not remember their true reason for existence . . . to help and heal the trees and animals and to be kind to the *payos* . . . I fear that a terrible fate awaits them. I see a sinister cloud swallowing Europe and taking them with it. Tell them that: warn them.'

Then she turned to me and touched my cheek. 'Don't let Diego bully you,' she told me. 'You are not a *paya*; you are one of us. You always have been. Remember you have the gypsy magic.'

A knowing smile came to her lips before she closed her eyes and took her final breath.

Francisca's wand and her herbs were placed alongside her in the coffin. Then the men dismantled her shack and everything else was burned. As I watched the smoke rise to the sky, I remembered her words: 'You have the gypsy magic.' The problem was, I wasn't sure if I believed in magic any more. Everyone I loved seemed to die before their time.

After Francisca passed away, I went to live with Manuel's sisters in their mud hut. The move saved my life, because two days later a freak wave washed over the beach, destroying several dwellings. Manuel was swept out to sea, along with some dogs and chickens. The dogs swam back to shore and the chickens were retrieved. But Manuel and his guitar were never found.

'It's the bad luck you brought on him by doing those *payos* dances!' Blanca accused me.

She and the other gypsies shunned me, until Diego decided to be my manager and announced that under his 'guidance' I would earn so much money that I'd soon be able to support the whole clan.

There was a club named the Villa Rosa where the best flamenco artists from around the country performed. The owner was a flamenco guitarist from Madrid, Miguel Borrull. The club soon became known as the 'Cathedral of Flamenco'. It was rumoured that rich *señoritos* would hire artists from the Villa Rosa to perform at their fiestas, where vintage wine flowed and dancers were sometimes paid in diamonds. It was even said that the King was known to frequent the club in disguise whenever he was in Barcelona. Rather than send me to auditions for the variety shows playing on las Ramblas, Diego set his sights straight on the Villa Rosa.

He took me there one chilly evening. I was wearing a dress loaned to me by Juanita: a typical gypsy frock in lime green with polka dots and ruffled elbow-length sleeves. It was a size too big for me and I had to keep pulling it back over my shoulders. Diego and I stood outside on the pavement, shivering. Despite his ignorance of the flamenco world, Diego had audacity and self-confidence. He had brought with him bags of mushrooms that the gypsy women had gathered that day, which he intended to use to bribe our way into the club by offering them to the flamenco artists who were performing there that night.

His first victim was a thin man whose bloodshot eyes and curly hair were the only things showing above the upturned lapels of his overcoat.

'Excuse me, señor!' Diego called out to him. 'My niece is a talented *bailaora*. If you watch her dance for a minute or two I will give you these—'

The man walked past us without stopping.

Diego didn't immediately recognise the woman who stepped out of a taxi and made her way towards the club, but I did. It was la Tanguera, whose impeccable sense of rhythm was admired by all who loved flamenco. She was famous for dancing the *farruca*, traditionally a male dance.

'Excuse me, señorita, could you show my niece a step or two?' Diego asked, affecting his most charming smile.

La Tanguera fixed her smouldering eyes on Diego and stretched herself to her full height. 'Nobody can imitate me!' she said, tossing her hair over her shoulders. 'Nobody!'

'Snob!' Diego muttered when the woman entered the club. But he wasn't to be deterred. His face lit up when a rotund man in a well-cut suit made his way along the pavement towards us. The man looked like a rich politician, not a flamenco artist, so Diego tried a different approach.

'Excuse me, señor,' he said, raising his clasped hands in a begging gesture, 'I have with me perhaps the greatest *bailaora* this country will ever see. You will be doing the world a great favour if you speak to el señor Borrull and ask him to let my niece dance in his club tonight. She will not disappoint him—or you and your esteemed friends!'

The man turned to look at me. I realised it was the flamenco singer, Antonio Chacón. His tenor voice was said to be so powerful it could carry through a bullring without the aid of a microphone. He glanced at my gaudy dress and my callused feet, which were turning blue in the rope sandals I was wearing because I didn't have proper dance shoes. I was expecting him to push us out of the way, but to my surprise, he smiled.

'Yes, why don't you come in and show don Miguel what she can do. We don't want to deprive the world of talent.'

I followed señor Chacón and Diego into the Villa Rosa unable to believe that Diego's scheme had worked. I was so overwhelmed to be in that esteemed place that I barely took in the Moorish tiles on the walls and the plaster arabesques on the ceiling. The club was crowded and I kept my eyes on the backs of señor Chacón and Diego so as not to get lost, but I did notice the polished bar stacked with wines and sherries in classy bottles. I gave a start when I recognised the matador Juan Belmonte speaking with the dashing film star Antonio Moreno, who had a successful career in the United States. The other lavishly dressed people were probably just as famous, but I had no idea who they were.

Señor Chacón led us to a room where the flamenco artists were sitting. The dancers were dressed in black with their hair elegantly pinned behind their ears. By comparison, I looked like some sort of strange sea urchin in my bright dress. My heart leaped to my throat at the sight of the guitarist Ramón Montoya holding his famous guitar, la Leona: the Lioness. The attractive dancer Concha la Chícharra was there that evening too. She was known for a rather risqué dance called *El Crispin*, where she stripped off various layers of clothing, supposedly searching for a flea.

'Don Miguel!' señor Chacón called out to a man who was sitting next to señor Montoya. The man looked up and raised his thick eyebrows.

'I have brought you a new talent!' señor Chacón said.

If I had not been standing next to señor Chacón, I doubt that señor Borrull would have looked at me twice. He rose from his chair and nodded to señor Montoya, who started playing a *farruca*. My heart dropped to my feet. I could feel la Tanguera's eyes boring into me. How could I dance something for which she was famous? But I knew this was my only chance to impress señor Borrull and the others, and I had to do my best.

I slipped off my sandals and placed them under a chair. I glanced once at Diego before lifting my chin and beginning to dance. I twirled my wrists, swung my arms and stamped my feet with all the passion I could muster. It was a long time since I had felt the dark angel, but something took me over when señor Montoya began to play faster and my feet moved with him. A surge of power and majesty ran through me. I was the mistress of this dance, not its slave. I forgot about impressing señor Borrull and danced with my full spirit.

When I finished, the effect on the room was electric. I held my proud stance as the artists shouted '*Olé!*' for me. Señor Chacón smiled at señor Borrull, who nodded his approval. Diego, who didn't know a *farruca* from a bowl of olives, folded his arms and smiled smugly, as if the victory had been his alone.

'Her!' a voice behind me said.

I turned to see a hollow-cheeked man with a hooked nose and red-rimmed eyes staring at me. His intense gaze gave me an eerie feeling, but it was clear from the excitement that ran through the room, and the two burly men standing on either side of him like guards, that the man was important.

'Señor Salazar,' señor Borrull said, putting his hand on the man's shoulder. 'This *señorita* has just started with us tonight. I don't know what else she can dance. She may not be up to your standard. Ask la Tanguera instead.'

Salazar laughed through his yellow teeth. 'You've forgotten that I am the best judge of what I want! That *señorita* burns with gypsy fire. Send her and Montoya for me.'

Señor Borrull looked worried but gestured for me to go with the men.

'You'd better be as good as that first dance,' señor Montoya whispered in my ear. 'El señor Salazar doesn't stand for games.'

'Who is he?' I asked.

Señor Montoya was shocked by my question. 'Oh God!' he muttered. 'He is one of the most famous breeders of fighting bulls in Spain . . . and also something of a gangster.'

I glanced at Diego, who ran his hand through his hair nervously. We were out of our depth now.

We followed the men up a staircase to a room decorated with wrought-iron chandeliers and with tiled murals of Moorish castles on the walls. The air was thick with cigar smoke and the hazelnut scent of fine sherry. The audience was mostly men, as it had been in the cafés in the barri Xinès where Manuel used to take me to dance, only this time the few whores present were wearing Jeanne Lanvin dresses.

Salazar signalled to the guests to make room so I could dance. He pulled a pistol from his jacket before sitting down in an armchair.

'Oh God,' whispered señor Montoya again. 'Can you dance an *alegrías*?'

I glanced at him. 'Yes.'

Most flamenco dancers specialised in two or three musical forms, devoting their lives to mastering every detail of that rhythm. But I was obsessed by dance in all its forms. I could have performed the Argentine tango or the American cakewalk if señor Montoya had asked me to; or, at least, my interpretations of them.

Señor Montoya seemed dubious but began to play.

I did my best to ignore the pistol in Salazar's lap and the stern expression on his face and began my *paseo*. Luckily for me, I could tell by the way the crowd shouted their encouragement that they appreciated gypsy flamenco. I raised my arms and arched my wrists, letting the dark angel take me. I felt myself transform. My torso grew heavy and solid. Horns sprouted from my head and my shoulders bulked up with muscle. I caught sight of myself in the wall mirror. My skin was black and my head was enormous. I had turned into one of Salazar's bulls . . .

My blood on fire, I rushed from the dark *toril* into the arena. I was dazzled by the light. The crowd roared. My heart thumped with fury and fear. The matador in his suit of lights was waiting for me along with his *banderilleros*. The matador raised his satin cape, testing my courage. A *picador* on a horse stabbed me in the neck. A searing pain burned through me and I could no longer hold up my proud head. Warm blood trickled down my legs into the sand . . .

I danced with ferocity, my anger burning up my insides. I wanted to live but I hated life. Injustice was all I had known. I must kill those who had hurt my family . . .

The spectators were a sea of brilliant colours. Women in lace mantillas waved their handkerchiefs. I could not win but I knew I must fight . . . I spun like a whip. Not once but twice. My hair flew from its pins. My feet beat the floor like war drums . . . I ran at my tormentors. My triumph was the glimmer of fear in the matador's eyes, even though it lasted only a moment and all was stacked against me . . .

The Villa Rosa's glamorous guests jumped from their seats, screaming and shouting. Salazar fired shots into the ceiling . . .

The barbed spears they jabbed into my shoulders drained my strength. I was outnumbered and alone. But I charged with all the courage I had left. An agonising pain ripped through my shoulder blades. The matador's sword had pierced my heart. I collapsed to my knees. My vision blurred. The spectators cheered. My last view of the world was thousands of white handkerchiefs being waved in victory as my life ran out of me . . .

I ended the dance with my right arm raised and my eyes cast down. Sweat poured down my face and back. My lungs pulsed, desperately trying to suck in air. There was stunned silence for a few seconds, before a man lifted his chair and threw it against the wall. Another picked up one of the splintered legs and smashed it into a mirror. The women sobbed hysterically. One of them tore her scarf from around her neck and shredded it in her hands. Her companion broke his wine glass and thrust the jagged vessel into his shoulder. My legs were trembling and the room was turning white around me. The people in the audience were demonstrating how deeply I had moved them.

Señor Montoya struck up another *alegrías* but I had nothing more to give. I looked from señor Montoya to Diego, and then fainted.

When I regained consciousness, señor Montoya and Diego were leaning over me. '*Alegrías* means "joys",' señor Montoya said to me, a scowl on his face. 'Wherever you went with that one, it was troubling.'

Diego, however, was beaming. It was clear from the loud voices around me and the murmurs of 'spectacular' that I had been well received.

The men helped me to my feet and I found myself face to face with Salazar. He took my hand and pushed a wad of notes into it. It was more money than I had ever earned in my life. Disoriented and confused, I turned to go.

He grabbed my arm and yanked me towards him. 'I warn the matadors who fight my bulls that it is dangerous to turn their backs on them.'

Salazar's grip was painful. At first I averted my eyes from his cruel face. I sensed his darkness was deep. But then I thought of the bull I had become during my dance and courage returned to me. I locked eyes with him. A smile curled his lips. My defiance seemed to please him. He laughed loudly and leaned his face towards mine.

'*Encaste, nobleza, bravura*,' he said. 'The most important quality I look for in my bulls is courage in the face of pain.'

He released his grip and I stumbled backwards. I kept my eyes on him as I backed out of the room. It was obvious that

Salazar had the devil in him. I did not know then just how much pain he would one day cause me.

Señor Borrull had invited me and Diego to return the next night to the Villa Rosa. Although I was excited to be in the company of the finest flamenco artists, I was afraid Salazar would pick me again for a fiesta. At least Diego had decided to spend some money on me, 'as an investment', and had purchased an elegant black dress with a ruffled skirt and white piping for me to wear.

I breathed a sigh of relief when Salazar wasn't at the club. Instead, I danced for some English and American tourists. The Englishmen said nothing, although they paid me generously, but the Americans were exuberant. 'Darling, you should go to New York,' a man in a white suit told me. 'Americans are having a love affair with Spanish dancers. You'll make millions!'

As well as dancing at the Villa Rosa, Diego and I were invited to other famous clubs in Barcelona: la Taurina; el Manquet; la Criolla. If a club wasn't busy on a particular night, the flamenco artists would perform for each other. No dance academy could have given me what I learned from watching the masters up close.

One evening the following year, a month after my nineteenth birthday, I was demonstrating my ability to do two or three turns and stop precisely on the spot when I sensed someone watching me. Out of the corner of my eye I noticed a man in a double-breasted suit sitting at a table in the corner. He had broad shoulders and his hands, which were clasped in front of him, were large and square. He wore a gold signet ring on one and a diamond ring on the other. The man gave the impression that he could crush someone in his grasp, but was too suave to do so.

I finished my dance, and was waiting at the bar for some iced water when the man approached me.

'You dance very well,' he said, in an accent that wasn't Spanish. What was it? French? German? He had the sleek brown hair and strong jaw of a younger man, but the droop of his hooded eyes and the grooves around his mouth made me guess his age to be about fifty.

'Do you want me to dance for a fiesta?' I asked him, hoping for an engagement for the evening. The man looked like he had money. Another epidemic of the Spanish flu was keeping the tourists away and I had an entire gypsy clan to support.

He shook his head. 'No, I'd like you to dance in my cabaret.'

The memory of the insipid acts Manuel and I had performed in variety shows when we were low on money didn't make me jump at the offer. If I ever danced in one of those places again, it was going to be on my terms.

'If you're looking for a "flamenco act",' I told him, 'you've got the wrong dancer.'

The man shook his head. It was hard not to be mesmerised by his eyes. They were the same cobalt blue as the water bottles the waiters placed on the tables.

'I'm not looking for a dancer,' he said. 'I'm looking for a *star*.'

The word made me think of great beauties like la Argentina: women who had four or five costume changes a show. Not poor girls like me, who borrowed their clothes.

'You think I could be a star?' I asked with a laugh.

The man shifted on his feet. 'I don't know,' he said. 'You're a bit of a rough diamond. I don't know what I'll get when I polish you.'

'Polish me?' I cried, lifting my chin defiantly. 'What if you can't polish me?'

'We'll see,' he replied, reaching into his jacket and taking out a card. He passed it to me.

The Samovar Club, las Ramblas, Barcelona

I had heard of the club. The best international acts performed there. So this man was serious. He turned to go.

'Excuse me, senyor,' I called after him. 'You didn't tell me your name.'

The man looked over his shoulder. A half-smile danced on his lips and his eyes shone brighter. 'My name is Maxim Tarasov,' he said. 'But in Barcelona they call me "el Ruso".'

That was how I met the impresario el Ruso: the Russian. The man who would change everything.

TWENTY

Paloma

It was both wonderful and daunting to be back at the School of the Opera Ballet. When I exited the Métro at the place de l'Opéra and stood before the rose marble columns of the Paris Opera House, a thousand memories flooded back to me. The first time I had seen the Beaux Arts building, considered to be one of the most beautiful in the world, I had been with my mother. I was only three years old at the time and I'd gaped in awe at the gilded statues representing poetry and music, and the bronze busts of the famous composers. When Mama showed me the stage where she had danced, I felt as though I had stepped into a world of magic and fantasy. I'd craned my neck to admire the grand chandelier suspended above the auditorium and to take in the Baroque opulence of the gold-leafed cherubs and nymphs that decorated the walls. When I entered the ballet school, it was the dream of dancing on the Paris Opera's stage that gave me the strength to endure the gruelling dance classes and brutal competition. On the occasions when ballet school life became overwhelming, all it required for me to pick myself up again was to imagine gazing out at the audience from that stage and taking my final curtain call to the sound of thunderous applause.

The entrance to the Ballet School was through a courtyard. When I crossed it, I suddenly remembered that Mama had once told me about a ghost she had seen one evening when she was hurrying from her dressing room to the wings. The apparition was of a dark-haired woman and it had rushed towards her from a door in the corridor. Mama had stopped in her tracks to avoid a collision with what she thought was another performer. Then, to her surprise, the woman had vanished into thin air. I wished I had asked her more about that encounter when she told me about it, but ghost stories were frequently exchanged among the ballet students—after all, the Paris Opera House was the setting for Gaston Leroux's Gothic novel *The Phantom of the Opera*—and the associated practical jokes of missing ballet shoes and moved pictures had made me cynical. Despite Marcel's assertion that all Spaniards see ghosts, I had never believed in their existence until la Rusa.

I made my way to the dressing room, where I changed into my leotard and tights and did some preliminary stretching before applying full stage make-up, including two sets of false eyelashes. The students of the Ballet School were expected to maintain a high level of grooming, but Mademoiselle Louvet, who would be helping me prepare for the examination, had standards that were even more exacting. She was from the glamour era of the ballet, when *étoiles* had the same status as film stars and took their roles very seriously. They always had to be beautiful and conduct themselves with decorum whether they were performing or not.

'You are not just dancers,' I remembered Mademoiselle Louvet telling my class one day. 'You are muses . . . you must inspire the human race to appreciate and live for beauty.'

I did have to smile though when I recalled Mama once telling me that Mademoiselle Louvet had been temporarily suspended from the Ballet in the 1930s for dancing in a Monaco nightclub like a 'common music-hall star'.

I was walking to the rehearsal room when a group of *petits rats*, as the young students of the school were known, passed me on their way to their afternoon dance class. The sight of them in their maroon wraps and leggings made me smile. They were about nine years old and the worst of the competition and strain hadn't yet begun. Ballet was still magic, beauty and fantasy to them. I envied them their innocence—and pitied them because I knew they would soon lose it.

Mademoiselle Louvet was waiting for me in the rehearsal room, with the pianist, Monsieur Clary. As to be expected, she was wearing full make-up with dramatically shaded eyes and elongated eyeliner and was looking chic in a shirtwaister dress and low-heeled pumps. I patted my hair to make sure it was perfect.

'Ah, *bonjour*, Paloma,' Mademoiselle Louvet said when she saw me. She kissed me. 'How lovely it is to see you again. I've missed your pretty face.'

Mademoiselle Louvet was my favourite teacher. There was nothing insincere about her. If she welcomed you with kisses, you could be sure that she was not going to turn on you later in a fit of bad temper.

'Are you warmed up? Are you ready to start?' she asked, guiding me to the barre.

I took my place, and Monsieur Clary began to play so I could commence my *tendus* and *glissés*. For an institution that stuck rigidly to the rules, the Ballet School was making an exception for me, and pulling out all stops by assigning one of its most highly regarded teachers as my coach. Although it was permissible for me to attempt the audition for the *corps de ballet* again externally, I was past the age where I could officially return for classes at the school or take the examination from there. Perhaps the school was helping me out of respect for the memory of my mother, who had been a popular student and who had gone on to be a star of the ballet, or maybe it was because they were angered that their best student should have been rejected from joining the Ballet because of unfair prejudices. Perhaps they believed that if I took the examination again, the judging panel, including Arielle Marineau, would have to concede to my determination.

After my barre and floor-work exercises, Mademoiselle Louvet had me perform *sauts de chats* across the room.

'Use the whole room, Paloma!' she called out. 'You are the queen of the stage!'

The two-hour lesson flew by. When it finished, I was left with the familiar feeling of exhaustion and exhilaration that made me love ballet.

'You've done well,' Mademoiselle Louvet told me, after we had thanked Monsieur Clary for playing for us and were alone again in the room. 'I expected that we might have some catching up to do . . . but if anything you've improved.' She took a step back and regarded me fondly. 'There's something different about you . . . Paloma, have you fallen in love?'

I felt myself blush. Had I fallen in love? Was that why whenever I thought of Jaime I couldn't concentrate on anything else?

'I've had a couple of flamenco lessons,' I said. 'The teacher invited me to stay for dinner one evening and the whole family danced. It was inspiring! But I think I'm going to have to give up the flamenco lessons to train for the audition.'

Mademoiselle Louvet shook her head. 'I don't know at what point ballerinas became elite athletes with no room for a life outside rehearsals. Of course in my day we worked very hard, but we also socialised with other artists and in that way fed each other's creativity.'

She smiled whimsically and began performing a gypsy dance from *Les Deux Pigeons*. Mademoiselle Louvet was in her sixties but she moved with expressiveness and grace. Her slim body and stately beauty had never turned to fat. I thought she characterised a gypsy convincingly. She curtseyed and I applauded her presentation.

'That was an enjoyable ballet to do,' she said. 'I modelled myself on the flamenco dancer la Rusa for that one.'

The sound of the name made my blood freeze. I had never heard of la Rusa until a couple of weeks ago. Now I sensed that I was being drawn into her life, and that she had intended it to be so. But why?

'I've heard a lot about la Rusa lately,' I said.

Mademoiselle Louvet drew in a breath. 'Oh, what a dancer!' she said. 'She was formidable! So regal and so proud! At the end of her performance she had people eating out of her hands.'

'Did you know her personally?' I asked, hoping to learn something about la Rusa from someone who had seen her in the flesh.

Mademoiselle Louvet shook her head. 'I watched her perform in authentic flamenco bars when I travelled to the United States, but she was not someone who taught students, or gave interviews, or mingled in society. It's remarkable, isn't it? She would appear on stage where she completely dominated her audience and had everyone at her feet, and then she would disappear. She was incredibly seductive, but there was something dark in her eyes too. A lot of Spaniards had that look about them. So many of them had seen things—or done things—during the Civil War that made it impossible for them to enjoy life again.'

I probed a bit more, but it was clear that Mademoiselle Louvet didn't know much more about la Rusa than I had already discovered.

'Anyway,' she said, rubbing my arm, 'do you have to rush off somewhere or do you have some time to come to my office? I have something I want you to hear.'

Mademoiselle Louvet's office had a view over the rooftops of Paris, and the late afternoon light streaming through the windows gave everything an ethereal glow.

'Here,' she said, placing two chairs near her record player and offering one of them to me. 'Being a dancer is not just about being in time to music,' she said. 'You have to feel the music with the essence of your being. It must circulate in your veins.' She placed the needle on the record and slipped her hand into mine before sitting next to me. 'Now close your eyes.'

The beautiful, nostalgic notes of Brahms's 'Intermezzo in A Op 118 No 2' filled the room. It was one of those pieces that made me see life as a crystal glass: so beautiful and yet so fragile.

Mademoiselle Louvet let go of my hand, and I opened my eyes to see that she had lifted her arms to the ceiling as if the music had become drops of rain and she was relishing their cool freshness on her skin. I thought of Xavier and the way Mamie had described him. I thought about Avi too. I was sorry that I had not known my grandfather as he had been when he was younger.

The music finished and Mademoiselle Louvet opened her eyes. A smile came to her face. 'I was sitting in my office listening to this very piece of music, when your mother came rushing in to tell me that her pregnancy had been confirmed.' She laughed at the recollection. 'Julieta was so happy, so full of life. She wanted you so much. Of course, everyone at the Opera was shocked when she resigned. "But your career, Julieta! Your career! You've only just been made an *étoile*!" they all cried.'

Mademoiselle Louvet stood up and gazed out the window for a moment before turning back to me. 'Do you know what your mother replied? She told them, "But mothers are the greatest artists of all. They create lives."' She sat down next to me again. 'Your mother was so happy, Paloma. As soon as your father found out, he proposed. Julieta had not one doubt that what she wanted most in the world was to be a mother to you.'

I stared at my hands. I knew that Mama had loved me deeply. I only hoped that she had been too sick to suspect Papa's betrayal of her—that she didn't die with regrets about him.

'Thank you,' I said to Mademoiselle Louvet. 'Thank you for telling me that.'

Although she was smiling, Mademoiselle Louvet had tears in her eyes. I was sure that there must have been many men who had loved her, yet she had never married nor had children. The retirement age of *étoiles* at the Opera Ballet was forty, but people were still coming to see Mademoiselle Louvet perform when she was in her fifties. They would probably still have been coming if she herself had not decided to retire and devote herself to teaching.

'You are truly one of the grand ballerinas,' I told her. 'But did you ever regret not getting married and having children?'

She touched my cheek. 'Never, darling. I made the right decision for me. To devote my entire life to ballet was what I was meant to do. Exactly as your mother knew that she was born to be a mother to you. We are not all the same. We must make the decisions that our hearts cry out for.'

My heart was crying out for something. But what? Ballet— or something else?

'Listen,' said Mademoiselle Louvet, 'let me tell you something. I've performed with the greatest ballet dancers of all time—people like Danilova and Chauviré. They were not great people because they were great dancers. They were great dancers because they were great people.' She took my hand and placed it on my heart. 'Strive to be a great person first, Paloma. Then you will succeed at whatever it is your heart tells you to do.'

I left Mademoiselle Louvet's office in a swirl of emotions, my thoughts alternating between Mama and la Rusa. I felt as if I were on the verge of solving some grand puzzle. The pieces were coming to me, but I had no idea where they all fitted.

I went to the administration office to pay for the private classes and to sign up for the final examination. After completing the paperwork, I was looking forward to going home. I was meeting Jaime for dinner and then we were going to see the flamenco guitarist who had known la Rusa. I needed a soak in a bathtub and a catnap first.

On my way out of the office, I ran into Madame Genet, who had been one of my teachers when I was a *petit rat*. If Mademoiselle Louvet was the type of ballerina I dreamed of being, then Madame Genet was the one I feared I'd become. Instead of being lithe, every sinew of her body seemed to be stretched tight. She was tense in her movements, not fluid, and even being around her made me feel anxious.

I curtseyed to her, but from the way she stared at me I thought she mustn't have recognised me. '*Bonjour*, Madame Genet,' I said. 'It's me, Paloma.'

The corners of her mouth turned down and she moved towards me. I instinctively stepped back. I'd received a few whacks from her in my time for not lifting my leg high enough. Madame Genet was overstrung and you never knew when she was going to lose her temper. She had been one of the most brilliant dancers with the Ballet, but her nerves had cracked during the opening night of *Swan Lake*. Odette had been the role she had always aspired to dance. She'd had to retire to teaching after that, and seemed never to have recovered from the bitterness of her disappointment.

Madame Genet brought her face close to mine. Her breath was a mix of stale smells—coffee, cigarettes and ham. 'I don't believe the school should let you take the examination again,' she said. 'Do you really think that after you have devoted another six months to practising and taken up Mademoiselle Louvet's precious time, you are going to succeed in a second examination?'

My skin prickled. I sensed what was going to happen next: Mademoiselle Louvet had lifted my spirits and now Madame Genet was about say something nasty to dash them. I glanced towards the corridor, wondering if I could make an escape without appearing rude. But I had to keep the school—and its teachers—on side. I had no choice but to hear her out.

'You were outstanding in your last examination,' she said. 'I've never seen a student perform so well under the pressure. And yet, despite the fact that the ballet director had seen you dance dozens of times before, every teacher at this school gave you the highest recommendations and the independent judges accepted you, still you did not make it into the *corps de ballet*!' Her voice rose in pitch. 'If Mademoiselle Marineau had enough influence to stop you getting into the *corps* last year, what do you think will have changed this time around? She is still the ballet mistress, and if she says she can't work with you, they won't hire you! That's it!'

Madame Genet stared at me as if she were waiting for an answer. I knew her anger had more to do with her own thwarted career than it did with my fate. And yet, how could I argue? I struggled not to cry. Everything she said was true. Maybe I— along with the director of the ballet school and the well-meaning teachers—was deluding myself that the Opera's ballet director would override Mademoiselle Marineau's influence this time. A tear fell down my cheek, followed by another. Soon I was sobbing. But Madame Genet was not inclined to be compassionate.

'Even if you were successful in getting into the *corps de ballet*,' she continued, 'Mademoiselle Marineau would make life hell for you. She hates you with a passion: all those years of playing second fiddle to your mother!'

'My mother is dead,' I said, trying to calm myself. 'Mademoiselle Marineau has not had a private conversation with me once for me to have given her any personal offence. If anything, she should be grateful. It is because of me that my mother retired at twenty-one. Mademoiselle Marineau was promoted to *première danseuse* after that.'

Madame Genet's eyes narrowed. 'And even then, your mother found a way to make Marineau second best.'

I didn't know what she meant. After her ballet career was over, my mother had raised me. She hadn't even taken up teaching, except to occasionally help Mamie. She had been entirely removed from Arielle Marineau's life.

'What are you talking about?' I asked.

Madame Genet's chin trembled and she glanced over her shoulder. Her cheeks were blotched, which happened when she was agitated. 'It's not my place to tell you,' she said, perhaps realising she had gone further than she had intended. She glanced in the direction of her office again and moved away from me.

'Please!' I grabbed her arm. 'If there is some reason I don't know about that will cause Mademoiselle Marineau to always reject me, tell me what it is!'

Madame Genet pushed me away. 'It's not my place,' she repeated. 'You will have to ask your father.'

'My father? What has he got to do with anything?'

But she was already rushing down the corridor as if she were trying to escape a dangerous animal. 'You'll have to ask him,' was all she said, before disappearing into her office and locking the door.

After my disturbing conversation with Madame Genet, I doubted a bath and catnap were going to calm me. I stopped at a café near the Métro station and ordered an espresso and a chocolate éclair. I didn't usually eat creamy things, and the richness of the éclair made me nauseous even though I only finished half of it. I paid the waiter and walked to the nearest telephone booth. The call I was about to make was not one I could place from home.

The telephone rang a number of times before a young man's voice answered. Pierre? I had never spoken to Audrey's son, but I guessed it must be he who had answered.

'I'd like to speak to my father,' I said. It felt strange to be talking to someone who now had a closer relationship to Papa than I did.

Pierre didn't answer straight away. Perhaps he was taken aback. I had never called before. 'I'll get him,' he finally said.

My heart thumped in my chest. I had expected that my father would probably be away on tour. It was months since I had spoken to him and I didn't feel prepared.

My father's voice came on the line. 'Paloma? Is everything all right?'

'Listen,' I said, 'I'm taking the examination again for the *corps de ballet*. I met Madame Genet at the school today and she was adamant that Arielle Marineau will still be against me. When I asked her why she should hate Mama so after all these years, she said that you would be able to explain.'

My father didn't answer.

'Do you know the reason?' I demanded. 'I'm about to do six months of intensive training, but Madame Genet says I'm wasting my time.'

My father sighed. 'Paloma, I'm leaving in an hour for the airport. I have some concerts in New York. But I will be back in a week. Will you come and see me then? This is not something I can explain over the telephone.'

A sick feeling churned in my stomach. So there was some reason beyond the Ballet for Mademoiselle Marineau to still hate Mama. But I had no choice except to wait a week before finding out the truth.

'All right, I will call you then,' I told him, and hung up the telephone. I didn't want to get into a discussion with my father about anything else. I certainly didn't want him to ask if I was coming to his birthday party.

I wasn't in a good mood when I met Jaime on rue du Faubourg Saint-Denis in Montmartre. I spotted him as soon as I'd parked Mamie's car. In a grey pea coat, floral shirt and flared tailored pants, he was an appealing mix of snappy dresser and Bohemian musician. His glossy hair glinting in the streetlights turned the heads of several women who walked past him. The idea that such a coveted guy was about to take me out to dinner should have been enough to pull me out of my ill humour, but I found it difficult to be optimistic when the dream of my lifetime was about to be thwarted for reasons I couldn't yet fathom.

'Wow! You look like you've had a bad day!' said Jaime, kissing me on the cheeks. 'Why the long face?'

I did my best to change my scowl into a smile. 'Is it that obvious?'

'Is it something you want to talk about?'

I shook my head. The last thing I wanted to do was bore Jaime with my problems. 'It's something I want to forget.'

He nodded and guided me towards rue Cail. 'Well, hopefully you'll like the restaurant I've chosen,' he said with a smile. 'I couldn't decide whether we should eat at a Catalan restaurant, an Andalusian one or a French one—so I booked a table at an Indian restaurant. I hope you like curry.'

'I do,' I said, trying to forget that the last time I'd been to an Indian restaurant was with my father in London. My mother would only eat French or Catalan food, and hated touring if it meant she'd have to exist on foreign foods for weeks. But my father was adventurous for a Frenchman.

The cocoon-like atmosphere of the restaurant Jaime had chosen, with its candlelight, vegetable-dyed tablecloths and embroidered mirror-work cushions, helped me relax. The music playing in the background reminded me that the gypsies were supposed to have originally come from India, and that was why there were similarities between Indian music and gypsy singing and dancing.

When we sat down at our table and the waiter handed us our menus, the scents of basmati rice and coriander wafting from the kitchen stirred an appetite in me that I hadn't had earlier. We ordered some dips, samosas and pakoras to start.

'So did you like my family?' Jaime asked. 'They certainly liked you.'

It pleased me to think that I hadn't alienated them with my usual awkwardness. 'I liked them very much,' I told him. 'I have the impression that you would do anything for each other.'

'Pretty much,' he agreed. 'And that's not the whole lot of them. Most of my relatives are still in Spain.'

'That must be hard . . . to be so divided.'

'I miss my sisters especially,' said Jaime, tearing a piece of naan bread. 'They are younger than me and every time I see them they have grown several inches.' He pushed the mint and yoghurt dip towards me. 'This is good, try it.'

I scooped the creamy mixture onto a piece of bread. 'Mmm,' I said, taking a bite. 'Garlic, ginger and coriander.'

We chuckled as we remembered how Carmen had tested her Andalusian food on me at dinner.

'Your grandmother is from Barcelona? She must have been a supporter of the Republic?' Jaime asked me.

'Yes,' I said, picking up my serviette to dab my mouth. 'She's only started talking about her life in Spain now that Franco is dead.'

'It's still too painful for many of them . . . tía Carmen rarely talks about my uncle.'

'What happened to him?'

'He died in gaol. He was arrested for protesting against the Franco regime. That's when Carmen and Isabel left the country.'

'How have you been able to come and go so freely?' I asked. 'If your uncle was a political prisoner, I thought they wouldn't let you go anywhere.'

'My father is an important surgeon in Granada,' he said. 'He hates the system, but he stayed because he saw his main purpose as saving people's lives. His position gives him special privileges but he thought I'd get a superior music education in France. The arts are tightly controlled in Spain, although that might change now.'

I looked at my plate thoughtfully. My life had changed significantly in a couple of weeks. There was a whole Spanish side of me that was coming to light. I saw that Jaime and I had much in common in regard to our displaced family backgrounds.

'Now, tell me more about your ballet,' he said, picking up his glass of water. 'When am I going to see you on stage?'

I winced without meaning to. Ballet was my great passion in life, but it also caused me a lot of pain.

Jaime sensed my discomfort. 'Is that what was worrying you earlier?'

I liked the way he looked at me, as if what I said and felt was of great interest to him. I had a sudden urge to tell him everything—about my father, about my failure to get into the *corps de ballet*, maybe even about the 'visit' from la Rusa. But the waiter arrived with our palak paneer and korma curry. As he placed everything on the table and refilled our water glasses, I decided to limit my confidences to the non-supernatural.

I told Jaime that my mother had been a star with the Ballet, and about my class with Mademoiselle Louvet and my encounter with Madame Genet. 'My father is away on tour, so I have to wait until he gets back for an explanation of why Madame Genet is so convinced the Opera's ballet mistress will have me rejected again.'

'Maybe your mother can explain what happened,' suggested Jaime.

I shook my head. 'She died a year and a half ago. Cancer.'

'I'm sorry,' he said, and I could see from the sympathetic expression on his face that he was. We were silent for a few moments.

I thought of the beautiful stage of the Paris Opera House and how every day of my life had been devoted to the dream of dancing on it. I recalled Madame Genet dashing my hopes that it would ever happen. The idea of that made me want to cry out. But I was used to keeping my feelings under control, and I'd probably burdened Jaime with enough already.

I glanced at my watch. 'Should we get going?'

Jaime nodded and signalled to the waiter for the bill.

The flamenco bar Jaime took me to was a former cellar, with panelled walls and long wooden benches. The entrance was down a steep flight of stairs. Manolo, whom we had come to see, was already playing. The musician's black bushy eyebrows contrasted with his white hair. The air was laden with cigar smoke and the fruity smell of sangria. The waiter, who appeared to know Jaime, brought us two seats so we could have a front-row view. Manolo was playing a fast rhythm. I was mesmerised by his nimble fingers.

'It's a *bulería*,' Jaime explained.

'*Burlar*' in Spanish meant 'to mock'. Because the rhythm seemed to change so dramatically from one moment to the next, it did fool the listener about where the piece was going.

'It is one of the most difficult *palos* in flamenco,' Jaime whispered to me. 'It takes years to master it.'

I watched the enraptured faces of the audience and felt as if I were waking from a long sleep. So there was another world outside of ballet. Normally on a Friday night, I would be at home reading a book or listening to music after a full day of ballet classes. I wondered what it would be like not to feel the constant pressure to excel—to have a normal life and a normal job and be able to come out with Jaime like this whenever I wanted. I thought of what Mademoiselle Louvet had said: 'I don't know at what point ballerinas became elite athletes with no room for a life outside rehearsals.'

After the performance, Manolo greeted Jaime and came to sit with us. Jaime ordered a bottle of wine.

'This is my friend Paloma,' he said, pouring the wine into three glasses. 'She's a dancer and is interested in knowing more about la Rusa.'

'Ah, la Rusa,' Manolo said, a dreamy look coming to his eyes. 'I toured with her. I was only a young man then and she was a star. The crowds gathered to see her wherever she went. In South America, they had to turn the fire hoses on people to keep them under control. I don't believe there will ever be another *bailaora* like her. She was a phenomenon.' He gave a little laugh. 'She was certainly a shock to refined audiences who were used to dancers like Anna Pavlova and la Argentina. Even Isadora Duncan was tame by comparison. But la Rusa . . . she was the opposite of "civilised". When you watched her perform, the building could have caved in and you wouldn't have noticed. She bewitched her audiences. She was magnificent!'

'And what was she like as a person as opposed to a performer?' I asked him.

Manolo sat back and took a sip of wine. 'She was famous but she was never a snob. After a show, she liked nothing better than to kick off her shoes and cook us all a pot of stew. She was also generous. When my wife and daughter were sick one year, I arrived at the hospital to find all the medical bills had been paid by la Rusa.'

What Manolo was describing seemed to me something of a contradiction: a woman who was a major star cooking soup in her kitchen like a housewife.

'My ballet coach said la Rusa was quite reclusive after the war—when she lived in America,' I said. 'Do you know why?'

Manolo glanced at his hands. 'Everyone was ruined after the Civil War. The Spanish . . . well, we love our music, our wine and our dancing, but we can be brutal. I don't think that war left anyone unscarred. La Rusa had stayed to fight. She remained in Barcelona until the bitter end. Most of the other entertainers had long left for America or Europe before things became too bad. Poets, artists and dancers were usually the first people on the execution list for Franco's Nationalists. She risked her life to fight for the Republic.'

I mulled over this information. 'Why do you think she stayed?'

He stared into the distance for a moment. 'I don't know why. Perhaps she truly believed in the equality of human beings and was prepared to die for it.'

What Manolo was telling me was interesting, but where did it all fit? I realised there was so much about la Rusa that was unknown. So much that would probably never be known. I wondered if her spirit had come to me so that I would start digging up her story. It was almost as if she wanted to be in my thoughts.

There was no easy way to ask the next question. I took a deep breath. 'La Rusa committed suicide in Paris. But Jaime says many people in the Spanish community think she was murdered. What do you say?'

Manolo's head snapped up. 'Yes, I've heard that too. But I don't know how someone could have lured her to the spot where she died, or pushed her under that train. She was too smart for that.'

I caught my breath. Train? I hadn't expected that la Rusa had died so violently. If she had committed suicide, I'd imagined a more romantic death, such as drowning herself in the Seine. Manolo was grimacing, as if some memory was troubling him.

'Did you see where she died?' I asked.

He nodded. 'A suburb outside of Paris. I went there later with some flowers. I was deeply sorry. I'd lost track of la Rusa after she left Europe. Maybe I could have done something to help her.'

His regret sent the three of us into reflection. Perhaps there were too many people in our lives we didn't appreciate enough until it was too late.

Manolo suddenly sat up. 'There was someone in Paris who had known la Rusa very well. He met her before she became famous. In fact, I think he helped her. He probably could have told you a lot more about her, but unfortunately he died a few years ago.'

I nodded. Once more, la Rusa was slipping away. She was exactly like a *bulería*: as soon as I thought I had understood something about her, everything changed again. 'What was his name?' I asked out of curiosity.

'Gaspar Olivero. He was a Catalan.'

The atmosphere in the room seemed to shift. I felt light-headed. Maybe the thick smoke and the wine were affecting me. I was sure I couldn't have heard correctly.

'Pardon?' I said. 'Could you repeat that name?'

'Gaspar Olivero,' Manolo said. 'He was la Rusa's accompanist for many years. They were the greatest of friends.'

I felt the blood rush to my feet. I turned to Jaime, who lifted his eyebrows.

'Does that name mean anything to you?' he asked.

'Yes,' I said, trying to catch my breath. 'Gaspar Olivero was my grandfather.'

Part III

Part II

TWENTY-ONE

Celestina
Barcelona, 1920

The Samovar Club was situated on las Ramblas, near the plaça de Catalunya. Diego and one of his sisters, Fidelia, came with me for my appointment with el Ruso. Diego and I had thought the Villa Rosa was luxurious so our eyes nearly popped out of their sockets when the doorman ushered us in. It was early afternoon, and even without the fashionable guests who would fill it later that evening to add glitz, we were amazed by the sumptuous velvet curtains and the golden columns which gave the space the appearance of a Russian ballroom. Surrounding the oblong dance floor were round tables decorated with linen cloths and silver candlesticks. Fidelia touched one of the dozen malachite urns that were perched on marble stands and muttered some gypsy obscenities. Diego gazed up at the crystal chandelier that hung over the dance floor, too overcome for words.

'*Bona tarda!*'

We turned in the direction of a marble staircase to see el Ruso coming down it with another man by his side. The stranger was wearing a silk suit with pleated pants. His hair was brushed back from his clean-shaven face and parted sharply at the side. When he saw us—me and Fidelia in our flamenco dresses and Diego in his ill-fitting suit—he didn't seem impressed.

'This is our choreographer, Vasily Zakharov,' said el Ruso.

Zakharov nodded in greeting but did not extend his hand. The idea of touching any of us seemed to disgust him.

Another two men appeared from a door at the rear of the club. The older one, a swarthy gypsy, was carrying a guitar. The younger man had copper-coloured hair. He smiled when he saw us.

'This is Gerardo Ruíz,' said el Ruso, indicating the gypsy. 'And this young man here,' he placed his hand on the red-haired man's shoulder, 'is Gaspar Olivero: our musical director and a genius composer.'

Gaspar Olivero shook our hands warmly. He had a ready smile and a pleasant manner about him. I was surprised that he was a musical director at such a young age: he looked a year or two older than me.

El Ruso turned to me. 'I thought you might show us one of your dances, senyoreta Sánchez. Gaspar will compose some numbers especially for you.'

I passed my shawl to Fidelia and walked up on stage. Gerardo followed me and set up a chair for himself. The others took seats at one of the tables, Zakharov screwing up his nose and placing himself as far away as possible from Diego and Fidelia.

'What do you dance?' Gerardo asked me. 'Shall I play a *bulería?*'

I sensed that he was challenging me by suggesting such a complicated rhythm, but I nodded because I danced everything.

'Are you really a gypsy?' he asked, adjusting his guitar.

I glanced at Diego, who nodded. 'Yes,' I replied.

'Where are you from?' asked Gerardo. 'You speak Spanish like a Catalan.'

'I am from the barri del Somorrostro.'

Gerardo looked away from me to el Ruso. 'Then she's a fraud,' he told him. 'Only gypsies from Andalusia know how to truly dance flamenco.'

El Ruso rubbed his chin and chuckled. 'Wait and see, Gerardo,' he said. 'Wait and see.'

The blood boiled under my skin. A fraud! I didn't need a guitarist! I could make my own percussion if I needed! Besides, my mother had been of gypsy descent!

Gerardo played and I danced with passion. Then I did something I had never done in front of Diego: I danced a series of furious *zapateados*, building to a frenetic climax before coming to a sudden stop.

'Good gracious!' said Zakharov, standing up. 'Did you see what she did with her feet?'

Diego nodded as if my explosive foot percussion was well known to him. I'd picked it up from watching the male dancers at the Villa Rosa and other clubs, and practised it when no one was looking. It was the first time I had tried the steps in public.

'She shouldn't dance like that,' Fidelia complained to Diego. 'It's not feminine. Those steps are for men.'

'I've never seen a man dance like that!' said Zakharov.

He was looking at me with awe, like a prospector who has struck a stream of gold.

'She performed those *zapateados* better and much faster than any male flamenco dancer I've seen,' added Gaspar. 'She's strong but she has dainty feet.'

El Ruso raised his eyebrows and looked to Gerardo.

'I humbly apologise,' the gypsy said to me. 'You are every inch the great *bailaora* that el Ruso said you were. But I agree with your friend that those steps are for men.'

El Ruso rose from his chair and leaned against the stage. 'That's exactly what I was explaining to you. She's not just another Spanish dancer. She is unique. We have to create an act that conveys that to the audience. I want them left breathless.'

He thought something over before saying to Gaspar: 'Could you fetch la senyora Dávilo, the wardrobe mistress? I want to see la senyoreta Sánchez dance those steps in a man's suit.'

'What?' asked Diego, rising from his chair, his machismo offended. Then he realised where he was and thought of the fee I might be paid. He sat down again.

'But that's been done before,' said Zakharov. 'La Tanguera danced the *farruca* in men's clothes.'

'Yes,' agreed el Ruso. 'But la Tanguera was masculine and she danced like a man. Here we have a beautiful woman who demonstrates feminine rather than masculine strength. I don't want her dressed like a matador. I want her wearing something . . . becoming but powerful at the same time! We have to let people see those magnificent feet. Otherwise it's like not being able to view the hands of a great pianist.'

Everyone turned and stared at me, as if they couldn't quite see who it was that el Ruso was calling 'beautiful'. The exception was Gaspar, who nodded enthusiastically.

'That's a brilliant idea!' he said. 'Her technique is feminine but her strength is powerful. I see her with ten guitarists and an orchestra behind her!'

El Ruso clapped his hands. 'A spectacular!'

'Flamenco, rest in peace,' said Gerardo. Fidelia murmured her agreement.

'Don't be such cynics. Art is always evolving,' Zakharov told them. 'It is not vulgar to be innovative!'

Ten guitarists and an orchestra, I thought. Wasn't I the girl who'd started out dancing to the sound of Manuel's old guitar and his sisters clapping their hands and banging their knuckles on tables? Hadn't I learned flamenco's rhythms from the sea? The idea of an orchestra amused me. Dancing was in my soul, not in my head. The truth was, it didn't matter who accompanied me, what I wore or what the audience thought. In the end I danced only for myself—and for the demon.

In the office afterwards, el Ruso and Zakharov showed me a contract. 'You can read it?' el Ruso asked.

I nodded, although my reading level wasn't quite up to deciphering a legal document.

'Then take it with you and go over it. How much do you want to be paid?'

I turned to Diego, who stared at the ceiling as if he were making a complex calculation. I knew he was probably considering the value of the marble busts and mahogany desk in el Ruso's office.

'Twelve *pesetas* a night,' he said. He'd doubled my usual earnings.

El Ruso and Zakharov exchanged a glance. Fidelia shifted in her seat, as if she expected the impresario to chase us out of the office for asking for such an audacious sum. But el Ruso made no objection. He rose from his chair and said to me, 'Please come back here at ten o'clock tomorrow morning so we can discuss your act further.'

I stood too and el Ruso cast his eyes over my worn dress and dirty sandals. 'You'll need some new clothes, as befitting an upcoming star at the Samovar Club, and a new hairstyle. La senyora Dávilo will see to that for you.'

The secretary closed the door behind us and I heard Zakharov laugh and say something in Russian to el Ruso. A long time afterwards, when I knew el Ruso better, I asked him what Zakharov had said to him that day that was so amusing.

El Ruso smiled when he recalled the conversation. 'We were surprised at your exorbitant asking price,' he said with a wink. 'Twelve *pesetas*!'

I smiled too. Diego was a terrible manager. The Samovar Club paid me sixty *pesetas* a night for my first season. Afterwards, when I was a star touring America, my fee was ten thousand dollars a show.

'Wow! Is that you, senyoreta Sánchez?' Gaspar cried when he saw me at the club after senyora Dávilo had finished with me.

I had spent the morning at the beauty salon being rubbed, steamed and pummelled. Now, instead of smelling of sea salt and the olive oil I used to smooth my hair, I exuded an assortment of fragrances: the witch-hazel astringent the beautician had said would 'stimulate my skin'; the lanolin and zinc day cream that was supposed to give me 'a glow' and act as a base for the powder she had patted over my face, neck and décolletage; and the petrolatum scent of the sticky underarm deodorant cream that she had assured me all the dancers at the club used instead of talcum powder. The hairdresser had left my hair long for my dance act, but had curled it with an iron and pinned it up to give the illusion of the short chic style that was in fashion.

'You look beautiful!' Gaspar exclaimed.

I twirled around to show off my Chantilly lace dress and beaded handbag, teetering on the boulevard heels of my pumps. 'I don't know,' I said. 'My face feels hot. I don't normally wear powder and lipstick.' Every time I blinked, I was conscious of the thick layer of cake mascara the beautician had applied.

Gaspar laughed that hearty, open laugh of his. 'You'll get used to it,' he said. 'You look gorgeous! You must let me take you out to a café. I want to show you off.'

The place he took me to was not like the cafés in the barri Xinès, which were havens for gangsters, police spies and anarchists. But it wasn't an upmarket place either, which surprised me. It was easy to tell from Gaspar's sharp clothes, manicured nails and relaxed manner that he was wealthy, even though he wore his good fortune lightly.

The café seemed to be full of actors and actresses, poets and idealists. We sat down at a table by an open window and the waiter brought us aromatic Cuban coffee in white cups. A group of students entered and disappeared into a back room. Gaspar noticed me watching them.

'That's the arts branch of the Socialist Club,' he said.

'Do you attend?'

He nodded. 'Sometimes.'

I studied him. 'Do you believe in an equal society?'

'I do,' he replied, not missing a beat. 'I would give my life to see humanity united in love, and for everyone to be properly fed and clothed.'

If Gaspar had been anybody else, I would have ridiculed him. What did a young man who wore tailored clothes and a gold tiepin know of the barri del Somorrostro or the barri Xinès? The previous day, I'd stopped Fidelia just as she was about to pick his pocket. But I sensed there was more to Gaspar Olivero than met the eye. He seemed to be that rare kind of person who could make himself agreeable to anyone anywhere.

'Are there many men like you in that club?' I asked.

'Men like what?' he said, his eyes twinkling at me over the rim of his cup.

I shrugged. 'Urbane, educated . . . rich.'

He laughed. 'Well, I have a good friend, Xavier, who plays piano sometimes for the social dances. I would have liked you to meet him: he is an aficionado of flamenco. But his father had some English idea of sending him away on a grand tour of Europe before he settles down to the family business and marries. I think he is in Italy right now.'

When Gaspar excused himself to go to the bathroom, I caught sight of my reflection in the wall mirror next to our table and jumped. I didn't recognise myself. I thought of the young society girls I had seen in the beauty salon, and for some reason Evelina Montella came to mind. How old would she be now? Twelve? Too young to have been one of them.

I recalled her beautiful mother, and remembered her father's words that day in the sweatshop: 'That is simply the workings of the economic system in which we live. Those who can pay reap the benefits.' Then I relived in my imagination my dead father lying in a pool of blood on a street not far from where I was now sitting. I saw my emaciated mother in her death throes; Anastasio being buried in an unmarked grave in Africa; Ramón and Teresa being marched into exile. A humanity united in love? Gaspar was dreaming. Humanity would never be united in love as long as people like the Montellas controlled the economy.

Gaspar returned and ordered us more coffee. 'Would you like something to eat?' he asked.

I shook my head. 'If you don't mind me saying, you seem very young to be a musical director. How old are you?'

'I'm as young as I look,' he said with a sheepish grin. 'But I credit my parents for fostering my musical talent early. They are both fond of music, and believed each of their children should follow their inclinations. I'm afraid that they've spoiled me. I don't think I'm cut out for serious work. All I've done is play music.'

'Is that really true? You give me the impression of someone who has many talents.'

He chuckled. 'And how do I manage that illusion?'

'Everything you do,' I told him. 'The way you walk, your manner of speaking . . .'

He blushed. 'Well, I don't know why, but I did seem to pick things up at school very quickly without having to study much.'

'It sounds like a good life,' I said, trying to imagine an existence where a person had so much money they didn't *need* it.

'Now speaking of talented people,' he said, giving the impression he was keen to move the subject away from himself, 'I'm excited about composing music for you. I want it to be brilliant. Could we work at the club together tomorrow afternoon? Zakharov's keen to get started on the choreography as soon as possible. El Ruso demands at least ten weeks of rehearsals before he launches any show.'

'Why?'

Gaspar looked puzzled. 'Senyoreta Sánchez, you do know what a choreographer is, don't you? Zakharov's going to plan out a dance for you.'

I thought about what Gaspar had said, then asked, 'How is he going to *plan out* a dance for me? I only ever have the slightest notion of how I'm going to begin a dance, and once I've started another part of me takes over.'

'You mean you never use a routine?'

'A routine? No,' I said, confused. 'Each flamenco dance has a certain structure and style of steps, but the dancer follows her own inspiration. Of course there are clues for the guitarist—the *llamada* break, or a particular posture that suggests what is to follow. Even so, a guitarist and a dancer who have worked together for a long time will be able to read each other with no visual clues at all.'

'But you do understand that part of your contract is to turn up to rehearse?' said Gaspar, leaning towards me. 'You can't just go out and do whatever takes your fancy on the night.'

'But that *is* flamenco,' I told him. 'You dance according to how you feel on that day and how the demon moves you. Do you understand?'

Gaspar's lips twitched, as if he were trying not to laugh. 'I do understand, senyoreta Sánchez. But I think Zakharov is going to have a fit!'

El Ruso's first extravagant gift to me was an apartment not far from the club. He took me there after my initial rehearsal session with Zakharov. My heels clicked on the parquet floor as I stared up at the bowed plasterwork on the ceilings. I leaned against a stone pillar and looked out the curved window to the street. An unsettling feeling came over me. I realised that I was inside one of the apartments I had seen being constructed when I had fled the police station the day Teresa and Ramón were exiled; the day Francisca had found me. Overcome by a sense that my life was fated, I turned away from the view.

'It's too much for me,' I told el Ruso. 'I'm used to simpler things.'

He studied me for a moment. 'I can't have a star at the Samovar Club living in a slum on the beach,' he said. 'The press will come and interview you. You must exude glamour and mystique in all that you do.'

'You don't know yet that I will be a star,' I told him. 'If I don't succeed, will you put me back out on the street?'

He walked over to the window and stood next to me. 'I've been an impresario for a long time now,' he said. 'You might be a rough diamond but you're a good one. After your season at the Samovar, I intend to tour you. Not just Spain but the rest of Europe and the Americas too. Maybe even Asia.'

We were quiet for a time, both lost in our thoughts. I could smell the citrus and bergamot notes of el Ruso's expensive cologne and the scent of fine cigar smoke on his clothing.

Suddenly he turned to me. 'Listen, senyoreta Sánchez,' he said, 'I was born into a wealthy family in St Petersburg. I grew up in a house full of servants and Kuznetsov porcelain. But after the Revolution, I lost everything. I came here and couldn't even afford a room with a bed. I existed in some cheap communal hall where everyone slept standing up, leaning on a rope for support. I didn't speak a word of Spanish let alone Catalan so I shone shoes and helped lug boxes onto the ships at the port. But within two years I had my first club. The year after I bought a bigger one.' He raised his eyebrows to emphasise his point. 'You see, a rich man can lose everything and become rich again because of the way he thinks. But a poor man will remain a poor man unless he experiences something that makes him strive for a better life.'

He stepped towards me and reached into his pocket for his wallet, then took my hand and placed a thousand *pesetas* in it. 'I know that Diego takes everything you earn. That is the life for a gypsy woman. But I'm not so sure you are a pure gypsy,' he said, looking at me with his penetrating gaze.

I didn't like him staring at me like that. 'What are you trying to tell me?' I said.

He threw back his head and laughed. 'I'm telling you to get used to being rich,' he said. 'Get used to having money . . . because if you ever lose it, you'll be able to build yourself up again.'

I tried to understand what el Ruso was saying to me. He sounded as if he thought we had a choice in how our lives played out. I had never seen things that way before. I didn't think my father had chosen to be poor. I didn't believe he'd wanted to die at the hands of a soldier on las Ramblas and leave me and Ramón as orphans.

'You're right that I'm not a pure gypsy,' I told him. 'But I'm not a pure *paya* either to be so motivated by the material world. I like to be well fed and to wear beautiful clothes, but apartments and money in the bank mean little to me. They are a trap.'

El Ruso merely smiled and placed his hat back on his head as he made for the door. 'You wait here. The decorator is coming by in a minute or so. Don't worry about the cost. Choose exactly what you like. He has strict instructions to give you whatever you ask for . . . believe me, having money and luxuries will grow on you.'

The decorator arrived a few minutes after el Ruso had left, carrying two bags of fabric swatches and books of coloured sketches. He introduced himself as Juan Bertrán. He was a short wiry man with thin blond hair swept over his balding pate. His suit was well-cut and he had the pampered skin and white teeth of a man who took care of himself.

'The first thing we should decide is style and colour,' he said, opening one of his bags. 'Are we looking at two or three tones?'

Senyor Bertrán showed me a number of sketches of drawing rooms that he had decorated. I studied the muted colours of the draperies, sconces and wing-back chairs and the modern light fittings, marvelling that people with money should choose such drab shades. I requested mustard-yellow walls, blood-red damask curtains and ottomans, and a chandelier for every room.

'Now,' said senyor Bertrán, wiping his brow with his linen handkerchief and walking around the apartment. 'The master bedroom is large enough for a king-sized bed. What about the guest room? How many people are you expecting to stay with you?'

I thought about his question for a moment before answering. 'Well, there's Diego, Fidelia, Raquel, Pastora . . . about fifteen people.'

Senyor Bertrán gaped at me. 'All at once?' he asked. 'You want fifteen beds in this apartment?'

I laughed. 'No! Fifteen beds won't fit! It's only a four-room apartment.'

Senyor Bertrán laughed too and wiped his brow again.

'Seven beds plus the king-sized bed will do,' I told him. 'The women are used to sharing with each other, and the children will all fit into one bed.'

Senyor Bertrán's mouth dropped open again. He looked like he was about to protest. But then he must have remembered el Ruso's instruction to give me whatever I wanted. He swallowed. 'Seven beds plus a king-sized bed,' he said, making a note in his folder before glancing up again. 'Now, will they be four-poster beds or modern ones?'

'What is this?' shouted Zakharov, banging his fist to his forehead and rushing towards the stage. 'I can't work like this!'

Gaspar lifted his hands from the piano keys and nodded to me. As he had predicted, Zakharov and I had come to logger-heads over the question of whether a dance sequence should be rehearsed or not at our second session together. Gaspar had composed beautiful music: atmospheric and full of changing moods. But instead of letting me use my intuition to guide me as to where I should move on the stage, Zakharov was doing ridiculous things like marking a chalk spot where he wanted me to stop and do a *llamada*.

'But what if I don't feel like doing it there?' I asked him. 'What if the moment calls for something else?'

'It won't call for something else,' he said, pushing back his hair and pointing to his chalk mark. 'Everyone will be ready for it to happen *there*—from the lighting men to the musicians.'

'I don't know what you call that,' I told him, 'but it's not dancing. It's some sort of miming to music; it has no genuine feeling.'

'Of course it will have feeling,' said Zakharov, looking indig-nant. 'You put feeling into it when you do it. Haven't you ever seen a ballet? Anna Pavlova dances precisely the same way each time, down to the merest flick of her eyes heavenwards, yet her performances are incredibly moving.'

'If that's the case,' I told him, 'then ballet is nothing more than a *simulation* of feeling. It's not real.'

El Ruso was called from his office to settle the dispute. He arrived with his secretary and his valet in tow. The valet must have been shaving el Ruso before he received the call because the impresario had the remnants of shaving soap around his ears and throat.

'She won't rehearse,' complained Zakharov. 'And she won't follow my choreography.'

'That's not true,' I said. 'I came here today on time, and I will come every day to dance. Don't insinuate that because I'm a gypsy I'm lazy.'

'She does the dance differently every time,' Zakharov told el Ruso.

'Because I *feel* differently every time I hear Gaspar's music!' I explained. 'There is so much to it. Yesterday I felt like a wild horse galloping through a wood. And today, the music made me think of the sea.'

'We've had this trouble with gypsy dancers before,' Zakharov told el Ruso. 'That's why we have never given them star parts.'

'I seem to remember that we didn't use gypsy dancers previously because they wouldn't adapt to our audience,' el Ruso replied. 'They wouldn't refine their steps or give up their mournful attitudes.'

'Exactly,' said Zakharov.

'But when I watched your first rehearsal with la senyoreta Sánchez, I thought she was very agreeable. Has she not learned the new steps you gave her?'

'She's learned them perfectly,' said Zakharov, throwing up his hands. 'It's where she is putting them in the dance that's the problem. Yesterday she was a horse and today she is the sea!'

El Ruso turned to me. 'Senyoreta Sánchez, didn't you tell me that you had no objections to using castanets?'

'No,' I told him. 'I have no objections.'

He walked towards the stage and beckoned me to move closer to him. 'Do you mind if Zakharov puts some classical Spanish dance movements into your act? Maybe some from folk dances too?'

I shook my head.

'And what about some dramatic Russian dance steps or Cuban ones?'

I shook my head again. Dance was dance to me: I loved to learn it all. To Zakharov's credit, he was a gifted dancer himself. There was so much he could teach me. All I wanted was to be able to express myself authentically. I didn't want to repeat my music-hall days with Manuel. I didn't feel bound to dance only gypsy *flamenco puro*, but I'd learned not to disrespect the demon either.

El Ruso turned to Zakharov and smiled. 'It seems to me you have a very cooperative performer to work with. Why don't you show la senyoreta Sánchez the steps you would like her to do, and let her decide where and when she does them in her performance?'

Zakharov looked horrified. 'You mean differently every time?'

El Ruso grinned and nodded. 'Differently every time . . . if she so wishes.'

After a rehearsal the following week, I waited until everyone else had left before approaching Gaspar at the piano. I showed him the thousand *pesetas* that el Ruso had given me.

'*Deu meu*, senyoreta Sánchez! You shouldn't be carrying that amount of cash around. Do you want me to open a bank account for you?'

I shook my head. 'I want you to take me to Alcañiz.'

Gaspar looked puzzled. 'What's in Alcañiz?'

'My brother Ramón and a friend of my father's, Teresa Flores García. They were exiled there after the uprising in 1909. Ramón said he would come back for me, but if he did, he was never able to find me.'

Gaspar stared at me. 'Returning would have meant the death penalty. Let's hope he didn't try it.' He glanced at the money in my hand again. 'You want to give him that?'

I nodded.

Gaspar picked up his copy of the rehearsal schedule from the top of the piano. 'All right,' he said, scanning the pages. 'It's meant to be just you and me the day after tomorrow, and then we have the following day off. We can say we are rehearsing at my home. We are going to have to leave early and stay overnight. Is that Diego character going to mind?'

'His sister will come with us.'

'Then I'll see you first thing Thursday morning,' said Gaspar.

I had known before I had asked him that Gaspar would help me. He was the only person I trusted fully.

I sat down to take off my dance shoes. 'I don't think my brother will recognise me,' I said, undoing the buckles. 'It's been ten years since I saw him.'

Gaspar smiled. 'He'll recognise you,' he said gently. 'There are certain things about people that never change.'

The morning that Gaspar was to take me and Fidelia to Alcañiz, I woke up long before my alarm rang. I didn't rest well in my new apartment without the sound of the waves to lull me to sleep. On top of that, Diego's other sister, Raquel, shared the bed with me and had snored most of the night. I'd tossed and turned, unable to stop thinking about Ramón and Teresa. Ramón would be twenty-one now. I wondered what he would look like. What would our first words be after all these years?

Diego's clothes were soaking in the tub in the bathroom, so I filled the sink with water and washed myself with a sponge. Being 'a star' meant my ablutions took longer. By the time I had curled my hair, filed and buffed my fingernails and applied my make-up, an hour had passed by. Fidelia was already in the kitchen when I went to make myself some coffee. She was assembling a picnic lunch.

'Do you think he will like tuna?' she asked.

The concierge rang to say Gaspar was in the foyer. I asked him to send him up to the apartment. A few moments later, Gaspar was at the door.

'Come in,' I told him. 'I'll fetch my bag.'

His eyes nearly popped out of his head when one of Diego's chickens ran between his feet. He looked at the laundry hanging in the hallway and the assortment of women sleeping on sleigh beds in the drawing room.

'Senyoreta Sánchez! How many people are living in this apartment?'

'Diego and his family plus my teacher Manuel's sisters and their husbands and children,' I told him.

Gaspar pinched his lips as if he were trying not to laugh.

'What's so amusing?' I asked.

'I don't think el Ruso will be pleased,' he answered. 'He wanted you to have this apartment to yourself. So you could concentrate on your work.'

'But this is my clan. I can't live in an apartment and leave them on the beach.'

'No, I suppose not,' he replied, his eyes twinkling. 'But aren't gypsies supposed to be nomads who live by their wits?'

I shrugged. That was what Francisca used to say—that my clan was inviting bad luck by staying too long in one place and not living the old gypsy way. Anyway, el Ruso had said he was going to tour me. I assumed my clan would be coming with me, so I guessed that would count as travelling for them.

It was early summer and the trip to Alcañiz was long and dusty. Fidelia slept most of the way while the tuna sandwiches she had made stank out the car. It was difficult to talk to Gaspar while we were driving because of the noise from the engine, so I spent most of the time looking out of the window. I had never been out of Barcelona before and my eyes were opened by the Spanish countryside. The mountains, plains, forests and clear skies were beautiful, but the poverty was not: the starving children on the roadside; the subsistence housing; the old people bent over by the loads of firewood they carried on their backs; the mangy dogs and rickety cats.

'The poverty gets worse the further south you go,' Gaspar said, when we stopped for a while to stretch our legs. 'Most of the farms there are owned by landowners who only employ labour for the harvests. That means in between harvests—or if a harvest fails—the peasants starve because they have no other sources of income.'

When we arrived in Alcañiz, I tried to see it as Ramón and Teresa would have experienced it when they first arrived after being exiled from Barcelona. A twelfth-century castle—once the headquarters of the Knights of Calatrava, who had ruled this part of Aragon—dominated the town, with ancient white houses clustered around its base. When we stopped in the marketplace and got out of the car, I felt we had stepped into a place where time seemed to have stopped. I looked at the Gothic and Renaissance buildings and the old Baroque church. It was nothing like Barcelona, which always seemed to be changing.

Some children gathered around Gaspar's car. He let them blow the horn a few times. 'Where are your mothers?' he asked. 'We need to find someone who can help us with some information.'

'My mother is over there,' said one boy, pointing to a young woman in a headscarf who was working at a fruit stall.

'*Buenos días, señora!*' Gaspar greeted the woman in Spanish. 'We are looking for some people who came here in 1909 . . . from Barcelona.'

I was thankful that Gaspar was taking over the search. My legs were shaking. Anticipating whether I was about to hear good news or bad news about Ramón and Teresa made my hands cold and clammy, even though my dress stuck to my back in the heat. I looked around, wondering if any of the young men were Ramón. I noticed some flower sellers at the far end of the market, but none of them was Teresa.

The young woman smiled. 'Yes, my mother knew them very well.' She turned to the man with her on the stall, who might have been her husband, and said something. He nodded. 'Come this way,' the woman said. 'I'll take you to my mother.'

Knew them very well? That didn't sound good. At the very least, it didn't sound as if Ramón and Teresa were still in Alcañiz. I put my hand on Fidelia's shoulder for support.

The young woman, who introduced herself as Sofía, led us down a narrow street to an old stone house. She shouted to an upstairs window. The shutters opened and a woman of about fifty years of age peered out. Sofía introduced her mother, Antoñita, to us and explained to her why we had come. Antoñita said she would come downstairs.

'Yes, yes,' she said, when she opened her door to the street and ushered us inside her house, which smelled of borax and old wood. 'I remember them very well. They were brought by the Civil Guard in September 1909.' She looked from me to Gaspar. 'You are not the first of the children who were left behind to come looking for them. Which ones were your parents?'

Gaspar indicated me. 'We are looking for this señorita's brother, Ramón, and her guardian, Teresa.'

'Ramón! Teresa!' Antoñita cried. She grabbed my hands and urged me to take a seat. 'You must be Celestina! They both talked so much about you. How happy poor Teresa would have been to know that you are all right!'

'What happened to Teresa?' I asked.

Tears filled Antoñita's eyes. 'Her heart gave out a couple of months after she arrived. The upheaval was too much for her.'

I felt pain in my own heart. It was the news I'd most feared.

'We buried her in the cemetery here,' Antoñita said.

It was a few moments before I could speak. I remembered Teresa's distraught face on the day she was taken away. She had cared for us after Papá's death. She had tried to be strong for us. As a child, I had taken these things for granted. But as an adult, I better appreciated the sacrifice she had made.

'And Ramón?' I asked. 'Where is my brother?'

Antoñita shook her head. 'I don't know. The Civil Guard came again one day after the exiles had been here for a few months. They took them all away. We have never been able to find out where.'

Sofía poured us a glass of wine each and sat down with us while Antoñita related the story.

'When the authorities brought the exiles here, they told us that they were dangerous criminals. I think they wanted to work us up into a rage in the hope that we would lynch them. But it was obvious those people were not evil. They told us their stories and we were moved. They had nothing, so we gave them what we could. But in the end, it was they who left us with the greatest gifts.'

I looked at Antoñita, trying to understand her meaning. She smiled and stood up to take something from the shelf next to her. She handed me a book. It was a Spanish translation of Jack London's *The Call of the Wild*.

'I had never learned to read,' Antoñita explained. 'One of the women, Carme, was a teacher. She taught me how to read and write, and she gave me this book. It was all she had with her. I still read a few pages of it every day. I'm so grateful to her.'

The wine Sofía had given us was Aragon wine: full-bodied and potent. My head felt dizzy but at least the wine numbed the grief that was racking my body.

'That's why the authorities took them away,' Antoñita continued. 'They thought the exiles were having too much influence on us, giving us revolutionary ideas. One day, without warning, the Civil Guard arrived, put them in horse carts and took them away.'

I rested my head in my hands. I'd never had the means to come to Alcañiz until now, and I was too late. Far too late. How would I find Ramón now?

'Your brother was a charming and resourceful boy,' Sofía said. 'I remember him well because we were close in age. I'm sure he will be all right wherever he is.'

Antoñita agreed. 'He was very clever indeed! He helped with the olive harvest and found ingenious ways to do things faster.' She put her hand on my arm. 'Would you like to see Teresa's grave?'

Gaspar, Fidelia and I followed Antoñita and Sofía to the cemetery. Teresa had been buried alongside Antoñita's parents. Her grave was decorated with bunches of blue and yellow wildflowers and some pink peach blossoms.

'My neighbours and I attend to it,' Antoñita explained. 'We felt sorry for Teresa, dying so far away from her home and being buried without her family around her.'

'Teresa was a flower seller,' I told her. 'At the big market in Barcelona. I'm sure she would have liked the display you've made for her very much.'

Antoñita and Sofía took Gaspar and Fidelia to see the other graves in the cemetery, leaving me alone to spend some time with Teresa. I could hear Antoñita explaining the history of the region to them as they went.

I kissed the white cross that marked Teresa's grave and leaned my face against it. It was still warm from the sun. I tried to think only of my love for Teresa and my sadness at her loss, but anger at the injustice of her exile and death burned inside me. One day I would find a way to get justice for her and Papá.

Afterwards, Antoñita took us to see the house on the outskirts of town where the exiles had stayed. I touched the walls and the Spartan furniture with reverence, knowing that Ramón had been here. I sat on a rusty bunk in one of the bedrooms and gazed out of the window towards the castle.

'Ramón,' I whispered, 'what happened to you? Where are you?'

That night, Antoñita insisted that we stay at her house. She cooked us corn cakes and garlic soup. After dinner, some of her neighbours came to meet us. They were eager to share their stories of how the exiles had taught them to read and write and also simple arithmetic. They spoke of their dreams of democracy.

'We've had enough of the monarchy,' Sofía's husband said. 'And dictators.'

The others agreed with him. 'It's time for a Second Republic,' they said.

The exiles had influenced them indeed!

An old lady with cataracts touched my arm. 'Teresa was very distraught to have left a little girl behind in Barcelona. She will be at peace now that you have visited her and shown her that you are all right.'

Sensing my emotional exhaustion, Gaspar drew the gathering's attention away from me and amused them by singing some songs and demonstrating how to dance the *sardana*.

Later that night, after everyone was asleep, I snuck out of the house and hurried down the road in the moonlight to the house where Ramón had stayed. Everything was so silent. I stood outside the house and danced a *soleá* for him. What else could I do to express the loneliness and alienation I felt?

'You see,' I told Ramón, lifting my leg and executing a turn, 'I have become a dancer.'

In the morning, we had to leave early again. Antoñita insisted that we take some sandwiches and olives with us. We thanked her for her hospitality.

Gaspar started up the car. As we were about to turn the corner, Antoñita came running out of her house.

'You left your money on the table!' she called to us. 'You left one thousand *pesetas*!'

Gaspar glanced at me. I shook my head. 'Keep driving,' I told him. 'I left it for her.'

He put his foot to the accelerator and drove into the brilliant Aragon morning.

On the night of my first appearance at the club, Zakharov brought red roses and champagne to my dressing room and then told me he was going home to bed. 'I can't bear to watch,' he said. 'El Ruso will tell me how it all went in the morning.'

It was fascinating to me that everyone else seemed to be on edge while I felt as calm as the sea on a still day. Gaspar's smile was stiff; and el Ruso paced up and down the corridor, before willing himself to go out and sit in the audience.

I wasn't the main act for the evening; that place was taken by the tenor Miguel Fleta. But I had been billed as the new surprise act and that had drawn a lot of people too. Senyora Dávilo had designed a stunning costume for me: shimmery black pants that were split from the knee to give a good view of my feet, and a silver-grey silk blouse, big-shouldered with ruffled full sleeves. The make-up artist had pinned my hair in a half updo with a red hibiscus behind my ear. The greasepaint she had plastered on my face was even heavier than the powder I was just getting used to applying, my eyes were outlined in thick black kohl and my lips were painted bright red. I felt like I was wearing a mask.

'She's not la Argentina, is she?' I heard one of the chorus girls say to another. 'She's not exactly going to charm the audience.'

Their viciousness didn't distract me. I flexed and stretched my toes and warmed up my wrists.

'Don't be nervous,' the nicer chorus girls said to me. 'You'll be terrific!'

It had never occurred to me to be nervous. There was going to be music and there was going to be dancing. It wasn't in my character to worry whether or not people liked me. They either understood the dance, or they didn't. That was all.

There was a knock at my door. 'Senyoreta Sánchez, ten minutes until you are on,' the stage assistant called. 'Please make your way to the wings.'

Senyora Dávilo brushed down my costume one more time while the make-up artist ran the power puff over my nose and chin. I opened the door and followed the stage assistant to the wings. As I passed the other dressing rooms, the performers peered at me. Their pay packets for the next few weeks depended on my success.

In the wings, I tightened the straps of my shoes. I still wasn't quite used to them. I had grown up dancing in bare feet, but el Ruso had insisted that no star of his would dance on his stage without shoes. Gaspar winked at me from his place at the piano.

The stage manager led me to the spot behind the curtain where I was to wait for the comedian who was on before me to complete his act. When the comedian had finished, he announced me.

'And now, the act that you have been anticipating: a young flamenco dancer plucked straight from the bosom of the gypsies who will thrill you with her vivacity and the virtuosity of her dancing. Ladies and gentlemen, I present to you Celestina Sánchez.'

The curtain rose. A hush fell over the audience. I couldn't see anything beyond the lights except for the occasional flash of diamond or gold jewellery. It didn't matter; I could *feel* the crowd. Their excitement was electric. I breathed in and summoned their energy into me, like an ancient tribesman singing in his catch of fish. Gerardo played the introductory *falseta*. I clicked my fingers, raised my eyes and took three steps forwards into the spotlight . . .

TWENTY-TWO

Diario de Barcelona, 2 July 1920

L *ast night, Maxim Tarasov, 'el Ruso', the inimitable impre-*
sario and owner of the glamorous Samovar Club, launched
his new show for the season. Known not only for his capacity
to attract the big-name stars to his Barcelona venue but also his
ability to discover new ones, Tarasov had filled his club to ca-
pacity with an audience anxious to hear the famed Miguel Fleta
and to see the touted 'surprise act': a gypsy flamenco dancer.

Fleta was in fine form, as to be expected, and the audience
was not disappointed when they also became witnesses to the
debut of perhaps the most astounding and intoxicating per-
former Barcelona has ever seen.

The curtain rose to reveal the diminutive Celestina Sánchez,
whose delicate physique transformed into a force of agility and
strength the moment she took her first step. Her technical ca-
pacity was impressive, with precise and percussive footwork and
a perfect sense of rhythm, but add to that an innate style that is
wild and sensual and you have all the makings for a tempest. A
pretty enough young woman, la senyoreta Sánchez transforms

*to a vision of beauty and passion when she moves, and hypno-
tises all in her wake. She had the audience enthralled with her
rapid spins, her graceful turns and the way her arms flashed like
fire around her body.*

*Accompanied by ten guitarists and an orchestra playing neo-
classical music composed by Gaspar Olivero, la senyoreta Sánchez treated to her audience to an alegría, a fandango and a soleá
before ending with a fiery farruca. Her costume was stunning,
the split trousers and her long wavy hair giving her athleticism
a sense of femininity.*

*Flamenco is an art whose dancers start at a very young age
and yet often do not come into their own until their fifties and
sixties. If last night was anything to go by, this young dancer, who
has been christened 'la Rusa' after the impresario who discovered
her, has even more thrills to offer future audiences . . .*

TWENTY-THREE

Paloma

I didn't sleep the night after I met Manolo at the flamenco bar and he told me that la Rusa and Avi had been good friends. I thought of how Mamie had described my grandfather when he'd been a young man: with alert eyes 'like a squirrel'. La Rusa's eyes were different: dark and full of secrets. Try as I might, I couldn't picture the two of them as friends.

I lay staring at my clock until it was time to get up and help Mamie prepare for the Saturday classes. When I walked into the studio, Mamie was already there, wearing a black dance skirt over her leotard and a pink scarf tied around her head. She had finished sweeping the floor and was wiping down the windowsills with a dusting cloth.

'Ah, good morning,' she said when she saw me. 'How was your outing with Gaby?'

'Mamie, I didn't go out with Gaby last night.'

My grandmother's eyes widened and she gave me a quizzical look. But she had too much faith in my sensible nature to think that I had done anything outrageous. A smile danced around the corners of her mouth.

'Have you met someone?' she asked. 'I've been wondering . . . you've been so *mysterious* lately.'

On any other occasion I would have loved to talk about Jaime. But I'd been visited by a ghost—and one that had once known Avi. It was hard to behave normally with that on my mind. If la Rusa had been friends with my grandfather, there was a chance she'd been friends with Mamie too.

'I've been taking flamenco classes,' I said. 'To improve my character dancing.'

The first part was true; the second part was a 'stretched truth' intended to protect Mamie's feelings.

'Did Mademoiselle Louvet recommend you do that?'

It wasn't a question I had been expecting and it stumped me. But I was tired of lying. It was as if flamenco was somehow shameful and should be hidden, like taking drugs.

'No,' I said. 'It was something I wanted to do myself.'

Mamie regarded me incredulously, but she hadn't reacted as negatively as I had anticipated. 'Come on, Paloma. You are a ballerina at the highest level. I hope you have a quality teacher. What style of flamenco are you learning? Spanish or gypsy?'

'Spanish,' I said. 'Probably something similar to the classical Spanish dances you were learning before you took up ballet.'

Mamie seemed relieved and went back to dusting—although there was something besides dust motes hanging in the air now. Mamie was acting nonchalant, but her shoulders were tensed; she looked like a cat that had been disturbed during a nap.

'The name of a dancer from Barcelona keeps coming up,' I said. 'She was supposed to be one of the greatest dancers this century. I wondered if you knew her. Her name was la Rusa.'

Mamie spun around. Anger flashed in her eyes. 'La Rusa wasn't a dancer!' she spat. 'She was a whore!'

My jaw dropped. In all my life, I had never known Mamie to react to anything this way; had never seen her attractive face scrunched into such livid lines. It was clear now it wasn't flamenco Mamie disliked. It was la Rusa.

Mamie glared at me. 'Don't ever mention her name again!'

'I'm sorry,' I said, berating myself inwardly. Hadn't I promised not to ask any questions about Spain to spare Mamie anguish?

'And how dare you go sneaking around my back?' Mamie continued, as if I hadn't spoken. 'Lying that you are out with Gaby! After all I've done for you!'

That moment with my grandmother staring at me, enraged, was one of the loneliest of my life. I couldn't bring myself to reply.

'Get out!' Mamie shouted, turning away from me. 'Go practise for your audition. Or go to your flamenco classes—or whatever it is you do these days. But don't come near me!'

I fled the studio and ran to my room. My heart ached so much that I could barely move my arms. Usually when I was distressed, I dealt with it by practising ballet. It was dance that had got me through my mother's death and my father's betrayal. But now the very idea of putting on my ballet shoes and standing at the barre filled me with revulsion. The degree of loathing I felt terrified me, as if I were a mother who has suddenly realised that she hates her child. I rushed to the bathroom and stood in the shower, but even the warm water running over my skin couldn't calm me.

I dried myself and pulled on a pair of jeans and a shirt. I left the apartment with no idea of where I was going. I ran down the stairs, tugging on my scarf and coat as I went. The students for Mamie's first class were arriving. '*Bonjour*, Paloma,' they said as they passed me. I did my best to smile and pretend everything was normal, but something was very wrong. I couldn't breathe.

Out on the street, I started to run with no destination in mind. If I could have stopped my mind racing, I might have considered that Mamie's fury wasn't directed at me. But I couldn't think. I couldn't stop.

I reached avenue Victor Hugo and headed in the direction of the Palais de Chaillot. I cut through the jardins du Trocadero and crossed the Seine at the pont d'Iéna. The Eiffel Tower loomed up ahead. 'A Spaniard without a ghost is like Paris without the Eiffel Tower,' Manuel had said. I passed the tourists studying their maps in the parc du Champ de Mars, and the joggers, rollerskaters, lovers, and students listening to Black Sabbath on their portable radios. I walked through the fifteenth arrondissement, only stopping when I came to l'hôpital Saint Joseph and I realised that I'd been walking for over an hour.

It occurred to me that I wasn't far from Carmen's apartment so I turned in that direction. I tried to remember if Jaime had said he was doing something today or not. As it was for Mamie, Saturday would probably be Carmen's busiest day for classes at the academy. Would Jaime be helping her there or studying at home?

I rang the bell to the apartment with little expectation that anyone would answer. But a moment later the door opened and Jaime stood before me wearing a turtleneck ski sweater and black corduroy pants.

'*Bonjour!*' he said, with a smile. 'Or should that be "*Bon dia!*"?'

I tried to return his smile but tears poured down my cheeks instead.

'What's happened?' he asked, guiding me inside the apartment. 'Did you ask your grandmother about la Rusa?'

'Mamie told me to get out of the studio. She's never been so angry with me before.'

Jaime touched my arm. 'Come up to my room,' he said. 'I found something I want you to hear.'

To reach Jaime's room, we had to climb a foldaway ladder in the studio. The space was a partly enclosed mezzanine. The walls were lined with shelves of books, records and flamenco memorabilia. An autographed poster of the guitarist Sabicas hung above the bed, which was covered in a red chenille bedspread. The light from the triangular window was muted by a pair of rust-coloured curtains.

Jaime indicated an oversized velour beanbag. 'Have a seat,' he said. 'Can I get you anything? A coffee?'

I shook my head and sank into the burgundy beanbag. The room smelled like sandalwood incense. I stretched out my legs on the shag rug and noticed the orange paper lantern hanging from the ceiling. There were so many shades of red in Jaime's room that I had the sensation I was resting inside a giant heart.

Jaime picked up a record off his desk. 'Do you know what this is?' he asked, showing me the cover. 'It's a recording of your grandfather, Gaspar Olivero, playing with a jazz band at the Samovar Club in 1928. That's about the time he met your grandmother, I think?'

Avi playing with a jazz band? Until a few days ago, I would not have believed such a thing.

'Most likely it was recorded on a gramophone disc before being converted to vinyl,' Jaime said. 'The sound quality isn't so good, but your grandfather's playing is superb!'

He dropped the needle onto the record and sat down next to me on the beanbag. Time seemed to stop as we listened to Avi play. I wondered what my father might have said about his performance. Although the recording was crackly, Avi's technique came across as clean with complex and profound improvisations.

My life has become so strange, I thought. It was as if the people in my family had been wearing masks and were suddenly revealing their true natures all at once—my father, Avi, and now Mamie. Why did my grandmother hate la Rusa so much? If they had been enemies, why had la Rusa visited me and given me the golden earrings?

The record finished and Jaime and I were quiet for a few minutes. Then Jaime turned to me. 'You look better,' he said. 'The colour has come back to your face. When I saw you at the door, you looked as if you'd seen a ghost!'

The irony, I thought. I shook my head. 'I had some sort of panic attack this morning,' I told him. 'Like the ones Mamie used to get when she was my age.' I rubbed my eyes and allowed myself to sink further into the beanbag. 'Every day, for as long as I can remember, I have always practised my ballet. But today, the very idea of it made me want to be sick. I don't know what's happening to me. I think I'm going crazy.'

Jaime rolled on his side and put his arm around my shoulders. I liked the feeling of him being so close to me; the warmth that he emanated. I wanted him to hold me tighter, but I was scared of that too.

'Sounds like burnout to me,' he said. 'Some people get it after ten hours, others after ten days, ten weeks or ten months. You're a bit slower than most: it's taken you ten years.'

I smiled. 'You always manage to make me laugh,' I said.

'I'm glad.'

Jaime's eyes focused on my lips, but then we both suddenly felt shy and looked away from each other.

'Seriously,' Jaime said after a while, 'you can't be a great artist if you are too uptight. You have to let things flow naturally.'

'Do you think I'm uptight?' I asked him.

He grimaced. 'Well . . . yes!'

If anyone else had said that to me, I would have been mortified. But I knew Jaime was right. I remembered Mamie's description of Avi, how she'd said the piano was an extension of his arms. Jaime was like that with his guitar. The music simply poured out of him. Did I ever feel that way about dancing? That it wasn't a strain? I realised that I did about flamenco—but not ballet. Not since I was a child anyway.

'I'm so tired,' I said, closing my eyes.

'Why don't you take the day off?' said Jaime. 'And not feel guilty for doing it?'

'A day off,' I said, grinning. 'And what am I going to do on my day off?'

'You are going to let me show you around Paris.'

I laughed. 'I was born here. I know Paris very well.'

'Do you? Well, I don't believe you've seen Paris with *me*. I think we should start with the view of the city from Sacré-Coeur.'

I sat up. 'I didn't bring my car.'

'Did you come by Métro?'

I shook my head. 'I walked.'

Jaime's eyes widened. 'You walked?' He gave a chuckle. 'Well, never mind. I have transport.'

I waited in front of the apartment building while Jaime went to the rear courtyard to get his 'transport'. A few moments later I heard the hum of a motor scooter coming down the street and turned to see him heading towards me on a Vespa. He brought it to a stop in front of me.

'Hop on,' he said. 'It will be a bit cold, but if you lean against me I'll keep you warm.'

I don't believe you've seen Paris with me. Indeed, I had never experienced my own city with my arms around a young man's waist, weaving in and out of the chaotic traffic with the wind in my hair. I felt as though it was *me* zipping around Paris rather than the scooter; I wasn't closed off to everything as I was in Mamie's car. I took it all in—the bare winter trees, the soft sunshine, the faces of the pedestrians. It was noisy and exhilarating. I hadn't felt so free since I had ridden a bicycle as a child, before I became fearful of injuring myself. Some of the students at the ballet school had owned scooters but I'd always declined their offers of rides home, too cautious to tempt fate.

We turned into boulevard Saint-Michel and stopped at a set of lights. I saw Gaby walking along with several shopping bags on her arms. Our eyes met.

'Paloma!' she called out. Her glance went from me to Jaime and her face broke into a smile. I just had time to wave to her before we took off again.

I blinked my eyes. I felt like I was in a dream. We reached the cobblestoned streets of Montmartre and I thought how wonderful it would be to live there: to open my window in the morning to see artists at their easels; the old matrons walking their dogs; the performers coming home from the clubs.

Jaime parked the Vespa and, arm in arm, we walked past the postcard and souvenir shops then up the steep slope to la Basilique du Sacré-Coeur. The beautiful Romanesque-Byzantine church was brilliant white against the soft blue sky.

'There are more stairs than I remember,' I told Jaime when we reached the top of the hill and the rooftops of Paris stretched out before us.

'I thought dancers were supposed to be fit,' he teased.

I squeezed his arm. It wasn't because I was unfit that I was breathless.

We found a bench to sit on and Jaime put his arm around me. I loved the sensation of his warm breath against my neck.

'So are you enjoying your day off?' he asked me.

'Very much!'

'And are you enjoying seeing Paris with me?'

I turned and looked at him. 'Yes.'

He leaned towards me. I closed my eyes when his lips touched mine. His kiss sent butterflies spinning in my stomach. We broke apart and smiled at each other. Then we kissed again, this time more passionately. We pressed our bodies together so tightly it was as if we were trying to melt into each other.

We stayed on the bench the rest of the afternoon, kissing and talking. Finally the winter light grew weaker and the air turned too cold to stay there.

'Would you like something to eat?' Jaime asked.

We walked down the steps holding hands. I felt different. The Paloma who had gone up to la Basilique du Sacré-Coeur was not the same one coming down from it. I had been distressed that morning, but now my brain had turned to dough and I was blissfully peaceful.

We stopped at the first café we found, which was full of tourists. Many Parisians hated tourists, but I loved seeing their animated faces and listening to their excited chatter as they shared stories of their sightseeing. I was glad that my city had such an enlivening effect on them. I was glad that today it had shared its magic with me. I had been training so hard these past few years that I had ceased to notice it.

Jaime and I ordered some tomato soup and bread. I reflected on his earlier observation that I was uptight. Then my mind drifted back to what Carmen had said in my first flamenco lesson—how the internal force of one's spirit needs to combine with the spirit of the dance and the music. She had called that union '*duende*'.

'Jaime, what exactly do flamenco artists mean when they talk about *duende*? In normal Spanish it means a poltergeist-like spirit.'

'Now, there is a contentious topic!' Jaime replied, rubbing his hands together. 'Few artists can agree on exactly what *duende* is and whether it exists or not. Some say it is essential to flamenco, while others say it is nothing more than a fanciful idea coined by the poet and flamenco aficionado Federico García Lorca. I'll tell you what I think it is: it's that moment when any artist, not just a flamenco one, transcends their ego and channels into their art something greater than themselves.'

'By something "greater than themselves" do you mean God?' I asked.

'Something spiritual and something universal,' he explained. 'It may be God or it may be something else. Musicians, dancers, writers, artists—they all talk about this moment of fusion between themselves and a greater force. Their audiences sense it too, and the effect is powerful. Athletes experience it as well: they call it "being in the zone".'

I thought about what Jaime was saying. My father had talked about a similar experience when he was giving a concert, although he had never given it a name. He'd told me how there were times when he'd been tired or unwell and had wanted to cancel a concert because he was afraid that he wouldn't play to his best standard. But when he went out on stage, suddenly something else would take over and he would give one of the most inspired performances of his career and the audience would be ecstatic.

'The gypsies never used the actual term *duende*,' Jaime went on, 'but I've read about how they often referred to a "demon" that would possess a performer at some point and transform a simple performance into an extraordinary spiritual experience. For them, that idea of *duende* was always connected to deep grief and the mystery of death.'

'You know, in that first class I felt something,' I told him, 'even though we were doing the basic first step. I had a sense of having danced flamenco before.'

He nodded. 'I saw it too. You had a profound connection to flamenco that made you stand out in the class. It wasn't only that you're a trained dancer; there was a presence about you. It's interesting, because while you have a family connection to Spain, it's through Catalonia. As you know, the Catalans are closer to the French and Italians in their way of thinking. But when you dance, you are pure Andalusian.'

I found what Jaime was saying interesting, but disturbing too. I had only seen la Rusa's ghost on one occasion, but what if she was around me all the time and I simply couldn't see her? Was that why she had given me the golden earrings, so that she could possess me through them? I thought about the research I'd covered at the Bibliothèque Saint-Geneviève: *Some ghosts are demonic and will possess you if you attempt to make any contact with them.* Hadn't Mireille Fourest's book also warned that ghosts retained the same personality they'd had when they were alive? If Mamie hated la Rusa so much, she must have good reason. The more I thought about it, the more I became convinced that la Rusa was evil and the golden earrings were a bad omen.

I was even more perturbed when Jaime brought up la Rusa at the same time I was thinking about her.

'You know, talking about *duende*, la Rusa was considered to be one of the most powerful possessors of it. I've read accounts of people crying and inflicting all sorts of harm on themselves because they were so moved by one of her performances. I do remember seeing a film with her in it—not one of her glitzy Hollywood ones, but a Spanish flamenco film made before the war. She really *owns* the dance she performs. There's probably a copy of that film in the Conservatoire's library. Do you want me to book a film room and we can watch it together?'

The idea of seeing la Rusa on film frightened me. It was one thing to listen to my beloved Avi on a recording years after his death, but to see la Rusa alive and animated . . . I wasn't sure if I could face that. It might be inviting trouble.

Jaime seemed to have a sixth sense for knowing when I was uncomfortable about something. 'What is it with you and la Rusa?' he asked. 'It's more than interest in her as a phenomenal dancer, isn't it? Does it have something to do with your grandfather?'

I wanted to tell Jaime the truth. But after the way I had shown up on his doorstep that morning, did I need to give him more reasons to think I was unstable? I knew that if I told him about la Rusa, he wouldn't be so insensitive as to laugh in my face, but I was worried it would turn him off me. I lowered my eyes.

'Come on, Paloma,' he said quietly. 'At some point you're going to have to trust me. You're going to have to let me inside that tough shell of yours.'

I took a deep breath. 'Every Spaniard has a ghost, apparently. And I've discovered mine.' I lifted my eyes to see that Jaime was looking attentively at me. I sighed and sat back. 'This is going to sound crazy.'

Jaime smiled. 'I'm Spanish. I understand crazy.'

I tried to imagine how the story of la Rusa's otherworldly visit would sound to me if I were in Jaime's shoes. Still, I took the leap, and relayed the story as factually as I could given the circumstances. I lost courage when I got to the part about the golden earrings, but something about Jaime's open face made me press on anyway.

To my great relief, while Jaime was astonished by my story he didn't seem to think less of me. 'I don't believe la Rusa's come to harm you,' he said. 'You would have felt the danger from her straight away. As it turned out, you took her for a living person at first. I'm sure the visit has something to do with her connection to your grandfather—and perhaps that explains your grandmother's negative reaction when you mentioned her.'

I reached out and squeezed Jaime's hand. After my initial misgivings, I was glad that I'd told him about la Rusa: I desperately needed a confidante and a friend.

It was seven o'clock and dark when Jaime dropped me back at the apartment in rue Spontini.

'Are you sure I can't entice you to have dinner with me?' he asked. 'Maybe we can go dancing afterwards? Have you even been to a disco? I'd like to see you knock some people out when you lift your leg higher than your head.'

I laughed. He obviously hadn't thought my story about my encounter with la Rusa to be so far-fetched that he didn't want to see me again. It's nice to have a Spanish boyfriend, I thought, and one who believes in ghosts.

'I would have loved to go with you to a disco,' I told him. 'But I need to sort things out with Mamie. And Saturday night has always been our special night together.'

'I understand,' he said, touching my chin. And I knew that he did. He kissed me, and then restarted the Vespa. 'Give me a call tomorrow, all right?' he said, before heading down the road. 'Let me know how you are.'

I quickly crossed the courtyard, afraid that la Rusa might reappear after we had spoken so much about her that evening. Conchita's light was on in her apartment and I could hear her listening to the radio. I was tempted to drop in and ask her if she knew why Mamie hated la Rusa so much, but something stopped me. Instead, I continued up the stairs to our apartment. All the lights were off when I entered it. For a moment, I thought Mamie might not be home. But I was relieved when I saw her keys were still on the hook.

She wasn't in the kitchen or the living room, although she'd covered Diaghilev's cage. There were no dishes in the rack. She must have gone straight to her room after the day's classes were over.

I knocked on her door. 'Mamie, I'm home. Are you there?'

There was no answer.

I knocked again. 'Mamie, do you want some supper?'

Silence.

'Mamie! Please say you are all right. I didn't mean to upset you.'

'I'm all right,' her soft voice came back. 'Just leave me alone.'

I went back to the kitchen and cut myself a slice of bread. I wasn't hungry, but I wasn't sure what to do with myself. I wavered from the pleasure I felt about the afternoon I'd spent with Jaime, to the guilt about not having done any practise for my audition, to the upsetting feeling of being alienated from Mamie. In the end, I went to my room to read for a while, so I could put my mind onto something else.

It was almost ten o'clock when Mamie knocked on the door.

'Can I come in?' she asked.

'Please,' I said, sitting up.

Mamie was pale. It was obvious from her puffy eyes that she'd been crying. She sat down on my bed. I put the cover over her shoulders to keep her warm.

'I'm so sorry, Mamie,' I said. 'I never meant to upset you. I won't bring her up again.'

Mamie shrugged. 'I am more shocked at myself,' she said. Then she sighed and stared at her hands. 'I didn't always despise la Rusa,' she said. 'There was a time when I admired her greatly. Your grandfather introduced us, you know . . .'

A faraway look came into Mamie's eyes. I sat back against the pillows, knowing it was time for another story.

*   *   *

For some reason, I had woken early that morning. The dawn light was seeping through the curtains of the bedroom I shared with Margarida. Although it was spring, the air was still chilly and I tugged the lace-trimmed quilt up to my neck and stared up at the ceiling light fixtures. With their domed glass and silver tips they reminded me of ramekins of crema Catalana, although Margarida said that to her they looked like breasts with elongated nipples. Gaspar Olivero's face loomed up in my imagination, as it did every morning even though I hadn't seen him for nearly a year. At first, when he didn't appear at the opera again or at any of the social functions hosted by the Cerdà family, I was worried my mother had warned him away. But when I asked Xavier about him, he said that Gaspar had finished his law degree, but instead of joining a firm he was making a successful career of playing music in venues around Spain and South America.

While my 'courtship' with Francesc seemed to be progressing well, according to the doyennes of Barcelona society, he too had a propensity for disappearing for weeks at a time for some sporting activity such as skiing and mountain climbing, or vanishing to Europe or America for car-racing and baseball. And here I am, I thought, not even able to walk to the end of the street without a chaperone!

I turned and looked at Margarida. How had my sister done it? How had she avoided the smothering supervision that went with being 'eligible' and secured for herself a kind of freedom unknown to all the other women in our circle? The latest idea she had was that Spain was soon going to be a republic again and she was going to join the parliament to represent women and the poor. I prayed to God that she wouldn't express that idea to Pare, otherwise my parents might lock *me* up and throw away the key! When I thought about it further, I saw that Margarida could enjoy her freedom because she cared nothing for marriage or having children. I wanted children, so I had no choice but to obey the rules.

I rested my hands behind my head. I had resigned myself to the idea that I would have to marry Francesc, but that didn't stop me thinking about Gaspar. I imagined scenarios where we would meet again at the Liceu, or at a soirée, and the Olivero fortune and name would somehow have been restored. Then my parents would agree that Gaspar and I were a good match. I had no idea how he felt about me—I couldn't be anywhere near as exciting as the exotic people he must be meeting on his travels—but losing myself in these fantasies helped me cope with being powerless to control my own destiny or to choose for myself.

I was drifting back to sleep when Mama's voice woke me. 'Margarida! Evelina!' The urgency in her tone roused me. I sat up to see her standing in the doorway in her dressing gown. 'Come quickly!'

She looked pale and frightened. My first thought was something had happened to Feliu. 'Is everybody all right?' I asked.

'What's happened?' asked Margarida, rubbing her eyes.

'Just hurry!' ordered Mama. 'Before the servants wake up!'

Margarida and I jumped out of our beds and tugged on our dressing gowns and slippers before following Mama out of the room. My worst fear came to life again when she led us towards Conchita and Xavier's apartment.

'Is Feliu all right?' I asked.

Mama turned and put her finger to her lips. 'Yes, he's fine.'

'Crazy Conchita hasn't stabbed Xavier, has she?' Margarida asked.

Mama spun on her heels. 'Whatever do you mean?' she demanded. 'A family does not make jokes like that about each other!'

Although it was unkind of Margarida to have said such a thing, I too had noticed that Conchita's behaviour was becoming more erratic. Immediately after Feliu was born, she had been a doting mother. But as soon as he began to crawl and then walk, her attitude towards him changed. She treated him in the same standoffish manner she treated the servants. Even at only a year old, he often seemed bewildered by her coldness.

We continued up the stairs and into the apartment. Xavier was in the drawing room with Feliu asleep in his lap. My brother's eyes were red-rimmed and the distressed expression on his face upset me. Mama led us into the bedroom where Doctor Castell was standing next to Conchita, who was prostrate on the bed with her wrists wrapped in bandages. She was lying still and staring at the ceiling; every so often she emitted a low groan.

'What is it?' I cried. I glanced at Margarida. Did she know something about Conchita that I didn't?

'This will not go beyond the two of you and your brother,' Mama whispered. 'I'm not even going to tell Pare or the de Figueroa family, do you understand?' Tears came to her eyes and she shook her head. 'And we of all families, such devoted Catholics!'

'I could organise a nurse to watch over her,' said the doctor. 'Her lacerations are not too serious.'

Mama shook her head. 'No, the four of us will do it,' she replied. 'We are her family now and we will take care of her.'

The following morning, I rose early to take over from Xavier in watching Conchita. 'Don't forget to come at ten o'clock,' I reminded Margarida as I dressed. 'I have a class with Olga this morning.'

'You can fuss over Conchita if you want,' said Margarida, 'but I'm not participating in this ridiculous charade.'

'You have to help,' I told her. 'Conchita's your sister-in-law!'

'She's a black hole, that's what she is,' replied Margarida. 'She's destroying Xavier! He sleeps on the sofa because Conchita doesn't want any more babies. She doesn't want to go out, but she complains when they stay in. She's made his life miserable.'

'She can't help it,' I said. 'Can't you see she's sick?'

Margarida sat up and glared at me. 'Sick or manipulative, Evelina? If you think she's sick, then you look after her. I say she's a drama queen who wants attention and expects us to be responsible for her. The sooner everyone stops pandering to her, the better.'

BELINDA ALEXANDRA

'But Margarida,' I pleaded, 'my ballet lesson—'

'It's your decision to give that up for Conchita and her antics,' Margarida replied, rolling over and pulling the covers up around her ears. 'Don't try to put that one on me!'

Conchita was quiet when I sat with her. She ate her breakfast roll thoughtfully, tearing it into small pieces and dipping it into her milky coffee. I watched her and tried to understand what made her so unhappy. In many ways, I related to Conchita. In the de Figueroa family, she was not only the eldest but by far the most beautiful of the sisters, which meant the pressure for a spectacular marriage had been placed firmly on her. Xavier was a devoted husband and father, but that didn't seem to be enough for Conchita. Maybe it was that, like me, she felt she'd never had any choice in her life. I thought about Gaspar and wondered if Conchita had loved someone else but had been pressured by her family to marry Xavier. Apart from their good looks and their wealthy backgrounds, Conchita and Xavier were different. She loved the prestige of being a Montella and Xavier hated it. If they had been free to chose, I doubted they would have chosen each other.

Conchita lifted her eyes to me. 'Evelina,' she said, 'go and open up my wardrobe.'

I thought that she may be feeling well enough to dress for the day, so I did as she asked.

'You see that dress under the organza cover? Take it out.'

When I lifted the cover, my breath was taken away by a shell-pink beaded dress with bell sleeves and intricate lacework around the cuffs.

'I want you to have it,' Conchita said.

'But no!' I protested. 'You've never even worn it!'

She shook her head. 'You'll have to take it in a bit, but it will look beautiful on you. Try it on.'

I did as she said and admired my reflection in the mirror. The sinuous skirt swirled around my legs when I moved, and the slightly tapered waist was more flattering than the previous year's straight styles. Conchita directed me to add a matching mesh hat with white flowers on the side and evening shoes from her wardrobe, then told me to go to her dresser and dab on some Chanel No 5. I had never felt so glamorous. I paraded up and down the room for her and she smiled with genuine delight.

'You should dress up like that every day,' she said. 'It's your turn to be a society princess. Once you get married and become a mother, people don't observe you the same way. You no longer bring expressions of enchantment to their faces when you walk into a room. All the enthralling possibilities you once represented are gone. There is only one predetermined fate for you.'

She pushed her dark hair back from her face. Even though she wasn't well, she was still beautiful. She didn't possess one feature that was less than perfect, from her straight nose to her slim feet. She's too beautiful, I thought. And it's become a curse for her.

I changed back into my ordinary dress and read the social section of the newspaper to Conchita until she fell asleep. I glanced at the clock. It was a quarter to ten. I would have to send someone to tell Olga I wouldn't be having my lesson today.

The bedroom door opened and I turned to see Xavier standing behind me.

'Has she been all right?' he asked.

His clothes seemed to be hanging off him and his shoulders were hunched. He looked as though someone had sucked all the life out of him. I thought about what Margarida had said that morning about how Conchita was ruining him.

'What are you doing here?' I asked. 'You are supposed to be sleeping. You were up all night with Conchita.'

Xavier slumped into the chair on the other side of Conchita's bed. 'Don't you have a ballet lesson at ten o'clock? I don't want you to miss it.'

'But you need my help,' I said.

Xavier rubbed his eyes. 'I don't expect you to suffer because of me. Conchita is my responsibility. I want you to go and enjoy your lesson.'

I moved to his side of the bed and sat on the armrest of the chair. 'What happened, Xavier? Why did she do it?'

A look of anguish came into his eyes. 'I don't know,' he said. 'No matter what I do for her, she is never satisfied. She seemed fine when we said goodnight. Then early yesterday morning I heard a cry come from the bedroom and I rushed in to find her arms covered in blood.'

Xavier and I sat with our cheeks pressed together for a few moments before he nudged me. 'You'd better get going.'

I embraced him. 'Thank you,' I said. I knew in that moment that I loved my brother dearly and that I would do anything to see him happy again.

By early summer, Conchita had recovered enough to be left on her own, and also to accompany Xavier to social functions or to join me and Mama for strolls along the passeig de Gràcia.

One morning, to my surprise, I walked into the drawing room to find Gaspar Olivero sitting there, talking with Xavier and Margarida.

'Evelina! Good morning!' he said, rising to his feet.

Something about him had changed. He had never been shy or awkward and he'd always been a gentleman. But as he stood before me in his pinstriped suit, every hair on his head combed into place, he exuded the kind of polish that must have come from rubbing elbows with some of the most talented people in the world.

'How are your ballet classes progressing?' he asked me.

The mere fact that he'd remembered I was learning ballet made my heart jump with joy.

'Very well,' I told him. 'My teacher is pleased with me.'

'And that prima donna doesn't give praise easily,' added Margarida, glancing from me to Gaspar.

'I dropped by to invite you all to come to the Samovar Club tonight,' Gaspar said. 'I have a table booked for us. The flamenco dancer la Rusa has returned from her world tour and will be giving her first performance in Barcelona in nine years.'

I had no idea who la Rusa was, but I would have gone to see a circus of fleas if it meant I could be with Gaspar again.

He turned to Xavier. 'You must bring Evelina tonight. La Rusa is a stupendous dancer. Her performances are wonderful, really wonderful.'

Xavier invited me to sit down with them, and a maid brought us some coffee and cakes. The conversation moved to Gaspar and his travels, but I didn't hear one word about the clubs in Cuba and Venezuela. All I could think about was what I was going to wear that night. Surely Xavier and Margarida would have to let me go with them to the Samovar Club if Gaspar had invited me? Neither had voiced any objection, which was a good sign.

When Gaspar left, I turned to my brother and sister.

'Can I really go with you this evening?' I asked Xavier.

'Mama would never hear of it!' said Margarida. 'The Samovar Club? They play jazz and people dance the Charleston there. It's too scandalous!' she said in a mocking tone.

I considered trying to make Margarida feel guilty that the reason I was so obsessively guarded was because of her. But I knew Margarida was impervious to guilt. I looked at Xavier, who seemed to be less decided on the matter.

'Please,' I begged him.

'Who is going to chaperone you?' Xavier asked.

'You and Margarida,' I told him.

Margarida laughed. 'As if Mama and Pare would trust me.'

'Then what about Conchita?'

Xavier shook his head. 'She won't want to come, Evelina. It's not her kind of place.'

'Well, that's it,' said Margarida. 'You can't come, Evelina.'

I was crestfallen. To go to the Samovar Club was the only thing I had wanted as much as ballet lessons. But I knew not to be so childish as to cry. I turned and walked out of the room. As I was shutting the door behind me, I heard Xavier say to Margarida, 'I don't see why Evelina can't join us. Mama and Pare don't have to know. We can sneak her out of the house. God knows, you did it yourself often enough!'

'She's not like me,' Margarida replied. 'She'll be seen.' Lowering her voice so that I could only just hear her, she added, 'I'd love her to join us, but it could damage her marriage prospects if the Cerdà family finds out she's been going out at night. It's one thing for me to go to places like that, but people expect differently of her.'

'Come on, Margarida!' said Xavier. 'How often have we seen Penélope Cerdà there? Or Soledad Manzano and the other society girls? They won't tell on each other. Francesc can't say anything if Evelina is there with you and me. He hasn't even formally proposed.'

'It's not Francesc I'm worried about,' Margarida replied.

'Who then?' Xavier asked.

Margarida said something I didn't hear.

'Well, forget Francesc Cerdà!' Xavier said. 'If he's so interested in Evelina, what's he doing in England this summer?'

Margarida sighed. 'You might have chosen differently if you had known about Conchita,' she said. 'But Evelina has no choice. I wouldn't wish on her what I've been through to walk a different path. Be careful with her. Gaspar might be able to flit here and there, but for a woman, one break with society and that's it.'

'The Samovar Club.' I rolled the words over my tongue as I lay on my bed that night. It conjured up exotic images of smoky-eyed women and Tyumen carpets.

I thought about Conchita, convinced that all her possibilities in life were gone. I wasn't a great beauty like she was, but I was in the bloom of youth. I didn't want to end up feeling the way she did. I wanted to believe that life would always be full of possibilities, no matter what my age.

I stood up and walked to the wardrobe, fingering the shell-pink dress Conchita had given me. 'It's your turn to be a society princess,' she had said. Not much chance of that, I thought. I am going straight from maiden to married woman, thanks to Margarida!

I thought about Gaspar Olivero. He had made a special point of asking Xavier and Margarida if I could go that night. What would they tell him? That I wasn't interested? What would he think then?

The house was still and silent. The servants had gone to bed. I slipped off my nightdress and stepped into the dress, admiring my transformed reflection. *A society princess*: it would only take a little powder and a dab of Chanel No 5. I smiled at my reflection and my reflection smiled back at me.

There was a taxi cruising down the passeig de Gràcia. It never occurred to me when I hailed it that it might be dangerous to travel about on my own without a male escort. The only danger I had ever been warned about was the moral kind. I did my best to affect a sophisticated air when I gave the driver my destination. Fortunately for me, the only thing dangerous about the driver was his daredevil nature. But careering through the streets of Barcelona at breakneck speed only added to the thrill of the evening. For once in her life, Evelina Montella was doing something she was not supposed to do!

When I arrived at the Samovar Club, the house band was playing and the dance floor was filled with glamorous men and women dancing the foxtrot. Everything seemed to sparkle and glimmer. The air was tinged with the scent of brandy, expensive tobacco and Bulgarian rose. The atmosphere was much more exciting than the staid luncheons and afternoon tea parties I usually attended. I told the hostess I was a guest of Xavier and Margarida Montella, and she led me to a private lounge with mirrored walls where I found my brother and sister drinking cocktails. Their eyes popped out of their heads when they saw me.

'No, no, no,' said Margarida, rising from her seat.

Xavier looked like he was trying not to laugh.

Margarida grabbed my arm. 'You are going straight home,' she said. 'I will not be responsible for leading you astray!'

She was surprised when I resisted her, and we found ourselves in a wrestling fight when Gaspar walked into the lounge. Margarida let go of me for appearance's sake. Gaspar was wearing a dinner suit with sateen lapels, and spats. He seemed to me more dashing than ever and it took all of my willpower not to ogle him.

'You're *all* here!' he said, grinning from ear to ear. 'I've organised a table at the front so that Evelina can see la Rusa's amazing feet.'

Margarida smiled at Gaspar, but threw daggers at me with her gaze when he wasn't looking.

'Are you playing tonight?' Xavier asked Gaspar.

'No, I took tonight off especially to see la Rusa again. I'll take you round to meet her after her performance. She's really something.'

'I've heard of her,' said Xavier. 'But I've never had the chance to see her perform. Apparently she's danced for the King and Queen.'

Gaspar laughed. 'Indeed! Despite two hours of lectures by the King's staff beforehand on royal protocol, she still treated him like he was anybody else on the street. His entourage was shocked, but I think he was amused. Even Alfonso knows when he is beaten in greatness.'

The hostess arrived to tell us that our table was ready. We turned to follow her.

I flashed my most innocent smile at Margarida. 'I'm staying?'

She shrugged. 'Just be discreet and don't do anything to draw attention to yourself, all right? You are only staying until la Rusa performs and then you are going home!'

On the way to our table, we passed Soledad Manzano and her sisters, who were sitting with the daughters of the Almirall dynasty. All of those girls were chaperoned as closely as I was but none of them seemed surprised to see me there. They merely nodded at me as if I were a member of an exclusive club who had been a bit late in paying her dues.

'I'm glad you could come tonight, Evelina,' Gaspar whispered to me once we were seated. 'I wasn't sure if they were going to allow you. Apart from Muslim women, Spanish women are the most carefully guarded in the world, even here in Barcelona.'

'Too true!' I said, and laughed. A thrill of excitement ran through me. So he *had* been keen for me to come.

'Where's Francesc?' Gaspar asked. 'Is he still in England? I haven't had a chance to catch up with my aunt and uncle yet.'

All the magic of the evening disappeared when Gaspar mentioned Francesc's name. For that night, at least, I wanted to imagine the possibility that I could marry Gaspar and dance the tango with him in Buenos Aires and listen to jazz all night in Havana. But by saying Francesc's name, Gaspar had shattered those dreams. Had he done it intentionally? After all, Francesc was his cousin. Or was it simply that Gaspar did not think of me the same way I thought of him?

I did my best to appear cheerful as the waiter brought us a supper of wild mushroom omelettes and artichokes with cream, as well as a bottle of fine champagne, which Margarida didn't let me taste. The show began with a Russian cabaret singer and a Spanish comedian. After dessert was served, the master of ceremonies introduced la Rusa as a hot-blooded gypsy *bailaora*.

The curtain opened and before us stood a woman with a mane of wavy hair and eyes like onyx. She was wearing a black dress with a red lace bolero jacket, and stood like a statue as the orchestra began to play. After a minute or so of utter stillness, during which the air of suspense in the audience became palpable, her eyes suddenly sprang to life and she bestowed a gaze on us that was at once haughty and dignified. Then she stamped her foot—one! two! three times!—like a bull preparing to charge, and began to dance in counterclockwise circles. I had never seen anything like it. Her castanets sounded like rattlesnakes; her feet beat the floor like bullets. Her fierceness challenged everything I believed about dance, about softness of movement and refinement. She was like a savage and yet every wild movement of her body was precise, from her turns to her *zapateados*.

The audience 'Ooh'd' and 'Ah'd' before falling silent, dazed by the sheer explosion of energy before them. As la Rusa danced, I found myself thinking, this woman is full of anger and violence, but I couldn't look away. I was as drawn in by her magnetism as everyone else was.

The music stopped, but la Rusa continued with some wild spinning turns before a furious finale in which she accompanied herself with her own percussive footwork and *palmas*, as the gypsies did when they danced. The audience rose to its feet, applauding and cheering.

La Rusa did not curtsey, as Olga had taught me to do in ballet, or make a humble bow as the Russian cabaret singer had done when she'd finished her act. She stood still, regarding us with her hands on her hips. In many ways the arrogant manner in which she looked down at us was shocking, but probably the most shocking thing about it was that it was justified. Unlike Conchita, la Rusa's features were not of perfect proportions— she had a large mouth, a broad nose and sharp cheekbones—and yet she possessed the kind of beauty that put women like Conchita in the shade. The sheer force of her conviction in who she was mesmerised the audience. She was the most captivating person I had ever seen.

I turned to say something to Xavier, but was taken aback by the expression on his face. He was regarding la Rusa as if a thousand thoughts were rushing through his mind at once. While I had been fascinated, it was clear to me that something much stronger had overcome him. The disturbing feeling I had experienced that day in the Old Cemetery when I had spied Xavier and Margarida at the paupers' plot returned to me: a dread of something sinister lurking in the future.

*　　*　　*

Mamie's voice slipped away and she became lost in her thoughts. I sat on the edge of my bed, spellbound by the image of la Rusa that Mamie's story had conjured in my mind. I decided that I would accept Jaime's offer to see the film of la Rusa dancing—I felt impelled to witness this force of nature for myself. From the description Mamie had given of la Rusa as a strong, self-possessed woman, I understood why it was hard for people who had known her to believe that she had committed suicide.

'Mamie,' I said, when I felt brave enough to speak, 'when you said that Xavier was betrayed by someone he once loved . . . a wild animal that he thought he'd tamed . . . did you mean la Rusa? Was she the one who turned on him?'

Mamie didn't answer me. She showed no indication that she had even heard me. After the argument we'd had that morning, I wasn't brave enough to repeat my question. It was left hanging in the air like an unsolved mystery.

Twenty-Four

Celestina

I hurried to my dressing room after my return performance at the Samovar Club, the sound of the audience's applause ringing in my ears. The star dressing room had been refurbished and was an elegant haven of full-length mirrors and Louis XV chairs. I pulled off my dress and shoes and wrapped myself in a silk robe before flopping onto the chaise longue. The room was quiet now that el Ruso had banned Diego and the others from visiting it. In New York, Raquel had started a fire while frying sardines in my dressing room in Carnegie Hall. El Ruso had footed the bill for the damage but hadn't forgiven my clan. 'When are you going to wake up?' he'd demanded. 'They are using you!' But el Ruso didn't understand how much I dreaded being alone: that noise and activity kept me safe from my memories.

Without the presence of my clan, the dressing room didn't smell of fish but of roses and lilies from the bouquets spread across the dresser and end tables. I rubbed my temples and closed my eyes, intending to rest for a while before joining el Ruso and some important guests for a celebratory dinner later. But even with the sound of the orchestra in the background and the clomping footsteps of the chorus girls running up and down the stairs, the room was too quiet. I sat up and wandered to the dressing table to read the cards that accompanied the bouquets. *You are the sparkling diamond of the city*, the Mayor of Barcelona had written.

There was a package too. I tugged away the ribbon and tore open the tissue paper to find a hand-embroidered shawl inside, with vibrant crimson roses stitched onto the cream silk and its four sides finished with hand-knotted fringing. It would have been worth a few thousand *pesetas*. I picked up the envelope that had been tucked inside the box, wondering who would have given me such a gift. Inside was an invitation to a bullfight signed by Salazar. My heart sank. I hadn't seen him since my Villa Rosa days and had hoped he'd forgotten me. I cringed when I remembered his cruel face and the deranged look in his eyes.

I sat down on the dressing table stool and rubbed my feet. Although flamenco, gypsies and bullfighting were intertwined, I had never been to a *corrida* and had no desire to go. Teresa, Carme and many other women in Damas Rojas had spoken vehemently against bullfights, calling them 'spectacles of torture and death'. I simply saw them as unfair. The bull had to face not only the matador but also *picadores* on horseback and *banderilleros* who repeatedly stabbed him to weaken him. I'd heard they even rubbed olive oil in the bull's eyes while it was still in the stall so it couldn't see properly. It was only when the bull was exhausted from blood loss and pain that the matador moved in for the kill. Where was the courage in that? If the bull killed the matador—which I would consider a victory on its part—it was still killed. The one-sidedness of the fight made me think of my father shouting his protests against the Civil Guard before being shot in the neck. I shuddered at the memory of his blood flowing out of him. Even after all these years it gave me a razor-sharp pain in my heart.

I shoved the shawl into the bottom drawer of my dresser. I'd burn it when I had the chance. There was a box of chocolates from Zakharov on my dressing table and I ate a sweet, creamy one to get rid of the bitter taste in my mouth.

A knock sounded at the door. I didn't answer at first. While I missed my clan, I'd set a rule that wherever I performed no audience members were permitted to visit my dressing room. In South America they'd had to position armed guards near my door to keep the crowds under control. Since I became famous, everybody wanted to know me—or at least to say that they had met me. Every word I muttered was noted down by reporters who jostled with each other to fire questions at me: 'La Rusa, what's your favourite food?'; 'What do you do on your days off?'; 'Describe your ideal man.' I preferred to greet my admirers and sign autographs at the stage door where I had some chance of getting away. I loved stimulation and to be diverted, but deep down I did not really like people.

The knock sounded again. 'La Rusa, I have some guests who want to meet you!' It was Gaspar's voice. I sighed. For Gaspar, I always made an exception.

'Come in,' I answered, tugging on a pair of slippers.

When I looked up to see who Gaspar had with him, I did not recognise the Montella siblings immediately. All I saw were three smartly dressed, youthful individuals with eager expressions. They bore the healthy, well-scrubbed look of people with money.

'La Rusa, let me introduce you to some good friends of mine,' Gaspar said, waving to them to come inside. 'May I present to you Xavier Montella and his sisters, Margarida and Evelina.'

At the sound of the Montella siblings' names I was hit by a confusion of feelings—a mix of anxiety and fury that made my mind whirl like a boat caught in a stormy swell. For twenty years, the Montella family had been the object of my hate and now its heir and his two sisters were standing right before me! The serpent in my heart uncoiled and rose in fury, but it did not strike. Why, I did not know. Perhaps its instinct told it to wait for the right moment.

The threesome took my hesitation as the reticence of a haughty star, which seemed to make them keener to tell me how much they had enjoyed my show.

'You were stunning, senyoreta!' Margarida said. I remembered her as the innocent girl who had held my hand without reservation before being scolded by her nursemaid.

'Your precision is inspiring,' gushed Evelina. She was graceful and refined, as I'd imagined she would grow up to be.

It was Xavier Montella who surprised me the most. I'd always supposed that he'd turn out a replica of his father: pug-nosed, self-assured and arrogant. But then I realised he must be the same Xavier whom Gaspar had mentioned the day he had taken me to the café after senyora Dávilo had transformed me: the Xavier who had been sent to Italy on a grand tour; who was an aficionado of flamenco; and who played piano for the Socialist Club. With his fine features and intelligent eyes, he was strikingly handsome. His eyebrows were the same chestnut colour as his hair. I found it disconcerting to realise that, up close, my arch-enemy was beautiful. I remembered the day I had seen him at the sweatshop with his parents and the way he'd looked at me, as if he were both fascinated and puzzled.

He was staring at me that way now and I realised that he had recognised me. I felt like a soldier who, after months of training, is faced with the enemy and finds himself unable to fire his gun.

'Thank you,' I managed to say. 'I'm glad you enjoyed the show.'

'I was the first person to compose music for her,' Gaspar said proudly.

I barely heard the young women as they prattled on: Margarida expressing how impressed she was to see a woman who was unafraid to dance in a masculine way; Evelina telling me about her own Spanish dance lessons. Only Xavier remained silent, his concentration on me intense.

'Well, we'd better leave you to get ready for your dinner,' said Gaspar finally.

He gave me parting kisses while the others shook my hand. Xavier's grip was warm and firm but I quickly withdrew from it so he wouldn't feel me trembling.

'Yes, thank you again,' I said.

After Gaspar and the Montellas left, I sat down at the dressing table, trying to catch my breath. I stared at my reflection before wiping away my make-up, smearing mascara and crimson lipstick over my face until I resembled an angry kabuki mask. What had I expected? What did I think I was going to do to the Montellas when I saw them again? Shout at them, accuse them and their kind of being murderers? If I wanted revenge, I had to be better prepared than that. I laid my head against the cold glass of the mirror, suffering a sense of helplessness so complete that it turned everything black.

The following night, after I had finished my act and was heading towards the stage door, Xavier Montella approached me.

'Forgive me, senyoreta,' he said. 'I would like to speak to you.'

What was Xavier Montella doing in the backstage corridor? Was he another deranged Salazar? But I didn't see the same madness in Xavier's eyes as I did in the bull breeder's. Nonetheless, I gave him the severe expression I saved for persistent admirers. 'I really don't have time,' I told him. 'I must get home.'

'Of course,' he said. But he didn't move. 'Perhaps you will allow me to take you to dinner?'

Is he out of his mind? I wondered. Could he really have no idea how much I despised him? Or did he, like so many rich men, think that all dancers were whores and easily bought?

Xavier smiled. 'Excuse me, senyoreta, for being so forward. I am sure that many men, captivated by your charms, invite you to dinner. But you see, I have a special reason for asking you. During the general strike of 1909 a boy and girl came with a woman to a factory owned by my father. The woman's name was Teresa Flores García. She was exiled to Alcañiz, along with the boy, where she died a few months later. The boy was taken with the other exiles to be sent to Valencia, but he escaped en route and was never found. I tried to discover the fate of the girl but she seemed to have vanished.' He took a step closer to me and peered into my face. 'You see,' he said, 'I believe that girl was you.'

I was careful to keep my expression impassive but it was difficult to do so at the mention of Ramón's name. My brother had escaped somewhere on the way to Valencia? I shivered when I remembered Gaspar saying that the punishment for an exile returning to Barcelona was death. Although I longed for my brother even after all these years, I'd resigned myself to the fact that we would probably never find each other again. It had been too long.

'Why are you so interested in the girl's fate?' I asked him. 'You obviously have used your contacts to find out about her brother.'

Xavier sighed. 'Because since that day . . . I have been haunted by her face: the hunger on it . . . and something else. She was about eight years old but she seemed ancient. As soon as I was old enough to do so, I made investigations about what happened to her. But I was years too late.'

Xavier's story was so strange. It was not what I had expected of him. He didn't sound like a presumptuous society man at all. Rather, he gave me the impression of someone who was deeply compassionate. But how could that be? To be a compassionate person and a wealthy heir was a contradiction in terms.

My gaze fell to his silk suit, then to his manicured hands and polished patent shoes. Anastasio's blood had paid for that affluent lifestyle. The serpent within me stirred and hissed a warning. There were plenty of starving, homeless children in the city. Why didn't Xavier Montella help them instead of obsessing about one young girl? I was not going to assuage his guilt by saying the girl had grown up to become an international star who divided her time between an apartment in Paris and a ranch in California, and who had jewellery boxes overflowing with diamonds and pearls. Mine was a miraculous exception to the fate of most of the homeless and orphaned children of the city.

I lifted my chin and stared Xavier in the face. 'You are mistaken,' I told him. 'That girl was not me. But I do know the family you are talking about. They were cousins of mine and that is why I resemble the girl. On the whim of a Civil Guard sergeant, she was not taken with her brother and guardian into exile. Instead, she was placed in an orphanage where she was beaten so badly she died.'

Xavier turned pale. The devastated expression on his face shocked me. For a moment I felt sorry for him. But my sympathy faded when I remembered my family and what had happened to them.

'Now, please excuse me,' I said, stepping past him and out the door.

That night I could not stop thinking about Xavier Montella. I remembered the boy at the sweatshop on the day of the general strike and the way he had regarded me with those earnest eyes. Then I remembered Xavier's tortured expression when I'd lied about the fate of the girl he had wondered about for so long. I rolled over and clutched a pillow to my chest. Why was it that as I had plunged my dagger into Xavier Montella's heart, it was my own heart that had cried out and bled? As if by stabbing him, I had mortally wounded myself.

The night after my encounter with Xavier Montella, I was leaving the club when he appeared in the corridor again. He must have been bribing one of the bouncers to get access to the dressing rooms; I would have to speak to el Ruso about it. I slowed my step. If I was truthful with myself, I was afraid of Xavier Montella. Perhaps it was an ancestral fear of the rich and powerful, handed down by my family who, before they had suffered as poverty-stricken industrial workers, had been starving peasants in Andalusia. They had been at the mercy of landowners and had no more rights than slaves. Although I was a woman used to holding my own, something about Xavier Montella made me feel like clay in his hands.

I took a breath and straightened my spine. No, I was la Rusa now, not a poor urchin, and I was not going to be afraid of anyone.

'Why did you lie to me?' Xavier demanded. 'Your name is Celestina Sánchez. Your brother was Ramón Sánchez.'

'Are you a police interrogator now?' I asked, determined that Xavier Montella would not put me on the defensive.

'I asked Gaspar what your real name was,' he said. 'Why did you tell me that you weren't the girl I saw at the factory that day? Why did you lie to me?'

His voice quivered, but there was no trace of anger in it, simply a distress that might have moved me if I hadn't hardened my heart. Whatever Xavier Montella wanted, I wasn't going to give it to him. I'd lost everything that was most precious to me because of his family.

'And in your investigation did you enquire what happened to the girl's father and older brother?' I asked.

Xavier held my gaze for a moment before answering. 'Your brother, Anastasio Sánchez, was killed in Morocco. I don't know about your father.'

The serpent reared its head, preparing to sink its venom into vulnerable skin.

'My brother was killed in Morocco defending the Montella iron ore mines!' I shouted at him. 'My father was shot when he protested that only young men from poor families were being sent to war, while the rich stayed home and played tennis and drove fancy cars they bought with the blood of others!'

The doors to the dressing rooms flew open when people heard my angry voice and the corridor soon filled with entertainers and chorus girls in sequined gowns.

'Are you all right, senyoreta?' asked Pepe, the Italian mime artist. 'Is this scoundrel bothering you?' He hadn't had time to clean off his white face make-up and the stars around his eyes. He pulled himself to his full height of five feet and puffed out his chest. 'Do you want me to get rid of him?'

I turned to Xavier. 'Yes, you were only a boy when that happened, I understand! But your car, your house, your education, your sisters' nice clothes and ballet lessons were all paid for with my brother's blood! And when you are head of your household, if Morocco should flare up again you will send more poor young men like Anastasio to their deaths so that you can go to the opera and keep a country villa!'

A troubled expression came to Xavier's face. He was breathing hard and his mouth moved as if he intended to say something but couldn't find the words.

'Now,' I told him, stepping back towards the performers who were waiting to swarm protectively around me, 'have the good sense to leave me alone!'

I strode back to the safety of my dressing room. Before I reached it, Xavier shouted at me: 'You are wrong, Celestina Sánchez! Everything you say and think about me is wrong!'

I did not see Xavier Montella for a long time after that night at the Samovar Club, but the memory of his distressed face continued to haunt me.

El Ruso took me on a tour of Spain, where I sensed restlessness amongst the people of Madrid, Valencia and Seville. The monarchist dictatorship of Primo de Rivera was becoming increasingly unpopular. While Spain's lack of integration into the global economy had softened some of the worst aftershocks of the Great Depression, unemployment was rife and some important public works were grinding to a halt.

While we were staying in Madrid, the owner of the theatre where I was performing, señor Sáinz, took me and el Ruso out to lunch in a restaurant on the Gran Vía. The wide boulevard with its ornate buildings and elaborately decorated shop windows was my favourite part of the city. El Ruso had bought me a Marin Chiclana flamenco doll there that morning and I placed her as a centrepiece on the table, where the waiters admired her frilly yellow and black lace dress and the rose she wore in her hair. As a child, I had never owned a doll and even though I was a grown woman, I couldn't take my eyes off her.

Señor Sáinz watched me savour a spoonful of the cool and refreshing gazpacho before asking, 'How do you find Madrid?'

'I always love coming here,' I told him. 'The people appreciate flamenco much more than they do in Barcelona.'

'That is true,' he agreed. 'The best of the best flamenco artists always gravitate here.'

As lunch went on, the conversation turned to politics.

'I'm thinking of moving to Paris,' el Ruso told señor Sáinz. 'There is something happening in Spain . . . it's the same sort of disturbed energy that one felt in Russia before the Revolution. I sense that at any moment all order could break down into anarchy.'

Señor Sáinz nodded. 'It's the same tension one feels in the atmosphere before a storm. While I think Primo de Rivera made some good decisions, he let this dictatorship go on too long. He should have moved the country towards a stable constitutional monarchy long before this.'

'The divisions in Spanish society between the rich and the poor, the army and the Church, are so great that the country is a giant fermenting vat which is about to explode,' said el Ruso.

The waiter brought our dessert of fruit flan and *tocino de cielo*.

'You know, the other problem is that things are never black and white,' señor Sáinz said with a thoughtful expression on his face. 'It's not always easy to guess who is your friend and who is your foe. Let me tell you a story about a gentleman I once knew. His name was Félix Gómez and his parents sent him to a seminary as it was the only way their son was going to get a proper education. Father Gómez was given a role as a teacher in an orphanage here in Madrid, and he was brilliant at it. He gave the poorest boys a better quality education than was offered in the most exclusive schools. He was not interested in indoctrinating them, but in encouraging them to use all their faculties. Even without patronage, several of the boys managed to succeed in the civil service and the army. Then Father Gómez made the mistake of asking a priest in a wealthier parish if he would sell some of his church's paintings to fund a school where Father Gómez's teaching method, which was proving so successful, could be taught to other priests. Father Gómez was summoned by the Archbishop, who accused him of being a socialist and dismissed him from the Church.'

The story hardly surprised me. I had seen from my own childhood that the institution of the Church had little to do with the Christian philosophy of loving and helping each other.

'The story does not end there,' said señor Sáinz, pushing aside his plate. 'During the recent riots, some revolutionaries, believing my friend to still be a priest who was disguising himself in plain clothes, bludgeoned him to death!'

I shifted in my seat. Señor Sáinz's story illustrated the worst of human stupidity. The revolutionaries had killed someone who had been an excellent educator and could have improved many people's lives. Furthermore, Father Gómez had not only been willing to help the poor but was passionate about doing so. But they'd killed him simply because they'd associated him with an oppressive institution.

I thought of Xavier Montella, and wondered if I was so dissimilar from those foolish revolutionaries.

TWENTY-FIVE

Paloma

After I awoke on Sunday morning and finished my barre and floorwork, I expected Mamie to begin telling her story again. But as we ate parsnip soup in the kitchen together for lunch, she barely glanced at me. Her introverted manner gave me the impression that she was either mulling over something before continuing, or that she was hesitating about finishing the story altogether.

I hung around the apartment, waiting for Mamie to say something. I moved Diaghilev's cage to the studio, and let him fly around while I cleaned his perches and food dishes. I sorted the cutlery drawer so that I wouldn't be too far away from Mamie, who was reading the newspaper at the kitchen table. But still she said nothing.

I carried the telephone to my bedroom and called Jaime. The sound of his voice made me happy in a way I had never felt before. It was as if I'd received some wonderful news, it lifted my spirits so much.

'Is everything all right?' he asked.

'Yes, Mamie and I made up. She spoke a lot about Spain last night.'

'I'm glad,' he said. 'I have to complete an assignment this afternoon but would you like to see a film with me during the week?'

Again that feeling that something amazing was happening to me tingled in my toes.

'*L'Important c'est d'aimer* is showing or there is an American movie, *Jaws*,' he said.

'*Les Dents de la mer*,' I told him. 'That's the French title.'

'Only the French could give a horror film such a romantic-sounding title,' Jaime laughed.

I laughed too. 'If the film was released in Spain the title would be twenty words long and give away the plot!'

'That's true,' said Jaime, still laughing. 'Maybe with every-thing that is going on we should see a comedy—to lighten things a bit. I've heard *Le Sauvage* with Catherine Deneuve and Yves Montand is good. I'll find out where it's screening.'

I told Jaime that I would like to see the film of la Rusa that he had mentioned as well. Then we talked for a while longer before Carmen needed to use the telephone.

'I'll let you know about the la Rusa film,' Jaime promised, before he hung up.

After returning the telephone to the hallway, I went back to the kitchen where Mamie was still reading the paper. She looked up at me. 'Who were you talking to on the telephone?'

'The nephew of my flamenco teacher. Jaime.'

Mamie studied me for a moment and then smiled. 'You were laughing a lot. Do you like him?'

I nodded.

Mamie indicated that I should sit down at the table. I took the seat opposite her. 'It's good to be in love,' she said, a thought-ful expression coming to her face. 'But it's complicated too.'

I sighed with relief. So she was going to tell me more about Spain after all.

When Francesc wrote to his parents that he was intending to stay yet another month in England, Mama decided matters had got out of hand.

'Does he think our Evelina is a wallflower who is going to wait for him all summer?' she said to Pare. 'As there has been no formal engagement, I am going to let it be known that we are happy for Evelina to be introduced to sons of other families.'

While my courtship with Francesc had been taken for granted, I had been given some reprieve from the rounds of afternoon teas, supper parties and balls the other debutantes had to attend. Now that Mama was on a mission to find me alternative fiancés, I appeared at social events with greater frequency: the Liceu, the de Figueroa family's summer ball, the Manzano family's garden party, tennis and croquet matches. I was everywhere except where I most wanted to be: with Gaspar.

When the Marqués and Marquesa learned that my parents were no longer considering Francesc exclusively, they must have panicked and written him a letter demanding that he return as soon as possible. Margarida and I were invited by Penélope Cerdà to spend a few weeks at the family's summer residence at S'Agaró on the Costa Brava.

'Please, Mama,' complained Margarida, 'don't sentence me to spending time with the aristocratic bores who hang around S'Agaró. They are so pretentious!'

'You should be pleased,' scolded Mama. 'The Marqués and Marquesa are spiriting Evelina away because they don't want to lose her as a future daughter-in-law.'

Margarida sighed. 'At least you can be happy, Mama, that your scare tactics are so effective!'

The Cerdà family's summer residence was a bougainvillea-covered villa perched on a headland overlooking the Mediterranean. Most mornings, Margarida hid herself away somewhere in the formal garden to read, while Penélope and I went to the beach to sunbathe and to swim in the calm bay. We were watched over by the gardener's stocky wife, who peeled potatoes sitting under an umbrella while Penélope and I spread our beach mats out near the rocks and turned our faces to the sun. Tans were fashionable that year.

'I was surprised when I saw you at the Samovar Club,' Penélope told me, looking around to check that there weren't any fishermen on the beach before slipping the straps of her swimming costume off her shoulders.

'You won't tell your parents, will you?' I begged her. 'I snuck out of the house.'

'So did I!' She laughed, tossing back her head. She had a long sleek neck, slender legs and the Nordic looks of her parents. I was grateful that she had lent me one of her fashionable thigh-length swimming costumes so I didn't have to wear the hideous knee-length tank suit my mother had packed for me.

'What did you think of la Rusa?' I asked. 'She was amazing, wasn't she?'

'Indeed she was!' agreed Penélope. 'What about those eyes of hers? They were the eyes of a woman who has *seen* things!'

'Her dancing was brilliant. I hope I will see her perform again soon.'

Penélope sat up and brushed the sand from her legs. 'Well, luckily for you Francesc likes to go out, so I'm sure you will have an exciting nightlife when you are married. I'm to be engaged to Felip Manzano, who rises at dawn to ride his horses. We are going to be in bed by ten o'clock! Still, he is very good-looking, so our children are sure to be beautiful.'

'How many children do you want?' I asked her.

She squinted in the direction of the water. 'Four: two boys and two girls. And you?'

I thought of cute Feliu with his button nose. 'As many as I can,' I replied.

We both laughed.

'Well, you'll be able to start a family soon,' said Penélope. 'Francesc has promised to return no later than the fifteenth of next month. I know for a fact that my grandmother's engagement ring has been sent to the jewellers to be cleaned and refitted. I have a sneaking suspicion that's for you because my mother asked your mother for your ring size.'

My heart sank. Another girl might have been thrilled that she was marrying the attractive son of a noble family, but I was despondent. All my fantasies of how Gaspar and I could be together had come to naught and the reality of what my future was going to be was starting to hit me. I lay back and turned my head, shading it with my hat as if I were protecting it from the sun when what I was really doing was hiding the tears that were welling in my eyes. Luckily for me, Penélope assumed I'd fallen asleep.

A few days later, I was playing in the garden with the Cerdàs' two sheepdogs, Fiesta and Torero, when I heard excited voices coming from the house. One voice in particular caught my attention.

'I've been staying with some artist friends in Cadaqués,' Gaspar was saying. 'I thought I'd drop by and see how everyone is.'

'Well, Margarida and Evelina Montella are staying with us. Why don't you join us for dinner this evening?'

I didn't hear the conversation after that, but a few moments later, everyone burst out of the house and headed towards me. Gaspar was wearing a blue blazer and white pants. His copper-coloured hair blew in the breeze. A playful glint danced in his eyes. I thought he was the most beautiful man alive. I realised that while I liked Francesc, I would never experience with him what I felt when I saw Gaspar: the thrills and butterflies of falling in love.

Margarida was called from the gazebo. 'Look who's here!' said Penélope, wrapping her arm around Gaspar. 'My long-lost cousin!'

'Why don't you young people go for a walk on the beach?' suggested the Marquesa. 'Gaspar's been working at nights. He could do with a bit of sun.'

The afternoon light was bright on the golden sand. The rocks beneath the clear water made the bay look like a map of the world. Margarida and Penélope found a common subject in the poetry of Lorca and walked on ahead of us, with the dogs leaping and prancing about them.

Gaspar lingered behind with me. 'You're more quiet than usual today, Evelina.'

My first instinct was to look away. I was so awed to be with him, I didn't know what to say.

'I hear Francesc is on his way back from England earlier than expected.' Gaspar stared at the water and sighed before turning back to me. 'He's a lucky man. I wish he'd appreciate it more.'

And then I knew. I could see it in Gaspar's eyes. He felt the same way about me as I did about him. But how could we even begin to broach this subject?

'I am lucky too that Francesc wants to marry me,' I said. 'But not lucky enough that . . .' I couldn't finish the sentence. I wasn't bold enough.

'That what?' asked Gaspar, looking at me with interest.

I had a lump in my throat. My tongue felt rough and I was afraid that if I tried to speak I'd only stutter. Once I said what was on my mind there would be no going back. If I was mistaken and Gaspar didn't feel the same way, he would never be comfortable around me again. Could I live with that? Wasn't it better to at least have him nearby even if I was married to Francesc? But I knew I could never be at peace unless I opened up to him.

'I'm not lucky enough to be marrying the man I really love,' I said.

Our eyes met. An expression flashed across Gaspar's face that was both elated and troubled. He'd understood my meaning perfectly.

'Maybe I should have done something,' he said, pursing his lips. 'Maybe I should have acted sooner.' He shook his head. 'I thought by going away . . . well, I didn't understand how you felt. I tried to forget you.'

'Gaspar . . .' But I couldn't say what I wanted to say. My heart was too full.

He glanced cautiously at the others, but they were busy throwing sticks for the dogs. I didn't care if they noticed or not. All I cared about was that Gaspar loved me.

'My life is not only music,' he said. 'Every country I visited, I wished you were there so you could see everything with me. I imagined you dancing in the streets with me for the Carnivale Rio, or drinking cocktails with me at the Park View Hotel in Havana.'

My heart leapt with joy. Every day that I had been thinking of Gaspar, he had been thinking of me. But he was sad.

'Francesc has everything I can't give you: a title, a family heritage, a fortune. Your father would never give me your hand even if I asked him.'

A pain stabbed my heart. If Pare had been so indulgent of Margarida, why couldn't he allow me to live the life I wanted too?

'Then we'll elope!' I said.

Gaspar shook his head. 'I would never put you through a scandal. It's not only about being happy now, but about being contented in ten, twenty, thirty years from now. Could you be happy with me if I made you desert your family? Think of the shame it would bring on them.'

I tried to fight my tears. It was awful being a Montella. We weren't a family: we were an institution. We didn't have individual rights to happiness.

'Evelina,' Gaspar said gently, 'don't give up hope. I'll ask Xavier. Perhaps he's guessed our feelings, I don't know. Maybe he will speak on my behalf to your father. I will work like a slave for you, Evelina. I will never leave you wanting for anything. But if I take the risk of asking for your hand and your parents don't approve, they may prevent me from seeing you again. Are you prepared for that? To gamble everything?'

'Yes!' I told him. 'Yes, I am prepared to lose everything on the chance I could win you!'

It was impossible to get through dinner calmly that evening, my stomach was so churned with excitement and anxiety. On the one hand, I liked being at the same table with Gaspar. I was blissful in the knowledge that our feelings were mutual. On the other hand, I felt deceitful. The Cerdà family had invited me and Margarida as guests with the expectation that I was soon to be their daughter-in-law. They would feel betrayed if I married Gaspar instead of Francesc. I tried to calm myself, but my mind was crammed with competing thoughts and my heart with confused feelings.

'Are you all right, Evelina?' the Marquesa asked me. 'You're quite pale.'

'It's that squid we ate for lunch,' said the Marqués. 'It certainly didn't agree with me. I'll have to speak to the cook.'

'Have faith,' Gaspar told me before he left that evening. 'Be strong for me, Evelina.'

I didn't fall asleep until late that night. I tossed and turned, and when I rose in the morning, I was burning with a fever. Margarida took advantage of my ill appearance to suggest that we return to Barcelona.

'She misses Mama too much,' she told our hosts.

'That's understandable,' said the Marquesa, smiling at me indulgently before whispering to her husband, loud enough for me to hear, 'I was the same on the eve of my engagement.'

I wasn't any calmer in Barcelona than I had been in S'Agaró. When would Gaspar speak to Xavier? What would Xavier say? If he agreed, when would he ask my father? And every day, Francesc's return grew closer. I lost several kilos in weight from worry.

One day, after my ballet lesson, Xavier asked to see me in the study. His face was solemn, but he was my brother and loved me so I tried not to worry.

'I guess you know that Gaspar has spoken with me?' he said.
I nodded. My throat felt dry. Why did Xavier sound so grave?

He looked at me with those eyes that matched mine perfectly
in colour, then he stared at his hands for a moment before saying,
'As you can see, Conchita and I are not happy together. If I could
wish you anything, Evelina, it would be a marriage that brings
you joy as well as security. Francesc is a good-hearted fellow but
he is not Gaspar.' He paused and smiled. 'I can fully understand
why you have fallen in love with Gaspar. If I had been born a
woman, I would have fallen in love with him too!'

My heart lifted.

Xavier reached out his hand to me and I took it. 'I know that
if you and Gaspar were allowed to marry, he would devote his
life to your well-being. He has offered to give up working as a
musician and take up law, or work for one of the Montella
companies, if that would make our parents approve of him. I will
speak to Pare and Mama, Evelina. I will put forward the case
for your happiness as strongly as I can. But also understand that
I may not succeed. Our parents have devoted their lives to building up the Montella fortune and name. We are not like other
people. The burden of our position in society means that we
cannot always do as we please.'

A few days after that discussion, Gaspar arrived at our house
looking more nervous than I had ever seen him. I met him in the
foyer and brushed his hand lightly, before he disappeared into
the drawing room to meet Pare, who thought Gaspar was coming to see him about a business proposal, having no idea of our
feelings for each other.

'I'll come and speak to you afterwards,' promised Xavier. 'Now
go to your room and have faith. Pray for us.'

As I lingered near the top of the stairs, I heard Xavier escort-
ing Mama to the drawing room. It was Catalan mothers who
decided on their children's wedding partners and it would have
been foolish not to include her in the discussion. I already knew
where Mama stood regarding Gaspar. My hope was that if

Xavier could convince Pare the match was suitable, Pare in turn might persuade Mama to agree.

I was glad that Margarida was out for the day. I found it impossible to settle my mind while my future was being decided downstairs. Dear God, I prayed. Please let me and Gaspar be together. I stayed in that agitated state for nearly an hour. But the longer I waited, the more hope I felt. I reasoned that if my parents had refused to give any consideration to Gaspar's proposal, the conversation would have been over by now.

I heard voices in the foyer and glanced out my door to see Gaspar leaving. Whether a proposal had been accepted or not, it was the custom for the suitor to leave immediately so the parents could discuss the matter with their child privately. When I ran back to my window and saw Gaspar getting into his car, I realised there was a flaw in our plan. I had not told him that I would be watching from the window and to wave if all had gone well. I chastised myself for not having had that foresight. All I could do now was brace myself for whatever news Xavier would bring.

Another half an hour passed before Xavier came to my door. His mouth was pinched. He shook his head. My heart pounded in a sickening way when I realised it was all over. I barely heard Xavier when he said that Gaspar had spoken from the heart and that he, my brother, had argued passionately that I should be given free choice in deciding on my marriage partner.

'Pare said that you have been promised to Francesc Cerdà and that was it. Mama added that it wasn't simply a marriage between two young people but a joining of two important lineages.'

'It's medieval,' I said.

Although I knew we'd had a slim chance of changing my parents' minds, the refusal came as a shock. I was wobbly on my feet. Xavier wrapped his arm around me. He didn't try to console me with words, understanding that there was nothing to be said. As a man, he had some chance of finding solace outside his unhappy marriage to Conchita, but there would be no such outlet for me. The truth was terrible: I was to be a prisoner. And what for? An alliance?

The image of Gaspar leaving came back to me.

'Gaspar!' I cried. I clasped Xavier's shoulders. 'Xavier, I must speak to him! Gaspar and I must at least be able to say goodbye.'

Xavier shook his head. 'He's gone, Evelina. He's going back to South America. It's for the best.'

I moved away from Xavier and sat down on the bed. So that nervous exchange of hope in the foyer was to serve as my last contact with Gaspar? I pressed the heels of my palms to my eyes but nothing could soothe my throbbing head.

When I looked up again, Mama was standing in the doorway. I stared at her, like someone peering through a fog.

'I'd like to speak to Evelina alone,' she told Xavier.

After Xavier had left, Mama came and stood next to me. 'Didn't I warn you not to entertain thoughts of someone who is beneath you, Evelina? You brought this unhappiness on yourself—and him.'

I glanced up at her. 'How can Gaspar be beneath me?' I asked. 'He is more intelligent and talented than all of us put together.'

Mama frowned. 'In social status, I mean.'

Her eyes fell to my hands. While waiting for Pare's decision, I had bitten my nails and they were now rough and shabby.

I turned away from her. 'That's important to you and Pare. It's not what matters most to me.'

Mama sighed. 'Maybe not now. But trust me, it's important. Do you think Pare and I are so callous as to not consider your happiness? Believe me, happiness runs out quickly when you don't have a decent home and can't give your children a stable life.'

'Gaspar is very successful—'

Mama raised her voice to cut me off. 'He has no name,' she said. 'His parents squandered away their place in society. And you are a *Montella*. Young love doesn't last, Evelina. What counts is mutual respect.'

I shrugged. Mama and I didn't seem to speak the same language any more.

'I don't think under the circumstances I should become engaged to Francesc Cerdà. It wouldn't be right.'

Mama prickled. 'The only people who know about this ridiculous state of affairs are your immediate family. I intend to keep it that way.' She grabbed my face and turned me so that we were looking into each other's eyes. Her fingers pressed into my skin so hard I was sure they'd leave bruises. 'You will accept Francesc Cerdà's proposal, do you hear? And you will be married before the end of September. Put your foolish notions about Gaspar Olivero out of your mind now. It's over! Finished! We will not speak of it again.'

The next two months of my life were a blur. Francesc returned from England and proposed. I accepted because I had no other choice. I felt a certain detachment as we went on the rounds of visits and I showed off the diamond and sapphire engagement ring that had once belonged to Francesc's grandmother. I didn't feel that the ring belonged to me, as I felt my own life no longer belonged to me. If I could not marry the man I truly loved, how could I be real? I was a spectator watching a game.

As I walked down the aisle of Basílica de la Mercè alongside my father, I could smell orange blossoms and lilies mixed with the scent of dust and damp stone that always permeated the baroque church's interior. In keeping with Catalan tradition, Francesc and his mother proceeded down the aisle in front of us. The dimness of the church and the halos of light from the chandeliers and candles added to the surreal atmosphere. I put one foot in front of the other, watching the hem of my lace dress sway with each step. I was lost in a hypnotic trance.

I glanced up and saw Mama sitting in the front pew, sobbing into her handkerchief. Margarida was weeping too. Only Xavier, dear Xavier, smiled for me, although his eyes were sad. Did he think he had failed me?

When Francesc and I were left at the altar to stand alone before the priest, my pulse pounded in my temples so violently that I thought I might faint. The aroma of frankincense from the priest's censer was overwhelming. I remembered Gaspar telling me the night we saw la Rusa that the incense was made from the hardened resin of the boswellia tree, and this hardened resin was referred to as 'tears'. Gaspar, he was always full of interesting facts, I thought. I saw his face before me, those alert eyes and ready smile. I heard his soothing voice in my ear: *Have faith. Be strong for me, Evelina.*

I glanced at the statue of Our Lady of Mercy. I had cried so much over my loss of Gaspar that I couldn't cry any more. There was no more hope. There was only surrender.

Francesc touched my elbow and brought my mind back to the present. 'You look beautiful,' he whispered.

He was so warm and kind that it bolstered my spirits a little. At least my parents weren't marrying me off to a monster. If I had never met Gaspar, I would have probably been happy to wed Francesc. It was a match that made my parents happy, the Cerdàs were pleasant people, and Francesc was handsome and possessed a fun personality. But I could not be happy now, and I was beginning to accept that I never would be. I thought of Conchita, sitting with my family and looking beautiful in her dress of turquoise silk. But her eyes were hollow and her mouth was stretched taut. Would I look like that ten years from now?

Although the church was crowded and the priest conducted a full Mass, the wedding ceremony seemed to be over in a few minutes. Before I knew it, my veil was lifted, the engagement ring that I had worn on my right hand had now become the wedding ring on my left ring finger, and Francesc and I were walking down the aisle as man and wife.

Outside, the early autumn light was fading. The guests cheered their congratulations and the feeling of being outside my body returned to me. Mama, Pare, Margarida and Xavier were standing together and I realised that I would never live with them again. From now on, I would be part of the Cerdà household. I looked at the Marqués and Marquesa and Penélope and suddenly they felt like complete strangers. And exactly how little I knew about my husband, I was soon to find out.

Mamie came back from her memories as the winter sky outside began to darken. I'd had no idea that she had been married before Avi. The troubles and the separation their love had endured cast them in a new light. Instead of being simply my grandparents, I saw them as romantic figures. I was dying to ask Mamie how, if she had been married to Francesc, she had ended up with Avi, but I was beginning to understand how complicated her life in Barcelona had been, and how many other people it had involved, and I knew that I had to be patient. I had to let Mamie tell the story her way.

She suddenly stared at me as if she had forgotten I was sitting with her. 'I knew something was wrong the first night of our marriage,' she said, a troubled expression on her face. 'After the wedding dinner, which finished in the early hours of the morning, Francesc and I returned to the Cerdà mansion where we were to spend the night before leaving for our honeymoon the following day. Our suite had been newly decorated and the walnut furniture contrasted beautifully with the cheerful yellow-papered walls. In the bedroom was a king-sized bed with monogrammed pearl-white pillows and a silver-grey satin cover. Francesc and I both stared at it.

'Mama had explained what was expected of me as a wife and, although I was exhausted, I brushed out my hair and put on the lace nightgown that had been part of my trousseau. Francesc fixed himself a nightcap. There were bowls of gardenias around the room, which gave the air a heavenly scent. Opposite the bed was a painting of blush-pink camellias, my favourite flowers. I knew Mama had put it there for me. I lay on the bed, feeling awkward and nervous. I wondered how different things might have been if I had married Gaspar. I imagined his soft lips kissing my neck, his warm hands gripping my waist . . . then I stopped myself. To think about a man other than Francesc now was a sin.'

Mamie paused for a moment, her eyes on my face. She seemed to be having trouble finding the words she wanted to say. I wanted her to go on but I was also afraid of what I might hear.

'Francesc turned off the light and undressed in the dark,' Mamie continued. 'The bed dipped with his weight when he slipped in beside me. I clenched my teeth, wondering what would happen next.

'"Well, it's a relief that ceremony is all over," he said at last. "It was more for our parents than for us."

'I giggled. It was so like Francesc to say something like that. "And for God, too," I reminded him. "It's important to be joined before God."

'"Yes, of course," he agreed.

'We became silent again. For a moment I thought he had fallen asleep, but then he got up again and went to the bathroom. I could hear him turning the taps on and off for what seemed like an eternity. I wondered what he was doing. I felt foolish lying in the dark, so I turned on the side lamp. After more splashing sounds from the bathroom, Francesc returned and seemed surprised to find that I was still awake. He climbed into bed next to me and stared at the ceiling. I stared at the ceiling too. Was it possible Francesc was as nervous as I was? He was older than me, and with all the travelling he had done, Mama had told me not to be upset if he seemed "experienced".

'Francesc lay still for another few minutes before a sort of resolve seemed to come over him. He reached across my chest and turned off the light. Then he made a move that was more like a doctor about to perform an operation than an amorous husband about to make love to his wife for the first time. He tugged up my nightdress and lowered himself over me. I gritted my teeth and anticipated the pain Mama had warned me to expect. But all I felt was something fleshy and soft rubbing against me. Absolutely nothing happened.'

I shifted uncomfortably in my seat. Why is Mamie telling me about her first sexual experience? I wondered, feeling a little queasy. Nobody likes to imagine their grandmother making love, and Mamie was normally on the prudish side about such things. I couldn't boast any experience myself, but thinking of the women's magazines I'd read, it sounded as if Francesc was nervous or had consumed too much alcohol during the dinner.

Mamie looked at me pointedly. 'Nothing happened the next night in Paris either—or the night after that. In fact, we never consummated the marriage. I was young and inexperienced but I knew something was terribly wrong, especially after Mama had told me to be understanding about the fact that men had strong appetites. Francesc wasn't interested in making love with me at all. Then, not long after we returned from our honeymoon, he told me that he was planning to go to the Moroccan Grand Prix.

'"Africa is no place for a woman," he said. "You'd better stay here. Penélope will keep you company."

'Although I tried to carry on as normal, the sense of something being wrong was always there. And the failure of this part of my marriage brought back the pain I had tried to suppress over Gaspar. Now it was so great, I was afraid it would engulf me. I distracted myself with ballet lessons, which I now took every day, bending and stretching myself to my limits. There was no one I could talk to about such things. How could I tell my mother or even a priest? Sex was considered something necessary for children, but shameful at the same time.'

Mamie paused a moment to go to the sink and pour herself a glass of water.

'So Francesc was impotent?' I asked. 'He couldn't father children?'

Mamie shook her head. 'He tried to be a good husband but he simply preferred men.'

I sat with my mouth open. I could hardly believe what she had said. 'Your parents married you off to a gay man?' I cried. 'How did you find out he was homosexual?'

'When he was away, I searched his study. I thought he might be in love with another woman. But then I found his diary and letters from male lovers.'

I couldn't believe a man had done that to Mamie. She was so sweet-hearted. And marrying under those circumstances was fraud!

'Did you have the marriage annulled?' I asked.

Mamie shuddered. 'No, I couldn't do that,' she said. 'It would have exposed Francesc in a terrible way. And besides, my parents certainly wouldn't have insisted on the marriage if they'd had any suspicion he was a homosexual.'

'But Francesc shouldn't have married you, Mamie!' I protested. 'That was dishonest! He did that for appearance's sake!'

'Oh, Paloma,' said Mamie, looking exasperated. 'You must understand that we are talking about Spain and not France. In Spain in those days, to be denounced as a homosexual could be fatal. The Church preached that the sin of homosexuality was worse than the sin of murder. Men of that nature were often beaten to death or locked away in mental asylums. Francesc would have done all he could to hide it. If Xavier, my parents and especially Margarida had not suspected his inclinations, then it couldn't have been so obvious. I don't believe Francesc's own family knew. And poor Francesc was full of self-loathing. His diary teemed with entries of guilt and self-hatred. I think Francesc half-hoped that marrying me would make him "normal".'

'Weren't you angry that you had been made to marry Francesc when it was Avi who loved you?' I asked.

'I couldn't bring myself to hate my husband, Paloma,' Mamie said quietly. 'Francesc was as trapped as I was. We had both been forced to marry within our circle, and Francesc was good to me. When he was in Barcelona he took me out to all the night spots, and he had no objection to my continuing to study ballet. He was also pleasant company, and when I accepted him for what he was, we did become friends. We just didn't have a physical relationship.'

'But, Mamie,' I said, still surprised that she wasn't bitter, 'you wanted children. Lots of them! That must have played on your mind.'

Mamie's jaw clenched and her brow furrowed. She looked away from me; and I knew that unless I was looking for another argument, the storytelling was over for the night.

TWENTY-SIX

Celestina

When I returned to Barcelona in January 1930, Primo de Rivera had resigned and King Alfonso had appointed General Dámaso Berenguer to prepare the country for new elections in a reinstated constitutional monarchy. But still the restlessness I had sensed in the people continued. General strikes and protests broke out on the streets, and there was a feeling of people wanting to go forwards rather than backwards.

I thought about my father and Teresa. I had grown up in a family where politics and making ends meet were the main discussions of the day. Ramón and I had spent much time with the women of Damas Rojas and in the revolutionary atmosphere of the Casa del Pueblo. I had been part of the burning of churches and the general strike in 1909. But after seeing Papá killed for protesting and Teresa exiled, I believed the idea that society could ever be made fairer was a myth. As long as humans were humans, they would always be looking for someone to exploit for their own gain. But maybe I had been mistaken?

I woke up one morning with a fever and muscle pains, which the doctor put down to having exhausted myself on my tour. He prescribed rest for a month and el Ruso had no choice but to cancel my shows. For the first time in my life, I took note of what was being discussed in the newspapers. It seemed to me that tolerance for the monarchy was dissipating and the Republican movement was experiencing a revival. *Full political democracy and universal suffrage are the only ways to create a just and fair society*, one journalist wrote.

Gaspar Olivero came to visit me at the Hotel Ritz where I stayed when I was in Barcelona, having long given up the apartment el Ruso had gifted me. I still supported my clan and took them everywhere with me, but, at el Ruso's insistence, they inhabited separate suites on a less prestigious floor. Fortunately for me, despite the complaints from other guests about the cooking smells that emanated from their rooms, they hadn't managed to set the hotel on fire yet.

'How are you?' I asked, welcoming Gaspar into my suite and signalling to my maid to bring us coffee and cakes.

'Oh, the same as ever,' he said. 'I'm back from South America but I will only be staying in Barcelona two days. Then I'm off to Paris.'

But he wasn't the same. For the first time since I had known him, I could see that Gaspar looked dejected.

'What's happened?' I asked.

'I am in love,' he sighed. 'But it's hopeless. She's married to another man.'

I had never experienced being in love myself. I'd had fleeting affairs on my tours, but usually I kept men at a distance because dancing was my true passion. I wasn't sure what to say to someone in Gaspar's position.

'We wanted to get married,' he explained. 'But her parents refused.'

'Why?'

'Because I'm not rich enough.'

'Not rich enough?' I repeated, raising my eyebrows. 'But you are very successful!'

'It's not enough, and not the right kind of money.'

I had no idea how the established rich defined money as the right or wrong kind and I was sure Gaspar would be better off not being part of such a pretentious family. But I could see from the tortured look in his eyes that he was taken with this young woman, so I remained silent, not wanting to hurt his feelings.

Gaspar changed the subject, pointing to the newspapers on my side table. 'I see you've been keeping yourself abreast of the latest political views.'

'Yes,' I replied. 'It seems that, in Barcelona at least, the people no longer want a king.'

'I'm going to a meeting of the Socialist Party tonight,' he said. 'Would you like to come? I'm sure that will be the topic of the night.'

I might have been reading the newspapers but I had no desire to go to political meetings. What good did they do? But I said yes because I was bored and Gaspar looked like he needed company.

The meeting was in the same café that Gaspar had taken me to when I was first engaged at the Samovar Club. I accompanied him to the back room, which was full of smoke and held an array of people. There were men in suits and men in overalls, and women of every age. Several people recognised me and whispered to their companions, who then sent glances in my direction. Fortunately, no one made more of a fuss than that. It must have given the meeting some cachet to have a star attend.

I turned in the direction of the platform that had been set up at the front of the room and was startled when I saw Xavier Montella sitting there with Margarida. I glanced down when Gaspar waved to them, then looked around the room, wondering how I could make my escape. But too many people had crammed in behind us: it would be impossible to push through the crowd to reach the door.

To my surprise, Xavier was one of the speakers for the evening.

'A government based on full democratic representation and the extension of civil liberties is the only way to break up the power of the self-serving oligarchy,' he told the crowd. 'Democracy will bring freedom of thought, freedom of the press, better education for all and an end to the demoralising poverty that plagues the lives of the majority of people in this country.'

When Xavier spoke he transcended himself, as I transcended myself when I danced. He has the demon too, I thought. It was obvious in the effect his words had on the audience: they applauded enthusiastically and stamped their feet on the floor. I thought of señor Sáinz's story of his friend the priest. Was that what I had done to Xavier—wrongly associated him with the oppressive ruling class when he was one of the few educated and passionate men who could transform society? Listening to him, I could almost believe it was possible for things to change and that perhaps Papá's sacrifice—and Teresa's—could have some meaning.

When Xavier had finished speaking, his listeners pressed forwards to shake his hand.

'Let's go and congratulate him,' said Gaspar.

I didn't follow Gaspar. Instead, I allowed myself to be pushed back by the crowd towards the exit. I still didn't know what to make of Xavier Montella and wasn't ready to apologise to him. As señor Sáinz had said, it was not always easy to tell who was your friend and who was your foe.

I reached the door, but before I left, something compelled me to look back. I turned, and at that moment Xavier lifted his eyes. Our gazes locked. Something like a bright light flashed between us: a demon. But not one that I had felt before.

The political developments in the next year were so dramatic that even I could not fail to be moved by them. Order broke down as inflation spiralled out of control, while the numbers of jobless workers continued to grow. Strikes and protests became such a daily occurrence that the middle classes began to lose faith that the monarchy and dictatorship could maintain a stable country. When I watched the workers march, I felt I was being transported back to 1909. But now, it seemed, the result was going to be different. Instead of the repression the striking workers had experienced after Tragic Week, the country was moving towards elections, and the Leftist parties were pushing for anti-inflationary legislation to link wages to the cost of living and mandate a shorter working day, as well as a number of health and welfare reforms. If the Left won, those rights would be granted by law and not left to the whims of the monarchy and dictators who crushed the workers whenever they tried to better their position.

After the April 1931 elections, the majority of the council seats went to pro-Republicans. It was a landslide victory. Two days later, the army high command made it known that it would not defend the monarchy. The King and his family left the palace and went into exile, and the Second Republic was proclaimed.

Workers burst from the factories and into the streets to celebrate. If Papá and Teresa had only lived to see this, I thought, as I watched the jubilation from my hotel. Republican flags hung from the windows, people danced in the streets and sang songs like 'La Cucaracha' and 'La Marseillaise' with the words changed to suit the occasion:

The King is gone
The Church is in retreat
Now the jackals have left
It's our turn to eat

I could not stay inside any longer. I had to be out there with the people in the streets, as if by joining them I was representing Papá, Anastasio and Teresa and all those who had been killed, gaoled or exiled for trying to create a fairer society.

When I reached the foyer, the concierge tried to dissuade me from leaving the hotel. 'My dear senyoreta, don't risk your life by going out there! Now that power is in the hands of the masses, we are at the mercy of barbarians!'

'My dear senyor Folguera,' I replied, walking past him, 'you forget that I *am* a barbarian. I shall be right at home!'

I was swept along by the crowds marching in the brilliant sunshine. People were hugging each other and crying. The police arrived, but they had come to join in the celebrations, not to repress them. A tram stopped nearby and the conductor invited people to jump aboard for free. I remembered the general strike of my childhood, when the workers and the women of Damas Rojas had attacked the trams after the guards on board had fired on them.

The celebrations continued all day, like a fiesta. There was a feeling of good will and brotherly love amongst the people. Is this really possible? I asked myself. Could a monarchy fall and a republic triumph without any violence?

As if mirroring my thoughts, a man near me turned to his companion and said, 'I only hope the Spaniards will be able to take advantage of this great opportunity they have been given . . . that it won't all collapse into factional fighting.'

The day grew warmer, and I looked for a café that might have a spare seat and where I could order a drink and absorb everything that had taken place. I was making my way across the street when I heard a voice behind me.

'Senyoreta Sánchez?'

I turned around to see Xavier Montella standing behind me. He looked dashing in a white suit and hat that brought out the colour of his eyes.

'I saw you at the Socialist Party meeting last year,' he said, 'but you left before I could speak to you.'

'I only went to keep Gaspar company,' I explained, lest Xavier get any ideas that I had become a revolutionary. 'You spoke very well.'

'And now everything we wished for has happened,' he said, glancing around us. Then he turned back to me and smiled. 'You look so pretty in that dress. Let me take you somewhere to celebrate.'

Me? Pretty? Hardly, I thought. Not compared to his sisters anyway—and probably his wife. I assumed that he had one. He was certainly of the age and class where a wife was indispensable.

'Why do I need to celebrate?' I asked him. 'It makes no difference to me who rules Spain. All I want to do is dance.'

His eyes narrowed on my face and he took a step closer to me. 'I don't believe that's how you really feel,' he said. 'I believe you only pretend not to have any compassion.'

'That's very opinionated of you.' I told him. His handsome face stirred something in me and I was doing my best to resist it. 'You hardly know me.'

'Then let me get to know you better,' he said, a teasing note in his voice.

My pulse quickened. I had that strange feeling again that I was like clay in Xavier's hands. Only I realised now it was not because he was rich and I'd been born into a poor family . . . it was for quite different reasons. But my pride wouldn't allow him to think he had got the better of me.

'All right,' I said, daring him. 'Take me somewhere you aren't ashamed to be seen with me. But remember, it's more difficult to be discreet with a star than it is with a mistress.'

He blushed, realising that I was alluding to his being married. But then, to my surprise, he said, 'I'm not ashamed to be seen with you *anywhere.*'

I stared at him, understanding now that like the crowds that were dancing and cheering around us, Xavier Montella and I were being caught up and swept away by something bigger than ourselves.

My defences weakened. 'Why did you pursue me?' I asked him, breathless. 'All those times I was so unfriendly to you . . . yet you kept coming back.'

Xavier gazed into my eyes and smiled. 'Because of what I sensed ever since I first laid eyes on you . . . that we were souls destined for each other.'

That light again! As the demon danced around us. I knew that what Xavier said was true. It was foolish to resist any more.

*   *   *

I have never understood how it is that a person can start life in one place and end up somewhere else entirely. How could I have been born in a slum to the poorest of poor families and now be residing in the Hotel Ritz? How could I have gone from hating a man to lying in his arms, the sheets crumpled beneath us, my thighs raw from our lovemaking, my skin still burning from his kisses? The gentle hue of late afternoon light washed over Xavier's sleeping face. I touched his eyebrows. One was slightly raised as if he were asking a question.

Xavier had taken me to the Casa Abela, where we had dined on croquettes and sautéed mushrooms. I marvelled at how quickly we had travelled from celebrating the Republic, to talking about flamenco, to returning to the Ritz where we embraced for the first time and covered each other with passionate kisses. I had sensed the wife and the child long before Xavier had mentioned them, but they were a world apart from this one: the world here in my suite where I lay with Xavier Montella.

Xavier opened his eyes and looked at me. 'Thank God!' he said.

'Thank God what?' I asked, propping myself on my elbow.

He rubbed his forehead. 'I thought I was going to wake up and find everything had been a dream.'

I lay my head on his chest and breathed in the fresh smell of his skin, still damp from the exertion of our lovemaking.

'How could we have been destined for each other?' I asked him. 'We are so different. I was born in barri Xinès and you were born in l'Eixample.'

'I don't know,' he said, closing his eyes again and drifting back to sleep. 'But now that I have you, I'm not letting you go.'

I remembered the tortured expression on Xavier's face when I had lied to him that Celestina Sánchez was dead, and how the pain I had caused him was like a dagger in my own heart. The memory of that had never blurred or softened; it remained crystal clear every time I thought of it. I knew then that whatever hurt Xavier would hurt me too. It's so strange, I thought, why some people fall in love like this and others don't. It was as random as the stars.

'I'll never harm you,' I murmured in Xavier's ear. 'I'll never do anything to hurt you ever again.'

By the second year of its birth, the new Republic was in trouble. While it had raised the hopes of the most wretched in society, it had also threatened the interests of those who were opposed to any redistribution of wealth and power—the monarchists, the Church, the army, the industrialists and landowners. While the world looked on in amazement, Spain went from a backward, conservative country to one where freedom of conscience was honoured, women were given the vote, civil marriage and divorce were permitted, education became compulsory and secular, and the Church and state were separated. But those who did not like the changes were bent on destroying the Republic . . . and soon, very soon, circumstances were to play into their hands.

In the October of 1933, I returned from a tour of Portugal to find Xavier waiting for me at the railway station. As soon as he spotted me, the light came to his eyes and he moved towards the carriage where I was sitting. How I loved these moments of re-union. We had been lovers for as long as the Republic had been in power, but every time we met again felt as fresh as the first.

I let him approach me, noticing that even his gait was attractive. He walked with his shoulders relaxed, his arms swinging. We couldn't kiss like lovers in public, but even the feel of his lips on my cheeks sent tingles down my spine.

'Where is everybody?' Xavier asked, looking over my shoulder. He was referring to my clan.

'They will be here,' I told him. 'They are gathering their things.'

No sooner had I spoken than Diego and his sisters alighted from the train along with Manuel's sisters. Their husbands and children followed. With Raquel's twins the latest additions to my clan, I was now looking after twenty-five people. The travellers waiting on the platform stared at the gypsies. Even when travelling on trains, the women wore their finest jewellery and tiaras; but they eschewed the Hermès suitcases I had bought for them and wrapped everything they owned in bundles tied with string.

Although el Ruso and Xavier had, between them, wrested control of my income away from Diego so I could keep it for myself, Diego still greeted Xavier like an old friend. The gypsies liked Xavier, but our affair was only possible because they considered me mostly a *paya*. If I'd been born a gypsy, they would have cut off my nose for sleeping with a married man. It also helped that Diego approved of Xavier because he had money and was generous with it.

'I've organised taxis for everyone,' Xavier announced, steering the group towards the exit like a tour conductor. He leaned towards me and whispered in my ear, 'For us, I have my car. I've missed you so much I'm whisking you straight to the apartment.'

In the chauffeured car, Xavier and I held hands underneath my coat.

'I've been invited to perform at the Samovar Club tomorrow night,' I told him. 'It's going to be Gaspar on the piano and me. Are you coming?'

Although I had been performing in grand concert halls for crowds of people for years now, I still preferred the intimacy of dancing in clubs and cabaret shows. And with Gaspar back in Barcelona for a month, I'd seized the opportunity to perform with my old friend again.

Xavier shook his head. 'I can't make the show but I'll meet you afterwards.'

I knew the reason. He'd promised to do something for Conchita.

I never made Xavier feel guilty about having to divide himself between two lives. I'd seen his wife once when el Ruso had taken me to the Liceu. She was sitting in the family box with Xavier: a foxy-faced beauty in form-fitting clothes. Very few people knew about my and Xavier's love affair. Xavier never treated me as a mistress, and I never badgered him to divorce his wife, even though it was now legal. Laws might change but attitudes didn't, and I much preferred our secret life to one embroiled in scandal. I might not have had him all the time, but when we were together Xavier and I were happy. He opened up the cold part of me and made it warm again. He'd brought me back to life.

'Margarida sends her regards,' he said.

'How is her arm?'

'On the mend.'

I found it unusual that Margarida had taken a liking to me. It wasn't only that she despised Conchita and thought Xavier was happier with me; her affection seemed genuine. I smiled as I remembered the day she'd invited me to join her on a teaching mission. With the support of the Republican government, she was going to tour the poorest villages in Spain with a group of artists and performers. The idea was that they would put on plays, give art exhibitions and talks, and show films to people who were still living as if it were the Dark Ages. While I loved performing and wasn't averse to living rough—I still preferred it to fancy hotel rooms—I couldn't imagine anything worse than touring the country with a gathering of intellectuals and poets. I hated the way the dance critics overanalysed my performances and, besides that, I'd never read a book in my life. I'd learned to autograph my name artistically, read the newspaper, and speak some English and French quite well. That was enough for me.

'The peasants need food and livelihoods, not high culture,' I'd told Margarida.

'Actually,' she'd said, straightening her spine and staring at me with her intense eyes, 'they need both—to feed the body *and* the spirit.'

Margarida had a passionate energy about her. I knew she was good at winning people to her cause. But she wasn't going to win me.

'I'll give your group money for the costumes and travel expenses,' I told her. 'But I'm not going.'

Margarida had written to me about the tour almost every day she had been away: *We performed to a full house tonight. Even though it started to rain, the peasants would not move. They were so enthralled by our performance.* But the bus she had been travelling on had overturned on its way back to Madrid and now Margarida was nursing a broken ulna.

The apartment Xavier and I secretly rented was off the carrer Gran. When we walked into it, the first thing I noticed was a vase of blood-red roses in the foyer. I turned to Xavier and smiled before sitting down in the drawing room and staring at the new painting above the mantelpiece. It was a distorted depiction of a woman painted in yellow, red and green oils.

'Where did you get that?' I asked.

'It's a Picasso,' replied Xavier. 'He's a Spaniard. Do you like it?'

'I don't know,' I told him. 'Perhaps it will grow on me . . . as you did.'

He laughed. 'Hopefully faster than that! I paid a small fortune for it!'

I kicked off my shoes and Xavier sat down next to me. 'I'm exhausted,' I said.

He rubbed my feet and blew on my toes. 'I've missed these feet. These delicate but powerful instruments. How did the Portuguese like your shows?'

'You've tamed me,' I told him, leaning back and closing my eyes. 'Reviewers no longer use words like "spitfire" or "hellcat" to describe me. Now they are calling me "refined" and "sophisticated". You've put out my fire.'

Xavier leaned over me, easing my skirt up over my hips and kissing my thighs. 'That,' he said, 'is yet to be seen.'

When we woke a few hours later, it was already dark. For some reason I had been dreaming of Teresa's flower stall, overflowing with geraniums and begonias. It took me a few moments to register where I was.

'It's six o'clock,' Xavier said, glancing at his watch. 'I'd better get going.'

I watched him put on his trousers and shirt. My show wasn't until ten. I had plenty of time.

'So what's been happening in Spain?' I asked. 'It's impossible to believe anything the Portuguese papers print.'

'For the Republic to survive it needs to raise wages and cut unemployment, but that's next to impossible in the midst of a depression,' he said, pulling on his socks. 'The workers are becoming impatient and are seeking more radical solutions. To keep the support of the middle classes, the Republic has to provide stability and order. They've come down too hard on some protests and now they've alienated the workers even more.'

'Did we change too fast?' I asked.

He shrugged. 'Yes, probably. But how can you not change quickly when people are starving?'

I thought of Teresa again and realised he was right. The Republic was something the Spanish people should have demanded when the French achieved theirs. We were hundreds of years late, although our transition had been less bloody. While King Alfonso had been tried in his absence for high treason, the sentence that had been passed down was permanent exile. Spain hadn't sent the aristocracy and other opponents to the guillotine.

'The Left is breaking up into factions of conservative reformers and extreme anarchists, while the disgruntled members of the Right are uniting,' Xavier said, straightening his tie. 'If the Left doesn't get its act together, they will lose the next election. Then I am sure the Right will dismantle the reforms that have been achieved and put the country even further behind than it was before.'

Xavier fixed his hair before kissing me goodbye. After he left, I rested my head back on the pillow. I could still smell the cedar scent of his aftershave. I breathed in the restful atmosphere of the apartment. It was a haven we had created in an unstable world.

'I hope that we always have this,' I sighed, before drifting off to sleep again.

Twenty-Seven

Celestina

Although el Ruso was now living in Paris, he still owned the Samovar Club in Barcelona. Zakharov had been made the manager. He was in the foyer when I arrived, looking as handsome as ever, although greyer around the temples.

'It's good to see you again,' he said, taking my hands and kissing both my cheeks before nervously looking around for my clan.

'They have a fiesta,' I explained. 'It's just me tonight.'

'*Well, look who is here!*'

I turned to see Gaspar rushing towards me. It was nearly a year since we had last seen each other, and we grabbed each other's hands tightly. Gaspar knew about Xavier and me, and was happy for us. But I felt sorry for him. I wasn't the marrying type, but he was—yet he hadn't settled down. Surely he wasn't still pining for the young woman who'd married someone else?

Zakharov glanced from me to Gaspar. 'You two have rehearsed this act, haven't you?'

Gaspar and I answered in unison: 'No!'

The three of us laughed. Zakharov had come to respect my need to improvise.

After all the challenges I'd had with highbrow conductors and orchestras who couldn't keep the *compás*, it was a relief to return to dancing with a single instrument played by someone who had known me as long as Gaspar had. Senyora Dávilo had dressed me on this occasion in gold and silver, and I performed against a black background with my hair swept back into a low chignon. I was relaxed, and improvised my performance from start to finish. It was true what the reviewers in Portugal had said: I no longer had to whip myself into a frenzy in order to dance expressively. The wild and the untamed were still in me, but I preferred to show my elegant, feminine side now.

Afterwards, I rushed to my dressing room. I was pleased with how well my new style had been received, but I was eager to clean off my stage make-up and freshen up before Xavier arrived. I sat down at my mirror and gave a start. In its reflection I saw the head of a man sitting with his back to me in the armchair. I swivelled around. The man rose and my blood turned to ice. It was Salazar.

'So you refuse all my invitations,' he said.

Although I hadn't seen Salazar for over a decade, he had never been out of contact. Wherever I performed in the world, he always sent expensive gifts and an invitation to a bullfight for when I returned to Spain. The gifts had unnerved me, but as Salazar had not appeared in person for all that time, I had disposed of them and put Salazar out of my mind.

'I only accept invitations given in person,' I replied. Then realised my mistake.

An amused look came into Salazar's eyes. 'All right,' he said. 'My wife has been dead for a year, so I can now invite you to my ranch. We'll raise bulls together. I'm trying to breed one with violet eyes.'

I'd been stalked in New York, and once a man in Paris had held a gun to his head and threatened to shoot himself if I didn't marry him. But neither of those encounters had terrified me as much as seeing Salazar now did. He had a demon too, but it was nothing like the one I danced with, or the one that had brought me and Xavier together. Salazar's demon was straight from hell.

'We'll have to do something about the peasants first,' he said, taking a step towards me. 'Do you know, the Republican government thinks that I'm going to share my land with them? Land that's been in my family for generations?'

'I believe the intention is to pay you for it,' I said coldly. 'And to prevent thousands of people starving to death each year. Land given over for hunting parties and the breeding of bulls doesn't feed the population.'

Salazar lifted his eyebrows. 'They are going to pay the land-owners according to what we've been putting on our tax documents, as if that's any indication of the land's worth!' He laughed. 'Don't they realise that peasants are nothing better than animals and a lot less noble? I've threatened those on my land that if they don't vote for the CEDA and the monarchists in the next election, I'll let them and their children starve.' He put a long, yellow nail to his nose. 'It's a delightful twist, don't you think? The Republican government gives everyone an equal say—and the peasants will vote against it for a little bit of sausage!'

I thought of my Andalusian grandparents, both of whom had died before they reached forty. They had lived at the mercy of men like Salazar. Still, I stayed quiet. I remembered how, when I'd danced at the Villa Rosa, Salazar had carried a gun. I assumed he still did. All I wanted was to get him out of my dressing room as quickly as possible. But he showed no intention of leaving.

'What this country needs is a man like the one they have in Germany,' he said. 'Hitler.'

I shrank away and moved towards the door, but he followed me. 'So you will come with me to the fight tomorrow?'

'I don't like bullfights,' I said.

'That's because you don't understand them. Come with me tomorrow and I shall explain everything to you: the nobility of surrendering oneself to death.'

I shivered. The demon around him was strong. I tried again to move away from him—and it. 'There is nothing to understand. They are just cruel.'

Salazar bit the side of his thumb. 'What sort of gypsy are you?' he asked, an annoyed expression on his face. 'Have you become a soft Catalan? Or should I say, has a *certain Catalan* softened you?'

I had no doubt that he meant Xavier. How did he know about us? His spying must have involved more than keeping track of where I was performing. The murderous look in his eyes chilled me and a terrible thought came to my mind. I saw Xavier arriving at my dressing room and Salazar shooting him. No sooner had I thought it than there was a knock at the door. Salazar and I both turned towards it.

I remained silent, terrified it might be Xavier.

'Senyoreta, I have some flowers for you,' came a female voice. 'Shall I put them in your room?' It was the club's maid, Consuelo.

Salazar shook his head, but I ignored him. 'Yes,' I answered.

Consuelo walked in with a bouquet of long-stemmed calla lilies that was taller than she was. She settled them in a vase on an end table before she realised that Salazar was with me. She glanced at my face and must have seen the fear there. Bless you, I thought, as she began moving noisily around the room, dusting everything in sight and violently fluffing the cushions.

Her frenetic activity made Salazar uncomfortable. He moved towards the door, where he grabbed my arm and forced me to look into his bloodshot eyes. 'So you think bullfighting is barbaric, do you?' he asked. 'What you don't understand is that some beasts . . . and some people . . . are born doomed.'

Salazar let me go with such force that I stumbled backwards.

He strode out the door and his demon scuttled after him. I realised now what the demon was. It was death.

Xavier arrived a quarter of an hour later with a bouquet of white roses. Salazar had so unnerved me that I collapsed in his arms.

'You've exhausted yourself again, haven't you?' Xavier laughed. 'You didn't give yourself much of a break after Portugal.'

I feigned a smile. I didn't want to tell Xavier the real reason for my alarm. To whom had Salazar been referring when he had said that some people were born doomed? I held Xavier to me as a chill prickled my skin. Dear God, I prayed, if one of us is doomed, let it be me.

Xavier was right when he said that I needed to rest after Portugal. But I found it impossible to settle my thoughts while Salazar's words rang in my head like a threat. I didn't go anywhere for a few days. I stayed in my hotel suite and read the newspapers to occupy my mind. I made Xavier call me every day even if I was seeing him that night. Salazar had disappeared from my life for months and years at a time before. I prayed he might disappear from it forever.

The articles in the newspapers were depressing: unemployment was rising and unrest among the workers and peasants was increasing. The brutality with which their protests were put down was causing many commentators to suggest that the only way forwards for the poor was through revolution, not reform.

One day, Evelina Montella arrived to visit me. I was touched that both Xavier's sisters frequently called on me; I had expected to be snubbed by them. Xavier had told me that, unlike Margarida, who openly despised her sister-in-law, Evelina was friends with his wife and doted on his son, so I was pleased that she viewed me without any resentment. Whether Xavier's parents knew of my existence or not, they didn't acknowledge it.

Evelina was wearing a white knitted dress and matching bolero jacket. While Margarida was boisterous, Evelina was quiet in a way I found intriguing. She reminded me of a rosebud—tightly closed but full of potential.

'Francesc is travelling again,' she said, when I invited her into the suite's sitting room. She did her best to smile, but I noticed the frown lines that had appeared on her forehead.

I wasn't surprised that Francesc Cerdà spent as much time away from home duties as he could. The fact that he preferred men to women was obvious to me. I had worked and performed with many homosexual men and enjoyed them as friends. But I couldn't imagine that Evelina and Francesc's marriage was bliss for either of them.

'I saw you dance at the Samovar Club the other night,' Evelina said in her soft, cultivated voice.

'Oh? Why didn't you come and greet me afterwards?'

She folded and unfolded her hands. 'It was late . . . I didn't want to bother you.'

She fell silent and I sensed there was something weighing on her mind that she wanted to talk about. Then it occurred to me that she might have witnessed Salazar leaving my dressing room. I hoped it hadn't given her the wrong idea.

'Xavier came to visit me afterwards,' I told her. 'You should have come too.'

But she wasn't listening. She took a breath and looked at me. 'I was wondering if you would teach me to dance flamenco.'

I was startled and didn't respond straight away.

Evelina blushed. 'It's presumptuous of me to ask a star like you . . . but you don't just dance flamenco, you embody it.'

I was flattered and confused. It was true I had become a polished performer, but flamenco was considered a lowbrow form of dance compared to Spanish dance and ballet. It wasn't a pursuit for upper-class women, let alone Catalan ones. Why did Evelina want to learn it? She'd never be able to dance it for anyone.

'I don't know if I can *teach* you,' I explained to her. 'I learned from watching others and from living with flamenco dancers. But I would be happy to try. When should we start? Now?'

Evelina looked surprised, then enthused. 'Truly?'

'Why not? I have nothing else to do today.'

I found a rehearsal dress for her to wear. She was a natural dancer. When I showed her how to use her arms, she mirrored me exactly. She had a good sense of rhythm. But she was all technique and no fire.

'I enjoyed that,' she said, when we had finished and the maid brought us coffee and cakes.

I had found her company pleasing too. Although there was something sad and a little repressed about her, she'd lifted my spirits.

'Why don't you come again tomorrow?' I asked her.

Her face broke into a smile. 'Truly . . . I'm not wasting your time?'

It touched me that she should speak so humbly to me. I remembered the first time I had seen Evelina, as a baby in a pram. She had been so pretty, like a fairy princess.

'Of course not,' I reassured her. 'I love everything about dance.'

'So do I!' she said, a sparkle coming to her eyes for the first time.

I watched from the window as she sent me a girlish wave before stepping into her chauffeured Bugatti. In many ways Evelina was my opposite: she was reserved and I was not; she was cultivated and I was a savage. What an unusual friendship we are making, I thought. I wondered if asking me to teach her flamenco might be the most daring thing Evelina had ever done.

Because Evelina progressed with the individual flamenco steps so quickly, we soon moved on to combining them into basic patterns. By the time we were a few weeks into our lessons, she was moving well enough for us to dance with each other.

'Don't try to imitate me,' I told her. 'Find something of your own.'

I could see that she understood what I was asking of her, but she had trouble executing it. I wondered if she had ever been given the opportunity to be her true self.

One day when we were dancing, the door buzzer rang. A minute later, my maid appeared and told me that Gaspar Olivero had come to see me.

'Tell him to come in,' I said.

I glanced at Evelina, expecting her to be pleased to see her friend. But she had turned pale and was standing frozen to the spot. I wondered what was wrong with her. Had she overexerted herself?

Gaspar strode into the room and stopped in his tracks when he saw Evelina. For a fraction of a second they held each other's gaze before looking away. Then I understood. The young woman Gaspar had been pining for all these years was Evelina Montella.

What followed was a stilted and awkward conversation. Gaspar told me he'd only dropped by for a minute because he was in the area. He looked towards the door as if intending to leave, but didn't move. Evelina said several times that it was a pleasure to see him again, all the while staring at her feet. I wondered if I should make an excuse to leave the room, or whether being alone was going to make everything worse for them.

Before I could decide, Gaspar said that he would call me later about doing another show at the Samovar Club and finally mustered the courage to actually leave us. I walked him to the door of the suite and kissed his cheeks. His skin was ice cold.

When I returned to the sitting room, Evelina was sobbing.

'I'm so unhappy,' she told me. 'I've been married for two and a half years and everyone keeps asking when Francesc and I are going to have a baby. This morning, the Marquesa hinted that maybe I should see her specialist. Even the old doyennes are whispering their fertility secrets to me at parties or at the Liceu. What I want more than anything else in the world is a child to love. Each birthday that passes without a child sends me into a depression—but Francesc won't come anywhere near me!'

The pain and despair in Evelina's voice touched me. So this was what she had been keeping inside her all this time. No wonder she was scared to express her true self. Ladies of the upper class were not meant to reveal family unhappinesses of any kind.

I sat down beside her. I didn't share her deep urge for a child; I had never experienced that maternal pull although I was thirty-two years of age. Xavier and I took precautions against pregnancy. Not being one to hold back my opinion, I clasped her hand and said, 'You know, even if a man prefers men he can still make a woman pregnant.'

Evelina shook her head and replied in a hushed voice, 'I've tried *everything*. He just can't.'

I sighed. Rich families and their marriages! Xavier was miserable in his, and now I'd learned that Evelina was unhappily wed too. No wonder Margarida had avoided matrimony altogether.

A few days later, when we were having coffee after our lesson, I brought up the subject again. I couldn't stand the pained look on Evelina's face any longer, and she seemed incapable of finding a solution to her unhappiness herself.

'What about Gaspar?' I asked her. 'You like him. He obviously likes you. Why don't you ask him to give you a baby? Surely Francesc can't object if he isn't up to the task.'

Evelina looked at me with a horrified expression on her face. 'I couldn't do that!'

One of the things that I found so amusing about her was that even though she was married to a homosexual man, she was still so easy to shock.

'Why not? It sounds like your husband would be relieved. It would stop any rumours about him.'

'But . . . I love Gaspar.'

I waited to hear why that was an obstacle to the plan.

Evelina shook her head. 'It wouldn't be right to tie him to me that way. He should be married and happy himself. I want him to forget me.' She burst into tears.

I brushed aside a strand of chestnut hair that was sticking to her cheek. Well, that suggestion didn't go well, I thought. Evelina and I moved in two different worlds. I promised myself never to try to give her my proletarian advice again.

'I'm sorry,' I told her. 'That was probably . . . not the right thing to suggest to you.'

She looked at me with tears in her eyes and shook her head. 'Apart from Margarida, you are the only true friend I have.'

I saw then that Evelina hadn't really wanted to learn flamenco at all. She had simply been looking for something to fill up her empty life.

The November 1933 election went exactly as Xavier had predicted. The Socialists and the Republicans refused to cooperate and it cost them their power.

The evening the result was announced on the radio, Xavier and I sat in our apartment, shocked and upset. Margarida arrived after dinner.

'Finally, women get the right to vote and what do they do?' she said angrily, flinging her coat onto the sofa. 'They listen to their priests and vote for the Right! The Church is the very institution that oppresses them! Haven't they read the story of Adam and Eve?'

'At least that's one step up from following their husbands,' I said, trying to inject some humour into the melancholy mood. 'Seriously, the working-class women would have voted for the Socialists if the Anarchists hadn't run such a successful campaign to discourage the working class from voting altogether.'

'The Right's victory seems a bigger landslide than it actually is,' said Xavier. 'Due to our stupid electoral law, the side that wins at the polls is given representation in the Cortes way out of proportion to the voting results.'

'One thing's for sure,' said Margarida, 'the Right are going to undo all the reforms that were started when the Republic came to power. Wages are going to be cut, landowners will have their estates restored to them, the peasants will be evicted, and women are going to be forced out of their jobs.'

I thought of my father and Teresa. 'The only way things will change for the poor in this country is with a revolution,' I said. 'I don't think anyone will believe in reform any more after this.'

Xavier, Margarida and I spent the rest of the evening debating whether revolution was the only recourse open to the peasants and workers. As we discussed the ins and outs of various political systems to help the most downtrodden elements of society, we didn't see that much more dangerous forces were lurking on the horizon. When Xavier and I climbed into our bed in the early hours of morning and embraced each other before falling asleep, we had no idea how swiftly and brutally things were about to change. And that the sweet life we shared was about to be cut short.

Twenty-Eight

Paloma

With Mamie keeping me on the edge of my seat with her stories about Spain, and the surprising developments in my relationship with Jaime, I hadn't given much thought in the past few days to what Madame Genet had said about me taking the examination for a second time. But when I arrived at the ballet school on Monday morning for my lesson with Mademoiselle Louvet, I was overcome by feelings of defeatism. What was the point of training until my body cried out in pain and my feet bled if it was all going to be for nothing?

'What's the matter today, Paloma?' Mademoiselle Louvet asked me, when I'd finished my barre work. 'You are not extending yourself completely or finishing off your movements. Why are you holding back? Last week you gave me everything.'

I bowed my head. I was a perfectionist and this was not what I wanted to hear. But I knew Mademoiselle Louvet was right. If I couldn't put my heart into what I was doing there was little point going through with the training.

'Can we talk for a moment?' I asked.

Mademoiselle Louvet sent me a concerned look. 'You can always talk to me, Paloma.' She nodded to the accompanist, Monsieur Clary, who took the opportunity to get himself a cup of coffee.

'Last week, after our lesson, I ran into Madame Genet outside the administration office,' I told her. 'She said that I haven't a chance in getting into the *corps de ballet* because Mademoiselle Marineau's prejudice against me will override all my efforts.'

Mademoiselle Louvet's beautiful face scrunched into a frown. 'It was quite out of place for Madame Genet to say that. If the head of the school has decided that you are fit to take the examination, then it really isn't any of Madame Genet's business. Mademoiselle Marineau said she didn't think you could take the load of a professional dancer, but you did that examination under the strain of having lost your mother less than a year before. Things will be much better for you the next time around.'

I wanted to believe what Mademoiselle Louvet was saying, but Madame Genet had been right when she'd said that I'd performed exceptionally well in the examination *despite* everything that had happened.

'Madame Genet said I didn't have a chance for personal reasons,' I told Mademoiselle Louvet. 'That the reason Mademoiselle Marineau hates me has something to do with my father.'

'Your father?' Mademoiselle Louvet looked thoughtful for a moment. 'Well, your father was the orchestra's pianist when your mother was dancing Giselle and fell pregnant to him. Mademoiselle Marineau was playing the role of Myrtha, Queen of the Wilis. They could have had some falling out about the music perhaps?'

The ballet *Giselle* was often interpreted as a battle of the sexes. The Wilis were the spirits of young women who had died before their wedding day and sought revenge on male victims by making them dance until their hearts gave out. The answer occurred to Mademoiselle Louvet the same time as it did to me.

'My father had an affair with Mademoiselle Marineau, didn't he? And he broke it off to marry my mother!'

Mademoiselle Louvet shook her head. 'I find it too hard to believe. Mademoiselle Marineau has been in love with the choreographer Christophe Valois all the years I have known her. Even though they have never married, I think he is the only man she's ever been in love with. Some would even go so far as to call it an obsession.'

'It's not my place. You will have to ask your father,' Madame Genet had said. Mademoiselle Louvet might find it hard to believe, but I was sure now that my father had been two-timing even then! I would never have thought my father capable of such a thing if he hadn't married Audrey so soon after my mother's death. He was due back in Paris on Wednesday, but there was no way I was going to see him now. His philandering had ruined my life!

I continued as best I could with my lesson. Afterwards, Mademoiselle Louvet and I went back to her office and she gave me her recording of Brahms's 'Intermezzo' that she had played for me after my last lesson. 'Listen to it,' she told me, 'and you will feel your mother's love.'

When I stood up to leave, Mademoiselle Louvet grabbed my hands. 'Promise me, Paloma, that you will put all thoughts that you could fail this examination out of your mind. I want you to give it *everything*. Ballet is like a love affair: you must surrender yourself to it fully, otherwise you will receive nothing in return. You must have faith, even if it cuts you like the Little Mermaid dancing on knives.'

I tried to keep Mademoiselle Louvet's advice in mind when I practised in the studio the following day. I pushed myself to my limits, but I couldn't get rid of the lump in my chest. Could my father really have ruined my dreams for good?

Only the sight of Jaime waiting outside the Conservatoire's library later that morning lifted my spirits. When Jaime smiled, his whole face came alive. He kissed me and took my hand.

'I've booked two films of la Rusa for us to see,' he said. 'One is a clip of her dancing at the Samovar Club as a young woman, and the other one is a routine she did for a flamenco film just before the Civil War.'

I waited anxiously as the projector whirred. The film jiggled until Jaime steadied it. My hand flew to my mouth when la Rusa appeared on the screen, alive and animated. It was strange to watch her: compelling and uncomfortable at the same time. The moments when she looked directly into the camera with her hypnotic eyes sent shivers down my spine. I could see in her the dancer Mamie had described: savage, violent and forceful in her movements. She had a lithe body but her technique was sharp and precise.

When she had finished her dance, she smiled at somebody. That intrigued me. In all the images I held of la Rusa in my head, I had not pictured her being happy. I looked at the corner of the screen and glimpsed a young man sitting at a grand piano. Avi! Seeing my grandfather, young and smiling, made me want to cry. He had no idea at that moment of the fate that was to befall him.

Jaime held my hand and gave me a few moments to collect myself before he wound on the second film.

'Are you all right?' he asked. 'This must be confronting for you.'

I rested my head against his shoulder. It was nice to have a boyfriend and Jaime was so kind. I wondered why I'd had to meet him now, when my life was in disarray and I was dealing with having been visited by a ghost.

There was no dialogue in the second film; the story was told through singing and dancing.

'The people in it are all la Rusa's gypsy family,' said Jaime. 'Apparently, wherever she went, they went too.'

I'd never thought of la Rusa as having a family either, I realised. She seemed different in the second film: she was older and more beautiful, with a nobility about her that made me think of an Indian princess. Her technique had changed as well. She was still explosive in her movements and powerful, but the sharpness of her steps had gone. She had softened.

I leaned forwards and studied her face with its gentler expression and the eyes that shone with joy. Did she look like that because she was in love?

Jaime and I went to a nearby café to talk.

'It's been such a strange time for me,' I confided in him. 'I've realised that there's so much I don't know about my own family. My grandfather, for instance—he was a successful musician and travelled the world. Conchita, who I had always thought was a family friend, is the widow of my great-uncle. I've just discovered that Feliu, a man who visits every few years, is my cousin. And then, there's Mamie. I had never considered for a second that she could have been married before Avi. And I sense that my grandmother hasn't told me half of it yet.'

'I can't imagine what that must be like,' said Jaime. 'No one in my family could keep a secret even if they tried. I've heard their stories so many times that they only have to say the first word of one and I can repeat the whole recollection for them. Your grandmother must have her reasons for not telling you those things until now.'

'That's what scares me,' I said. 'I get the impression that even with Franco dead she doesn't feel "safe" talking about Spain.'

'I can understand that,' said Jaime. 'I grew up in Spain under Franco. My father is a respected surgeon but because of my uncle's activities we were always under surveillance. It was like being under house arrest. Life was hell for those who had sided with the Republic during the Civil War. One of our neighbours had been a celebrated architect, but he couldn't get a job under Franco's regime and eked out a living selling marquetry boxes to tourists.'

Jaime had an afternoon class and had to return to the Conservatoire. He paid for the coffees and then he stood up and kissed me.

'You're not alone with this mystery, Paloma. I'll help you.'

*　*　*

I had a few hours to spare before my flamenco lesson with Carmen later that evening, so I went back to the Bibliothèque Sainte-Geneviève and looked up old newspapers, trying to learn what I could about la Rusa's death. Her body had been found on the train tracks on the outskirts of Paris, in an area that was scrubland back then but was now a growing suburb. There was a question mark over whether the death was suicide or not because when the police went to her apartment to look for a suicide note, they discovered it had been cleared.

I was out of my depth, but I decided to go to the Prefecture of Police and pretend I was researching a book on la Rusa's life.

'I'm sorry, Mademoiselle,' the police sergeant said, 'but we do not have a record. Investigations into suicides may be destroyed after twenty years have passed.'

I found it hard to believe that the records of the investigation into the death of a famous figure would have been destroyed, particularly when there was controversy around her death, but as I wasn't being honest about writing a book, it wasn't the time to get into an argument with a policeman. I was turning to go when I noticed another, older policeman standing near a filing cabinet and sending furtive looks in my direction. I was sure that he was listening to our conversation.

I turned back to the sergeant at the desk. 'You said records *may* be destroyed. Why would some be kept and others not?'

'Various reasons, but in the case you are speaking about, probably because foul play was ruled out.'

I caught the train to the station nearest to where la Rusa's body had been found. The station hadn't existed in 1952; according to the newspaper reports, la Rusa had caught a taxi to the village and then walked to the isolated spot by the tracks. No one remembered seeing her.

I alighted from the station in the late afternoon. The suburb consisted of high-rise buildings, a laundromat and a few stores. The buildings had a run-down look about them although they couldn't have been more than five years old. There were some cars parked alongside the station. One of them caught my eye: a brown BMW Longue. I noticed it because Mademoiselle Louvet had one like it in white. Although this car was an older model, it was polished and stood out from the battered Renaults and Citroëns. There was someone sitting in the driver's seat, but I couldn't see the face clearly because the windows were tinted.

I walked alongside a low concrete fence until it ended and there was nothing between me and the tracks but some overgrown grass and weeds. I was suddenly overcome by a feeling of desolation. Why had la Rusa, the greatest flamenco dancer of all time, come to this spot to end her life?

When I arrived for my flamenco lesson with Carmen, she told me that she was inspired to teach me the *farruca*.

'It's not a dance I usually show beginners,' she said. 'But I feel there is something you are suppressing. Perhaps this dance will bring it out.'

I glanced at Jaime, but he shook his head to let me know that he hadn't breathed a word about la Rusa to his aunt. 'It's not my secret to tell,' he'd promised me.

As I followed Carmen's lead, I saw that the *farruca* was everything that la Rusa had expressed in the first film that Jaime and I had watched that afternoon. The footwork was aggressive and the music shifted dramatically from one mood to another.

'Wow, you are on fire!' said Carmen, looking at me with admiration.

Indeed, dancing the *farruca* made me feel majestic and powerful; a sharp contrast to the defeatism I'd experienced the day before. If only I could make those feelings last, I thought. But I knew that as soon as I went home the strength would fade and I'd return to my normal anxious self.

'I'm sorry I can't stay for dinner tonight,' I told Carmen after the lesson. 'I've promised to help my grandmother with some things.'

I was torn between wanting to stay longer with Jaime and his family and my eagerness to hear more of Mamie's story. I was afraid that if there was too long a break between her reminiscences, she would change her mind and not tell me any more.

'You are welcome in our home any time,' Carmen said, kissing my cheeks. 'And your grandmother is welcome here too.' Then she added with a cheeky smile, 'She might have to change her mind about flamenco now!'

I glanced at her, wondering what she meant.

Carmen laughed. 'Jaime told me about the both of you,' she explained. 'I'm pleased. You are a well-brought-up girl. I've ordered my nephew to treat you with respect.'

I felt myself blush, and glanced at Jaime, who smiled and shrugged his shoulders.

'He does,' I told Carmen. 'He's very good to me.'

While Jaime walked me to my car, I filled him in about my visit to the police station and the place where la Rusa had committed suicide. 'It was such a sad, lonely spot. If it was la Rusa who betrayed Xavier, perhaps she deeply regretted it. I hope to find out more tonight.'

Jaime and I kissed before I climbed into the car. As I was about to start the engine, he knocked on the window. I unwound it and we kissed again.

'In future,' he said, serious for a moment, 'if you want to do any detective work, take me with you. You've got a man now. I'm here to protect you.'

I waved as I pulled out from the kerb. 'You've got a man now; I'm here to protect you.' It was such a Spanish male thing to say, I thought with a smile. But it felt good too.

To my dismay, after I drove home like a maniac and bounded up the apartment stairs, Mamie was already in bed when I arrived. I had to wait until after dinner the following evening, when we had cleaned the dishes and sat down with a pot of tea in the lounge room, for Mamie to begin to tell me what had happened to her brother.

'When I realised that Xavier and la Rusa were in love I suffered a dilemma.' She shook her head and glanced at her hands. 'I know it was wrong in the eyes of the Church, but how could I deny my brother this one happiness? He looked after Conchita well and saw to her every need; he was devoted to Feliu; and a dutiful son to our parents. But when he was with la Rusa . . . it was as if the real Xavier had emerged, the piece he could save for himself. He shed the skin that had been suffocating him and came alive.'

'Are you saying that la Rusa liberated him?' I asked her. 'Initially anyway?'

I thought of the spirit of freedom I had experienced while riding on the back of Jaime's Vespa—the sense of breaking out of restrictions and rules. I wondered if that was how Xavier had felt when he was with la Rusa. The idea made me sympathise with him.

Mamie stood up and walked to the window, where she stared out at the street. 'I was enamoured of the woman myself,' she said. 'La Rusa had this shining charisma and presence! Although she was a passionate person, she had a superhuman ability to contain herself. How was I to know the blackness within her?'

'Did Conchita ever find out?'

Mamie shook her head. 'Not at first, but eventually, yes. Xavier was head over heels and would not have been so discreet if it wasn't for la Rusa. She was careful that as few people as possible knew about them. She was always trying to protect Xavier. I liked her all the more for that.'

'Even so, Conchita knew?'

Mamie nodded and came back to sit on the sofa. 'It doesn't take much for a woman to suspect these things: a little hearsay, a whimsical smile on her husband's lips, hairpins in his pockets. There were some terrible fights. I remember Conchita screaming at Xavier once: "So that whore of a dancer has you eating out of her tough little hands, does she? She's glamorous and exciting in your eyes and I'm just some old shoe. But you are stuck with me whether you like it or not! If you ever try to leave me, my father will have you killed!"

'Her rages and threats of suicide would cause Xavier to try to be more discreet, but Conchita always knew and she hated la Rusa with a passion. Although it was normal for Spanish men of Xavier's position to have mistresses, and many men treated their wives more cruelly than Xavier treated Conchita, she was consumed with jealousy. She was convinced that la Rusa had used black magic to captivate Xavier. "She is a gypsy, after all," Conchita once told me. She could not see her own role in creating a cold, sexless marriage and blamed la Rusa for everything.'

Mamie looked like she was about to say something else, but instead rubbed furiously at her wedding ring. 'Xavier was ten years older than me and seemed happy for the first time in a long time. I had to trust him to manage his life. Besides that, the changes in Spain that were taking place around us were so great, I often felt that our daily lives were on the verge of being engulfed by them.'

Despite the troubles the Republican government suffered, there were many Catalans who regarded the early years of its rule as a kind of Golden Age in which culture and art blossomed. Even Pare, while not happy about having to pay higher wages and deal with worker unrest, was pleased that the Catalans had won greater autonomy for themselves and now had authority over the local police and civil service, local government and education. The Catalan language was once more official, and there were plans for new hospitals and better housing and recreation areas for the workers. 'For too long Barcelona has been held back by Madrid,' he said.

Although he maintained conservative views, Pare did not forbid Margarida from running for parliament in the February 1936 elections, although he did warn her that: 'It will be the last nail in the coffin of any hope you may have of marriage. A man will never take a woman involved in public life for a spouse.'

Given that Margarida had never been the marrying type, I think that prediction suited her. She preferred to undertake her battles outside the home, where the right-wing candidates she was up against tried to dismiss her as 'a lesbian and a whore'. Despite the fact that Margarida had never encouraged violence as a means to an end, her opponents attempted to turn middle-class voters against her by claiming she was an anarchist. Even some members of Margarida's own party resented her disdain of tradition. While they mired themselves in battles over seniority and so much bureaucratic detail that their reforms became useless, Margarida sidestepped party politics and put all her energy into making life better for the men and women in the street.

'Margarida has won twice as many votes as her nearest opponent!' Xavier shouted the day we all sat around the radio waiting for the election results to be read out.

The Left swept into power again. The Anarchists, having witnessed the damage absenteeism had done in the previous election, had urged the workers to vote this time. Margarida was among a handful of 'new women' who had won places in the Cortes. I was happy for her, although it meant she would now be spending time in Madrid and I would miss her.

'Well, she set out to win and she did it!' Pare cried proudly. 'Although I would have preferred it if she had joined the Catalan Party rather than the Socialists.'

'Just be happy for her!' Xavier told him.

Pare grinned.

I looked at my father. He had just turned sixty. Was he mellowing with age? Still, I couldn't imagine he would be as pleased if *I* had run for parliament.

Not everyone was happy with Margarida's new-found prestige. The person who was most angry of all was Conchita's father, don Carles, whose fascist sympathies had led him to become a prominent member of the Falange, along with the bull breeder and gangster Ignacio Salazar.

'You are supposed to be good Catholics!' he shouted at my father. 'And you are sending this country to hell!'

Don Carles cut off all relations with our family, including with his own daughter.

'Look at the trouble your sister has caused,' Conchita complained to me. 'Fortunately, my father has already honoured my dowry!'

When I look back on those times, the sweeping changes Spain was experiencing appeared to be heightening everyone's essential personality: the passionate became more passionate; the material, even more self-seeking; the timid, more frightened; and the treacherous . . . more dangerous.

But in 1936 I was too blissful to worry much about politics or family rifts. I was pregnant at last. And the baby was Gaspar's.

I had not seen Gaspar for three years, since the day he came to visit la Rusa while I was having a flamenco lesson with her. My feelings for him were so intense that I hadn't been able to bring myself to look at him. I knew then that I would never love anyone the way I loved Gaspar. But our situation was hopeless and I avoided him so that I wouldn't inflict more pain on him than I already had. While his work brought him to Barcelona from time to time, I had the impression he too was staying away as much as he could. Then fate brought us together again in January 1936.

An important part of the Catalan revival was to bring music and art to the workers of the city. One day, when Francesc was in Madrid, I went with Margarida to listen to a concert Xavier had organised in a community hall in the barri Xinès. Pau Casals, the famous cellist, was playing, along with other musicians. We hadn't told Xavier that we were coming. If we had, I'm sure he would have warned us that Gaspar was on the program.

When the master of ceremonies announced Gaspar Olivero's name and I saw the man my heart longed for walk onto the stage, I literally stopped breathing.

'Do you want to leave?' Margarida whispered to me.

I shook my head. 'No, really, it's all right,' I assured her.

But it wasn't. Along with other Spanish compositions, Gaspar performed 'The Maiden and the Nightingale' by Granados, the piece he had played at the Cerdà family's supper the first time I'd met him. Every moment of that evening came back to me in vivid detail. I remembered the intense expression on his face, and the way the piano had seemed to be a continuation of his arms. I recalled the calming effect he'd had on me when I'd panicked and fled to the dining room.

Gaspar finished playing and the audience rose to applaud him. He stood up from the piano and bowed. He straightened and for a split second our eyes met. The feeling of something unfinished, something longed for but never realised, pierced my heart.

'Let's go,' I said to Margarida.

We stood up to leave, but before we could reach the door, we were mobbed by people who had recognised Margarida as one of the new Socialist candidates running for the Cortes.

'Good on you for standing up to the landowners!' a man in a coat patched at the elbows told her.

'Please ask for better working conditions for women,' begged a mother clutching a small child.

While most people gathered around Margarida were supportive, one man wearing overalls folded his arms across his chest and said to her, 'You've never belonged to a union, you've never worked in a factory and you think you can represent us!'

If someone had confronted me that way, I would have shrivelled on the spot. But Margarida was made for politics.

'That's true,' she agreed. 'But I can read and interpret the legal documents that your employers throw at you and, because of that, I can stand up for your rights.'

A young man in a tram conductor's uniform gazed at her admiringly. Even though my sister towered a good foot over him, it didn't seem to bother him. 'You're very beautiful for a politician,' he said. 'Why aren't you married?' He flashed her a flirtatious smile.

It occurred to me that if Margarida had been so inclined, she would not have hesitated to marry someone from the working class. She was brave enough to defy society's norms. I wasn't. That was how I'd lost Gaspar.

Despite our attempts to reach the door, more people gathered around Margarida, giving her suggestions for reforms or asking her to solve a personal issue. Margarida wasn't fazed by the attention or the demands. She looked everyone straight in the eye and told them what she honestly thought.

I remembered a story that la Rusa had told me that illustrated my sister perfectly. La Rusa said that she had met my sister and me when Margarida was a child and I was a baby in a pram. Our nursemaid had taken us to the flower markets where la Rusa was helping a friend of her father's with her stall. Margarida had held out her hand to the little urchin la Rusa without a moment's hesitation. That was Margarida all over. She was different to everybody but she could get along with anybody. She had even managed to twist my strict father around her finger. The exceptions, of course, were Conchita and don Carles: certainly there was no love lost there.

'Evelina?'

The sound of Gaspar's voice jolted me from my thoughts. When I saw him standing in front of me, I realised that time and distance had not changed the intensity of my feelings. The longer we were apart, the stronger they grew. I realised what I had been waiting for and what I had let slip through my fingers because of my lack of boldness.

'Come to see me this evening,' I whispered to him. 'Francesc and his parents are in Madrid.'

My voice sounded strange even to myself, but in that moment I was determined not to allow myself to be thwarted ever again.

A serious expression came over Gaspar's face. Hadn't he heard me correctly? Did he disapprove? I stared at him, trying to understand the source of his hesitation, but before we could speak further, the crowd around Margarida swelled even larger and we lost sight of each other.

That night at dinner, I pushed and prodded at the rice and tomato on my plate until I admitted to myself that I had no appetite. Penélope was married now, and I was alone in the house. I sat by the fire, my heart racked with pain. Gaspar had not sent a message and it was now ten o'clock. He wasn't coming. My feelings for him were so powerful that I hadn't counted on the fact that his for me might have faded. Then a terrible thought came to me: what if Gaspar had married since I had last seen him and nobody had told me?

I sent the servants to bed early so I could be alone in my misery. But no sooner had I returned to my chair in the drawing room than there was a soft knock at the front door. I rushed to open it and found Gaspar standing before me. A feeling of radiant happiness washed over me, dispelling all the self-doubt of a moment before.

I ushered him inside, and we studied each other's faces affectionately for a long while before he said, 'I'm sorry I couldn't come earlier. I had another concert to play at this evening. I wasn't sure if I'd be able to get away!'

I shook my head. So that had been the source of his hesitation. It didn't matter. Nothing mattered now that he was here. I invited him to the drawing room and we both sat down in the chairs by the fire.

'I've sent the servants to bed,' I told him. 'But I can make us some tea.'

Gaspar gave me a long and tender look. He stood up and tried to say something, but for once he was lost for words. Instead, he pulled me to him and pressed my cheek to his chest.

I could not believe that Gaspar was holding me in his arms, that anything about the moment was real. I had been married for seven years but I had no sexual experience. Yet everything seemed natural. I was peaceful and happy when I led Gaspar to the bedroom and we pressed our bodies together. The passion that I had been denied burned over my skin. Even when we got older and life took its toll, I never lost the flame in my heart for Gaspar that was ignited that night.

When dawn broke the next morning, Gaspar and I lay in the tangle of bedclothes and gazed into each other's eyes.

'I love you,' he whispered. 'But we won't be able to go on like this—not after Francesc returns.'

In his voice I heard a mingling of joy and sadness. It matched my feelings perfectly.

For the next week, Gaspar and I did not think about Francesc returning or being separated again. I went in disguise to his apartment, telling my household's servants I was staying with my parents. There we made love until our skin was raw from kisses and our flesh bruised from our ardent embraces. It was the most heavenly and heady seven days I have ever known.

The day Francesc and his parents were due back and Gaspar and I had to part, I did not feel as devastated as I had expected. From Gaspar's tranquil manner, it seemed that he felt the same way. To have had a week of each other was more than we'd ever expected life to grant us; and although I would always wish for more, I felt gratitude for what I had been given.

Only, as it turned out, Gaspar had left me with something more than sentimental memories.

'You are sure you are going to have a child?' Francesc asked me.

I nodded.

He fell silent, spreading his fingers on the desk in front of him and contemplating them for a while. If Francesc had been a typical man, there would have been a terrible scene over my 'unfaithfulness'; there would have been shouts, tears and recriminations. But I could only guess at what he was thinking.

Although Francesc had never been able to perform his duty to me as a husband in a physical way, and we had been sleeping in separate bedrooms for a few years now, we had never spoken of our unconsummated marriage to each other. We had both been conspirators in the secret. Now, even indirectly, we had to admit the truth to each other. I realised that la Rusa had been correct when she had said that my falling pregnant to Gaspar would relieve Francesc from the suspicion that something wasn't right in our marriage. So now Francesc and I were to be schemers in another secret: pretending that the child was his.

'You were discreet?' he asked.

'Yes,' I told him, unable to meet his gaze.

'Someone of good breeding, I hope? Someone who won't talk?'

I nodded. For some reason, I could not bring myself to tell Francesc that the father of my child was his cousin. But, to my surprise, he guessed.

'Was it Gaspar?'

I nodded, feeling my face redden.

'Very well,' he said, standing up. 'When you feel ready, we will announce it to my parents.'

I was relieved. So Francesc would recognise the child as his own.

He gave me a peck on the cheek. It was the second-last intimate conversation he and I were ever to have together.

After we announced my pregnancy, Francesc treated me with courtesy but kept me at an even greater distance than he had before. At first, I wondered if he was hurt that I had been unfaithful to him with Gaspar. But then I realised from the way he looked whenever he saw my growing stomach that my body revolted him even more than it had when I was a virgin. While it hurt me to be found so repugnant, I bore it with grace. My greatest wish had been granted. I was aware of it every time the child kicked inside me.

I was in the seventh month of my pregnancy when the Civil War broke out. I was visiting Mama and Conchita when the news came to us.

While Mama and Conchita were embroidering clothes for the new baby, Feliu and I were reading a book. At eight years of age, Feliu was a miniature version of Xavier. Whenever Xavier was with him, Feliu knew that he had his father's undivided attention. They both had a special glow in their faces when they spent time together.

When we had finished reading, Feliu turned to me with a serious expression. 'After the baby is born, will you still love me?' he asked, looking at me with his big eyes.

'I'll always love you!' I assured him. 'You are my special Feliu.'

His question moved me—and saddened me too. I glanced at Conchita. She wasn't a bad person. I enjoyed her company and she could be generous, but why was she so cold to her son? Couldn't she see how much he needed her love? Conchita's whole life was spent pampering herself, fixing her hair in front of her dressing table, choosing beautiful gowns. But who got to enjoy the spectacular results? She had distanced her husband with her vanity and selfishness and she couldn't even give any affection to her own child.

The telephone rang and I heard the maid summon Margarida, who was up from Madrid for a while. After a few minutes of silence, I heard Margarida shout, 'But this is serious! The workers have to be armed! The first thing the army will do is seize the telephone and radio buildings—they must be stopped!'

Mama and I exchanged glances. I was tempted to run to the study to see what had happened but then Xavier came home.

'Pare!' he called, rushing into the room. 'Is Pare at home?' he asked us. From the pallor of his face, I could see something was wrong.

'What's happened?' I asked.

'There's something going on,' he said. 'There has been an uprising of the army in Morocco and it seems to be spreading to garrisons all over Spain. Members of the government and other prominent people have been arrested here in Barcelona this morning.'

'So it's a rebellion by the army against the Republic?' I asked.

Mama looked up from her sewing and sighed. 'We've been through all this before,' she said. 'I suppose we are going to be banned from using Catalan in public again?'

Margarida finished her telephone conversation and joined us, along with Pare. 'No, Mama!' she said. 'This is not a rebellion like the one led by Primo de Rivera. He at least was a reasonable man. The general at the heart of this is Francisco Franco.'

I recalled the name and it sent shivers down my spine. In 1934 there had been a revolt by miners in Asturias. It was put down by Franco, whose methods were so brutal and so ruthless that when the Left returned to power in 1936, Franco lost his position with the War Ministry and was sent to the Canary Islands where it was hoped he wouldn't cause any more trouble.

'If the army isn't loyal to the Republic how will the rebels be stopped?' asked Pare.

Margarida sat down next to Mama. 'The Republic needs to arm the unions and the workers. They are the ones who will fight for it,' she said.

Mama raised her eyebrows. 'But the Anarchists will use the opportunity to turn this chaos into a revolution if you give them guns.'

'That's right,' said Margarida. 'But perhaps a revolution in Spain is preferable to a country crushed by a brutal army. The rebels claim that they are saving Spain from the "Reds" and from anti-Christian forces, but what they really want is power. I can't see their aim as being a better standard of living for the Spanish people.'

We fell silent. Margarida's words had a strangely prophetic ring to them. I looked at my family and the menacing shadow of doom I had sensed over the years washed over me. Only this time, it was much stronger.

Mamie looked at me with sorrow in her eyes. She kept touching her shoulder as if it pained her, a gesture I had never seen her make before. I sensed her exhaustion and, although it meant that I would be left in suspense again, suggested we recommence the storytelling tomorrow.

In truth, she had left me with plenty of new information to digest, not least that my mother had initially been brought up as the daughter of Francesc Cerdà, not Avi. I couldn't wait to hear how that issue was resolved.

TWENTY-NINE

Evelina

*D*earest Margarida,

    I have almost told Paloma all she needs to know about the fate of our dear brother and the Montella family. But as I relate the story, I realise that I must be careful. Sometimes Paloma misses the obvious, but at other times she is very sharp. I do not want to reveal to her the one thing she doesn't need to know. If she found out, it would destroy her peace of mind for good . . .

THIRTY

Paloma

When I arrived at the cinema where I was meeting Jaime to see *Le Sauvage*, I got more than I'd expected. Jaime was standing in the foyer, looking handsome in his butterfly-collar shirt and platform shoes, but he wasn't alone. Carmen was there too, with Isabel, Vicenta, Ernesto and Mercedes. The only adult missing was Félix, who was at home minding Ricardo and Víctor.

Jaime kissed me chastely on the cheeks. 'I'm sure you know the saying: *Fall in love with a Spaniard, fall in love with his family,*' he said. 'Now that they know we are seeing each other, I don't think we are going to have much chance of being left alone if we want to go out at night.'

I grinned at the irony of it. I thought about what Mamie had told me so far about her family in the 1930s: Xavier having a mistress; Mamie herself being unfaithful to her homosexual husband. And here were Jaime and I in 1975—the days of sexual liberation and women going braless—being chaperoned by his family.

I greeted Carmen and the others with kisses before we walked into the cinema. Although I laughed along with everyone else at the antics of Catherine Deneuve as Nelly, a woman desperate to avoid going through with a marriage, I couldn't help thinking of Mamie and what she must have felt being forced to marry someone she didn't love.

After the film, when we gathered in a café for a glass of wine and I looked at the happy faces of Jaime's family, I thought of Mamie again, at home alone. She had forbidden me from riding the Métro late at night, preferring that I took her car instead, but she hadn't mentioned anything about me going out alone with Jaime. She had seemed happy for me when I told her about Jaime, but she hadn't asked me anything about him. It could have been because she had faith in my sensible nature, or perhaps it was because her parents had interfered so tragically in her love life that she didn't want to do the same with me.

When it was time to go home, Jaime was allowed to walk me to my car while everyone waited for him back at the cinema.

'You don't mind, do you?' he said, grimacing. 'They do it because they care about us, not because they are prudes. They don't want us to move too quickly and then regret it. I think they really like you.'

I shook my head. 'I'm happy they care about us. Besides, it makes me think of what it must have been like for la Rusa. Didn't you say she went everywhere with her gypsy clan?'

Jaime nodded. 'I'm not sure if they were as crazy as my family—but maybe.' He grinned before kissing me briefly on the lips. 'I'll call you tomorrow, okay?'

On my way home, I thought about Jaime's family again. They were so involved and 'together' in everything they did. My mind drifted from Xavier, to Mamie and Avi, to Mama and Papa, and then to Feliu. Why was my family so shattered?

I arrived home and found Mamie was still up, sipping a cup of tea. She was ready to tell me more of her story. Perhaps she would be able to explain the mystery of my fractured family.

'I have always believed that the Republican government could have won the war against Franco,' Mamie said. 'Once the decision was finally made to arm the workers, they fought with spirit. After all, the Anarchists and Communists among them had years of street-fighting experience. They were helped by those members of the army and police who had remained loyal to the Republic. Franco's forces became known as "the Nationalists" but they didn't have the whole nation's support. At first, they were simply called "military rebels" because that's all they really were. The Loyalists managed to defeat Franco's coup in the major urban centres, including Madrid, in a matter of days. This meant the gold reserves and the communications networks remained in the hands of the Republican government. The military coup could have been stopped as quickly as it began—only we were betrayed.'

I knew my Spanish history well enough to understand the betrayal Mamie was referring to. Franco's 'Nationalist' army requested help from its Fascist allies, Germany and Italy. The Germans and Italians seized the opportunity to test the weapons they had been developing in a real war and within days the rebels received military equipment and transport. But when the Republican government turned to Britain and France for help, it was faced with their policy of non-intervention.

'As well as his military officers, Franco's army was made up of Moroccan mercenaries and soldiers of the Foreign Legion,' explained Mamie. 'They swept through the country, torturing, butchering, raping and executing any who stood in their way.

'Because of his language skills and the time he had spent abroad, Xavier was asked to join a diplomatic mission whose purpose was to convince the other European powers to help the Republic.

'As things were precarious in Spain, I went with Mama to stay in Paris until the baby was born. We rented an apartment on avenue Hoche by parc Monceau. There, the war and the shadow that was falling over all Europe seemed far away. The French were living with a sense of *joie de vivre*, as if happiness and pleasure could somehow ward off evil. Feliu had come with us, and it was with great mirth that we listened to his stories when he returned each day from exploring Paris with his governess. "Tia Evelina," he would say, snuggling up to me on the sofa, "the sweet shops here are even more wonderful than on the passeig de Gràcia! The macarons are so sweet they make my lips tingle!"

'Xavier came to visit us while we were staying in Paris. He was despondent after yet another of his diplomatic missions to the city had failed to achieve anything further for Spain.' Mamie cleared her throat and took a sip of tea, preparing herself to finally tell me about the downfall of Spain—and her family.

'The Germans and Italians are flagrantly ignoring the non-intervention pact while Britain and France are sticking so firmly to it that they are breaking international law,' Xavier said, venting his frustration. 'The legitimate government of Spain has a right to defend itself, but they've put in place an embargo preventing any country from supplying us with matériel. In the meantime, the Italians transport arms to Franco unchallenged by the Royal Navy! The Americans are as bad. Their government adheres to non-intervention while private companies like General Motors and Texaco are providing goods to Franco on credit!'

I was upset by that news, and also to see Xavier looking so defeated. At thirty-seven years of age, he was still handsome but there were dark circles under his eyes from a lack of sleep and he hardly smiled any more.

'Your father says the allies are afraid that if they help the Republican government it will place them in direct conflict with Germany and Italy—and that could bring about another European war,' Mama told him.

Xavier examined his knuckles. 'I used to think that too, but now I see things differently.'

'How?' I asked, pouring him a cup of coffee.

'The British and French hope that the Fascists will exhaust themselves in Spain and therefore will be incapable of starting a larger war. We are to be sacrificed to that end.'

'Margarida proposed to the Cortes that Spain should grant Morocco independence,' I told Xavier. 'She said that it would stop the flow of Moroccan soldiers into Franco's army.'

'Oh no,' said Mama, slicing some cake. 'That would completely alienate the British and French.'

'My opinion is that we should give up caring what the British and French think,' said Xavier. 'They are never going to lift a finger to help us anyway. In fact, I have come across some reports that suggest Franco was flown into Spain by British intelligence officers. It's time we looked in other directions for support.'

'The Soviet Union, you mean?' I asked him.

'There's been a workers' revolution of sorts in Spain, so that would make sense,' he said. 'The problem is supply. Russia can't easily transport weapons to Spain by sea, and they don't have the production capabilities of Germany. Right now I'm negotiating with the Mexicans and buying military supplies on the black market. But that means the Republic is paying ten times as much for equipment as the rebels are.'

Xavier went on to explain how the lack of military supplies was crippling the Spanish government. 'The Republic's General Rojo is a genius strategist and far superior to Franco, but he is constantly thwarted in his attempts to regain Republican territory. He never knows if the required arms will arrive for a planned offensive.'

Xavier told us a terrifying story about a shipment of arms from Poland that was so defective, most of the casualties on the Republican side were caused by the soldiers' own weapons exploding or misfiring. Later, the backup shipment that he had bought from Mexico turned out to be a collection of rusty guns taken from museums.

* * *

I went into labour on 7 November 1936, two weeks past my due date and the day the battle for Madrid commenced. As I strained and panted to bring new life into the world, I thought of all the lives that were now being extinguished on the battlefield. In the early hours of the morning, Julieta was born. I cried when I saw her. I named her after my maternal grandmother.

Not long after Julieta's birth, we began to receive a frequent visitor to the apartment: la Rusa. She was living in Paris, which meant she and Xavier could be more open about their relationship. Although Mama absented herself when la Rusa came to visit, she made no objection to me receiving her. That was the contradictory etiquette to which we adhered: Mama liked la Rusa because she made Xavier happy, but, out of loyalty to Conchita, she could not *appear* to approve of her.

La Rusa seemed lonely in Paris. She usually lived and travelled with a large group of gypsies, but a few months earlier Margarida had warned her that gypsies in Germany were being rounded up and sent to work camps where the conditions were horrific. With the rise of Fascism all over Europe, la Rusa wasn't going to take any chances. She sent her clan to California, where she kept a property near Los Angeles. I expected her to follow them soon; many Spanish entertainers had already left for America. So I was astonished when, a few days before Christmas, during a visit with Xavier, she told us she was returning to Spain to drive ambulances for the Republican army.

'The brave people of Madrid held on to their city despite the massive onslaught by the rebel army. I have to help them!'

'It's too dangerous,' Xavier protested. 'Unless this international ban on selling arms to Spain is lifted, the Republican army and its supporters are going to be slaughtered!'

'How can I desert Spain,' la Rusa said, her eyes flashing, 'while every day I see foreigners going to fight for our country? Ordinary men and women—British, Americans, Russians, Poles,

Jews, anti-Fascists from Italy and Germany—all risking their lives to help us even though their governments will do nothing! They are fighting for a system of rule that gives equal value to all citizens. The kind of society my father and brother believed in. The kind *you* have always believed in.'

'We are wrong to let them fight for us,' said Xavier, 'when we can't give them decent weapons.'

This decision of la Rusa's was the one thing I ever saw her and Xavier argue over. Still, although Xavier tried to persuade her not to go, I think he was secretly proud of her. I was in awe of her. Her courage was inspiring.

The day la Rusa departed Paris, I accompanied her and Xavier to the station. I left Julieta back at the apartment with Mama; I did not want her out in the winter chill. As Xavier and la Rusa made their farewells, they could not have looked more like a couple in love. They held each other for a long time, before staring into each other's face. La Rusa's eyes were brimming with tears and my brother's lips trembled when he said, 'In all my life, there has only ever been you.' It was hard for me to watch two of the strongest people I knew look so vulnerable.

La Rusa took my hand and squeezed it before she climbed into the train. When the whistle sounded and the train began to pull out of the station, she put her head out of the window so she could wave to us as it departed. Although she kept her gaze fixed on us, I had a feeling that she didn't really see us. Her mind was somewhere else.

It would be nearly a year before I would meet her again.

La Rusa wasn't the only one who wanted to return to Spain. When Julieta was three months old, Mama decided that we should go back too. The front was still far from Barcelona, and Catalonia was so close to France that many of the city's inhabitants felt certain that if the Nationalist rebels truly threatened it, the French would intervene.

'Pare and Margarida need us,' Mama said. She was not a woman to be apart from her husband for too long. She was of the breed of wife who put duty above comfort.

When Mama and I, Julieta, Feliu and his governess returned we found a revolution of sorts had taken place. After the Anarchists and Communists had defeated the military coup in the city in 1936, they had taken control of everything and the weakened parliament had not tried to stop them. Now, Anarchist and Communist flags hung from the railway station and the buildings around it.

Because our family cars had been commandeered to drive militia men to the front, we had to wait in line at the taxi stand. All the taxis had been painted in the Anarchist colours of red and black. We engaged two vehicles: one to take us, and the other to carry our luggage. The drivers made no attempt to help us lift our bags into the taxi, and I had to open the door for myself although I was holding a baby in my arms. Mama was about to scold the drivers for their lack of manners when we saw the note pinned to the back of the front seat. It said that as all citizens were now equal in Barcelona, taxi drivers expected to be treated with respect. Mama glanced at me and raised her eyebrows.

Once we pulled out of the station, it didn't take us long to realise that taxis were not the only form of transport that been painted red and black. The trams and trucks had been repainted too. Restaurants were now canteens for the workers, and shops and cafés had signs on them stating they had been collectivised.

'Oh my goodness!' Mama gasped, before checking herself.

We passed by the gutted and burned frame of a church. The remnants of a statue of Mary were scattered on the pavement. I felt a strange mix of sorrow and anger when I saw one of Christ's nail-pierced hands tossed in the gutter.

'There will be no more churches,' the taxi driver told us. 'They are being torn down.'

Mama paled. I took her hand and held it.

While I could understand the anger at the corruption of the clergy, I couldn't bear to think of Barcelona's beautiful churches and cathedrals being destroyed. Our family had made several donations to the construction of the Sagrada Família. Although it wasn't to everyone's taste, I loved the whimsical cathedral. I had grown up watching it develop like a giant tree with each passing year. The bell towers were now finished, along with the cypress spire. I shut my eyes against the terrible vision that it might have been painted red and black—or even worse, dynamited.

There were other noticeable changes in Barcelona: there were no priests or nuns to be seen; and when we pulled into the passeig de Gràcia, there were no well-dressed people either. Everyone was wearing workers' overalls and badly tailored coats. Perhaps the clerics and the rich had fled the city? Or were they walking around in disguise? I wasn't sure that I liked Barcelona this way, but then in the whole trip from the station to our house, I hadn't seen any beggars or homeless children on the streets either.

When the taxis pulled up outside my family's home, I had a terrible premonition that it had been divided up into flats for the working class, as I had heard the Soviets had done to mansions and palaces in Moscow. I wondered what Xavier and Margarida would say if that had happened. They might have liked it, having always been more egalitarian than me. I didn't like the idea of children starving on the street, or of their parents working like slaves in factories, yet at the same time I was shocked to realise how much I enjoyed the status quo. I wanted to wear beautiful clothes and live in a fine mansion. I might wish for good things for others, but I didn't want to lose what I had.

I was relieved to discover that the biggest change at home was that the menservants had left for the front and the maids greeted us with 'Salud', which was considered more revolutionary than Buenos días or Bon dia.

Unlike the people on the streets, Conchita was stylishly turned out in a dress with diagonal stripes and a tailored jacket with white piping. Despite the fact that she had not seen Feliu in months, she was as stiff and formal with him as ever. 'Run along with la senyora Tortosa now,' she told him, patting his head in an absentminded way. 'I've got some things to discuss with your grandmother and aunt.'

When Feliu and his governess had left the room, Conchita turned to us. 'You can't imagine how bored I've been here without you two,' she said. 'One can't go out on the streets without hearing those insipid revolutionary songs. Barcelona isn't fun any more!'

She peeked at Julieta, who was asleep in my arms. 'She's dark, isn't she?' she said. 'People would think she was mine not yours and Francesc's. He's so blond and you are fair too.'

I prickled at the comment. Having been away from Conchita, I'd forgotten how caustic she could be sometimes, even to people she liked. There were plenty of dark beauties on Mama's and Pare's sides of the family.

Mama's personal maid, Maria, appeared and offered to bathe Julieta for me. 'You and la senyora Montella must both be exhausted,' she said. 'I will bring you some tea.'

'Well, thank goodness Maria hasn't changed,' Mama said when the maid was out of earshot. 'I half expected her to tell you to bathe Julieta yourself.'

'Look, Mama,' I said, sitting down next to her, 'it is all a bit strange, but I guess we'll have to get used to it. It's far better to have the city run by the Anarchists than to be invaded by Franco's army. They are murderers.'

I shivered, although it was warm in the house. What I had read in the French papers on the train had shocked me. When Málaga fell to the rebel forces, Italian troops had pursued the fleeing civilian population for miles before massacring them. Such brutality made everything that was going on in Barcelona mild by comparison. Instead of throwing bombs, the Anarchists were trying to create a society of equality and peace where everybody had food and a home.

'But the churches,' Mama wept. 'I agree that it is better for people to be educated and fed, but do we have to become heathens?'

I put my arm around her, wondering if it would have been better if we had stayed in Paris. 'Go rest for a while, Mama. You are exhausted from the trip.'

I turned to Conchita. 'I'm not sure who to go see first: Pare or Francesc.'

'Go to your father,' Conchita replied. 'He is the one who needs you most.'

I couldn't find another taxi, so I caught the tram to the outskirts of the city where Pare's main textiles factory was located. Revolutionary songs blasted from the tram's speakers the whole trip. People kept staring at me, at my handmade shoes and tailored clothes, and I realised that I was going to have to find some different attire if I didn't want to draw attention to myself. Near the factory tram stop was a women's clothing store. I bought a shapeless coat to wear over my dress. The material was scratchy and stiff and I could smell the chemicals that had been used to dye it. I felt dowdy in it but I reminded myself that people all around the country were dying, and that kept my discomfort in perspective.

I found Pare in his office, which he now shared with his secretary and clerk.

'Let's go for a walk,' he said, when he saw me.

He took me around to the side of the factory where we sat on a bench. 'They've collectivised all the Montella factories in Barcelona,' he said, looking more bemused than angry. 'Almost all the other factory owners have fled or joined the Nationalists. But I'm not going anywhere. I built these factories up from nothing, and even though nobody wishes to call me "senyor" any more, I'm not going to let them run my life's work into the ground.'

'I don't like Barcelona this way,' I told him. 'It's lost its charm.'

'Don't worry,' he assured me. 'The revolutionary atmosphere is dying down. It's much calmer now than it was a couple of months ago. I think the government is finally understanding that they have to get the workers under control. The Republic could have been harnessing Barcelona's industrial power to manufacture matériel for the war effort. I think the workers here need to wake up to the fact that it's more important to repel the massive death squad that is marching towards them than worrying about whether or not people speak to them nicely.'

'Do you really think Franco's army will reach Barcelona?' I asked. 'The Republican army seems to have regained some ground.'

Pare shook his head. 'Franco is taking his time, letting the Republicans exhaust themselves. He doesn't want to destroy the infrastructure of Spain. What he wants to destroy is his enemies. And if he has to kill two-thirds of the Spanish population to do that, it seems to me he is prepared to do so.'

On our way back to the passeig de Gràcia together, I thought about what Pare had said. He wasn't a revolutionary or a leftist; he was a die-hard Catalan who hated Barcelona being beholden to a centralist government. That was why he hadn't deserted his factories. But if the Nationalists reached Barcelona, he would certainly be executed as a traitor for keeping his industries running.

I did my best to put those thoughts out of my mind when we arrived back home and Pare laid eyes on his granddaughter. 'She's a true beauty, all right,' he said, cradling her in his arms and touching her hands and feet. 'Look at her delicate fingers and toes.'

When I returned to the Cerdà household, Francesc was waiting there for me. The furniture, what was left of it, was covered in white cloths and all the servants were gone.

'They are fighting in the popular army,' Francesc said. 'Poor devils! The maids have all taken roles in the factories and transport.'

'Where are your parents?' I asked.

He motioned for me to come into his study. 'May I see her?' he said, indicating Julieta. I pulled the blanket away so he could see her rosy face. He smiled. 'She's very beautiful, Evelina. You should be proud.'

Francesc had aged since I had last seen him: the grooves around his mouth had deepened and he looked tired. He'd always appeared so healthy and fresh.

'My parents, along with Penélope and her husband, have decided to leave for Argentina,' he told me. 'Barcelona isn't what it used to be and, although we are a noble family, we don't support murderers. I know I can't ask you to leave your family, Evelina, so I want to grant you a divorce.'

My heart plummeted. 'But I've just had a child. You can't abandon me.'

He lifted his hand in a reassuring gesture. 'You have been a wonderful wife, Evelina. I can't say a word against you. I'm only doing this because the Republic has made divorce legal and there is no shame in it any more. I know that you have not been happy with me. Gaspar is Julieta's father and you should be free to marry each other.'

I stared at him.

'I'm made for different things,' he said. 'We both know it.'

I was overcome by a profound sadness. I was sorry that Francesc and I could not have been so open with each other from the beginning.

'Now,' he said, rising to take some papers from his desk drawer, 'unfortunately, the properties that came with your dowry have been collectivised. But I have bought you a house in France, in the Dordogne, and deposited some money for you in a Swiss bank. I want you to go back to France with Julieta and your family. Gaspar, the fool, returned to Barcelona after you left and volunteered. He's now an officer in the Republican army. I don't know where he is but I will try to get word to him. I hope you will be happy together.'

I don't know which overwhelmed me more: Francesc's generosity in freeing me to be with Gaspar, or the dangerous position Gaspar had put himself in. Please don't let him be killed, I prayed. The idea that Gaspar could die before he had a chance to see Julieta made me weak in the legs.

'In the circumstances, I think it is best that I return to my family home,' I told Francesc.

He nodded. 'I imagine that your parents will be upset. I haven't told mine yet. But it's for the best, Evelina. We both know that.'

Francesc and I embraced. He walked me to the door and we embraced again. Francesc might not have been an ideal husband, but he was a fine human being. I knew that I would never say a bad word against him.

The Republic of Spain amazed the world. Despite suffering a military revolt, it had rapidly created a disciplined army. In spite of the high-technology arms supplied to the rebels by Germany and Italy and the lack of similar support from its supposed allies, the Loyalist army, along with Madrid's courageous civilians, had repelled Franco's forces from the city to the rallying cry of '*No pasaran!*': they shall not pass. By some miracle, the government was even able to re-create a sense of normality in the country's non-combatant zones. But the Republic was bleeding and its strength could not last. It was the charging bull— courageous and noble, but the odds were hopelessly stacked against it.

Franco and his forces pushed forward into the Basque country, Santander and Asturias. In April 1937, Guernica, a market town of no military significance, was firebombed by the German Condor Legion as a test to see what damage shrapnel bombs and machine-gunning from the air could inflict on a civilian population. Barcelona and other Spanish cities were bombed too. Still neither Britain nor France would come to our aid.

By October, Republican Spain was cut in two halves. There was the Catalan north-east; and the centre-south, which encompassed the cities of Madrid and Valencia. The government, which had already relocated from Madrid to Valencia, now moved to Barcelona.

This meant Margarida was back living with us when Xavier returned from another unsuccessful mission to France. It was the first time all of us had been together in the house for over a year. One afternoon, we gathered in the drawing room to discuss the progress of the war, except for Conchita, who was nursing a headache, and Feliu, who was having a lesson with his governess.

'Things are going from bad to worse,' Xavier said, pouring us each a glass of black-market wine. 'It looks as if both the Russians and the British intend to make deals with Hitler. They should know that what the Germans did in Guernica is what they intend to do to the rest of Europe.'

'What will happen if they sign pacts with Hitler?' I asked.

Xavier's mouth turned into a grim line. 'The Soviets will withdraw all aid to us. Then we will have nothing but our bare hands to fight with.'

'Things are so dire,' said Margarida, biting at her nails, 'that I go around with an insane kind of optimism that they simply have to get better.'

Despite the enormous strain she had been under as a member of a government at war, I was relieved to see Margarida had lost nothing of her black humour.

'Well, those stupid street battles between the Communists and the other factions of the Left didn't help,' said Pare. 'For a moment there it looked as though we were going to have a civil war within a civil war.'

Xavier turned to Margarida. 'The Anarchists are saying that they are not being as well supplied with weapons as the Communists because the government doesn't want a revolution; and the Communists are under order from Russia not to cause one.'

'The approach we are taking is that we need to win the war first, then we can worry about revolutions,' Margarida told him. 'That's why the Loyalist army is gearing up for another offensive.'

'In God's name, why?' asked Pare. 'We should focus on controlling what we've got and making a compromise with Franco. He can have his part of Spain and we can have ours.'

I knew that my father felt that as long as Catalonia was safe, nothing else really mattered. He wanted to get back to business as soon as possible.

Margarida's face became serious. 'We are not dealing with someone who makes civilised compromises. When the Republican side captures rebel soldiers, we feed them and treat them according to military conventions. The democratic justice system still prevails in our zone. When Franco's forces take over a village that has shown any sort of resistance, they kill everybody without question or a trial. Franco is not interested in saving lives. Therefore we have two choices: either we fight until the growing tension over Czechoslovakia finally brings about a European war and the British and French need us as allies against the Germans; or we get the hell out of here!'

I thought of Gaspar. The last I'd heard of him was what Francesc had managed to find out: that he was alive and well, but posted on the dangerous Aragon front. I could flee to safety but what would happen to him? It frightened me to even consider it.

I turned to Pare and Mama. 'I think we should leave for France as soon as we can. Margarida and Xavier will go with the Republic to form a government in exile, but we should go now. I have that property in the Dordogne.'

'And leave everything?' Mama asked, horrified.

'*Everything* is not worth our lives, Mama. Plenty of people have already departed the country.'

'The Cerdà and the de Figueroa families might have cleared out,' said Pare, his eyes blazing, 'but we are the Montellas! *We own Barcelona*. If Franco wants it, he's going to have to negotiate with me!'

'Don't be a fool!' Xavier told him. 'Franco hates Catalonia and all it stands for. He will crush it and you will simply be a pebble under his feet!'

* * *

A few weeks later, I met la Rusa again. She had come to Barcelona on leave. When the military coup had first broken out, women had fought alongside their husbands and brothers in the militias. But as the Republic began to organise a professional army, women were called up to the home front to take men's places in factories, transport and on farms. However, la Rusa's role as an ambulance driver kept her close to the front. Xavier had told me that her ambulance was constantly fired upon by German and Italian planes and that she had witnessed stretcher bearers blown to bits by them. 'The government keeps offering her a role as an entertainer to the troops,' he'd said. 'But she refuses. She says she wants to fight with the "real people". Besides that, the army medical unit wants to hold on to her: she's proved to be a skilful driver.' What Xavier didn't tell me was how much la Rusa had changed.

I found her waiting for me in the café where we had arranged to meet. She was wearing khaki overalls with a red-cross armband and no make-up. Her thick hair was hidden under a beret and, apart from her dramatic eyes and sensual mouth, she looked like any other woman in the street. Her hands and fingers were devoid of jewellery. The only adornment she wore was a pair of golden hooped earrings: the kind the gypsies favour. It was hard to believe that she was one of Spain's most popular entertainers.

'Xavier asked me to take you and your family over the border to France if the rebels reach Barcelona,' she said, reaching into her pocket and taking out a packet of cigarettes. She lit one and stared at me. 'Your parents won't go now? That's foolish. If you go now, you can simply catch a train. You won't have any trouble getting into France. If you leave it too late, the French might close the border.'

She spoke like she danced: in short, staccato bursts of energy.

'I can't leave without my parents,' I said.

'Eventually they are going to have to leave,' she said. 'Unless they have a death wish!'

La Rusa had always had a hard edge to her personality, but now I sensed a layer of armour around her that was so thick I doubted I would ever be able to penetrate it. In the whole time I had known her, I'd never seen her put a cigarette in her mouth. Now she was chain-smoking and the tips of her fingers were stained yellow. They were Lucky Strikes: foreign cigarettes. She must have had a good contact on the black market. Most people these days were smoking dried maize leaves.

'Why do you say that?' I asked her.

She didn't answer my question directly. She only repeated what Margarida had said. 'If the rebels come, you'd better get away. If you don't value your own life enough, then at least think of Julieta.'

While in Barcelona, la Rusa had agreed to do some performances at the old Samovar Club. It seemed strange that in the midst of bombings and the prospect of death, the people of Barcelona still liked to be entertained. Xavier, Margarida and I went to see her at the club a few evenings later. The place was shabby and run-down now. The columns were covered in hand marks and the floor was in need of a polish. The glamorous women in their evening dresses and furs had disappeared too. La Rusa's audience consisted of soldiers and workers.

When the band walked onto the stage, I half expected Gaspar to take his place at the piano. But of course he wasn't there. The thought that anything could happen to him was like a stone in my heart.

La Rusa's vigorous dancing meant that she had never had a spare ounce of fat on her, but it seemed to me that she was even thinner now: I could see her rib bones through her dress. Her face looked taut with fatigue but she'd lost nothing of her forceful energy. She still managed to mesmerise the audience with her rapid footwork and fiery arm movements. When she finished, she stared down at us as she always had, with that attitude of triumphant arrogance. But I saw something else in her eyes, a kind of cruel passion. Any trace of softness that she'd ever possessed had disappeared. She looked wild, bitter and tragic.

'I thought la Rusa was put on leave to have a rest.' Margarida whispered to Xavier. 'Before the push into Teruel.'

'She doesn't know the meaning of rest,' Xavier said, forcing himself to smile. 'She reminds me of those ex-soldiers who used to come to Barcelona after the Great War: the ones who had seen so much horror that they could never settle down again.'

After her performance, la Rusa joined us at the table. Xavier lit a cigarette and she took a few puffs before handing it back to him. 'I go on duty again in a few days ,' she said.

Xavier didn't look pleased by the news but he didn't say anything.

'How is the morale of the men?' Margarida asked.

La Rusa's face darkened. 'How do you expect it to be?' she snapped. 'You've taken away their revolution. They were fighting for a better life. What should they fight for now? Franco or the Republic? Either one is just another form of capitalism. After the war, everything will be the same for them—the rich will be rich and the poor will starve.'

'It won't be that way,' said Margarida, looking affronted. 'Whether it's a revolution or reform, the Republic will be much better for the workers and the poor than Franco ever will be!'

La Rusa didn't seem to hear my sister. 'You know, there was a soldier I picked up from the military hospital after an offensive,' she said. 'His intestines had been blown out of his abdominal cavity and the doctor had stuffed them back inside as best as he could. The man was dying but do you know what he said to me: "I don't regret for one moment going to fight. For once I was treated as something better than peasant dirt!"' La Rusa looked from Xavier to Margarida with piercing scorn. 'While you've been pushing your pens around your desks and making trips to and from Paris, I've seen the men who have been dying for a promise . . . for an ideal . . . for a *lie*. They've been betrayed!

Why do you think you have to conscript people for the army now?'

Margarida glanced at Xavier. She looked puzzled and hurt.

Xavier put his hand on la Rusa's arm. 'You're tired,' he said. 'Let me take you home.'

La Rusa stood up without protest. But when Xavier took her arm, she didn't press herself against him the way she used to do. They didn't look like lovers any more.

'They used to be so happy together,' said Margarida, watching them leave the club. 'This war is killing everything!'

THIRTY-ONE

Evelina

There were moments of light in the darkness: flashes of beauty in the horror. At dawn, when the roosters that now lived on almost every balcony on Barcelona began to crow, I would hear Feliu running around in Xavier and Conchita's apartment upstairs. 'Pare! Pare!' I would hear him call excitedly to his father.

My parents had reacted surprisingly calmly to my divorce. Perhaps we'd all developed a greater perspective on everything. Even Conchita stopped being at Xavier's throat all the time, and as a result he stopped avoiding her. And Margarida no longer bothered needling Conchita.

Xavier was going abroad less frequently these days. 'The Soviets have given up on us,' he had told me after his latest trip. 'Stalin is more interested in what's happening in Europe and the Japanese invasion of China. We are a lost cause. Even Britain looks like signing a treaty with Italy to keep Mussolini from getting too cosy with Hitler. I've told the committee since the beginning that they were wasting time with the English.'

'Have you given up on the Republic?' I asked, remembering how he had always been an idealist.

Xavier looked at me seriously. 'Sometimes I feel as if we all boarded a plane that we knew was going to crash but we got on anyway,' he said. 'And other times I feel like the dying soldier that Celestina told us about. I don't regret for a second that we tried to build a better country, that we experienced moments of greatness. Perhaps our sacrifice will inspire future generations— or at least help them to learn from our mistakes. It's for Feliu's sake that I continue now and won't give in to defeatism.'

In March 1938, we all went to the Liceu one evening to see a ballet by the Spanish composer Salvador Bacarisse: *Corrida de feria*. I was entranced. It was as though I was a young girl again, sitting in the family box. It made me realise how much I had missed ballet. At the end of the night, I overheard Conchita and Xavier talking while we were waiting for our coats.

'Are you going away again?' Conchita asked.

'I have to travel to Paris next week,' Xavier said, looking around to make sure Mama and Pare were out of earshot. 'We've got one last ace up our sleeve, although it won't please Pare. We are going to offer Catalonia to France. If they annex us, I don't think Franco will challenge it. The French will gain a wealthy industrial region and a port.'

Have we come to that? I thought. Selling ourselves off to the French?

'I'm sorry that our marriage didn't turn out to be all we had hoped,' Xavier added. 'But I will always make sure that you and Feliu have everything you need. If Barcelona looks like falling before I've had a chance to fetch you, I will give instructions to Evelina about how to move you all to a safer place. Please promise me that you will do everything she asks.'

The following evening we were together at dinner again, except for Pare who had sent a message that he had to work late at the factory. Some materials he had been waiting for had only just arrived and he wanted to move them into the factory in time for the morning shift. I stared at my plate of rice and pickled vegetables, knowing that I should be thankful for the cache of black-market goods Xavier had been able to secure when the rest of Barcelona was surviving on ever decreasing rations of bread.

We had gathered in the drawing room after dinner when we heard the air-raid sirens start. Barcelona had been bombed several times before, especially the port. I thanked God that Pare wasn't at any of his factories in that area.

'We'd best go to the cellar,' Xavier said.

He called the servants and we all calmly walked down the stairs. While we believed Franco to be a tyrant, none of us expected him to order the destruction of the city centre. It wasn't one of his tactics to destroy important buildings. But it soon became obvious that there was something different about this raid.

'The air sirens are sounding so often, I can't tell when one raid is finishing and another is starting,' Margarida said.

Xavier frowned. 'The explosions are close by. It doesn't sound as if they are only targeting industrial areas.'

The sirens and explosions continued through the night, and it wasn't until the following afternoon that quiet descended again. As soon as we returned upstairs, I picked up the telephone receiver but the line was dead.

'Pare!' I said to Xavier. 'I must go and see if he is all right!'

'You can't go by yourself,' he replied, taking our coats from the cupboard.

The horror we found out on the streets would remain in my nightmares forever. Buildings had been reduced to rubble. Those that remained standing had shattered windows. Shop grilles had been twisted out of shape; trams had been overturned. The air was thick with smoke. Soldiers and policemen with shovels and pickaxes were digging into the rubble. I wondered what they were doing, until I heard the screams coming from under the ruins.

Xavier grabbed my arm and steered me away. 'The buildings are unstable,' he said. 'Stay in the middle of the street.'

Trucks were moving through the city, collecting bodies or body parts. I saw a policeman pick up a woman's arm, its hand still clutching a purse.

'The housewives were lining up for the food rations. They refused to go to the shelter because they didn't want to lose their places in the line,' a man standing nearby told us. He was covered in dust.

I moved as if in a dream. Was this Barcelona? Was this destruction possible? My understanding of the world and how things worked was turned upside down. The front was still far from Barcelona but the war was already here.

The trees, which had been coming into their spring leafiness, were hung with all kinds of things: clothes, tyres, a man's leg torn from the thigh. The city stank of blood and charred flesh. We passed an orphanage where the bodies of dead children lay in lines on the pavement outside. Apart from the cuts and burns, they looked as though they were sleeping.

Xavier saw a colleague from the diplomatic committee standing in the doorway of his apartment building. 'I can't believe Franco did this!' Xavier said to him. 'I thought it was the people he hated. I thought he'd try to keep the city itself intact.'

'It was Italian planes that did it,' the man replied. 'Continuously coming and going from Majorca. Mussolini wants to demoralise us.'

The damage became worse the closer we got to Pare's factory. 'Oh dear God!' I said when I saw the main building. Half of it was gone. The rest was black from a fire that was still smouldering. The police were pulling bodies from the wreckage. A makeshift morgue had been set up in one of the storerooms on the site.

'We are Xavier and Evelina Montella,' my brother told the policeman standing in front of the storeroom.

The policeman shook his head. 'I don't know if your father is in there,' he said. 'With some of them it's hard to tell if they are male or female.'

'I'll go in,' Xavier said to me. 'You stay here.'

My legs went weak. I crouched down on the pavement, not ashamed to be seen in that undignified position. Surely Pare could not be dead. We were supposed to leave the city before it became dangerous. I tried to imagine the best possible scenario. When the bombings first started, Pare had ordered shelters to be built around all his factories for the workers. I hoped he had used one of them himself the previous night.

Xavier was gone for a long time. Surely that must be a good sign?

I stood up as two policemen came out of the factory carrying a stretcher. The body on it was covered in white ash and at first I thought they were carrying a statue. They came closer and I recognised Pare's broad forehead and moustache.

'Oh God, no!' I cried, running towards the stretcher. 'Stop! Stop!'

'Is it someone you know?' one of the policemen asked as they lowered the stretcher to the ground.

I knelt beside Pare, tearing my stockings on the rubble. He seemed unhurt apart from a gash above his eye. I took his hand. As I did, I was sure that his face twitched.

'He's still alive!' I said. 'Look! He moved!'

The policeman placed his hand on my shoulder. 'Is it your father, senyoreta? I'm sorry but he is dead.'

Xavier came out of the storeroom. When he saw me next to the stretcher, his face dropped. He rushed towards me.

'It's Pare,' I told him. 'But I'm sure he moved.' I peered again at Pare's face for a sign of life.

'Senyoreta,' the policeman said softly, 'it's an illusion from the shock. I assure you that he is dead.'

I heard the other policeman whisper to Xavier, 'The back of his head is missing. We had to leave his brain behind.'

Xavier crouched down beside me and wrapped me in his arms. 'Come, Evelina,' he said, his voice trembling. 'Pare wouldn't want you to remember him this way.'

I couldn't move. 'Pare!' I cried as Xavier gently lifted me to my feet.

He walked me towards a button shop whose proprietress was standing in the doorway and surveying the damage to the factory with a distressed look on her face.

'Is it your father?' she asked us. 'He was a good man. I've done business with him for years.'

Xavier grimaced. 'Can my sister stay here with you a moment? I have to go back and make arrangements.'

The woman nodded. 'Can I get you anything?' she asked, helping me to a chair. 'I wanted to boil some water but there is no electricity.'

She talked about the raids and how the terrible whistling of the bombs as they dropped had broken her nerves. She praised my father for the air-raid shelters that he had funded for the neighbourhood.

'He dug them alongside the women and children when they were constructed a few months ago,' she said. 'Did you know that?'

I shook my head. I hadn't known that. My father wouldn't have done something so egalitarian before the war. Obviously what was happening in Spain had changed him.

'Those shelters saved our lives,' the woman said. 'But your father and his workers didn't have enough warning before the main factory was hit. The pilots must have cut their engines and flown in silently. There was supposed to be a blackout, but unfortunately the factory was lit.'

The woman meant well but I barely heard her. All I could think about was that I would never see Pare again, and that the crypt at the Old Cemetery would have another Montella.

Pare's death left us with a sense of solitude and anxiety, but no one more so than Mama. 'I don't want to live,' she said. 'There is no point to my life.'

'Mama, think of your grandchildren,' I told her. 'You must be strong! They need you.'

I thought that Pare's death would convince Mama to leave Barcelona. Instead, it made her refuse to do so. 'I can't leave Leopold,' she said.

She insisted on visiting the cemetery every day, despite the danger from further air raids. I couldn't justify asking one of the maids to risk her life by going with her, so I went instead, leaving Conchita in charge of the children. Every time we left the house, I kissed them knowing it might be the last time I would see them. One day, the sirens sounded as we were leaving the cemetery, and Mama and I had to spend three terrifying hours in a crowded, lice-ridden shelter with rats scurrying across the floor and the ground shaking. The whole time I wondered if we would return to see the house on the passeig de Gràcia in ruins.

With Xavier and Margarida away from home much of the time, and Mama unable to function from grief, I had to take charge as mistress of the house. While I could barely think for myself, I had become responsible for everybody.

'Mama, we cannot go to the cemetery any more while the war is raging,' I told her. 'We have to look after the living.'

Mama's face collapsed and she slumped in her chair as if I had punched her. I hated myself for being so cruel. To not visit Pare's grave would make Mama feel disloyal. But what could I do? Although I grieved for Pare too, I had to think of the children.

In late spring that year, it was clear that things were getting worse.

'What's going on?' I asked Margarida. 'There aren't enough weapons to go around and now they are calling up young boys and fathers with children!'

Margarida looked exhausted. She was drained from the late nights she had been spending in parliamentary discussions and debates.

'Our prime minister thinks that one last heroic effort on the part of the Republican army might finally persuade the allies to help us,' she said. 'The Republic's northern army is going to cross the Ebro River in one massive offensive.'

'But we don't have the aeroplanes and weapons that the rebels do,' I said, horrified. 'It will be suicide!'

'Exactly,' she said bitterly. 'We are going to send an army of babies and old men to their deaths to get the world's attention!'

The crossing of the Ebro River turned out to be the final catastrophe for the Republic. After initial gains, the Loyalist army was driven back by the air power given to the rebels by the Germans and Italians. Our old planes and faulty weapons were no match for the ten thousand pounds of bombs that were dropped daily on Republican lines. The northern army of the Republic was wiped out. Then Republican Spain received the most humiliating blow of all: the British signed the Munich Pact with Nazi Germany. If Britain was prepared to sacrifice Czechoslovakia, there was no chance of her coming to our rescue.

Margarida came to see me the morning she received the news about the Munich Pact. She had a message from Xavier in Paris: *It's over for the Republic in Spain. The only thing to do is to continue the fight from across the border.*

'What does he mean?' I asked her.

She leaned forwards and lowered her voice. 'It means Xavier will be carrying out espionage work. He's given up on the government but not on Spain. They will have to try to "remove" Franco and other top generals. It is the only way the Spanish people will be able to rise again.'

While I admired my brother, I was painfully aware that those who had attempted to assassinate Mussolini and Hitler had met horrific ends.

Conchita walked into room and began searching around for something. I would have continued the conversation but Margarida stopped until Conchita found the scarf she had been looking for and left again.

'Be careful not to mention any of this to her,' Margarida said. 'I'm sure she was trying to listen in on us then.'

'Conchita? She doesn't understand the war. She probably hoped we were gossiping about something.'

'Yes, but she might say something to one of her sisters. Don't teach a parrot anything you don't want it to repeat.'

I sighed. Margarida might not be going out of her way to antagonise Conchita any more, but she was never going to like her.

'Listen,' Margarida continued, 'la Rusa is also involved in this plan. She's been conveying messages across the border. Xavier is returning to Spain but he must stay in hiding. As la Rusa is more mobile, he has charged her with getting you, Mama, Conchita and the children out of Spain. When the time comes, make sure everyone cooperates with her, especially Conchita.'

'When is she coming?'

'I don't know,' Margarida said. 'I can't imagine it will be too soon. I only hope it won't be too late.'

By winter, life in Barcelona was bleak. Coal could not be found anywhere. There was barely any food. Cats and pigeons began disappearing from the streets. People collapsed from hunger while waiting in line for rations. Feliu broke out in boils from a lack of nutrition. It seemed only thanks to Mama's fervent prayers that he survived the infection.

I gave our servants money and told them to start making their way to the house in the Dordogne. Feliu's governess listened to me, but the others returned to their villages. I was later to learn that returning to places where they were known proved fatal for them.

Word came that Franco's forces were heading our way. The Republican general staff prepared for the attack on Catalonia. People were leaving the city by whatever means they could—in carts, on bicycles, on foot if necessary. Still there was no message from la Rusa. Then I learned that those fleeing were being fired upon by German planes. Perhaps la Rusa thought that method of getting out of Spain was too dangerous. Although I was now mistress of the house, I had no idea how to get three women and two children safely to France. Dear God, I prayed, don't let la Rusa have been killed.

Margarida arrived to collect a few things. She was spending more and more time in government meetings. 'You wouldn't believe what President Roosevelt has announced to the American press,' she said.

'Oh God, what?' I asked. 'Are they going to attack us too?'

She shook her head. 'Roosevelt says that now dark forces are descending on Europe it appears that the embargo forced on Republican Spain was a "grave mistake". Despite all the treaties to avoid war, Hitler is set on invading Poland.' She paced around the room. 'The truth of what Xavier and the Republic's diplomatic delegations have been trying to tell the Americans, French and British since 1936 seems to be finally dawning on them: the fall of Republican Spain will put them in a position where they are surrounded by hostile states.'

'So they will help now?' I asked hopefully. 'All is not lost?'

Margarida shook her head. 'They will be busy defending themselves now. It's too late for the Republic. The bull has been forced to its knees and the matador is poised for the kill. We can't escape the sword now.'

The rebel offensive on Barcelona was launched two days before Christmas, when the weather was bright and cold. Franco's army advanced at a rapid speed. The fortifications that had been established fell quickly under the massive air attacks. The Republican government called up reserves and a week later ordered the mobilisation of all citizens of both sexes between seventeen and fifty-five years of age. But given the hopeless circumstances, who was going to fight? Especially when the government itself abandoned Barcelona in January to relocate to Figueres. Those who could flee the city then, did.

With the Republican government gone, the right-wing supporters and Falangists who had been lying low were free to come into the open. They looted shops and settled scores. The families of Republican soldiers were dragged out of their houses and shot or thrown into prison. One day, while out getting rations, I came across the corpse of a man who had been hacked to pieces. Who could have imagined such sights in Barcelona?

A few days away from entering the city, Franco issued a decree that anyone who had 'actively or passively opposed the Nationalist movement' was a criminal. That definition covered our entire family. Because Catalonia had been a stronghold of the Republic, it was to be humiliated in every way: the Catalan dialect was forbidden and replaced by Castilian, 'the language of the Empire', including within the churches; and even our folk dance, the *sardana*, was banned.

'I'm ashamed ever to have been part of this government,' Margarida said the day the last of the official Republican envoys left Barcelona. 'They've told the citizens to defend the city with their lives while they are fleeing in their cars for their apartments in Paris!' She beckoned me to follow her to the study. 'I've made contact with la Rusa—she's going to be here in a few hours. I'm taking some wives and children of Republican soldiers across the border, but I'll meet up with you in Figueres. Are you packed?'

'You aren't going with the government officials?' I asked.

She shook her head. 'I'd be embarrassed to flee like that. I intend to help as many people as I can on my way out.'

I nodded, proud of my sister, but also fearful for her safety.

'Right,' she said, looking about the study, 'we'd better get to it. We have to burn all evidence of my involvement in the Socialist Party, Xavier's role in negotiations with France, and Pare's pro-Catalan literature.'

'But it's obvious that you were in government,' I said, watching her empty drawers and pile documents into the fireplace. 'Your picture was in the newspapers.'

'That's not the point,' she said, glancing at me. 'It's to protect you. If for some reason you are stopped on your way to France, you and Mama must say how disappointed you were in me. That you didn't approve of a single thing I did. You must disassociate yourselves from me and Xavier entirely.'

'But I'm very proud of you,' I told her. 'You are a far better woman than I will ever be!'

Margarida straightened. 'That's not true, Evelina. You and I are different, that's all. You have a strength all of your own. I could not have helped Mama, Conchita and the children the way you have been doing.'

I ran across the room and embraced my sister as though I would never let her go.

'Come on,' she said, touching my cheek. 'We'd better get through this stuff before la Rusa arrives. She will want to leave as soon as possible.'

We threw file after file into the flames. When I saw Xavier's Socialist Party card, I hesitated. 'He was so proud,' I said. 'He wanted to do so much.'

'He's *still* doing something for his country,' said Margarida. 'He hasn't given up or fled.'

When we were finished with the documents, Margarida hurried to the hall to grab her coat. 'I won't have time to say goodbye to Mama,' she said, kissing me. 'Tell her that we will meet again soon at the border.'

We embraced before she rushed out into the cold air. I didn't budge from the doorway until I saw Margarida disappear around the corner. Even then, I hesitated before closing the door. I wished we were going with her, but she had important work to do and we had la Rusa to help us.

To my great relief, la Rusa finally appeared that evening. She wasn't wearing her uniform but a black coat and hiking boots. She wore a navy beret over her hair and a navy scarf around her neck. I noticed the thick golden earrings: they stood out against the brownness of her skin.

'I have a van waiting for us on the outskirts of the city,' she said. 'We are going to have to walk there. So bring only what you can carry.'

Mama and Conchita came down the stairs to see who had arrived. Conchita's eyes narrowed when she recognised la Rusa.

It was the first time, to my knowledge, that the two women had been in such close proximity to each other.

'Thank goodness you're here!' Mama said, kissing la Rusa's cheeks.

'I had one last duty to perform,' la Rusa told her. 'The Republican soldiers in Vallcarca hospital were deserted by the staff. I saw them attempting to flee, men without legs and arms crawling on the street, terrified of what Franco's troops would do to them if they remained in the city.'

'So you put them ahead of us?' Conchita asked. 'My goodness, how sincere you are. Does Xavier know that his family are a lesser priority?'

La Rusa regarded her contemptuously. 'Those men fought bravely for the Republic. They were deserted and left to die. I used my van to take them to a Red Cross station.'

'Well, I hope you will defend us as bravely,' said Conchita with a strange smile.

I could have slapped her. How Xavier could have conceived that his mistress and his wife would be able to cooperate on such a dangerous journey, I didn't know.

La Rusa stared Conchita down with her piercing eyes. 'Xavier believes that the Republic lost the war due to inferior armaments,' she said. 'But I know differently. It was a loss of spirit. How could the men go on fighting knowing that their women and children back home were starving, while families like yours feasted on black-market goods? Those men were like my brother who died in Morocco. They were tricked into fighting for their class enemies. Even the bravest souls lose courage when they don't know what they are risking their lives for.'

'And the point of this story is?' said Conchita, folding her arms.

I jumped with fright when la Rusa pulled a revolver from her coat and pointed it at Conchita's face.

'When I was transporting those injured soldiers to the Red Cross station, two government officials tried to commandeer my van to drive themselves across the border. I shot them,' she said matter-of-factly. 'Just as I will shoot anyone who endangers this mission. I've been asked to get you out of Barcelona and that is what I will do. Understood?'

I was relieved that Conchita remained quiet for once. I don't know what she had wanted to do to la Rusa—intimidate her with her wealth and place in society? This was hardly the time for a showdown with her husband's mistress.

La Rusa lowered her gun and put it back in her coat pocket. 'Now go get the children,' she told us.

Although her manner was intimidating, I trusted la Rusa could get us out of Barcelona safely. It was devastating to be abandoning my home, my city and my life, but la Rusa's strength of purpose helped me conquer my emotions.

I roused the children from their sleep. With Julieta in one arm and Feliu clinging to the other, I stepped out onto the street. Mama was grasping the handles of the small cart in which I'd packed blankets and basic supplies. 'Put Julieta on top,' she suggested.

Julieta was two years old and heavy to carry but I didn't want to let her go. She was fidgeting less than she normally did and the warmth of her body pressed against mine gave me comfort on that bitterly cold night.

The city was deserted: either people were hiding, or we were amongst the last to leave. Torn party cards and burned piles of documents littered the street. I realised this might be the last time I ever saw Barcelona.

Mama looked nervous, and my pulse thrummed in my ears, but la Rusa was chillingly calm. I turned to her but she wouldn't meet my eyes. I was wondering why she wouldn't look at me when I heard the sound of car engines starting up.

Two vehicles approached from a side street. The first was a plain black car, but the second was a Bentley with wood panelling on the doors. It could be anyone, I told myself. Just another family leaving the city. But as I thought it, a man jumped out from a doorway in front of us. Mama screamed. The cars stopped and three policemen leaped from the first one. In a few seconds we were surrounded.

'You Montella women!' the larger of the policemen shouted. 'You are under arrest as enemies of Spain!'

He grabbed Mama and pushed her towards the black car. I was shocked to see my mother being treated so roughly. I tried to pull the policeman off her while still holding on to Julieta with one arm. He turned around and punched me in the face. The pain was so sharp that I thought he had broken my nose. Dazed by the blow, I didn't resist when the man who had jumped out from the doorway seized my shoulders and pushed me into the car after Mama. Conchita and Feliu were thrust inside after us. In the confusion, I didn't see what had happened to la Rusa, but she wasn't in the car with us as it sped away. I tried to glimpse the second car, which was falling behind us. All I could see was the chauffeur; he was wearing a Nationalist army uniform.

THIRTY-TWO

Evelina

We were taken to a prison; not Les Corts as that was already full, but a convent that had been converted for the purpose. Conchita and Feliu, despite our protests, were led away with another group of women, while Mama, Julieta and I were put in a cellar with other women as disoriented and as dishevelled as we were.

Our cart had been confiscated when we were arrested, so we had no blankets to sit on, only the stone floor. The coldness of it made my kidneys ache. Poor Mama! It broke my heart to see her. Always so elegant and composed, she stared at her surroundings with a bewildered look on her face. I took my scarf and rolled it into a pillow for her, and we slept that night with Julieta cradled between us.

The next day, some nuns brought us a meal of gruel and stale bread. One of the nuns, seeing that we had a young child with us, returned with a cup of goat's milk for Julieta. I was about to thank her when she put her finger to her lips. It didn't take me long to realise why. The Mother Superior of the convent was a sadist.

That afternoon she came to speak to us. 'You are here be-cause you have committed crimes against Spain and against God,' she said with a spiteful glint in her eye. 'Those of you who cannot be reformed will be executed.'

It took a moment to register what she had said. When we realised the meaning of her statement, a stunned silence fell over the group. My stomach sank. If they shoot me, I thought, what will happen to Julieta? Will they kill her too?

'And you can be sure that your men will be hunted down and shot like rabbits,' the Mother Superior continued. 'Franco will cleanse Spain of evil, and we are his helpers in doing so.'

A woman with a pale, freckled face spoke up. 'I worked in the hospital, helping to deliver babies. That's all I did. I never belonged to any party.'

'You delivered *Republican* babies; that is enough,' the Mother Superior replied, lifting her eyes heavenward.

When the Mother Superior left, the prisoners started to tell each other their names and what they had been arrested for. The group was a mix of dressmakers, housewives, factory workers and shopkeepers. There were even three schoolgirls who had been arrested with their mother. Most of the women had committed no crime other than to have been related to a man who had leftist leanings, or who had fought in the army, even if he was con-scripted.

I was surprised when Mama spoke up.

'I am Rosita Montella,' she said. 'The wife of the late Leo-pold Montella. We are a faithful Catholic family. We have con-tributed significant sums to the construction of the Sagrada Família and other public works. I supported Carmelite chari-ties. And yet we are here too, imprisoned in a convent of all places.'

The other women stared at Mama in awe. I had thought it would be better not to reveal our social standing, but I realised that the women's frowns came not from the fact that they de-spised us but because a terrible truth had dawned on them. If the women of one of the most powerful families in Barcelona had been imprisoned and possibly condemned, what hope did anybody else have?

That evening, an officer of the Civil Guard and a policeman came to our cell and read out ten names. A young pregnant woman was first on the list. Another of the women, assuming she was to be released, went to pick up her bundle of belongings.

'You won't need those,' the guard told her.

When the woman realised what the guard had meant, she hesitated for a moment and then passed her bundle to Mama. 'Live for your children and grandchildren no matter how short the time is,' she told her.

It was awful to look into the faces of women marked out for death. Some of them wept for their loved ones but most of them remained quiet, having resigned themselves to their fate as soon as they had been arrested. Only the pregnant woman screamed and struggled. 'Let my child be born first!' she shouted. But she was subdued by the policeman. I hated myself, but I wanted the women to leave as soon as possible. I was terrified that if they lingered, the guard would choose more of us.

The women were led away and the cellar door was locked again. There was a grille near the roof of the cellar. By securing my feet between some of the stones in the wall, I was able to climb up to it and peer out onto the ground of the courtyard. I saw the women being led towards a truck and ordered to get into it. The woman who had given Mama her belongings stumbled and had to be lifted on board.

After the truck had left, I climbed down and sat on the floor with the others. About half an hour later, shots rang out into the night.

'They must have killed them in the rail yards,' one woman said.

I wondered if Conchita and Feliu were all right. Then my mind went blank. I could not fathom the reality of the situation.

'What do you think happened to la Rusa?' Mama asked me later.

I shook my head. 'I haven't allowed myself to think of her. She was a famous figure on the side of the Republicans. They probably shot her straight away . . . or tortured her for information.'

I cringed at that last possibility. La Rusa was the only person who knew Xavier's whereabouts. But she was strong and she loved my brother; I put my faith in that.

That night, as I lay with Julieta pressed against me, I wondered if it might be better to suffocate her now to save her from prolonged suffering. If I left it too late, I might not be able to help her. A more courageous woman would have acted on that thought, but I did not have the strength to do it. I wept myself to sleep.

Although another ten women were executed the following night, more arrived to take their place. The pace of the killing seemed to be speeding up, but there was no apparent logic to it. There was a priest at the convent, but I didn't believe any of those killed were allowed confession or received absolution. I realised how awful that must have been for the religious ones. What I had seen had not made me lose my faith in God—he simply seemed very far away—but I had no love left for the Church or its rituals.

The new arrivals brought stories of merciless killing sprees carried out by the sons of aristocratic families against peasants and workers.

'The port and dock areas are brimming with bodies,' one woman told us. 'And there are hundreds of corpses in the fields outside the city. Entire families in some instances.'

I didn't think the nightmare could get any worse, until one night I heard trucks pull up in the courtyard. There were so many of them that I thought they were intending to finish us all off that night. Then I heard men's voices.

'Pedro, who bred song canaries,' one voice called out.

'Juli, who baked the best bread in la Barceloneta,' another yelled.

I realised what was happening. The men were condemned prisoners who had been brought to the women's prison to be processed by the superintendent. They were calling out their names and something about themselves with the idea that the women prisoners would hear them, but not enough information that the Nationalists could identify their relatives. Perhaps they were hoping that through some of us, their families might find out what had happened to them; they would not be anonymous bodies in a mass grave.

With so much death around me, it would have been easy to give in to hopelessness. But, for the sake of Mama and Julieta, I refused to let the situation get the better of me. To remain calm, I would close my eyes and picture our home on the passeig de Gràcia. In my mind, I walked through the rooms, touching the damask curtains and running my hands over the furniture. Pare was at his desk and Xavier was at the piano. What is he playing today? I'd ask myself, before a hauntingly beautiful nocturne came to my ears. I'd imagine Olga giving me a ballet lesson in the ballroom and me performing dazzling *fouettés* for her. Margarida was usually to be found in the library reading a book, while Mama arranged bouquets of sweet-smelling gardenias. Conchita was invariably sitting before her mirror fixing her hair, while Feliu crouched on the rug playing with a toy train. I'd feel the weight of Julieta's body as I lifted her from her cot and brushed my cheek against her feather-soft hair. I knew heaven once, I told myself, and now I know hell.

On the fifth night of our imprisonment, after the lists had been called, I kept my mind from dwelling on the women who would shortly be lined up against a wall and shot by imagining Xavier ten years from now. It was always my hope that he was safe. In my fantasy, he and Feliu had been reunited and were now adventurers together—flying across the globe, exploring the jungles of the Amazon, sailing the seas to Australia. I imagined that

Margarida had become a famous writer and was living in a cottage somewhere with dozens of cats. She would write about us, and we would live on in her fiction.

Of course, I was to realise later how misguided my day-dreaming turned out to be. Feliu would never have been reunited with his father. The children of Republicans were put in orphan-ages where they were forced to wear the uniforms of the Na-tionalists and spit on pictures of their parents.

'Xavier, who loved his family and worshipped the music of Granados.'

I opened my eyes and sat up, convinced that I was imagin-ing things. Surely that wasn't Xavier's voice I had heard? I hadn't noticed the trucks bringing the men into the courtyard. They were much later than usual, and the few women left in our cell had gone to bed assuming that there would be no executions of male prisoners that night. Mama and Julieta were asleep too.

'Let my family know that I die a man of clear conscience who devoted his life to make Spain better for all people,' Xavier's voice went on. 'Tell my son to rise above the memory of my fate by becoming the finest human being that he can.'

I was tempted to wake Mama, but what good would it do for Xavier to know that we were here? It was far better for him to go to his death thinking that we hadn't been able to reach him but were all safe somewhere.

I climbed to look out of the cellar grille. The men had been unloaded from the truck directly in front of it. One of the guards had given them a cigarette to share. Xavier was standing so close to the grille that I could push my finger through it and lightly touch the hem of his trousers. My fingertip felt the cloth and for a split second we were reunited, then he was marched away. All fell silent again. The moonlight glistened over the stones of the courtyard.

A short time later, shots rang out into the still air and I knew that my beautiful brother, Xavier Montella, who loved his fam-ily and worshipped the music of Granados, was dead.

With Xavier's death, I could no longer maintain my outer appearance of bravado. My grief at his execution was so great that everything drained out of me. I sat there, awake and still, until dawn. Mama had no idea what had taken place, while I knew that our hour had come. When the officer of the Civil Guard and the policeman arrived at first light to fetch us, I wasn't surprised. It was usual for the women of a family to be executed the day after their men, although they had never come so early before to issue the death call.

I held Julieta with one hand, and with the other helped Mama to stand. Mama was pale with dread. She faltered and came close to fainting. I kissed Julieta, and regretted not having been brave enough to kill her earlier. For a moment, I considered passing her to one of the remaining women, but something stopped me. All I could do was pray that our deaths would be quick and that she would not suffer.

We were taken to the prison office, where the superintendent, a heavy-set man with bloodshot eyes, and the Mother Superior were waiting for us.

'Know this,' the Mother Superior told us. 'The Montellas were once one of the great families of Barcelona. But you chose to side with the Reds and betray Spain. You are nothing now. The Montella name will be wiped from all records, your properties will be divided and auctioned off to the highest bidders. History will forget you and you will live no better than prostitutes.'

If we had heard those words a few days before, they might have had an effect. Now, we were too numb to care.

'Go!' the Mother Superior ordered.

To my surprise, there was no truck waiting for us in the courtyard; only Conchita and Feliu. Conchita's eyes were wide open with terror. Feliu was not the boy that he had been before we were arrested. He tucked his chin into his neck as if he didn't want to look at the world any more, and when Conchita tried to take his hand he swiped at it like an animal. Was he behaving that way because he knew that his father was dead?

'I managed to make contact with one of my father's friends in the Falange,' Conchita said under her breath. 'He signed our release documents, but he said it's not safe for us to go back to the house. The ways things are, we could be arrested again in twenty-four hours.'

I led her away from the others. 'Do you know about Xavier?'

She nodded. 'They brought him here last night. Feliu recognised his father's voice calling from the courtyard.'

I hadn't thought it was possible I could feel any more grief, but I did then. Poor Feliu. I hoped that he would remember the words his brave father had said for him.

'I haven't told Mama,' I confided in Conchita. 'I don't want to just yet—we have to get out of here first.'

Conchita nodded. She looked upset about something, but I sensed it wasn't Xavier's death. I thought of la Rusa and how much she had loved my brother. She would have cried rivers for him. Julieta came to me and rested her head against my leg. I pulled her closer.

'What about la Rusa?' I asked Conchita. 'Do you know what happened to her?'

Conchita's eyes flashed. 'Don't be so stupid as to worry about her!' she spat. 'Who do you think betrayed us? Your la Rusa led us straight into a trap!'

'No,' I protested. 'La Rusa would not do something like that.'

'Truly? Well, according to my father's friend, she is a spy—for the Nationalists!'

I knew what she was saying was ridiculous, but I was too tired and weak to argue with Conchita further. I had to think about getting everyone to safety. Despite the warning from her father's friend, I couldn't see any choice for the moment but for us to return to our home.

Barcelona was a charnel house; the streets around the rail yards were splattered with blood and the stench of death was everywhere. We passed a church that was pockmarked with bullet holes and I wondered if perhaps Xavier had been killed there rather than at the rail yards. I realised that I would never know.

We passed the body of woman lying in a doorway with her baby in her arms. They looked and smelled as if they had been there a week. I was sure the authorities had left them there on purpose to terrorise the population. But as we got closer to the passeig de Gràcia, the atmosphere changed. Banners hung across the streets and from the windows proclaiming: *Franco, Saviour and Father!* Priests and nuns were everywhere, as were men with the Falange insignia embroidered on their coats. A truck holding women and children drove past; the women were giving the fascist salute and cheering. Their hair was clean and curled and they wore lipstick. They looked healthy and well fed, not at all like people who had been living on rations. Where had these Franco supporters been hiding? I recognised Soledad Manzano and Maria Dalmau's younger sister and looked away, although it was doubtful they would have recognised us in our starved and dirty state. So the 'good families' of Barcelona could rest in peace again now that all had been restored to normal. The poor would always be poor and they were free to exploit them once again.

I thought of Xavier. He had been one of the most privileged men in Spain and yet he had given his life trying to create a fairer country. The realisation that he was now lying in a mass grave somewhere, while the vacuous and self-interested were parading around in victory, was perhaps the bitterest of all the pills I'd had to swallow since the Republic had lost the war.

As soon as we entered the house, I regretted returning to it. The chandeliers had been smashed to smithereens; someone had taken an axe to the piano; and obscene words had been scrawled over the paintings, although many of them were priceless originals.

'It must have been the Moors,' said Mama. 'Those savages don't have a clue.'

The desecration of our home was the final blow for her. She sat down on the bottom step of the staircase and refused to move.

'Quickly,' I told Conchita, 'grab some necessities and some warm clothes. We'd better hide in the pantry and make our way to the border tonight.'

'We are in no fit state to walk to the next town, let alone the border!' she said.

I was in no mood for her to be difficult. 'We just have to. We either take the chance or die here.'

Most of our clothes had been stolen, but I found some woollen dresses and coats in the maids' cupboards. All our money from the safe had gone too, but by rummaging through desk drawers, handbags and coat pockets we managed to collect a few *pesetas* each.

'I hope this is still worth something. Inflation could have got much worse, or they might even have changed the currency already,' I said.

I tidied myself as best I could and tucked my hair under a hat before going back out to see what food I could buy. I avoided the shops of our neighbourhood, where I might be recognised. My legs were swollen from a lack of food, but I did my best to appear well and to keep moving. I found some women lining up for food. I checked to make sure they weren't using Nationalist ration cards before standing with them. The prices were black-market ones and all I was able to purchase was a loaf of bread and some olives.

Conchita's incredulity that we were going to try to reach the French border had been justified. The roads were probably blockaded now. We could be shot on sight. And yet the thought of going back to prison was far worse. If only I could think clearly, I lamented. But no matter how hard I tried, I could not concentrate. Poor la Rusa, I thought. She would have been able to help us.

On my way to the next store to buy matches, I saw a car turning the corner. I recognised it straight away and stepped back to hide in a doorway. There were so few cars left in Barcelona anyway, but this one could not be mistaken. It was a Bentley with wood-panelled doors. A sick feeling rose in my stomach when I saw the driver in his Nationalist army uniform. The passenger was a beautiful woman in a white mink coat. The car passed slowly by and I was sure that I must be hallucinating. But the dark hair and tawny skin were unmistakable. It *was* la Rusa.

I stood with my mouth open, feeling like the victim of an appalling joke. Conchita's words came back to me: 'She is a spy—for the Nationalists.' For a long time after the car had passed, I couldn't move. Did I need any more evidence that la Rusa had handed us over to the authorities? She had intended to send Julieta and Feliu to their deaths! Rage exploded in my body, worsened by my awareness of my impotence to do anything to change what had happened. We had trusted that whore! La Rusa had betrayed us; but even worse, she had betrayed Xavier, who had adored her. I finally saw la Rusa for what she was and what she had always been: a beast in the guise of a woman.

I don't know how I found my way back to the house. I was overcome with pain and anger. Parts of my body seized up with hatred and fury, as if I were a corpse going through the process of rigor mortis. The only thing that kept me putting one foot in front of the other was my desire to be with my family again, to protect Julieta and Feliu, to stay alive even if only to spite all those who wanted us dead.

As I approached the house, I spotted a man in a black coat and hat crouching near the servants' entrance. He must be one of the Falangists, I thought. My blood froze. He hadn't seen me, but I couldn't turn and walk away from my family. I had no choice but to confront him.

'What are you doing here?' I demanded.

He straightened and his eyes flew open with surprise. 'Evelina?'

I stared at the man's unshaven face and straggly hair without recognition, and then our eyes met. He was gaunt and pale like me, but that alert gaze was unmistakable. Gaspar! I ran to him and he clutched me in his arms.

'Evelina,' he said over and over as he kissed me. Then he took my face between his palms, suddenly sad. 'You know that Xavier is dead?'

I nodded, too worn out to cry.

'I heard you'd been put in prison. I came here every day to wait for you in case you were released. I thought that when they executed Xavier . . . well, you are here now.'

'Oh, Gaspar,' I cried, 'you should have left. It's too dangerous for you to be in Barcelona now.'

He shook his head. 'Life without you would have no purpose. I'm glad I took my chances. Where is your family?'

'Inside the house,' I told him. 'Except for Pare. He died in the air raids.'

Gaspar clasped me to him again. I understood then how the kisses of those who have survived a terrible ordeal are much more intoxicating than those of ardent lovers.

'We must wait until nightfall,' he told me, 'but I know a way out of the city and a route that will take us past Figueres. We will get to France that way.'

When Mama saw Gaspar, she rose to her feet. 'Thank you for coming to help us,' she wept as she kissed his hands. 'We have been through a nightmare. Are you taking us to Xavier?'

Gaspar glanced at me. I shook my head.

'Yes, senyora Montella,' Gaspar said, helping her to one of the few unbroken chairs. 'Xavier is already in France. Could you eat some of the food Evelina has brought and then rest? We have a difficult journey ahead of us and we must begin tonight.'

After Mama had eaten some of the bread and olives, I went up to her room to see if I could find any blankets. By some miracle, Mama and Pare's bedroom had not been ransacked.

'I want to rest here,' Mama said, coming in behind me.

I turned around in surprise. 'But you can't, Mama. We must all hide together downstairs.'

She shook her head. 'I'm tired of being frightened. Let them take me if they want.'

BELINDA ALEXANDRA

I was too exhausted to argue. I helped her take off her shoes and slip under the covers. Her feet and hands were icy cold so I rubbed them for a while.

'I gave birth to all of you in this room,' she said. 'Xavier and Margarida together, and then you.'

'Sleep, Mama,' I said, kissing her forehead. 'I'll come and get you when we have to go.'

When I returned downstairs, Conchita and Feliu were already asleep in the pantry. They had gathered material from the ripped cushions in the drawing room as mattresses and were using the coats we had found as blankets. It was freezing in the house, but they slept apart from each other. You would imagine in these circumstances, Conchita might try to comfort her son and put her arm around him, I thought.

Gaspar was sitting in the kitchen, bouncing Julieta on his knee. She gurgled with delight when he tickled her cheeks.

He looked up at me. 'Francesc wrote and told me everything,' he said.

'That Julieta is yours?'

'*Ours*,' Gaspar corrected me with a grin.

His face had lost all its boyish ease, but it made me happy to see him smile nonetheless. I sat down next to him and rested my head on his shoulder. 'I wasn't sure if you got his letter.'

'I wrote to you many times, but I suspect most of the letters the soldiers wrote never reached their families. The planes were shooting at every vehicle, even the mail trucks. I saw la Rusa once when I was on the front. She was driving an ambulance that was full of holes . . .' He noticed my frown. 'What is it?'

'La Rusa is the one who betrayed Xavier,' I said. 'She told the police where he was hiding.'

Gaspar stared at me and shook his head. 'It's not possible. She wouldn't do that. La Rusa lived for Xavier.' He shivered before adding, 'Unless they got that information from her under torture.'

I told him about the Bentley that had followed us the night of our arrest and how la Rusa had disappeared. Then I told him about what I had seen that morning. Gaspar flinched as he wrestled with his disbelief. But then his doubt became realisation.

'She was the only one who knew his whereabouts,' he said, his hands clenching into fists. 'She's the only one who could have betrayed Xavier.'

We lapsed into silence for a long time. Julieta fell asleep against Gaspar's chest.

'She's our hope,' he said, kissing the top of her head. 'She's the one who will give us a reason to go on.'

As night fell, I went upstairs to wake Mama. I touched her shoulder but she didn't respond. 'Mama?' I said.

She slowly opened her eyes and smiled at me. 'Evelina,' she whispered. 'Promise me that you will marry Gaspar and be happy. He's a good man.'

I kissed her cheek. 'I promise, Mama. But now we must go.'

She shook her head. 'I'm so tired, Evelina,' she said, before inhaling sharply. She gasped as if the air had caught in her throat. Her eyes froze and then half closed. Her body went limp.

'Mama! Mama!' I screamed.

Gaspar rushed into the room. I watched as he tried to revive Mama by wrapping her warmly and breathing into her mouth. I stared at her face for any sign of life. But it was too late.

When I realised my mother was dead, my legs gave way beneath me and I sank to the floor. 'Mama!' I sobbed. 'Poor Mama.'

Gaspar kneeled beside me and held me in his arms. 'We have to leave her, Evelina,' he said gently. 'We can't approach a priest and there is no time to put her in the crypt.'

Later, I would see that Gaspar had made the right decision: the Montella family crypt had been demolished by the new regime and the bodies of my family were thrown into a mass grave. But that night, the only comfort I could take was that we were leaving Mama tucked up in bed in the home she had loved.

I was so distressed by Mama's death that Gaspar had to help me down the stairs. He opened the front door for me and we joined Feliu and Conchita, who was holding Julieta, in the laneway. Together we started the long and dangerous journey to France. I turned back only once to catch a glimpse of the passeig de Gràcia and the city that had been my home. I whispered a prayer for all the souls that had perished there. I hoped that one day they would rise again and dispel the darkness that had descended on Spain.

THIRTY-THREE

Paloma

Mamie was exhausted after telling her story. I kneeled in front of her and stroked her hands. Her skin was ice cold. Now I understood why she had never wanted to talk about Spain before. The tragedy of what happened was too over-whelming.

'Mamie?' I said. She was so pale I thought that she might faint.

'If it wasn't for your grandfather being such a good talker, I doubt any of us would have survived,' Mamie suddenly began again. 'The French would have put us in one of their barbaric refugee camps, where people dropped dead like flies. We lived in the house in the Dordogne for a while, but then we sold it and tried to start our lives again in Paris where Gaspar could get work playing the piano . . . Well, that was until the Germans invaded.'

I shook my head. 'No wonder Conchita lost her mind.'

Mamie shrugged. 'She tried to reunite with her family in Portugal, but her father rejected her. He said Xavier had brought too much shame on them all. She did her best to make a new life in Paris: she remarried and tried to be a better mother to the twins than she had been to Feliu. But then, of course, there was the accident. I think Feliu leaving home at fourteen made her realise that there are some things about the past that can never be fixed. She sort of gave up on life after that.'

'I'm sorry for that,' I said. 'I wish that Feliu had been more a part of our family.'

Mamie nodded. 'His father would have wanted that . . . but everyone has to make their own decisions. I think Feliu wants to forget his childhood.'

I got up and sat next to her. 'I still don't understand why la Rusa betrayed Xavier . . . or why she turned against the Republic and joined the Nationalists.'

'Don't you?' said Mamie, staring into the distance. 'It's because deep down she had always hated my family, even though she tried to make it appear otherwise. She blamed us for the death of her father, a revolutionary who was killed in the riots over Morocco in 1909, and the death of her brother who was sent there to defend the mines. When the Republic turned against the revolutionaries, she turned against it. She was treacherous and full of anger.'

'But she too came to live in Paris after the war,' I said. 'Did she ever try to contact you?'

Mamie looked at her hands. 'She wrote to me many times wanting to see me "to explain".' My grandmother shook her head in disgust. 'Can you imagine? She wanted me to assuage the guilt she suffered. The woman had my brother's blood on her hands! I never replied. Then, many years later, she committed suicide.'

The whole tragic story burned itself into my heart. I had never met Xavier or Mamie's parents, yet I felt deep sorrow at their fates. I wished that I had known all these things earlier, and that I had talked to Avi more about his life. Maybe I would have made a greater effort with Feliu if I had understood the cause of his reticence.

I glanced at Mamie. I saw her in a different light now. Her dignity, her kindness and tranquillity had always been qualities I'd admired, but knowing that she had retained them despite having suffered so many horrors made me love her even more.

'Mamie, I'm so proud of you,' I said.

My praise seemed to alarm her.

'No,' she said, refusing my compliment, 'I am proud of *you*. Just as Julieta was the reason your grandfather and I could go on, you are the reason that I get out of bed every day. Seeing you happy is the most important thing in my life. As long as I have you, I can bear everything else.'

I pressed my cheek to Mamie's, and we sat on the sofa together until the sunrise began to dance over the rooftops of Paris.

'That's how I feel too,' I said. 'As long as I have you, Mamie, I can bear everything else.'

I would have stayed with Mamie that morning, but my lesson with Mademoiselle Louvet was scheduled for nine o'clock and I couldn't miss it. While rushing around getting myself ready for the day, I checked in periodically on Mamie who remained in the living room. She was so still and quiet. I wondered what she was thinking.

'I love you, Mamie,' I told her, when it was time for me to leave. I gave her a hug. 'I'll see you this afternoon.'

Out on the street, I noticed a brown BMW Longue parked opposite our building. The window was wound down and I noticed there was a man sitting in it smoking a cigarette. It reminded me of the day I had gone to see the place where la Rusa had committed suicide. I was still intrigued about why she had betrayed Xavier. Despite Mamie's explanation, something niggled at me. I couldn't help thinking that an important part of the story was still missing.

Although I'd had no sleep, I felt strangely enlivened as I made my way to the Métro station. The colours and shapes around me were more vivid than they ever had been before. The windows of the patisseries and dress shops shone like crystal; commuters rushing for their trains were more animated and noisy; the golden sand and turquoise water of a travel advertisement for the Caribbean leaped out at me. In the train, I observed the other passengers with interest instead of ignoring them as I usually did. I wondered about the lives behind their impassive faces—the joys, the tragedies, *the secrets*.

Mamie's story had overwhelmed me. In Paris, there were reminders everywhere of the horrors of the Second World War: bullet and shrapnel holes in buildings; plaques to commemorate fallen Resistance fighters; memorials to call to mind the victims of the Holocaust. Why did the war in Spain seem even worse than all that? Was it because Spaniards had killed Spaniards—that neighbours, friends and families had turned on each other? Or was it that the clergy, who were supposed to be the representatives of a loving and merciful God, had joined in with the atrocities? What are we human beings? I wondered. We are capable of creating such beauty and yet we are responsible for so many horrors.

Then I thought of la Rusa, 'treacherous and full of anger'. Her betrayal of Xavier had disturbed me most of all. I still had no idea why her ghost had visited me. Was she hoping for some sort of absolution? If so, then why visit me and not Mamie? I rested my head against the window, feeling the vibration of the train hum through my skull. Mamie had mentioned several times the golden earrings that she had seen la Rusa wearing towards the end of the war. Were they the earrings she had given me? If so, what did they mean? I shivered and decided that I no longer cared. I would throw them into the Seine at the first opportunity.

Despite the cacophony of emotions coursing through me, I managed to give Mademoiselle Louvet my best effort in my lesson. My muscles were strong but fluid. My lines were perfect. I felt unstoppable.

'Well done,' she said afterwards. 'What you gave me was full engagement. Keep dancing like that and you are on your way to the Ballet!'

But when I changed back into my street clothes, the feeling of being overwhelmed returned. I walked around the jardin des Tuileries to gather my thoughts. The bare winter trees reminded me of Mamie's description of the aftermath of the Italian bombing of Barcelona and how it had changed her idea of the world and how things worked. The story of her family had done the same for me. I thought about what Xavier had told her: 'I don't regret for a second that we tried to build a better country—that we experienced moments of greatness. Perhaps our sacrifice will inspire future generations—or at least help them to learn from our mistakes.'

Part of me felt weighed down by the horror of what human beings could do to each other, while another part of me longed to soar, to make a positive impact on the world. There were so many thoughts rushing around my head, I needed to talk to someone to make sense of them. I wondered if Jaime would be at home.

'Paloma!' cried Carmen when she saw me at the door. 'What a lovely surprise! Jaime isn't here but I'm having lunch. Would you like to join me?'

While Carmen ladled out some vegetable soup for me, I looked around her beautiful apartment. I couldn't help feeling that I had been led to flamenco, that there was some connection between the appearance of la Rusa and my decision to take classes. If I hadn't started the flamenco lessons, I wouldn't have met Jaime and Carmen and the others, and they were becoming a second family to me.

'What's upsetting you?' Carmen asked, placing the bowl of soup in front of me and handing me a spoon. 'Tell me, Paloma. You look anxious.'

'Mamie told me about her life in Spain,' I said. 'She's never said anything about it before; it's only since Franco died. I can't imagine what it's been like for her to carry all that sadness around with her for years. All my life I've been striving for a role in the Paris Opera Ballet—it's been my obsession. And when I failed the audition last year, I became depressed and introverted. But when I think of my grandparents and their families . . . they never even had a chance to live their dreams. I was offered places with New York and London ballet companies. I refused them because I had my heart set on the Paris Ballet. Now I feel foolish for not understanding how lucky I am just to have been able to dance.'

Carmen reached across the table and squeezed my hand. 'Don't be too hard on yourself, Paloma. You're only eighteen. But if your grandmother's story has given you an expanded view of life, she's not done you a disservice in telling it.'

I sighed. 'I don't know what to do with all these feelings I have. I'm not even sure that I want to audition for the Ballet any more. Everything suddenly seems so trivial.'

Carmen thought for a while before speaking. 'The story of the Spanish Civil War is powerful . . . that's why many people who experienced it can't bring themselves to talk about it, in case the listener doesn't understand the impact of it. But it sounds as if you have.'

'There is no justice in it,' I said. 'Now Franco is dead, the newspapers are proclaiming a "New Spain" where everyone has to forgive each other and forget the past. But how could someone like Mamie ever forgive what was done to her family?'

Carmen nodded. 'I agree, Paloma. I will never forget that the love of my life died because he stood up for human rights. What makes it worse is that at least Mussolini and Hitler got what was coming to them in the end. But where was the justice for Spain? Franco lived to be an old man, pandered to and courted by the very countries that betrayed the Republic.'

'That's true,' I said. 'Perhaps that's why part of me feels so weighed down by it all.'

'Franco's killing didn't stop with the end of the war either,' said Carmen. 'His orders for the execution of his opponents continued right up to a few days before his death. But when the unfairness of it gets to me, I recall an inscription that I once read on a grave here in cimetière du Père-Lachaise: *All honourable causes eventually succeed even if at first they fail.*'

'I like that,' I said.

'Spain is going to become a democracy,' Carmen said. 'While no one can expect the older generations to forgive, the younger ones have to find some way of making sense of the past and moving the country forwards. I'd like to be part of that process, even though I don't know how yet. They have plenty of flamenco teachers but not enough dance companies.' She smiled and touched my cheek. 'Maybe you and I will form our own flamenco-ballet company one day and through dance assist the healing process in Spain,' she said.

'Perhaps we will,' I said, suddenly feeling that my world was opening up to a whole range of possibilities. It didn't have to be the one ballet company for the rest of my life.

Carmen glanced at her watch. 'I have a student coming in ten minutes, but I have a cancellation tonight. Why don't you come and have a lesson? I'll teach you some steps that will lift your spirits—and I know a certain young man who will be very happy to see you!'

I thought of Jaime and smiled. 'I'll be very happy to see him too.'

As Carmen and I reached the door, I said to her, 'I really like that inscription from the cemetery: *All honourable causes eventually succeed even if at first they fail*. Do you remember whose grave it was? I want to go and see it for myself.'

Carmen smiled. 'That's easy. It's the inscription on the grave of Spain's most famous flamenco artist: la Rusa.'

Carmen's revelation about the inscription on la Rusa's grave added to my bafflement. How could such a hopeful sentiment come from someone who had taken her own life? Of course, the inscription could have been requested by a well-meaning friend who still thought la Rusa was a heroine of the Republic, but I kept sensing that there was something vital to the whole la Rusa story that I'd missed.

I stopped by Micheline's kiosk to pick up Mamie's newspapers on the way home: *Le Monde* and *Libération*. Mamie had read the liberal newspapers for as long as I could remember but now I understood why: her experiences in Spain had given her a keen social conscience and she had been strongly influenced by Xavier and Margarida.

I thanked Micheline, then stopped in my tracks on my way to the apartment. Margarida! I recalled the details of Mamie's story of her last days in Spain. She hadn't mentioned what had happened to her sister. Had Margarida made it across the border? I did a mental calculation: my great-aunt would be seventy-six if she was still alive.

My heart beat quickly as I rushed home. Since Mamie had started talking about Spain, I'd discovered I had a cousin in Feliu—maybe I had a great aunt somewhere too! I thought about the way Mamie had described Margarida. She sounded like a fascinating woman. It would be wonderful to meet her. I burst through the apartment building doors, eager to speak with Mamie, but came to a standstill when I saw my father pacing the courtyard. It took me a moment to recognise him. Papa used to have long hair and sideburns, and usually wore turtleneck sweaters and corduroy pants with cat hair on them. Now he was sporting a short back and sides cut and was wearing a bullet-grey suit, navy overcoat and patent leather shoes. He looked more like a suave French businessman than a pianist. Was Audrey dressing him these days too? More importantly: what was he doing here? Then I remembered that I had promised to call him when he returned from his tour. I hadn't because there wasn't any need: it was obvious he'd had an affair with Arielle Marineau. I hated him for turning up like this.

'What are you doing here?' I was keen to get what I anticipated would be an awkward encounter over with so I could go talk to Mamie.

My father turned around, flinching at my hostile tone. 'Paloma!' He leaned forwards to kiss me but I backed away.

'Do you want something?' I asked.

He ran his hand through his hair, what was left of it. 'I'm sorry,' he said.

What was he apologising for? If it was for betraying Mama and marrying Audrey, it was much too late.

'I've come from the hospital and things don't look good,' he went on.

At first I wondered if he was re-enacting a conversation from when Mama was dying, but then the truth hit me. A sick feeling gnawed the pit of my stomach. 'Mamie?'

Papa nodded. 'She collapsed in one of her classes. The students called an ambulance.'

The whole world seemed to fall into slow motion. I hardly heard the rest of what Papa said as he guided me towards his car because the blood was humming so loudly in my ears.

'Audrey is ringing the parents to let them know the classes are cancelled,' he said, opening the passenger door to his Triumph sports car and helping me into its black interior. 'She will find a teacher who can take over until we sort out what to do about the school.'

My father climbed into the driver's seat and looked at me a moment before switching on the engine. 'I'm sorry, Paloma,' he said. 'I know how much Mamie means to you.'

I turned my face to the window so that I wouldn't have to talk to him. It was starting to rain. Droplets slid down the glass and disappeared into the window seals. 'As long as I have you, Mamie, I can bear everything else,' I'd told my grandmother that morning.

Mamie's doctor met us in the corridor. He was a tall man with such pale skin that the fluorescent lights showed up the blue veins under it. 'She's out of intensive care,' he said. 'It was very serious for a while there, but she's stabilised. We still have to assess what damage has been done to her heart.'

I was allowed see Mamie briefly. She was hooked up to oxygen and drips, and her face was grey. It was the first time I had ever seen my grandmother actually looking old. My legs trembled when I approached the bed. I stood beside her and stroked her arm lightly. Mamie opened her eyes.

'I'm sorry, Mamie,' I whispered. 'It's because I made you speak about Spain. I didn't know you had a bad heart.'

'It's what gets us Montella women in the end,' she said weakly. 'Our hearts.'

I remembered her story of how her mother had passed away. I couldn't bear to imagine life without Mamie. 'Please get better,' I begged her, my voice sounding small in the sterile room. 'We won't speak about Spain any more. We'll talk only about the future.'

She gave me a nod and a slight smile. 'Only the future,' she repeated.

Papa and I drove back to the apartment in silence. It was only after he had pulled the car into the kerb that he turned to me. 'Audrey says you should come and live with us while Mamie is in hospital.'

At a moment like this, I couldn't stand him mentioning his new wife: the woman who had replaced Mama. 'So we all do what Audrey says these days?'

My father ignored my comment. 'When Mamie comes out of hospital, I'll arrange a nurse for her. But for now you have to prepare for your examination. It's better that you concentrate on that instead of fending for yourself.'

'That would be nice,' I said sarcastically, 'if you hadn't ruined my chances of getting into the Ballet!'

Papa looked at me incredulously. 'What the hell are you talking about?'

'Arielle Marineau hates me and I've finally worked out the reason why. You had an affair with her and then dumped her when you found out Mama was pregnant with me.'

Papa slapped his hand on the dashboard. I jumped. 'Because that's the sort of bastard I am, isn't it, Paloma?'

I stared at him, rage building up inside me. I had told myself that my father no longer meant anything in my life. But it wasn't true. He still had the power to hurt me.

'Yes, you are a bastard!' I screamed. 'A bastard for cheating on Mama when she was dying, and a bastard for marrying Audrey before Mama's body was cold in the grave!'

A change came over my father's face. His jaw set and his nostrils flared, and he seemed to look straight through me. For a wild moment, I thought that he might hit me. But he didn't. Instead he leaned across me and shoved open the door, letting in a sharp blast of winter air.

'Get out, Paloma! Go fend for yourself if that's what you want! Get out!' he shouted.

I stepped out onto the pavement. Papa slammed the door shut. He glared at me for a moment before speeding away.

I watched his car turn the corner. It was the wrong time to have started an argument, but the anguish had been bottled up inside me ever since Mama died. My grandmother's sudden illness was bringing up the memories of what it was like to lose someone I adored. I wanted the kind of father who would put me first. Who was honourable and who had never cheated on my mother. But it was too late for that: my father wasn't that man and never would be.

At home, I took Diaghilev and the telephone to my bedroom and locked the door. The apartment felt empty without Mamie and the fight with my father had left me in tears. I lay on the bed, exhausted but also scared that la Rusa might choose tonight to make another appearance.

I rang Carmen to tell her I couldn't have a lesson and Jaime answered the telephone.

'I'm coming to get you,' he said when I told him about Mamie. 'You're not staying there on your own.'

Mamie had to have surgery and she remained in the hospital for over a month. Every morning I woke up with the dread that she might have passed away overnight, as had happened with Mama.

Carmen rang the hospital for me early each morning before I left the apartment. When I heard the words from her: 'The nurse says that your grandmother is fine', I wanted to fall to my knees and thank God.

I kept up my training for the examination, but my visits to Mamie were a much more important part of my day. I sat with her while she ate breakfast before going off to my class with Mademoiselle Louvet and returned after dinner each evening to read her the papers.

'You're the granddaughter every woman wishes for,' Mamie told me.

One evening, after she had started showing significant improvement, I brought Jaime to meet her.

'So you're the young man who's been looking after Paloma?' she said.

'As much as she will allow me to,' said Jaime with a dashing smile. He placed the roses he had brought on the beside table.

Mamie smiled. 'She's stubborn, that's for sure.'

'Are you two going to gang up on me?' I asked them.

They shared a conspiratorial smile. Jaime sat down in the chair next to Mamie's bed. 'Where does Paloma get her stubbornness from?' he asked. 'Not from you, I am sure. Maybe from her grandfather?'

A strange look came over Mamie's face. For a moment, I thought she might be feeling ill. But the expression passed and she smiled again. 'You should know yourself, young man,' she quipped. 'That defiance is a Catalan characteristic and Paloma has Catalan blood in her veins.'

Afterwards, when Jaime went to search for a vase to put the flowers in, Mamie leaned towards me. 'I like him,' she said. 'His family are Andalusians?'

I nodded.

She looked thoughtful for a moment. 'Well, he's a gentleman anyway. Do your best to make each other happy. You never know what life might bring.'

*   *   *

My life became a whirlwind of intensive training, visiting Mamie in the hospital and staying with Jaime and his family.

It was an adjustment living in Carmen's apartment. I was used to quiet and a lot more space, but I loved being part of a lively household. Sometimes Jaime, Carmen, Isabel and I would be up talking or singing and dancing until late at night—or until one of the neighbours complained. I found myself tapping out flamenco rhythms on the Métro, in the café when I waited for Gaby, on the tiles when I took a shower. Flamenco helped my spirits during an anxious time in my life.

Jaime had given his room over to me and made a temporary bed for himself on the sofa. 'It's good practise for touring,' he said with a chivalrous smile.

I loved sleeping in Jaime's room. Before I turned the light out each night, I'd look at all the flamenco paraphernalia and other objects that he'd collected that meant something to him. One night I noticed on his desk the pewter bat pendant I'd seen him wearing at the first flamenco class I'd attended. I picked it up and climbed down the stairs and went to the living room. Jaime was still up, playing a melody softly on his guitar.

I showed him the pendant. 'I'm curious about this,' I said. 'Is it something from southern Spain?'

He shook his head, and moved his blanket aside so I could snuggle up to him on the sofa. 'A friend of mine from the Conservatoire gave it to me. He believes in Native American symbolism and in that culture bats represent intuition, dreaming and vision. But they also give the ability to see through illusions or ambiguity.'

I leaned against Jaime and examined the pendant again. For reasons I couldn't explain, I was fascinated by it.

'Why don't you wear it?' Jaime suggested, taking the pendant from me. I lifted my hair so he could fasten the clasp at the back of my neck.

'Thanks,' I told him, pressing my cheek to his. 'I do have the feeling I'm not seeing something clearly. Maybe the bat will help me.'

Although I was training several hours a day for my ballet examination, I still found the energy for lessons with Carmen. Maybe I will go to Spain with her one day, I thought. Maybe I will become a flamenco-ballet artist and start a new version of both arts. One thing was certain: I was going to grab any opportunity that came my way—whether it was to have lessons with a magnificent ballerina like Mademoiselle Louvet or to live with a family of flamenco artists. People had died terrible deaths in Spain and I lived in a country where free speech was considered a national characteristic. I had no excuse not to be making the most of my life.

One morning when I was visiting Mamie, she asked me about Papa. 'When I collapsed, Madame Carré called your father. He came straight away. The first thing that he said to me was not to worry about you. He'd look after you. Well, where is he?'

Audrey had organised another teacher to keep Mamie's studio going, but she didn't make any further contact with me and neither did Papa. After the way we had parted, I would have been surprised if Papa ever contacted me again.

'I sent him away, Mamie. We don't get along any more.'

Mamie looked into my eyes for a long while before saying, 'Maybe you need to forgive him, Paloma. After all, he is your father.'

I thought about Mamie's change of heart towards my father on my way to ballet class and wondered what had caused it. When I had first told her that he was seeing Audrey, she'd been as shocked as I was that he could be serious about a woman so soon after Mama's death. I wondered what had caused her to feel differently about Papa now. Perhaps she was afraid that if she died, I'd be without a family of my own.

That evening, I found Feliu's telephone number in her address book; he lived in Marseilles. He was family, wasn't he? Yet I knew so little about him. He was in his late forties now. Was he married? Did he have children? Was he happy?

I listened to the phone ring, not sure if he would be home.

'Hello.'

'Feliu?'

'Who's this?'

I wanted to tell him I was his cousin. That Mamie had told me all about what had happened in Spain, and that I understood his pain now and wished there was some way I could help him. Instead I said, 'It's Paloma Batton. I wanted to let you know that Mamie is in hospital. She's had heart surgery.'

Feliu was silent. At first I wondered if we had been disconnected.

'I'm sorry,' he said finally. 'Which hospital is she in? I will send her some flowers.'

I gave him the address of the hospital with a sense of disappointment. I had hoped that he would say he was coming to Paris. There was so much that I wanted to ask him. From Mamie's story, I had the impression that he had once been very attached to her; that she had been more of a mother to him than Conchita.

I went to see Conchita on my way from the ballet school one day, to make sure she was still receiving her deliveries of food. I sat with her for a couple of hours to keep her company. I saw her in a different light now too. I surprised her with my warm embrace and told her that I loved her. She was no longer simply an eccentric, aging beauty, a friend of Mamie's; she was family to me in a way she had never been before. I admired her because she had survived something terrible. I wanted to ask her how it was that she had come to think of Franco as a great man when her husband had been executed by his forces and she herself had been gaoled and exiled. I was aware that there were some liberal monarchists, not only fascists and Francoists, who would have a different perspective of the Spanish Republic's weaknesses and their own stories of atrocities committed by the Republican army. But Conchita was even older than Mamie and much more fragile. I didn't want to risk causing her the same agony of remembrance that had triggered Mamie's heart attack.

After my visit, I went up to our apartment. Mamie had asked me to bring a few of her things to the hospital. I walked into her bedroom and realised that I hadn't been in there since Avi had passed away. While my room was austere, with white walls and curtains, Mamie's room resembled a 1930s film star's dressing room, with a mirrored dressing table and a Swarovski crystal chandelier dangling from the ceiling. I could smell her signature lily-of-the-valley perfume. I sat on the quilted satin bedspread and imagined Avi as a nightclub musician and Mamie as a glamorous socialite. They'd lost those parts of their pasts but somehow kept a remnant of them alive in their bedroom.

I went to Mamie's armoire and took out a bathrobe for her. Then I saw the oriental silk dressing gown next to it and swapped them. Why shouldn't Mamie be glamorous in hospital? I found a headband and a cosmetics bag in the dresser drawer. I looked for something to put everything in, and noticed a travel case on the top shelf of the armoire. I stood on tiptoes and tugged it out. Something sharp fell on my head and thumped to the floor. I looked down to see a large journal lying open near the bed. I picked it up to put it back and the words on the open page jumped out at me:

> But as I relate the story, I realise that I must be careful. Sometimes Paloma misses the obvious, but at other times she is very sharp. I do not want to reveal to her the one thing she doesn't need to know. If she found out, it would destroy her peace of mind for good . . .

The entry was unfinished. My eyes flew to the top of the page: *Dearest Margarida.*

I sat down on the bed and flipped through the journal. There were dozens of entries addressed to Margarida. I looked up at the shelf and saw more journals stacked there. They had been hidden by the travel case. I stepped up on the ottoman and took them down. The entries dated back to 1939 and detailed every significant event in Mamie's life since that time, including Mama's marriage and my birth. Mamie must have copied into her journal all the letters she had sent to Margarida. So Margarida was alive! But where was she?

I flipped through the journals and found several references to Australia. I searched the armoire for Margarida's replies to Mamie but couldn't find any. I felt as if I knew everything and nothing at all. What did Mamie mean when she wrote that I sometimes missed the obvious? What had I missed in her story? Something about her? About Xavier? Or about la Rusa?

When I went to visit Mamie that evening, I was in two minds whether I should ask her about Margarida. Her sister would want to know about Mamie's condition, but if I brought up the journals—which were obviously private—Mamie might get angry with me again. I didn't want to risk anything that might cause further strain on her heart.

In any case, Mamie was in the television room when I arrived, so there was no chance to speak to her privately.

I sat down next to her and held her hand. She still looked frail. I realised I could never ask her about Margarida without the fear of making her ill again. I guess I'll never know, I thought, and sighed inwardly.

A week after my discovery of the journals, I saw my second ghost. He was waiting for me in the hospital foyer as I was leaving after visiting Mamie. The night receptionist had gone on an errand and the lights in the foyer had dimmed. The ghost rose from a chair in the waiting area. He had Mamie's honey-coloured eyes and fine features: Xavier! My heart missed a beat and my blood turned cold. I stood frozen as he walked towards me.

The night receptionist returned to her desk and nodded to the apparition. I realised then that he wasn't a ghost at all. It was Feliu! Mamie had said that he was the spitting image of his father. Now that I knew about Xavier, I could see it.

'Paloma?' he asked, reaching out to shake my hand. His flesh was warm and firm: he was real. 'You've grown up,' he said. 'You were only fourteen or fifteen when I saw you last. How is tia Evelina? I got into Paris just now: too late for visiting hours unfortunately. But the nurse said you were with her.'

Now I understood who Feliu was, I found myself staring at him. The skin on his hands was rough and freckled. There was nothing about him to suggest that he had once been the son of the debonair heir to one of the richest families in Barcelona. There was a sadness in his eyes too. It was a terrible thing for an only son to be estranged from his mother, especially as she was getting older. But how could I judge Feliu? He must have had his reasons. After all, I was an only child too and I was also estranged from my only remaining parent.

'Would you like to have dinner with me?' I asked him.

Instantly, that twitchiness that reminded me of a sparrow returned to Feliu. I sensed that he was uncomfortable around anyone from his family, even me.

'I have to go,' he said, turning towards the exit. 'I have an early morning start.'

I knew I had only a few seconds to ask anything that might help resolve the questions I had about Mamie's story.

'Excuse me,' I said in a pleading voice. 'I found copies of letters Mamie wrote to her sister, Margarida. They go back to 1939, and the latest was dated just last week. It appears she is living in Australia. I'd like to write and tell her about Mamie. Do you know where she is now?'

Feliu winced. 'Tia Margarida?' He shook his head. 'Maybe the letters are a way of helping tia Evelina cope. They were very close.'

My stomach turned. 'Cope?' I repeated. 'So Margarida is dead?' I swallowed. Please let her have died peacefully, I prayed, but I sensed something dreadful coming. 'What happened to her?'

It looked for a moment as though Feliu was going to cry, but his voice remained steady. 'I only know what oncle Gaspar told me.' He hesitated and looked at his hands. 'Tia Margarida drove a group of Republican refugees to the border in January 1939. When she reached Figueres, she learned that we had been arrested. She returned to Barcelona to try to orchestrate our release, but she was caught and arrested herself.'

My legs went numb. I had to take a seat.

'What you have to understand,' said Feliu, moving a step towards me, 'is that Franco's army was full of right-wing extremists. Women like tia Margarida, who played a part in public life, who cut their hair short and wore modern clothes, were abhorrent to them. They had a special way of dealing with women like that: they shaved their heads, raped them and paraded them through the streets before killing them.'

I felt as if my intestines were twisting inside me. 'Is that what happened to Margarida?'

Feliu nodded.

'And Mamie knows that?'

'Oncle Gaspar found tia Margarida's body while he was waiting—hoping—for our release from the prison,' said Feliu. 'They had hanged her in the music room of our house. He cut her down and placed her body in the Montella crypt. Oncle Gaspar never wanted Mamie to know, but some other Spanish refugees told her. That's probably why she started writing in 1939. It must have been her way of dealing with what had been done to tia Margarida—to convince herself it had never happened, and that tia Margarida was alive and well in Australia.'

I could barely breathe. Mamie must have known too that Margarida's body was tossed in the mass grave along with those of her grandparents and father. I thought of Mamie's story about finding Xavier and Margarida standing before the paupers' pit on the Feast of All Souls and pitying the nameless who were buried there. I had to lean towards my knees until the lightness in my head disappeared. I hadn't thought Mamie's story could have got any more tragic, but it had. Poor Mamie, writing to a sister she had loved and would never see again.

I looked up to ask Feliu about la Rusa, but he was already gone.

THIRTY-FOUR

Paloma

It was a strange Christmas season without Mamie, who was still in the hospital, but at least I spent it with Jaime's family. And we all visited Mamie together before going to Christmas Mass, taking her a chickpea and spinach stew that Vicenta and Carmen had cooked for her.

'We can't let your grandmother eat that tasteless hospital food on Christmas Eve,' Vicenta said.

'Look, Evelina,' said Carmen, after I had introduced everyone. 'we've made you a delicious stew.' She lifted the lid off the casserole dish and sent the smell of cumin and paprika wafting around the ward. She glanced at Mamie's nurse. 'It's not spicy, honestly.'

Mamie barely managed to fit a word in as Vicenta and Carmen talked to her about every topic under the sun: the decreasing quality of the goods at the Christmas markets; the increasing number of tourists coming to Paris in winter; how Jaime had broken his arm as a child and everyone thought he'd never be able to play guitar.

'Our children and grandchildren are much stronger than we ever give them credit for,' Vicenta said.

When it was time to leave, Mamie called me back as the others were heading out the door. She looked deeply into my eyes and I sensed there was something she wanted to tell me. But the nurse came in with Mamie's medications and noisily tugged the bed curtain around us, indicating that I should go.

'I'll see you tomorrow,' I said to Mamie, kissing her forehead.

When I arrived the next morning, I hoped that Mamie would tell me whatever had been on her mind the day before. Instead, she gave me the news that the specialist had come to see her and thought she would be well enough to return home in early January. I sat with her while she ate breakfast, but the only other thing she talked about was how much she liked Jaime and his family.

The new year came and went. I didn't go to my father's fiftieth birthday party, and I wasn't surprised that there were no more pleas from Audrey to attend. True to his word, my father arranged a nurse to care and cook for Mamie when she came out of hospital, and he had the bills sent to his address.

The new teacher, Jeannette, was popular with the students and Mamie decided that she would keep her permanently. 'It's probably time I retired,' she told me, 'and let someone younger take over.'

I didn't ask Mamie any more about Spain and she didn't bring the subject up either. I had come to believe that what she had written in her journal about me missing the obvious was in reference to Margarida. Every time I thought of what Margarida must have suffered at the hands of the Nationalists, I wanted to cry. But I didn't let it destroy me, as Mamie had feared. Instead I drew on the pride I felt in being part of a family of strong women. I gave everything I had to my training, but I no longer felt that the Paris Opera Ballet was the only company in the world worth joining. I was more motivated by the idea of developing myself fully as a dancer—and of showing Arielle Mari-neau that she hadn't broken me.

Once I was confident that Mamie was on the mend, I could throw myself entirely into my preparation. The months flew by and it was summer before I knew it. I slept well the night before my examination, not like the previous year when I had tossed and turned all night, going over every step of my variations in my mind. I'd had to put on extra make-up the following morn-ing to hide the circles under my eyes. I hadn't let Mamie drive me to the audition either; I'd insisted on going alone. But this time, as I double-checked my bag and pointe shoes to make sure I had everything, I was glad Carmen and Jaime were taking me to the Paris Opera House.

I heard Carmen's Fiat as soon as she turned into the street: Hot Chocolate's 'You Sexy Thing' was blaring from its radio.

'Are you ready?' asked Mamie, poking her head in the door. 'It sounds like they are here.'

I stood up and embraced her. 'You can come this year,' I told her. 'Are you sure you don't want to?'

She shook her head. 'I'm the one who would be tense,' she said with a laugh. 'You go and do your best. You will be great.'

Carmen and Jaime were waiting for me in the car. Jaime got out and kissed me before climbing into the back seat. 'I don't want you to get a cramp in your legs sitting here,' he said with a grin.

When we arrived at the Opera House, I smiled at the golden statues and rose marble columns. The building was an old friend. Carmen parked the car and we all got out. She and Jaime were going to wait in a nearby café while I did the examination.

'You all right?' Jaime asked.

'Surprisingly, yes.'

'Good,' he said, kissing me passionately on the lips even though his aunt was standing right next to us.

Carmen cleared her throat and we stepped apart. 'When we next see you, Paloma,' she said, 'you will be a member of the *corps de ballet*.'

I crossed the street and turned to wave to them. So much had changed, I thought. Jaime and I had spoken about what me joining the *corps de ballet* might mean for our relationship.

'There will be long hours of rehearsals and performances and less time to spend together,' I'd told him. 'Are you worried?'

He'd shaken his head in response.

'No?'

He smiled. 'You never know what's going to happen in the future . . . but right now I know this is something that you have to do and I'm proud. It feels right to be with you . . . I'm sure we will work out the minor details as we go along.'

It feels right to be with you too, I thought now, and waved to Jaime and Carmen one more time.

After changing into my tights and leotard in the dressing room, I went to the classroom that had been assigned for warm-up exercises. The other students greeted me with nervous smiles or blank stares. I didn't know them well because they were in the year below me. I was competition they hadn't been expecting. Even under their make-up, their faces were pale with tension and everyone was sweating. I felt for them, understanding exactly what they were going through: the dry mouth; the urge to get started before your nerves got the better of you; the feeling of dread that after all your work and sacrifice you may not make the cut. I was a year older but I felt ten years wiser. This day would decide whether or not I was accepted into the Paris Opera Ballet, but it wouldn't decide whether I would be happy or not. Only I could decide that.

When we were directed to enter the Salle Bailleau, I thought with excitement rather than trepidation: This is it! I was prepared. All should go well for me.

The judging panel was sitting at a table at the front of the room. As well as the director of l'Opéra national de Paris and two independent judges, there was Raymond Franchetti, a much-admired former dancer and the current director of dance, Claude Bessy, the director of the Ballet school . . . and Arielle

Marineau, the company's ballet mistress. I did my best to avoid eye contact with her.

We were given our places to commence the adagio part of the examination, which we would do together as a group to demonstrate form and strength. The Opera's beautiful auditorium was directly below the examination room, and I imagined that I had been given a place right above the crystal chandelier. Mademoiselle Louvet had trained me to give two hundred per cent to all my exercises 'because on the day of the examination, your nerves will cut you down to one hundred per cent'. That had been true the first time I had taken the examination, when my limbs had felt heavier than usual, but not this time. My *développés*, *arabesques* and *fondus* were beautiful and fluid. I felt as relaxed as if I were dancing for Mademoiselle Louvet alone. Even when we had to hold the poses for a long time, I did not lose my form.

The first solo piece I had to perform was Aurora's variation from Act III of *The Sleeping Beauty*. It was probably the purest of the classical ballets and was usually the first full evening role a ballerina performed. It was also a part that involved incredible stamina and Mademoiselle Louvet had chosen it to show the judges that I could bear the load of a professional dancer. 'Make sure you stay present with every step,' she had advised me. 'Don't be in a hurry to rush to the next one. Keep everything clean.'

As soon as Monsieur Clary began to play and I took my first step, I knew that things would go well. 'Think of a rose when you dance this part,' Mademoiselle Louvet had said. My balance was perfect. Because of Mamie's stories about Spain, I understood Aurora's journey from innocence to womanhood; she'd had to accept that not all in the world was good.

I finished and waited for the panel to write down their comments. Then I was allowed to go and dry off before my next piece, which was the Kitri variation from *Don Quixote*, Act III. I was looking forward to it because I thought I could give the part a distinctly Spanish flavour. Just as I was about to begin, the lights in the room started to blink and several of them went out. The judges looked up.

'How quickly can we get that fixed?' asked Monsieur Franchetti.

'I'll call the attendant,' said Mademoiselle Bessy, rising from her seat.

'I'm sorry, Mademoiselle Batton,' said Monsieur Franchetti. 'This is most infuriating during an examination, but we must take a break.'

I went to the water fountain outside the room to take a drink.

'You were beautiful,' said Mademoiselle Louvet, touching my shoulder. She directed me away from the other students, who were gathering around the fountain. 'Don't let their energy distract your concentration,' she said, leading me to a curtained-off area with a sink and a chair. 'Wait here a moment. I'll come and get you when they are ready.'

I sat in the chair and took a few deep breaths, keeping my mind focused on my performance and hoping it wouldn't take too long for the lights to be fixed. I leaned my head against the wall. The coolness of it was soothing. Then I realised I could hear voices speaking inside the Salle Bailleau.

'She is delicate and lyrical,' a woman's voice said. 'But she's limited. The ballet is full of sweet dancers with good technique. Her mother was a *bravura* dancer—strong, powerful, exceptional in every way. From start to finish you could not take your eyes off Julieta Olivero. As her daughter, Paloma Batton is always going to be compared unfavourably to her, and that is not going to be good for her or for the ballet.'

It was Arielle Marineau speaking about me to another judge. A nauseous feeling rose in my stomach. Suddenly all the self-doubt that I'd managed to push away came rushing back. While I no longer believed that the Paris Opera Ballet was the only company worth dancing for, I still dreamed of being an *étoile*. What was Marineau saying? That I was not an outstanding dancer? That I never would be? What more could I possibly give?

Relax, I told myself, she's just a woman who is bitter about your father dumping her! But the more I tried to calm my nerves, the worse they became. I did a pirouette to get my mind back on my next variation, but almost fell. *I had never fallen in my practise, not once!* I tried again. I lost my balance again. My limbs began to tremble as blind panic ran through me. I thought of Madame Genet, whose nerves had cracked the opening night of *Swan Lake*. Would I end up like her—creeping around the corridors of a ballet school, embittered and dreaming of what could have been?

'They are ready for you,' said Mademoiselle Louvet outside the curtain.

'I'm coming,' I told her.

I bent over to get the blood back to my head. *I'm never going to be a première danseuse. I'm always going to be in the* corps de ballet. Suddenly, chills ran through my body, as though I was coming down with influenza. I straightened, closing my eyes to get rid of the white dots in my vision. When I opened my eyes, la Rusa was standing in front of me, staring at me with her dark, hypnotic gaze. My blood turned cold. Oh God, I thought. Not now!

'What do you want?' I hissed at her.

'*Duende*,' she whispered. 'Let your demon help you.'

I remembered the conversation I'd had with Jaime: *duende* was the 'demon' that possessed a flamenco dancer and transformed her performance into an extraordinary spiritual experience.

La Rusa vanished, and at the same time so did my fear. A sense of calm washed over me. I held my head up. It no longer mattered how the panel judged me. All that mattered was that I danced from the core of my being.

I returned to the examination room and took my place on the floor. Never had I been so poised, so in control of myself. I imagined myself the way Mamie had described la Rusa standing before her audience at the Samovar Club: majestic, dignified, captivating.

When the music commenced, I *became* Kitri: vital and mischievous. I stabbed my pointes, my *pas de chats* were tight, every movement of my body was precise. I jumped with energy and performed the rapid turns with a spirit I had never possessed before. When I finished, I held my head high, haughty and sure of myself, not the delicate rose of the previous variation.

When the examination was over, all the entrants curtseyed to the panel and to Monsieur Clary, then we ran outside to collapse in the corridor, breathless and panting. When the secretary came out half an hour later to post the names of the successful candidates on the announcements board, I knew mine wouldn't be there so I didn't bother to rush forwards with the others. I no longer cared about failing. I thought about la Rusa and the spirit that had taken over my performance. I knew that I wanted to feel that way every time I danced.

Mademoiselle Louvet came out of the examination room. 'The judges want to see you,' she said.

That didn't sound like good news. I was sure they were going to tell me that I had danced well but not well enough to make it into the company, so I should stop trying. But when I stepped into the room after Mademoiselle Louvet, the judges turned around and applauded.

'Bravo, Mademoiselle Batton!' said the director of l'Opéra national de Paris. 'You are not only highly polished, you have incredible charisma. And that's not something anyone can teach, although we compliment Mademoiselle Louvet on what she has done with you.'

Charisma? I was astonished. No one had ever described me as 'charismatic' before. 'Beautiful' and 'delicate', but never more than that.

'The energy you emanated was contagious,' said Franchetti enthusiastically. 'Last year we felt you were holding something back from us. But this year you gave us everything.'

'You've been accepted into the *corps de ballet*,' said Claude Bessy, who had championed me from the beginning and made all the exceptions for me to take the examination for the second time through the school. 'You've achieved exactly what you wanted.'

I did my best to respond to their comments courteously, despite my utter surprise at the result. I thanked them and turned to leave. Before I reached the door, Arielle Marineau stepped forward. Our eyes met. The other judges turned to one another and started to talk and gather their papers.

'Congratulations,' she said. 'I look forward to working with you. If you keep giving me performances like the one in your second variation, you won't be in the *corps de ballet* long. You are star material.'

'Thank you,' I said, not quite able to take in what I was hearing. But while her praise sounded sincere, I detected a touch of frostiness in Arielle Marineau's manner. She'd been able to rise above her prejudice on this occasion, but I could not afford to get off on a bad foot with the ballet mistress over something that had happened in the past. 'I believe that you may have some ill feelings towards my father,' I told her. 'I hope it won't get in the way of our relationship. He and I are estranged.'

'Your father?' she said, looking genuinely surprised. 'Why would I have ill feelings towards *your father*? The man is a saint!'

Although I was exhausted after the examination, we celebrated my success with a flamenco party in Mamie's studio. I was surprised when Mamie joined Carmen in a slow gypsy tango. I almost begged her to stop on account of her heart, but the doctor had said that mild exercise would be good for her and she seemed to be enjoying herself.

I recalled that she'd had flamenco lessons from la Rusa. I was shaken by my second encounter with the ghost. But I was puzzled too. La Rusa hadn't given me the impression that she was a malevolent spirit. Nor did I feel that she wanted something from me. If anything, she had helped me. But the same question remained: why?

Of course, the other thing that was bothering me was what Arielle Marineau had said about my father. What did she mean he was 'a saint'? Those weren't the words of a woman scorned.

The following afternoon, I went to my father's apartment in avenue de l'Observatoire. The concierge telephoned Audrey. After a moment's pause, he turned to me. 'Madame says to go up.'

I walked up the fleur-de-lis-carpeted stairs to the second-floor landing, where Audrey was waiting for me. She was wearing a powder-blue jumpsuit with white beads and white platform shoes. Her dark hair was teased up behind her white headscarf. Even though it was Saturday, she wore winged eyeliner, thick black mascara and pale pink lipstick. She looked like an aging Bond girl. But I didn't want an altercation with Audrey today.

'I'd like to see Papa, please,' I said to her.

Audrey didn't reply. She opened the door for me and I followed her into the hallway. The apartment was as chic as I had expected, with terracotta stone floors and ornate moulded ceilings. The white walls were classic raised-panel wainscoting, but the furniture and art were modern. There was a framed print of Tretchikoff's *Fighting Zebras* above the mantelpiece in the sitting room, which must have been a talking point because the artist was considered by many as rather kitsch. The thing that took me by surprise was that Audrey's company appeared to occupy most of the space in the apartment. There was an office for her, plus another two rooms containing desks for employees and filing cabinets. There was a small boardroom too. I hadn't realised that Audrey ran her business from home.

My father was reading in a room at the rear of the apartment. Audrey obviously hadn't warned him I was coming. She ushered me into the room and shut the door behind me.

Papa appeared more tired than surprised to see me. He didn't stand up and kiss me. He didn't offer me a seat, but I took the armchair opposite him anyway. He looked more like his old self in his reading glasses and jeans. There were cat hairs on his sweater. I glanced around the room and spotted a tiger-striped tabby curled up on the windowsill.

'I passed the examination yesterday,' I said. 'I've been accepted into the *corps de ballet*.'

'Good,' Papa said matter-of-factly. 'You deserve it.'

When he didn't say anything more, I was stumped. The Ballet represented everything I had been working towards since I was eight years of age. Papa took off his glasses, as if he were impatient to hear what I'd come to say.

'The apartment is very nice,' I told him.

He nodded. 'It's a bit showy, but half of it belongs to Audrey's company and I guess publicity is all about image. I have a music studio the next floor up.'

'It must have a nice view.'

He nodded again but made no attempt to elaborate.

I rubbed my hands on my skirt. 'I met Arielle Marineau after the examination yesterday. She said she thought you were a saint. I guess that means that you didn't dump her for Mama. But something happened . . . something more than old rivalry. Otherwise she wouldn't have rejected me so unfairly on my first attempt.'

Papa looked away.

'Please tell me,' I said. 'I'd like to know the truth.'

My father gave a gruff laugh. 'Would you, Paloma? You don't want the truth. You want to live in fantasy land, just like your mother.'

His words stabbed at my heart. But I stayed calm.

'Mamie told me everything that happened in Spain,' I ventured. 'It was terrible to hear it, but it made me appreciate her much better and also realise how much I have to be grateful for. I think the truth is good.'

Papa sighed and shook his head. 'Really, Paloma,' he said, 'it's much better for you to go on believing that I am a bastard.'

I felt myself pale. In the same way I had sensed I was going to hear something terrible about Margarida, I now began to suspect that there was something about Mama I didn't know. I lost my courage at that. Perhaps Papa was right: it was better that I didn't know. Mama was my heroine, my ideal. But I'd set the ball rolling now.

'Your mother and I . . .' Papa began. 'Well, we loved you very much. In fact, you were the reason we stayed together as long as we did.'

'But you weren't happy together?' I asked.

I looked into my father's face and saw that it was true. If I was honest with myself, I had sensed it a long time ago. They were not the perfect couple. Mama had seemed happiest when Papa was away, and my father had toured more than his true nature would have wanted.

'I loved your mother,' he said. 'But she didn't feel very much for me other than as the father of her child. When you were away at ballet school, our lives were empty. She didn't like me being around, but she didn't want a divorce either in case it hurt you. We went on for years like that.'

'I'm sorry,' I said. 'I didn't understand what it was like for you.'

Papa looked surprised that I was handling an ugly truth so well, but he pursed his lips before continuing. 'No, because you adored your mother. In your eyes she was everything.'

I nodded. 'But I loved you too, Papa. And it doesn't explain why Arielle Marineau held a grudge against me.'

Papa looked away from me again. Mama, I thought, what did you do?

'Please,' I insisted. 'I want to understand.'

Papa hesitated, then said, 'Your mother . . . well, she and Christophe Valois . . . they had an affair.'

Christophe Valois, the choreographer? Arielle Marineau's long-time lover? Of all the things I had heard in the last few months, this shocked me the most. My mother had an affair? She must have been very discreet, I thought, because although the ballet world thrived on gossip, I hadn't heard even a hint of this.

'For how long?' I asked.

'About four years before she became ill.'

'And when did you meet Audrey?'

'The year before your mother died. She organised the publicity for my Australian tour. Her husband had suffered multiple sclerosis and died of complications a few years before we met. We began talking and we found we had a lot in common. We both love animals. Audrey is a volunteer fundraiser at the Société Protectrice des Animaux.'

I felt as if my life was constantly being torn down and reconstructed. I hadn't known I had a Spanish cousin; I hadn't known about Mamie's family; I hadn't known my mother had been having an affair. I hadn't known even trivial things about the woman my father was now married to: that she helped abandoned animals and liked kitsch art. I began to wonder if Audrey was to my father what la Rusa had been to Xavier.

'But you were still with us when Mama was ill,' I said. 'You took her to her medical appointments. You were there until she died.'

Papa stood up and stared out the window. 'That's because that bastard Valois abandoned her and went back to Arielle as soon as it was confirmed that Julieta had cancer. She was alone with only you and Mamie. Your grandmother was in pieces, and you were too young to go through all of that on your own.'

'But what about Audrey?'

'She encouraged it,' he replied. '"You must put your daughter first," she told me. "She's so young and this is a terrible thing to have happened." She'd seen how hard it was for Pierre to witness his father's slow, painful death.'

'Audrey let you pretend that you and Mama were still happily married! Why?'

'I think she hoped that one day you would be the daughter she had always wanted but never had. I don't think many women would have behaved so nobly.'

'No,' I agreed. 'No, not many women would put a man's wife and daughter first even in that situation.' I looked up at him. 'Is that why you married so quickly after Mama's death? To make it up to her?'

Papa shook his head. 'Audrey said we should wait, but I wanted to give you a stable home life as soon as possible. I thought that you and Mamie could both come here. I believed you'd like having a brother in Pierre and a mother figure in Audrey. But it went terribly wrong. I underestimated how badly you would take things. You think I always do what Audrey wants? Well, that was an occasion when I should have listened to her.'

I was so astounded by what I was hearing that at first I couldn't say anything.

Then it occurred to me how badly I had misunderstood my father's intentions. 'But you didn't explain any of this to me,' I said. 'How was I to know?'

I was about to stand up and embrace him, so that we could begin our reconciliation, but Papa frowned.

'How *were* you to know? Indeed!' he said. 'You moved out to go live with Mamie as soon as I mentioned Audrey. You walked away from me every time I went to see you to explain. I assume that you didn't read any of dozens of letters I sent to you and you even convinced Mamie I was so terrible that she hung up the telephone whenever I called. When Audrey tried to speak with you, you treated her with contempt. What else could I have done? When I tried to explain, you didn't want to listen!'

I stared at my hands, feeling as if a heavy weight was bearing down on my shoulders. It was true. Every time he'd tried to speak to me, I'd pushed him away. I hadn't even given him a chance.

'You're right,' I told him, tears choking my voice. 'I don't understand why I did that.'

My father put his hands on his hips. 'I didn't understand why either,' he said. 'Until I drove you home from the hospital after Mamie's heart attack . . . and I realised how much you despised me. If you had any kind of love for me, you would have demanded an explanation. Instead, your expectations of me were so low that you assumed that I was simply a bastard.'

'I'm so sorry!' I said. I almost couldn't bear to hear any more. Yes, I had been upset about Mama's death, but why had I been so cruel to Papa?

'You're sorry?' my father continued, his voice growing louder. 'I lived with a woman who was cold to me for seventeen years, Paloma! I did it for nobody's sake but yours! What a fool I am! All so you could look down on me with the same contempt your mother did!'

There had once been a time when Papa couldn't stand to see me cry. But even though the tears were streaming down my cheeks, he looked away from me and out the window. Avi had often said that there are some things in life that a mere apology couldn't fix, and it was obvious that my relationship with my father was one of them.

My father's revelations about my mother and my own realisation at the lack of understanding between us was as devastating as my failure to get into the *corps de ballet* the year before. It was difficult to adjust my picture of my mother. I didn't love or miss her any less, but I could see that she wasn't as perfect as I had thought. If I hadn't held my mother on such a pedestal, I might have been more generous to Papa.

'I feel as if I've been knocked down and gone over a few times by a steamroller,' I told Jaime. 'How could I have been so wrong about my own father?'

'Your father was hurt,' he said, putting his arm around me and kissing the top of my head. 'But it sounds to me like you both love each other very much. I'm sure now you've gone to see him that he will think things over. Just give it a bit of time.'

I wanted to believe Jaime, but the truth was that I had never seen Papa look at me so dispassionately. It was as if the feelings he had for me had died. And after the way I had acted, how could I blame him?

My rehearsals with the Ballet would begin in a few weeks and I had to be in good form. But one thought kept playing over in my mind: I had been wrong about my father, completely wrong, and that convinced me that I didn't know everything about la Rusa's betrayal of Xavier either. The only way to find out more was to try to make contact with her ghost myself.

The light shimmering through the trees of cimetière du Père-Lachaise gave the place an atmosphere that was both tranquil and tragic. Chopin, Proust, Colette and Édith Piaf were buried here, along with Molière, Oscar Wilde and Honoré de Balzac.

The attendant at the gate had marked on the cemetery's map the location of la Rusa's grave. Jaime checked it, then pointed in the direction we had to go.

'If there was a soundtrack for this cemetery,' he asked me, 'what would it be?'

'Something hauntingly beautiful,' I said. 'I know . . . Tchaikovsky's "Symphony No 6, *Pathétique*".' I remembered it was one of the pieces that Xavier had played at the Cerdàs' supper where Mamie first met Avi.

La Rusa's gravestone was black granite and it was covered in flowers. She was supposed to have betrayed my great-uncle and yet for some reason I found it comforting that she was still venerated by lovers of flamenco.

'It's poignant that someone who became such a recluse later in life is buried in one of the most densely populated areas of the cemetery,' I said.

Jaime squeezed my hand. 'Are you all right here for a while? I'll go visit Jim.'

He was referring to Jim Morrison from The Doors, who had died a few years before. Jaime was a big fan.

'I'll be fine,' I told him.

I watched Jaime walk away up the winding path. The golden

earrings tingled in my pocket. I had explained to Jaime that I wanted to see la Rusa's grave but not that I wanted to try to contact her. I had shared everything about Mamie's story with him, but for some reason I wanted to keep this part to myself. I hoped that la Rusa would appear again so I could ask her why she had visited me. It was strange, but since she had helped me at my examination, I was no longer afraid of her.

I took the earrings out and examined them in the sunlight. They looked in every way like an ordinary pair of hooped earrings. Who could believe that they had crossed worlds? Mamie's heart attack had made me forget my intention of throwing them in the Seine. I was glad that I hadn't.

'La Rusa . . . Celestina,' I whispered.

I waited for a response. But there was none: only the rustling of the breeze through the trees.

Jaime returned about half an hour later. 'Fans keep stealing the markers for Jim's grave,' he told me. 'But it's still easy to find because of all the people standing around it. The cemetery has even placed a security guard there.'

I knew that Jaime had to leave to play guitar for Carmen's advanced classes, but I wanted to stay by la Rusa's grave a little longer. Although cimetière du Père-Lachaise was a place for reflection and peace, there were sometimes reports of muggings and rapes occurring there. But there were plenty of summer tourists wandering around, so I felt safe to be on my own.

'Will you give me a call later on?' Jaime asked.

I nodded, and we kissed. Although Carmen and the others weren't there, I had a strange sense that someone was watching us.

'*Hasta luego!*' Jaime said, and waved before heading in the direction of the exit.

I waited a while longer, but when la Rusa didn't appear, I decided to leave by the porte de la Réunion gate so I could visit the memorial for the Second World War deportees and Resistance fighters. I paused for a moment to remember Avi and how he had 'lost' his music in a German prisoner-of-war camp. The suffering of Spanish Republicans hadn't finished with the end of the Civil War.

'You seem very interested in la Rusa.'

I spun around to see a man standing behind me. My blood went cold. There was something menacing in the way he'd asked the question. What did he want? He appeared to be in his seventies and was short with a round face and body. But he looked physically powerful. What was he? A mugger? A rapist? I didn't have anything valuable on me except for the golden earrings. And then I realised that the man had spoken in a marked Spanish accent. Something about his clothing struck me too. He wasn't shabbily dressed but he wore his clothes badly. The leather jacket and crocodile-skin shoes seemed expensive but were all wrong on a man his age. A gold chain nestled in the hairs of his barrel chest. There was an underworld air about him. Was he a drug dealer? I found myself wishing that I had left the cemetery with Jaime.

'You are not a reporter, in any case,' the man said. 'You are a descendant of the Montellas.'

I didn't like the way he said 'Montellas', as if it gave him a bad taste in his mouth.

'Who are you?' I asked, feeling braver now that I was sure he wasn't a rapist. I was obviously known to him in some way.

He fixed his eyes on me. 'I am Ramón Sanchez. La Rusa was my sister.'

A blow to the head couldn't have stunned me more. I stood with my mouth open.

Ramón's eyes darted from me to the memorial and back to me again. 'Why is a Montella wanting information about my sister?'

Now I knew who he was, I had no hesitation: I reached into my pocket and showed him the earrings.

He seemed startled by the sight of them, but quickly recovered. 'You'd better come with me,' he said. 'I'm parked over there.'

I turned to where he was pointing. Outside the exit was a brown BMW Longue. It was the car I had seen when I went to visit where la Rusa had died; and again outside my apartment building.

'You've been following me?'

'I wanted to know who you were and what you wanted. I have something of great importance to tell you.' He sounded less antagonistic and more awe-struck.

I wondered again how he'd known who I was. Then I remembered the policeman who had kept staring at me the day I went to the prefecture pretending to be a reporter investigating la Rusa's death. Now Ramón's earlier comment made more sense to me. It must have been the policeman who informed him. I still wasn't sure that going with him was a wise idea. Should I telephone Jaime or Carmen first? Then I realised that the man standing before me could answer every question I had. He could tell me why la Rusa had appeared to me.

Ramón drove me to Orly, an outer suburb of Paris. It wasn't far from where la Rusa had killed herself. He parked the car and I followed him into his apartment building, feeling that I was getting more and more out of my depth.

His apartment on the tenth floor made me wonder what he did for a living. My gaze moved from the shag-pile rugs to the brown leather chairs. A Marantz stereo system took up one wall of the living room. Like Ramón's dress style, everything in the apartment looked expensive but somehow in poor taste. Through a door I saw another room with an open trunk bursting with flamenco dresses and an antique Spanish dressing table. I no longer had to wonder who had cleared out la Rusa's apartment.

'Take a seat,' Ramón said. 'Would you like a drink? I would.'

I shook my head. His attitude towards me had improved markedly and I wondered why.

Ramón headed towards his bar to mix himself a Cinzano Bianco. He returned and sat uncomfortably close to me. His spicy aftershave made me want to sneeze. 'So how did you get those earrings?'

'Your sister gave them to me.'

'I buried them with my sister.'

Ramón stared at me intensely, but I wasn't sure if that meant he believed me or not. After all, who could believe my story? Was he going to accuse me of graverobbing?

'How many times have you seen her?' he asked me.

'Twice.'

To my surprise, he nodded. 'She said she'd return with them, although I didn't understand everything that she was explaining to me then. I didn't understand that she was going to kill herself.'

'My grandmother thinks la Rusa betrayed her brother, Xavier, during the Civil War. That she was responsible for his death.'

Ramón hesitated a moment at the mention of Mamie. 'Of course she does,' he said, staring into his drink. 'It didn't matter how high my sister rose or what she became, she would always be worthless in the eyes of the Montellas. Well, let me tell you, my sister was the most loyal person I've ever known. She was loyal to her family, she was loyal to her gypsy clan, she was loyal to her country. And, despite what Evelina Montella believes, she was loyal to the man she loved . . . and the child that they'd had together.'

'A child!'

'Yes,' said Ramón. 'A dark beauty who would grow up to dance magnificently.'

I turned away from Ramón. A thought was jabbing into my mind like a needle no matter how hard I tried to resist it. Mamie's journal entries to Margarida came back to me: *I do not want to reveal to her the one thing she doesn't need to know. If she found out, it would destroy her peace of mind for good . . .* I didn't know if I had the strength to bear my life being turned upside down yet again. But was there any choice?

I turned back to Ramón. 'If you know something, please tell me. Your sister is visiting me for a reason. I don't think it's because she wants something. I think it's because she wants to help me.'

'Yes,' he said, looking at his hands. He sounded gentler and less bitter. 'That's exactly what she would do.' He looked up at me again, his eyes misted with tears. 'After all, you are her granddaughter.'

THIRTY-FIVE

Celestina

Despite the care that Xavier and I had taken, I discovered in March 1936 that I was pregnant. After the doctor had confirmed my pregnancy, he assured me that under the new Republic abortion was legal.

'I can recommend a reputable clinic,' he said, which I assumed, even in those days of social equality, meant it catered for women of means. 'You're healthy. You'll recover quickly,' he promised me. 'You can go home again that night and no one need ever know.'

I returned to my hotel suite and sat for a long time staring out the window. How could this have happened? I had no mothering instincts at all; children had never interested me. There were other considerations too. Even though I was wealthy and famous, I had none of the power of the privileged classes. Senyor Montella and his wife tolerated me. Even Conchita, though she had words to say about me, had stopped protesting my existence. In her eyes I had saved her from more babies after she had produced an heir in Feliu. But if I were to start having children with Xavier at a time when laws about property were rapidly changing and even illegitimate children might have claims, they would turn against me. Then what would that mean for Xavier and me? It appeared that the doctor had been right: abortion was the only option available.

I got up from the window and paced the room. The idea of destroying something that was part of Xavier sent a shudder through me. My stomach churned with panic. No, I couldn't kill this child. What could I do? Go to France and give birth discreetly? Give the child to someone else to bring up?

Yes, that's much better, I thought, and calmed down a little. But then doubts assailed me again. Was that a life for a child? To be fed and clothed but never to have parents? I thought of my own childhood after my parents had died: I had been unhappy and alone.

Xavier was away on business in Switzerland, so I couldn't confide my troubles in him. Never in my life had I been so conflicted about what to do. Then one morning Evelina Montella came to pay me a visit. When the maid showed her in, I noticed that Evelina looked pale and shaken. I hadn't heard from her in a few months and I wondered what had happened.

'Please, sit down,' I said, inviting her to take a place on the sofa.

Even after my maid had left the room, Evelina didn't speak. She stared in front of her like a person who has suffered a shock.

'Evelina, what is it?'

'I lost it,' she said. 'I lost my child.'

She brought her hands to her face and sobbed hysterically.

Child? What child? At first I wasn't sure what she had meant and then the truth dawned on me. 'Evelina, are you saying that Francesc gave you a child and you miscarried?'

'It was Gaspar's child,' she replied, taking her hands from her face. 'We were together in January and I conceived his child. Like you said I should.'

What I was hearing sounded so uncharacteristic of Evelina that I was astonished. I hadn't *told* her to have an affair with

Gaspar. I'd simply suggested it could be a solution for her. And that conversation had taken place years earlier.

'I was pregnant to Gaspar but I lost the child,' Evelina repeated slowly. It was as if she was trying to get the facts of the matter clear in her own head. 'I felt its heart beat for a short time and then it stopped. A few days ago, everything gushed out of me including the tiny unformed baby in its sac. The doctor said there is something wrong with my uterus, that I will never be able to have a baby.'

Evelina began to sob again and I put my arm around her. I felt pity for her, remembering what she had said to me once: 'What I want more than anything else in the world is a child to love.' Was God playing some sort of joke on us? Why had I become pregnant against my will while a woman who desperately wanted a child had lost the one she was carrying?

Then it occurred to me that maybe God was not playing a joke at all. Maybe Evelina's problem was the solution to my own dilemma.

'Does Francesc know?' I asked her.

'About the baby, yes . . . Not about what happened. He is away.'

'But he was all right with accepting it? I mean, it does look much better for you to have a child than not—as long as people think it belongs to him.'

'Yes, he was all right with it,' she said, sadly.

'And nobody else knows that you lost the baby besides the doctor?'

Evelina shook her head. She was puzzled by my question. 'I didn't go to the Cerdà family's physician. I was too ashamed.'

I stood up and took a deep breath before speaking. 'Evelina . . . I think there is a way I can help you.'

Evelina didn't respond at first. She was too caught up in her grief. I sat down next to her and took her hand. 'This is probably the most unselfish thing I've ever done, but I want to do it for you,' I told her.

I watched Evelina's expression change from despair, to surprise, to pensiveness, then slowly to joy as I told her my plan.

'The baby won't be Gaspar's,' I said, 'but you will have a child to love. And one that shares your family's blood. And,' I added with a smile, 'who might even turn out to be a good dancer.'

Evelina grabbed my hands and kissed them. 'I now know what a true friend you are,' she said, her eyes brimming with tears. 'You are the answer to my prayers.'

She and I made our arrangement. Only Xavier and Evelina's mother were to know. Everyone else could be fooled if she padded herself convincingly and mimicked the symptoms. I would go to France when I began to show, and she could join me at the close of her supposed pregnancy. She could use the good reputation of French doctors as an excuse to give birth to her first child in Paris.

After Evelina left, I was stunned at what had taken place. How perfect, I thought. Evelina would be a beautiful, doting mother, and the child would be brought up in the midst of Xavier's family without anyone except Xavier and his mother being any the wiser. A sense of calm came to me: I had made the best decision for the life that had taken root in my womb. But when I undressed for my bath that evening and placed my hand on my stomach, a sense of loss swept over me; a feeling so profoundly sorrowful it was as if I had pledged not only the baby but my soul.

'I wish we could have kept the baby,' Xavier said when I told him. 'But you did the best possible thing in the circumstances, and my sister is blissfully happy.'

Most of the time I felt that way too. Evelina would be the perfect mother; I was simply carrying the baby for her. She feigned everything so well, from the dreamy look that came to her face whenever she rested her hands on her belly, to the fainting spells, which, ironically, I never experienced. But sometimes I felt angry in a way I hadn't expected. This child would be brought up in the Montella house, Xavier's house, but I would not be there. I would be on the outside. When I thought like that, I almost hated Evelina. I wanted to tell her, 'The baby is growing under *my* heart, not yours!' But most of the time, I numbed myself to all emotions. I had to accept things as they were. After all, this had been my choice.

I had always been slim, but the baby hardly showed under my flamenco skirts and loose dresses. No one seemed to suspect my pregnancy. I decided to take myself and my gypsy clan to Paris in the summer of 1936. They had grown to over forty adults and children now. Once there, I took a separate apartment, hoping to continue to keep my pregnancy hidden. Still, I wondered how I was going to absent myself for the birth.

Being so preoccupied with what was happening inside me, I hadn't paid much attention to what was going on in Spain, where dark and dangerous forces were at work. No sooner had my clan and I arrived in Paris than we heard that a military uprising had taken place in Spain. It was unbelievable to me. The mood in Barcelona had been festive when we'd left: the city was about to host an alternative Olympic Games to those to be staged by Hitler in Berlin. The city had taken on the air of a popular beach resort and had been crowded with athletes and foreign tourists. How could a military coup take place in such a holiday atmosphere?

I sent a telegram to Xavier but did not receive a reply. I didn't know then that the army had disrupted communications.

I read the French newspapers with trepidation and a sense of outrage. The coup had started in Morocco and spread to Spain in the form of garrison revolts. There had been some hesitation by the Republican government in arming the workers, but once they were given weapons, both men and women formed militias along with the loyal elements of the police and army. They managed to quell the revolts in industrial areas like Barcelona and Madrid, but Spain was not out of danger. The Republic had been weakened.

'Franco and his army had no right to attack the legitimate government of Spain!' I shouted, even though there was no one to hear me.

While the mainstream French newspapers preached the need to stay calm lest intervention on the part of France bring on a full-scale European war, French workers and students took to the streets. *If Fascism isn't stopped in Spain, it won't be long before the whole of Europe is burning,* read the pamphlets they handed out. Every day, volunteers from around the world arrived in Paris, preparing to go to Spain to fight for the Republic that had been the dream of my father, Anastasio and Teresa. I ached to think the Republic had been attacked, but I was in no condition to do anything to help now that the baby was kicking and moving.

Xavier was eventually able to send a telegram, but he arrived in Paris before it did.

'I'm here on a diplomatic mission to try to persuade the French to change their policy of non-intervention,' he told me. 'They are afraid to do anything without the British, who in turn are scared of provoking Hitler.'

When I listened to Xavier's stories of how the workers had fought the army in Barcelona and brought down the coup, I felt as if a flame ignited in me. I wanted to be there fighting with them.

That night as we lay together, Xavier rested his head on my stomach. 'It will be fine, won't it?' he asked me. 'We'll respect Evelina and Francesc in how they bring the child up . . . but it will be special knowing that it is a little bit of you and me.'

It comforted me that Xavier felt that way. I had never thought that I wanted a child, but as the baby moved inside me and became real, I found the idea of giving it away much harder.

'Listen,' said Xavier, 'I have some unpleasant news. I think you'd better send your clan to America. Through the committee I'm on, we've received intelligence that the Nazis have set up a central office "For the Suppression of the Gypsy Nuisance" in Berlin. They are passing new race laws by the day. The Romani people are being herded into work camps to make armaments. According to the reports, they are being forcibly sterilised there.'

'What?' I couldn't believe what I was hearing. 'But surely my clan is safe here in Paris. They can hardly be accused of being criminal vagabonds when they live in an apartment near place Vendôme.'

'There are Nazi supporters all over Europe, even here in France,' said Xavier. 'They'll be better off if they leave the continent altogether.'

It broke my heart to think of sending away the people who had been my family for the past twenty-seven years, but I sensed what Xavier had said was right. Paris had a liberal atmosphere in many ways, but it was true that there were plenty of right-wing extremists, and gypsies were always easy targets for racists.

I arranged for my clan's passage to New York, from where they would travel to California. It was windy the day that they set sail from Le Havre. Although they were travelling on the luxurious *Île de France,* the women were nervous about the trip. Gypsies have a terror of dying at sea.

'If the waves don't get us, the sharks will,' lamented Blanca.

Manuel's other sister Pastora, who was a great-grandmother now, wept openly.

'You'll be all right,' I assured her. 'It will be like when we travelled to South America on tour.'

'Yes, but you came with us then,' she said, wiping her face with the back of her hand. 'I'm more terrified that something bad is going to happen to you than to me. My dreams have been full of bad omens.'

Diego was nearly seventy now and he'd mellowed with age. Perhaps it also had something to do with the fact that, due to Xavier, I controlled my entire income now so he'd had to become more accommodating if he expected to be kept like a king.

'I hope we will see you soon, little *paya,*' he said, resting his hand on my shoulder. 'Keep safe, eat a bit less and dance a bit more: you are starting to put on weight.'

When I returned to my Paris apartment, I found a note from Xavier saying that he'd had to return urgently to Spain. So I was alone again, with only my memories and the baby inside me.

In late October, Evelina and her mother came to Paris to await the birth of the baby. I had organised a Spanish midwife for my time when it came. If I was going to suffer, I wanted to suffer in my heart language. I went into labour on 7 November, the day Franco's forces began their assault on Madrid. The pains were severe from the onset and didn't subside. Evelina and her mother arrived to give me support. The midwife, a woman with muscular arms and a downy moustache, shouted orders at me as if I were a cow she was trying to herd into a field. I pushed and strained to steer the baby through my narrow pelvic area. I had never imagined it was possible to endure such physical agony and not die.

Finally, in the early, quiet hours of the morning, when I didn't think I had any strength left, the baby emerged into the world.

'A girl!' Senyora Montella's eyes misted with tears when the midwife held the child up.

I glimpsed the baby's dusky skin and mop of black hair. I couldn't believe that she had come out of my body. The midwife bathed her and handed her to Evelina. My heart sank.

'I'm naming you after my maternal grandmother,' Evelina whispered to the child. 'Julieta.'

Now the agony of the birth had subsided, a different kind of pain gripped me. What had I done? How could I have given something that Xavier and I had created away? Only the happiness in Evelina's eyes gave me any comfort.

'Promise me,' I said, grasping Evelina's arm, 'that you will always let me see her. You will never keep her away from me?'

'Of course,' said Evelina, stroking my brow. 'You have given me the greatest gift. Julieta will be yours too, *secretly*.'

The following day, my breasts ached for Julieta. I offered to feed her, but senyora Montella had already organised a wet nurse.

'It will look better that way,' she said, picking up her handbag.

So the day after I had given birth to the child I had carried for nine months, she was taken away from me. After everyone had left, I was alone in the apartment. Even my maid was not there; I had sent her away before the birth.

A telegram arrived from Xavier saying that he would come as quickly as he could. But I was alone in a way I had never been before. My family were dead; my gypsy clan was on the other side of the world; my lover was married to someone else. I paced back and forth in the room. For the first time it struck me that without the noise and activity of people around me, my life was bleak and pointless. I stood by the window and stared out at the street, wringing my hands as tears flooded my eyes.

The new year arrived but brought no joy. Losing Julieta gave me an overpowering wish to die. Every time I walked past the Seine, I imagined filling the pockets of my winter coat with rocks and throwing myself into it. I had lost my urge to dance, and my heart bled for Spain. The news was bleaker every day. Málaga had been attacked by the rebels, who had committed horrific atrocities against the people. I watched Xavier and Margarida come and go from Paris on diplomatic and governmental business, trying to save the Republic.

What's the point of living if one's life has no purpose? I wondered. I knew I had to stop feeling sorry for myself. No more! If I wanted a purpose in life then I needed to do something useful.

'No, Celestina,' Xavier said when I told him that I wanted to drive ambulances, if not for the army then at least for the rear echelon troops. 'Do you know how dangerous that is? Franco does not differentiate between soldiers and civilians. Even if you are transporting injured women and children, the rebels will still bomb you.'

I took his hands. 'Why is it acceptable for others to risk their lives but not for me? Am I superior in some way?'

He rubbed his face. 'No . . . it's not that.'

'Then what?'

He shook his head and looked at me with tears in his eyes. 'I couldn't survive if something happened to you.'

I pressed my head to his chest. I felt the same way about him.

I remembered the joy of the people on the streets after the April 1931 elections, when the Republic was first declared. 'How did it ever come to this?' I whispered. 'How did this insanity ever get unleashed?'

When Xavier realised that he wouldn't be able to change my mind about serving in Spain, he organised for his French chauffeur to give me driving lessons.

'Is Mademoiselle thinking of competing in the Concours d'Elegance this year?' the chauffeur asked.

The Concours d'Elegance was a prestigious event where society ladies displayed their Bugattis and Rolls-Royces.

'No, I want you to train her more like someone preparing for the Grand Prix *and* the Monte Carlo Rally,' said Xavier. 'She needs to know how to drive fast in all conditions. Mademoiselle Sánchez wants to serve the Republic as an ambulance driver.'

The idea both amazed and impressed Xavier's chauffeur.

'I drove an ambulance in the Great War,' he confided during my first lesson. 'If you want to drive ambulances, you'll also need to know how to fix them.'

He gave me instruction on the parts of an engine and showed me how to empty and refill the radiator so it wouldn't crack in freezing temperatures overnight.

'And you have to learn to drive in the dark with the headlights off,' he told me. 'That's probably the most important thing you're going to need to know.'

Xavier bought a Ford truck and had it fitted out with stretchers.

'It's waiting for you in Perpignan, to drive across the border,' he told me. 'There is a pistol hidden in the box beneath the driver's seat. You can't imagine how difficult it is to get one in Spain, and you'll need it for self-protection. The bullets are under the bandages in the first-aid kit. The supply kit is stocked with iodine, soap, matches and cigarettes.'

'Cigarettes? But I don't smoke.'

'Cigarettes—real cigarettes—are useful for bartering in Anarchist-run villages where money has been abolished,' Xavier explained. 'Is there anything else from the volunteers' manual that you need?'

I shook my head. 'You always look after me so well,' I told him.

He grabbed my hand and pressed it to his cheek. 'One day, when things are better in Spain, I will devote my entire life to looking after you.'

My poor Xavier. How could he fulfil such a promise? He had too many other people who depended on him. He was the heir of an important family, and he couldn't divorce Conchita and bring shame on his son. I wouldn't have asked him to give me any more than he already had.

The next day, Evelina accompanied Xavier and me to the railway station. I was taking a train to Perpignan, from where I would collect my ambulance. I hoped that Evelina would have some news to tell me about Julieta: how she had grown; how she squealed with delight at bathtime; how she always reached for her favourite toy. Anything! I was desperate for anything. But Evelina said nothing.

Xavier's lips trembled when he kissed me. 'In all my life, there has only ever been you,' he said.

I embraced him and told him that it was the same way for me. Evelina turned to me and I squeezed her hand before I climbed into the train. 'Kiss Julieta for me,' I told her.

Evelina nodded but said nothing.

When the whistle sounded and the train began to pull out of the station, I leaned out of the window so I could wave to Xavier and Evelina again. Why was Evelina so reluctant to speak to me of Julieta? Has she fooled herself that the baby is actually hers? I wondered. Had she created in her mind a world in which she had carried Julieta for nine months in her womb and given birth to her? I was happy that Evelina was bringing Julieta up, but I could not forget that the child was the physical manifestation of my and Xavier's love.

When I arrived at the Barcelona barracks with my ambulance, I was already a seasoned driver. The journey over the Pyrenees had been a challenge and I saw why Xavier had made me do it. Keeping my attention focused on the road was difficult enough when I was travelling alone and not in immediate danger; what would it be like with passengers moaning and screaming in agony at every bump while enemy planes bore down on me?

The officer who signed me in kept glancing at me, on the verge of recognising me, but I'd been careful to dress as plainly as possible. I was constantly receiving requests from the military office to entertain the troops to keep up morale, but that wasn't what I wanted to do. I was finished with Hollywood-style extravaganzas and variety shows. If I danced anything in the future, it would be strictly *flamenco puro*.

'I've seen many British and American ladies arriving with converted cars and trucks, but you are the first Spanish woman to offer her services. How did you obtain the ambulance?' the officer asked me.

'I took a collection from the factory where I worked in France,' I told him. 'A fellow worker taught me to drive.'

He nodded. My fictional account of comradeship appealed to his communist sensibilities. 'Well, you've come at the right time,' he told me. 'We need ambulances more than ever.'

Franco was making another attempt to encircle Madrid by crossing the Jarama River and cutting off the city's communications with the new temporary seat of the Republican government in Valencia. The Republican troops, reinforced by the International Brigades, fought valiantly to prevent the Nationalists from succeeding in their aim. The casualties on both sides were severe. My first assignment was to ferry wounded soldiers from a field hospital to a convalescent hospital that had been set up in an abandoned monastery.

When I arrived at the convalescent hospital, I was greeted by British and New Zealand doctors and nurses, who were relieved to learn that I could speak what they called 'quite passable English'.

'Everything is in short supply,' the head surgeon, Doctor Parker, explained to me. 'I often have to work in unsterile situations and hope the patient makes it. On more than one occasion I've left a bullet or a piece of shrapnel where it is, believing that the patient's body will cope better with a foreign object than it will a case of septicaemia.'

I was shocked to learn that soap, the item most needed for basic cleanliness, was almost non-existent at the hospital. Doctor Parker and his team nearly fell to their knees and kissed my hands when I gave them my carton of *savons de Marseille*.

Initially my duties involved transporting convalescent soldiers and some civilians to hospitals further afield, to make room for the more severely wounded. But war in many ways was like a hurricane: the wind could change suddenly and destruction could come from any direction. One day I was driving back to the convalescent hospital with my ambulance loaded up with supplies. I also had two British nurses with me. The nurses were catching up on sleep when a noise like a thousand bees sounded in the distance. Seasoned by war, both women snapped to attention. One of them pressed her face to the window and looked at the sky.

'Ours?' her companion asked nervously.

The nurse answered with: 'Get out! Head for the embankment!'

I turned the engine off and ran after them, then slid down the side of the embankment on my haunches. There was a natural hollow that we could squeeze ourselves into for protection. I copied the way the nurses huddled themselves into a ball, covered their ears and opened their mouths to reduce the effects of concussion. The explosions rocked the ground and threw us against each other. For once, I had a full tank of petrol; I was terrified a bomb would hit the ambulance and it would explode. I hadn't expected the planes would fly so low. There were two of them. I could see the face of one pilot as his plane swept past us.

'Italians,' said one of the nurses. 'Lucky for us! They're bad shots.'

I stood up to see what had happened to my ambulance.

'Sit down!' the women shouted at me. 'They'll be back! There's nothing those bastards like better than a non-military target!'

Sure enough, the planes turned and came for us again. This time they opened fire, riddling the ambulance with bullets before disappearing into the distance. I stared in horror at the damage to my vehicle. What would have happened if I'd been travelling in the other direction with patients on board?

To my amazement, the ambulance was still in working order and the nurses and I could continue on our way. When we arrived at the convalescent hospital, dozens of vehicles were parked outside and orderlies were hurrying to and fro with stretchers. There had been another offensive.

The officer in charge sent me straight to the field hospital. 'Be careful,' he said, eyeing the bullet holes on the roof and side panels of my Ford. 'We've lost two ambulance drivers already.'

When I reached the field hospital, I reported for duty, then opened up the back of the ambulance, ready to receive patients designated for the convalescent hospital.

'We don't have any idea who's ready to go,' said a medical officer, ushering me into the hospital.

I was swept into the triage area, where a nurse handed me a pair of scissors and told me to cut off the uniforms of the wounded so the nurses could assess them and get them ready for surgery. Everybody on hand was brought in to help the nurses in this way, including the hospital's housekeeper and cook. All blood had to be mopped up quickly, lest it spread infection. Even worse, one of the surgeons could slip in it and break a much needed hand.

I found myself seeing up close what shrapnel and bullets could do to the human body. Some men's limbs and abdomens looked as if they had exploded from within. Many had been lying on the battlefield for several hours before the stretcher-bearers could get to them and their wounds were crawling with maggots. It terrified me to see how quickly gangrene could set in. There were other wounds—chest wounds, head wounds, severed spinal columns, massive burns. For years, the screams of the wounded and the smells of faeces, blood and infected flesh stayed with me.

'You're an ambulance driver?' one of the medical officers asked me. When I nodded, he waved me into the operating theatre.

Minutes later, I was carrying out legs, arms, hands and other body parts and throwing them onto a fire. There was no time to be shocked. No sooner had one group of men been treated than more ambulances were returning from the front.

We worked through until the evening. Then my ambulance was loaded up with men who could be transported that night. As we were about to leave, a Spanish medical officer performed a blood-pressure check on the wounded. One of the men was removed.

'He's dying,' the medical officer told me. 'I saw him in surgery. His stomach was slit open by shrapnel and all the intestines came out. The doctor squeezed them back into his abdominal cavity and sewed him up again.'

I looked at the young man on the stretcher. He had chiselled features and dark, broody eyes. I thought instantly of Anastasio.

This soldier was about the same age that my brother had been when he was shipped off to Morocco. I helped the medical officer carry him back inside to the now empty triage area. I could see from the colour of young soldier's skin that he was fading. I hated the thought of him dying alone. A priest had been with Anastasio when he died. I sat down next to the young man and took his hand.

'I don't regret for one moment going to fight,' he said. 'For once I was treated as something better than peasant dirt!'

'Is there anything I can do for you?' I asked him. 'Is there someone you want me to send a special message to?'

'I'd like to kiss a beautiful woman.'

Despite the circumstances, I laughed. 'I think all the beautiful women are busy right now. Will I do?'

'You're the most beautiful woman I've ever seen,' he said.

I leaned over and kissed his burning lips. 'Is there anything else you'd like?'

What a question to ask a twenty-year-old man, I thought. Perhaps he would like to have lived the next sixty years of his life, with a wife and a family and food on the table.

'Do you have a cigarette?' he asked me.

I reached into my pocket and took out one of the Gauloises Xavier had given me to use for bartering. I helped the man sit up so his head was resting in my lap, then I put the cigarette between his lips and lit it for him.

'Hmm, this is good,' he said. 'I would have been happy with the eucalyptus-smelling shit they've been giving us. But this . . . what is this?'

'It's a French cigarette,' I told him.

'Who would have thought,' the soldier said, half smiling, half wincing with pain, 'that one day I would be lying in the lap of a beautiful woman and smoking a French cigarette?'

A few minutes later, he died. The medical officer returned and we carried his body down to the washhouse where several other recently dead soldiers were lying. I was about to return to my ambulance when the officer touched my arm.

'They've run out of anaesthetic here,' he said. 'I heard that when a field hospital further up the line ran out of anaesthetic, the Spanish doctor there did the most humane thing he could for the dying. He had them taken outside and he put a bullet in their heads. Do you think he will be tried?'

'I hope not,' I said.

Before climbing into the driver's seat of my ambulance, I gave each of my passengers a cigarette. I smoked too as I drove, partly to stop the tears that were threatening to blind me, but also to get rid of the stench of blood and rotting flesh that seemed to have settled in my pores.

I had to drive through the night without headlights. We passed a village that had been bombed that day. It was close to midnight, but men and women were still digging frantically with whatever tools they had, or their bloodied hands, to get their families from under the rubble. They only had a partial moon and candlelight to guide them. Could anybody who had not witnessed anything like this ever understand? I wondered. I thought of Xavier, who was working without sleep to procure weapons and help for the Republic: even he had never seen what it was like so close to the battle.

I had received a letter from him a few days earlier, telling me that his family didn't fully understand the danger in Spain and that his mother and Evelina had returned to Barcelona a week after I had departed Paris. He asked me to take responsibility for them if the city was ever in danger and he was away. For now, the front was still far from Barcelona and I'd heard that the city was carrying on largely as normal. But things could change quickly. I thought of Julieta and winced. I'd have to somehow persuade Evelina to go back to Paris with her. But meanwhile, there was nothing I could do until I was given leave.

I arrived at the convalescent hospital as dawn was breaking. One of the patients had died on the journey, but Doctor Parker informed me that an ambulance had arrived earlier with all the patients dead, so mine was considered a successful journey.

'The driver hit a shell crater and that was it for the lot of them.' He glanced at my stomach. 'You're bleeding by the way.'

I looked down to see that my hip was covered in blood, my own blood.

'Let me treat the patients you've brought me,' said Doctor Parker. 'And then I'll take a look at you.'

I lay on the examination table and he prodded at my wound. 'It appears you caught a piece of stone,' he said. 'It's only started bleeding because you've been moving around.'

'We were bombed on our way to the field hospital. It must have happened then.'

'Often medical staff get injured and don't notice,' he said. 'It's the adrenaline.'

Despite heavy losses and the lack of equipment and supplies, the Republican army and the International Brigades held the Jarama Valley. Other places became of greater importance and the field and convalescent hospitals moved frequently. By June, Bilbao was taken and the proud Basque country fell to Franco's army. I was so overcome by the tragedy of the situation I danced a *seguiriya* in the courtyard of the convent we were now using as a hospital. It was the most solemn of the flamenco rhythms, and I used sharp, blunt movements of my feet to express my grief. Some Spanish patients noticed me and began to accompany me with *palmas*. Soon others joined in with them. I finished the dance in a fury of steps so wild that the wound in my side opened again.

Doctor Parker made a point of admonishing me while sewing me up again. 'La Rusa. Now I understand who you are,' he said. 'You are certainly a fine dancer, but I'd prefer you to keep your performances for our scheduled social occasions. It doesn't do well for the patients to get too excited.'

I smiled at Doctor Parker. I had come to admire him, and was grateful in my heart that he had left the comfort and safety of his practise in London to come and help us. But it amused me to think that there could be any such thing as 'too excited'. As long as the British thought that, they would never understand the Spanish.

One day in October, after Gijón and Avilés had fallen and the Republican government had moved to Barcelona, Doctor Parker came to me as I was repairing one of the tyres on my ambulance.

'Lift up your shirt and show me how that wound is going,' he said. He took one look at it and said, 'I want you to go back to Barcelona for some rest. If you keep lifting things, that's never going to get better.'

'Franco doesn't rest,' I told him. 'How can I?'

'Because if that wound doesn't heal properly, you won't be any good to anyone,' he said. 'You're one of the best drivers. We need you. But we need you in good health.'

So I took his advice and returned to Barcelona. I was angered to find that the revolutionary fervour that had characterised the city when the coup had first been repelled had faded. The government had taken back control from the workers, ordering the police to disarm them. There had been an explosion of street fighting in the city when the police were used to eject the workers' committee from Barcelona's Central Telephone exchange. Many of the Anarchist leaders were being arrested and accused of rebelling against the Republican state while it was at war.

The glaring differences between the wealthy and the poor had become obvious again too. The blockades had led to shortages in the stores, but if you had money you could buy what you wanted on the black market. There were no cigarettes, except the ersatz kind, to be found in Barcelona's shops. Although I hated the black market, I paid a wad of cash for a few cartons of Lucky Strikes. If a dying soldier requested a cigarette, I wanted to make sure I gave him a good one. I myself had become addicted to them: they kept away the stench of death, which seemed to remain on my skin no matter how much I scrubbed myself.

I had given Xavier's and my apartment over to a group of refugees from the south, so I booked myself into a hotel and, for the first time in a long time, soaked myself in a bath. I looked at the red-blue wound in my side and thought how many times I had come close to death. I closed my eyes and remembered the earrings that Francisca and I had buried when I was a child.

After my bath, I dressed in the new overalls I had bought for my work and made my way to the park by the beach. To my relief, the palm tree where we had buried the earrings was still standing, and when I dug into the sandy soil I found them easily. I washed them in the ocean, then put them in my ears, feeling the weight of them. The earrings had been in my family for generations; my mother had told me they were passed from mother to daughter. Whoever took them to the grave could return three times after death to help someone they loved.

But this supernatural crossing between the worlds could only occur for one woman, so it was obvious none of my fore-mothers had chosen to wear the earrings at the time of her death. I understood why. The idea of returning from the Other-world was something anyone with gypsy blood feared in case they could not go back and would be left to haunt this world forever. Only the most courageous woman would attempt it. As I faced death every day, I decided to wear them. Perhaps someone I loved would need me one day.

Xavier was away from Barcelona for a few days, so I called Evelina to see if she would meet me. I hoped she would bring Julieta, but was afraid to ask her. I longed to see the little girl, although I accepted more and more that she wasn't mine and that I had made the right decision in giving her to Evelina.

To my disappointment, Evelina came alone. She was wearing a navy flannel suit with wide lapels and a polka-dotted cravat. She looked so pretty and so untouched by the war that the sight of her made me feel tainted. To get rid of the feeling, I smoked more, despite the disapproval on her face.

I tried to convince her that her family should leave. She seemed concerned about the war, but didn't want to go anywhere without her parents. *If not for you or them, then for Julieta*, I wanted to scream.

Like most people in Barcelona, she seemed oblivious to the type of enemy we were facing. I wanted to tell her about the village I had been to where a German pilot had flown a captured Republican plane overhead and dropped leaflets. Thinking they were messages from the government, the people of the town, including the entire population of children, had run out of their houses to collect the papers. The plane had returned and machine-gunned the lot of them. But I knew if I told Evelina the story, she wouldn't believe me. If things ever became really dangerous, I promised myself, I'd drag the whole Montella family across the border if I had to.

A few nights later, I danced at the Samovar Club. I was supposed to be resting, but I was too haunted by the images of what I had seen. I enjoyed performing for the workers and soldiers much more than I ever had dancing for highbrow society. It took me back to the days when my clan and I had been real gypsies, living by our wits in the barri del Somorrostro and performing in flamenco bars.

Xavier brought along Evelina and Margarida, who had returned to Barcelona when the government relocated there. Having had to evacuate from both Madrid and Valencia, I'd expected Margarida would have had a better idea of the conditions of war. I was shocked when she asked me about the morale of the men on the frontline.

I eyed the little banquet of olives, pickled vegetables and fresh bread on the table: black-market goods. The sight of them filled me with outrage. I loved the Montella siblings, but I was sure they thought the rations a hardship. For some of the soldiers at the front, it was the best they had ever eaten in their lives. A soldier's ration was a feast compared with the starvation they had known as peasants. And now their hope of a social revolution was gone. What were they fighting for?

'How do you expect it to be?' I snapped. You've taken away their revolution. They were fighting for a better life. What should they fight for now? Franco or the Republic? Either one is just another form of capitalism. After the war, everything will be the same for them—the rich will be rich and the poor will starve.'

Margarida coloured with anger. 'It won't be that way,' she answered. 'Whether it's a revolution or reform, the Republic will be much better for the workers and the poor than Franco ever will be!'

I thought about the young soldier who had died in my arms and as I described him to the Montellas I wished I could fully explain to them the powerlessness and humiliation of being poor. But as well intentioned as they were they could never understand. They had only ever been rich.

Xavier took me back to my room at the hotel, making the excuse to his sisters that I was overtired. I followed him mechanically.

'Celestina,' he said, shutting the door behind us and taking me in his arms. 'Tell me what's going on. What are you thinking?'

I wanted to tell him about the horrors I had seen, to explain that the only thing that helped me face them was thinking about him . . . and Julieta. But I didn't. I couldn't say anything.

Xavier caressed my cheek then led me to the bedroom. We made passionate love that night. When he tried to withdraw, I wrapped my legs around his waist and wouldn't let him. The only thing that could comfort me about losing Julieta was to make another baby with him. But with the war and all the hardships it wrought on my body, it wasn't to be.

'Why are you crying?' Xavier asked me afterwards.

'All those men are going to die,' I told him. 'All those men fighting for the Republic are going to perish. And plenty of civilians too. It's true, isn't it? As much as you try, Xavier, you can't get us better weapons. You can't get the British, French and Americans to help us.'

He leaned over me and stared into my eyes. Every detail of him that night was etched in my memory: his skin that smelled like tea and vetiver; the warmth of his breath; the hard, muscular strength of his arm around my waist.

'Even if every one of us who believes in the Republic dies, somehow our spirits will live on,' he said. 'They will emerge somewhere in another generation . . . and it will be us, *our* spirits, spurring them on to create a better and fairer world. Everyone who lays down his or her life for the Republic does not do so in vain, Celestina. Not one of those lives will be wasted. No matter the sacrifices, no matter the appearance of defeat, it will all add to the progress of the human race. In my studies of history, there is one thing that repeats itself again and again and which gives me faith: All honourable causes eventually succeed even if at first they fail.'

Thirty-Six

Paloma

After Ramón had finished relating the story that la Rusa had told him, I fell into a kind of shock. La Rusa, not Mamie, was my grandmother? Yes, I could believe that la Rusa had given birth to my mother. The similarities were obvious. I remembered Mamie's description of la Rusa's dancing: powerful, hypnotic, majestic. They were the words the ballet critics had used to describe my mother. No one in the history of the Paris Opera Ballet had progressed as quickly from *quadrille* to *étoile* as Mama had. I was astounded. So many emotions and questions rushed at me, I didn't know how to face them. I loved Mamie deeply but I was her brother's granddaughter. I felt that I had lived the past eighteen years as one person, and now I discovered I was another. I didn't feel angry at Mamie, only confused. There was no doubt that she loved me fiercely—and that she had loved Mama in the same way. Had she been afraid that if she ever revealed the secret, she would have had to share Mama with la Rusa—or lose her altogether?

Considering that Mamie believed la Rusa was responsible for Xavier's death, I could understand why she had kept the facts

465

of my mother's birth from me. But was it ever possible to know what was truly in another person's heart, even someone we loved? I didn't know. All I knew was that there had been too many assumptions made about who did what and why; just as I had wrongly drawn conclusions about Papa and Audrey.

My heart pounded in my chest. '*All honourable causes eventually succeed even if at first they fail.* Did your sister request that you put that on her gravestone?' I asked Ramón.

'It was stated in her will.'

I realised that I had to review much of Mamie's story. What Ramón had told me explained many of the things that had mystified me. 'From what you are saying, it sounds as though la Rusa loved Xavier very much. I believe you when you say that she didn't betray him.'

Ramón studied me before taking a deep breath. He seemed relieved.

'Let me relate to you what happened in January 1939,' he said. 'And you will see how wrong Evelina Montella was for ever believing that of my sister.'

Thirty-Seven

Celestina

In October 1938, at the height of the Battle of Ebro, the League of Nations pressured Republican Spain to demobilise the International Brigades and repatriate them back to their home countries. The Republican government hoped that if it agreed, the League of Nations would also force Franco to dismiss the Italian and German troops fighting in Spain. But Franco had no intention of quitting.

Although Doctor Parker and his staff didn't want to leave, they had to obey orders or face losing their citizenships. I helped them with handing over the convalescent hospital to a group of anti-Fascist German and Italian doctors who couldn't return to their countries due to either the racial laws that were being passed by Hitler and Mussolini or because of their political beliefs.

The German surgeon who would be heading the hospital shook Doctor Parker's hand. 'This was the last "great cause",' he lamented. 'The last chance to fight for democracy in Europe. If the rest of the world understood what the Nazis intend to do, they would have been here too.'

The evening before Doctor Parker was due to leave, he came to see me. 'You should go too, la Rusa,' he said. 'The battle here is lost. You can do more for your country by becoming an international ambassador for Republican Spain. But first, get the people you love out of Barcelona.'

I gave my ambulance to the new staff to use and returned with the transport convoy to Barcelona. Xavier was there when I arrived. The family from the south who'd been staying in our apartment had left for America. From the balcony, we watched the farewell parade of the International Brigades. People threw flowers and blew kisses to the men and women who had come from all around the world to help us. I was grateful for all the International Brigades had tried to do, and to the many who had given their lives for the Republic, but my spirit felt like a dead weight in my body.

'It really is all over, isn't it?' I said, turning to Xavier. 'There is nothing more that we can do.'

Xavier's face hardened. 'There are certain Russians who believe the way to solve the Spanish problem is to assassinate Franco.' My eyes met his. I waited for him to continue. 'I've agreed to find means for their agents to infiltrate Spain and get close to him. I'm going to need you, Celestina, to carry intelligence reports for me into Paris.'

Xavier's determination to keep fighting had a powerful effect on me. While I had lost my faith in the idealism of the Spanish Republic, I cared about the fate of the Spanish people. The international press could argue the pros and cons of the Nationalists and Loyalists all they liked, but Franco was a brutal murderer. He needed to be stopped.

'Yes!' I told Xavier. 'I will do whatever is required.'

He embraced me. 'Good! You're the only one I trust; the only one with the required nerve.'

I knew what the stern expression on his face meant. The mission we were undertaking was precarious. But I did not allow myself to dwell on the risks nor on the horrific fate either of us could suffer if caught. I simply felt an ache in my heart at the idea that this might be the last day we would ever spend together. I pressed myself to Xavier's chest, holding him with all my strength.

'Whether the mission succeeds or fails, we will meet in Paris,' he said, kissing the top of my head.

'Yes.'

'But . . . if I don't make it to Paris,' he said quietly, 'please promise me that you will watch out for my family.'

I closed my eyes tightly to hold back the tears that threatened to come. But I wouldn't cry. I refused to believe that anything could go wrong.

'You'll make it to Paris,' I said. 'And there isn't anything I wouldn't do for you—or for your family.'

Because of the non-intervention embargos imposed on Spain by the allies, Xavier had to resort to negotiating with Barcelona's underworld bosses to traffic illegal weapons into Spain for the Republican army. It was a murky world and he hated being involved in it; he knew well that the men with whom he did business would as happily supply Franco at the right price. There was, however, a crime syndicate that seemed to be an exception to this rule. One of its members was a man known as el Garbanzo, the Chickpea, who had definite Loyalist leanings. It appeared that he also had a network of informers willing to help the Russian agents get close to Franco.

One of my first assignments was to make contact with el Garbanzo to obtain a list of Franco's aides whose loyalty could be bought. Through one of Xavier's agents, it was arranged that I would meet el Garbanzo at an address in the barri Xinès, the slum area of Barcelona where I had been born. It was unsettling to be walking those gloomy, narrow streets again. The overcrowded apartment buildings, some in ruins due to the bombings, and the rank smell of rotting garbage and rat droppings brought memories flooding back to me: Papá and Anastasio leaving at dawn for the factory; my mother slicing the bread thinly; Ramón and me playing make-believe in the streets.

The apartment where I was to meet el Garbanzo gave the appearance of never having received sunlight. The walls were water-stained and damp and the entrance smelled like a drain. Then a disquieting feeling came over me. I glanced up and down the street. The spice merchant had been replaced by a seedy-looking café, but this was the street and the apartment building where I had grown up. When I was a child, there had been no building next door—it had collapsed in some heavy rains—which was why I had failed to recognise where I was at first. When I stood before the apartment number I had been given, a sense that I was moving towards some kind of destiny prickled at me. I was the only person in the network who didn't use a false name; it was all too obvious who I was. Surely it couldn't be pure coincidence that this meeting had been set up in my childhood home.

I knocked on the door. It was answered by a gaunt-faced man with thin-rimmed glasses and the air of a funeral director about him.

'I'm here on el senyor Pinto's business,' I said. Senyor Pinto was Xavier's codename. Xavier and el Garbanzo had never met and never used their real names; they communicated through go-betweens.

The man beckoned me inside. The apartment had not been inhabited for a while judging from the layer of dust on the floor. Blending with the smells of decay and mould was the aroma of an expensive cigar. It was then I noticed a man wearing a three-piece suit sitting on an upturned crate and gazing out the window. From his beefy frame and puffy cheeks, I gathered he'd been given the name el Garbanzo because he was so round. Then our eyes met and a flash of recognition ran through me. When I blinked and he was still there, I gave a startled sob. Ramón!

I knew for certain that el Garbanzo was my brother even though thirty years had passed since we were parted. Gone was the bright look on his face, the way he had always observed the world with wonder. He had bags under his eyes and deep grooves around his mouth, and the puppy fat he had carried as a child had turned into a pot belly. Yet I recognised him as only siblings can: intuitively. It was as if I had summoned him out of my imagination. I had been thinking about my childhood and my brother had appeared.

At the sight of him, I forgot my original reason for coming to the apartment. I ran towards him and reached out my arms. To my horror, Ramón shoved me away. I stared at him, bewildered. Why had he called me here, to this apartment, if not to be reconciled with me?

Ramón's lips tightened. He put down his cigar. 'I didn't think you'd realise it was me,' he said.

'Where have you been?' I asked him. 'You promised to come back for me!'

He considered me a moment before speaking. 'I did return to find you. I risked my life to escape when the authorities came to take us away from Alcañiz after Teresa died. All I could think about was that I must get back to Barcelona and save my sister. But when I returned, I couldn't find her.'

'I was supposed to go to Juana,' I told him. 'But I had no idea where she lived—'

'Juana was arrested and exiled herself shortly after Teresa,' said Ramón, cutting me off.

My heart sank lower as Ramón described to me how he had searched every night in the barri Xinès, staring into the faces of the child prostitutes, terrified that one of those forsaken creatures could be me. He told me how he had worked for the drug criminals, talking his way into their circles while all the time looking in orphanages and workhouses. In the end, he began to believe that I may have been one of the victims of Enriqueta Martí, the woman who murdered street children and used their bones and fat to make youth-enhancing face creams for Barcelona's high society.

Ramón looked at me in such a pointed manner that at first I didn't know what to say.

'It wasn't on purpose that you couldn't find me,' I told him. 'I was with the gypsies. I danced in flamenco bars in the barri Xinès. How could God have been so cruel to let us pass like ships in the night?'

'A dancer?' repeated Ramón, with a sarcastic laugh that stabbed at my heart like a knife.

He told me that when he became older and had more power as a drug trafficker himself, he had called in people who owed him favours to trace what had happened to me. 'They found you and, as I feared, you had become a whore . . . only not a whore to sailors and perverted old men. You were the willing whore of *Xavier Montella*!'

I lowered my eyes and dug my nails into my hands. The word 'whore' burned into me. So this is the reason for his hatred, I thought. This was why, although he knew where I was, he had never made contact with me.

'You don't understand,' I told him. 'I love Xavier Montella. I'm not his whore.'

Ramón's eyes flashed with anger. 'I remember the Montellas, Celestina,' he said. 'I recall the way even their servants snubbed us. I keep forever in my mind the fact that Anastasio was sent to his death to defend their mines in Morocco, and that Leopold Montella said that such an injustice was simply the workings of the economic system. And . . . I can never erase the image of Papá being shot for protesting against that system. *I remember*, Celestina, even if you have chosen to forget!'

'I've not forgotten!' I cried.

My eyes filled with tears. In all the time I had hoped that Ramón and I should find each other again, I had never imagined it would be like this. The look of contempt on his face crushed me. I wanted to tell him that I had searched for him at Alcañiz, and that when I couldn't find him I had danced a *soleá* for him to express my sorrow. But I saw it would not do any good.

'Why, if all this time you have been shunning me, did you want to see me now?' I asked. 'You knew who was being sent to see you, obviously.'

Ramón didn't answer at first. He seemed to be studying me.

'And yet,' he said, 'your heart can't be completely black. According to my informers, you drove an ambulance for the Republican army. A woman in your position could have gone and lived in any city she wanted.'

'That is true,' I said. 'I have not forgotten as much as you think I have!'

For a moment, the hard look on Ramón's face softened. The expression that came to his eyes was the one I used to see when he brought me a piece of cake from the markets or lifted me up in his arms when I was a child. I wanted to embrace him again; to show him how much I still loved him. But then the severe look returned.

He reached into his pocket and handed me an envelope. 'It's only because of the respect I have for el senyor Pinto that I trust you with this list.'

I grabbed the envelope and fled the building. I ran through the maze of streets, desperate to find a place with sunlight. Finally, I came to a square with a fountain where enough sunlight came through the surrounding buildings to heat up the cobblestones. I stood there for a moment, absorbing the sun's warmth. The tears came. Ramón! My brother Ramón!

I remembered the way he used to charm the women at the flower market, his talent for persuading people. If we had not been poor, he might have become someone great rather than a criminal. I bore the truth of my brother's unsavoury profession much better than his rejection of me. The idea that Ramón, my childhood companion and protector, despised me hurt me the deepest.

I wiped the tears from my eyes. I have to go back, I thought. I have to make Ramón understand that Xavier Montella is a social reformer. The irony that the man Ramón was working with *was* Xavier Montella was too much for words. I looked back in the direction of the apartment. Would Ramón change his mind about the Montellas if I revealed senyor Pinto's true identity? But real names were not to be exposed under any circumstances. I had no choice but to keep Xavier's identity secret so as not to jeopardise the mission.

There was nothing I could do other than to let Ramón's barbs pierce where they had landed. Once again I had lost my brother, only this time I feared it was for good.

In November, the Ebro front collapsed. The Republican army of the north was defeated. As Franco began his march into Catalonia, it became increasingly difficult for me to carry out intelligence work. As each successive town fell, Nationalist supporters who had been clandestinely undermining the Republic came out openly. They turned on Republican soldiers and denounced Loyalist supporters. Barcelona, being a city with many places to hide, was full of this kind of treachery; and I had to be cautious as I was easily recognised.

It was also time to get Xavier's family out of Barcelona. Xavier was in Agullana near the border, from where he intended to help us safely across into France. On my last trip to France I was able to buy a van, but making my way back to Spain proved to be an arduous journey. The Germans were bombing the roads, and I was driving against a tide of refugees fleeing towards France in whatever type of transport they could find: buses, lorries, horse-drawn carts, bicycles.

The day I reached Barcelona is one that I will never forget. As I was driving past Vallcarca Hospital, I nearly hit a man in pyjamas. I looked to the entrance and saw patients staggering out of the building. Some appeared to be victims of the bombings, but many were clearly wounded soldiers. I saw amputees using their elbows to drag themselves along the ground because they were terrified of what would happen to them if they fell into the hands of Franco's army. They called out to people to help them but no one would stop. Of all the horrors I had seen in the war, the sight of those men disturbed me the most. These soldiers had given their youth and their limbs to defend the Republic and now they were being abandoned.

I had passed a Red Cross station on my way to Barcelona. I calculated how many men I could fit in my van and how much petrol I had left. I could take ten at a time and I had enough fuel. I helped aboard those least likely to get anywhere without a vehicle, and told the others, who would surely freeze in the cold, to go back inside and wait for me to return. Those men shouted at me that I was deserting them and rushed at my van, throwing themselves against the sides and windows. I had no choice but to press the accelerator and move forwards.

When I returned several hours later, some of the patients had waited for me while others had taken their chances. I doubted that any of those who had fled would have the strength to cross the Pyrenees, especially in winter. I prayed that someone else had taken pity on them and helped them, but from what I had seen of the behaviour of those fleeing Barcelona, I doubted that would be the case.

It took me a day to transport all the patients to the Red Cross station. When I returned to Barcelona, I parked the van near a building that had been bombed, covered it with blankets and threw rocks and dirt on top of it. I set off through the city, moving like an alley cat. The atmosphere was dark with fear. I passed several houses that were burning, with no one on guard to put the flames out.

I reached the Montella household about eleven in the evening. Evelina, pale-faced, opened the door.

'Only bring what you can carry,' I told her. 'The first part of our journey is on foot.'

Senyora Montella threw her arms around me when she saw me. 'Thank goodness you are here!' she said, kissing my cheeks. She welcomed me as warmly as one would a daughter.

Her real daughter-in-law, Conchita Montella, looked on with undisguised revulsion. It was the first time I had met her. Her features were beautiful—luminescent skin, round, dark eyes, arched eyebrows—but she was like a piece of ice. In all the years I had been with Xavier, he had hardly mentioned her. Now I saw the reason why. What would there be to say about her?

She was overdressed for our escape: in her flannel blazer, sweater, pleated skirt and a pair of fashionable Russian boots, she looked as if she was going for a drive in the countryside rather than taking part in an evacuation. From the way she regarded me, I sensed she intended to make things difficult. If that was the case, she'd be risking all our lives.

I told the women about the shameful scene I had witnessed at Vallcarca Hospital. Evelina and her mother looked upset, but Conchita said coldly: 'And the point of your story is?'

She had a kind of stupid madness about her. I understood why Margarida—always brazenly straightforward—didn't like her. I could also see that she was going to try to undermine my authority the whole trip. I needed to put an end to that plan immediately.

I pulled out my pistol and aimed it at her face. It gave me a jolt of pleasure to see her pupils dilate. I told her that I had shot two government officials who had tried to commandeer my van to transport themselves across the border. It wasn't true, but it had the desired effect: Conchita shut her mouth.

Evelina went to fetch the children.

When she returned with Julieta in her arms, the sight of the girl's mop of dark curls made my heart melt. I glimpsed her beautiful face above the scarf that Evelina was wrapping over her chin and cheeks. She had my dark colouring and Xavier's fine features. I knew I would do whatever I had to in order to get her to safety.

So that I wouldn't get distracted from that purpose, I didn't allow myself to look at Julieta again once we were out in the street, nor at Evelina who carried her in her arms, nor even at Feliu, who was the spitting image of his father.

The temperature of the air seemed to have dropped markedly in the past half hour. Vapour poured from our mouths when our breath met the icy air. Barcelona was silent except for the soft squeak of the wheels of the cart into which Evelina had packed supplies, and the click of Conchita's heels. Evelina and senyora Montella wore hiking boots, like I did. If we had to get out of the van and run from bombs, Conchita's boots would be a hindrance.

I was about to guide the women down a side street when I heard car engines starting up. A man jumped out of a doorway in front of us, yelling that we were under arrest. I reached for my pistol, but before I could fire, two men jumped on me from behind. I struggled as they wrestled me into a car. The last I saw of the Montella women and children, they were surrounded by police who were forcing them into the other car.

I was driven to a hotel, where the two men dragged me to a room on the second floor. The wine-coloured wallpaper gave everything a hellish hue. There was a man standing by the window. He turned and I was overcome by a sense of foreboding when I recognised him. It was Salazar.

The men pushed me into a chair and handcuffed my wrist to the armrest.

'You can go now,' Salazar said, dismissing them with the fascist salute.

His hate-filled eyes fixed on me. We stared at each other for a moment without speaking.

'You drove an ambulance for the Republican army,' he finally said, in a voice seething with anger. 'I think we can assume where your loyalty lies.'

He picked up a piece of paper from the desk and began reading out Franco's Law of Political Responsibilities: '*All those who actively or passively opposed the Nationalist Movement will be answerable for their actions.*' Salazar looked at me. 'The punishment for what you did is death.'

I knew what Salazar wanted from me. He wanted me to throw myself into his arms and beg for his protection. He wants me to suffer for rejecting him, I thought. Well, I can suffer, as long as Julieta and Evelina and the others are safe.

I was afraid that if I spoke, the abhorrence I felt for Salazar would come out in my voice. And if I wanted my child and my friend and her family to be unharmed, then I had to avoid antagonising him. But not speaking was my first mistake. Silence was as infuriating to Salazar as a bull that wouldn't charge.

'You have other unwise loyalties besides the Reds,' he sneered, circling the chair I was trapped in. 'Your lover, Xavier Montella, is plotting to kill the Caudillo.'

Against my will, I stiffened. Oh God, how had Xavier's mission been discovered?

Salazar laughed when he saw my reaction. His bloodlust was clear in his malicious face. I resigned myself to the idea that I would probably be tortured. I knew about such atrocities from being near the front. I had seen the body of a peasant who had been forced to lie in the shape of a cross while the Nationalist soldiers hacked off his limbs because he wouldn't give away the location of deserters. But I would bear any horror if it kept Xavier safe.

'I'm going to ask you to rethink your loyalties and tell me where Xavier Montella is,' said Salazar.

'I don't know.'

'You don't know? According to our sources, you carried intelligence for him.'

My mind raced for a way to deflect the attention away from Xavier and back towards me.

'No,' I said. 'I only promised to help his family.'

'You promised to help his family?'

Was it fear and exhaustion that had caused me to make such a foolish slip? I realised too late that I had made everything worse by drawing attention to the others.

'Xavier Montella loves his family, doesn't he?' Salazar said. 'His mother, his beloved sister and niece, his adored son, and his wife—well, he may not be as ardent about her as he is about his lover, but he respects her as the mother of his child.'

I felt like an animal trapped by a hunter. I did not fear death for myself; I had faced it many times, and I could have borne anything if the ones I loved were safe. But I saw from the interest on Salazar's face that instead of saving the people I loved, I was leading them to their demise.

'You see,' he whispered, 'you have a choice. If you tell us where Xavier Montella is, we will let his family go. If you don't, we'll kill them.'

'I don't know where he is,' I repeated.

'Yes, you do. And I will give you another choice. For each minute you delay, I will give the order for one of them to be shot. Starting with the little girl.'

'What?' The blood began to pulse in my ears. I couldn't breathe.

'You heard me.'

'Why are you doing this?' I asked. 'Because I loved Xavier and not you? Are you tormenting me for that?' I tried to stand up but I couldn't: I was still handcuffed to the chair.

'Perhaps,' Salazar said, shrugging his shoulders. 'But there are always plenty of bulls for the kill, and I told you: some creatures are born doomed. You should be grateful that I am giving you this choice.'

The nausea in my stomach made me feel faint. My mind stumbled over the word 'choice'. What choice? I loved Xavier with all my heart and soul. I loved my child and Evelina too.

'What do you want from me?' I screamed at Salazar. 'What do you want?'

'I want you to choose,' he said coldly. 'Tell me where Xavier Montella is and I will have his family released as soon as we've captured him.'

I barely heard what Salazar was saying. My mouth turned dry and I struggled to speak. 'If you release his family from prison, how do I know that you won't order them killed if they try to escape to France?'

Salazar grinned. 'You have no idea of the power that I hold over all your lives. You aligned yourself with the wrong people, la Rusa. For every day that you show yourself publicly being driven around in *my* car, dressed as *my* whore, I will grant your precious Montella women two days to make their escape.'

I couldn't think. My throat felt thick, as if I was choking. I wished Xavier was with me to tell me what to do.

Salazar reached for the telephone and began dialling to give the first execution order. Julieta! Little Julieta with her mop of dark curls! I saw Xavier resting his head on my pregnant stomach. *It will be special knowing it is a little bit of me and you.* The truth was I knew exactly what Xavier would have told me to do in this situation, but I couldn't bear to think of it. Xavier! Xavier! My heart cried out. He and I were doomed, but Julieta could live on.

'Give me el senyor Rovira, the supervisor,' Salazar said to the person on the line.

The room began to spin around me.

'Agullana!' I cried out. 'Xavier is in Agullana!'

It took them five days to find Xavier and bring him to Barcelona. During that time, I lived like someone whose soul had left her body. The woman that Salazar had conquered was not the magnificent, majestic flamenco dancer of the past. She was a ghost.

The night they shot Xavier, Salazar took me to see his corpse. The expression on Xavier's dead face was a contradiction of bewilderment and peace. I fell to my knees and kissed his cold lips. 'Forgive me, my darling,' I said with tenderness and remorse. A bitter sadness took hold of me. I threw my arms around Xavier's body. How could I go on without the man I loved?

'Kill me too,' I said to Salazar. 'Finish what you've started!'

Salazar pulled me away and I watched as Xavier's body was thrown on a truck with dozens of others to be buried in a mass grave. I knew then that a part of me was gone forever: something that could never be replaced.

As I was driven around Barcelona in Salazar's Bentley, dressed in furs and diamonds, I viewed the crumbling city with empty eyes. I saw piles of Catalan books being burned; the signs that hung in shops and offices banning the Catalan language. *No ladres: habla el idioma del imperio español. Don't bark: speak the language of the Spanish empire. Castilian.* Priests said Masses continually to 'cleanse the city of the sin of Bolshevism'. Over ten thousand Republicans were murdered in the first five days of the city's 'liberation'. Sporadically, fighting broke out as the bravest remnants of the Republican army continued to perform desperate rearguard actions such as blowing up bridges and important buildings.

I witnessed the mass executions of the captured anti-Fascist Italians and Germans who had fought on the side of the Spanish Republic. I heard rumours from the hotel staff that Republican pilots from the north were trying to reach Madrid, which was still resisting, and that some International Brigaders were also attempting to return. But the flicker of hope faded when Madrid fell and Britain, France and the United States recognised Franco as the legitimate leader of Spain. It was as if Xavier and all he had hoped for had been executed again.

I would have taken my life long before that, but for the hope that with every day I played Salazar's game, somehow I was giving Julieta, Feliu and Evelina another chance to live. Although, in truth, if they hadn't made it into France a few days after being released from prison, they were most likely dead.

Like most men who hunger for domination and destruction, Salazar turned out to be impotent. Our role of whore and master was entirely for show. Part of our charade was for me to appear dressed for dinner each night, which we ate in Salazar's hotel suite. One evening, he didn't answer my knock and I opened the door to find him splayed on the floor in a pool of blood. It seemed Salazar was not immune to old scores from his criminal past. He had been murdered the way a matador destroys a bull—with a sword through the shoulder blades and into the heart. His killer had also mutilated him in the same way a vanquished bull is mutilated after a fight: his ears and penis—in lieu of the bull's tail—were presented on a platter next to our supper.

I expected that I would be accused of the crime, and sat for a while in a chair, staring at the body. No doubt I would be slowly garrotted for my act.

But as time passed, my will, or perhaps the desire not to die at somebody else's hand, forced me to my feet. I walked to the wardrobe and put on one of Salazar's suits, flinching at the smell of hair oil and sweat that permeated the fabric. I added a hat, shoes with two pairs of socks, and a short overcoat. My disguise was so poorly assembled that I should have been stopped in the foyer, but no one noticed me when I walked past.

No one paid any attention to me on the street either; they were too absorbed in the Nationalist soldiers' victory parades or in looting the houses of those who had fled. I walked on-wards as if protected by some angelic force that had made me invisible.

When I reached the outskirts of the city, I found my van where I had left it. I brushed off the rubble and pulled away the blankets. To my amazement, the engine started. I filled the tank with the jerry can of petrol I had saved for our escape, pumped up the tyres and drove out of Barcelona. I expected at any turn to be stopped by a patrol, but there were no barriers to my escape. I was skilled at driving at night without lights and I had become an expert at dodging bombers. I kept driving until I reached the border. The French had closed it, unable to cope with the thousands of refugees who had fled to their country. It was guarded by Senegalese battalions armed with machine guns. But I was a ghost and ghosts can go where they please. I left my van at the border and slipped across into the moun-tains undetected.

I managed to make contact with el Ruso, who had remained in Paris after retiring from show business. He spoke to a government contact in Perpignan who in turn sent his official car to collect me. I was given a change of clothes, and was relieved to burn Salazar's suit, but not before I emptied the pockets and carefully poured the soil I had collected in the mountains into a handkerchief. The soil of Spain was all I had left of my home.

THIRTY-EIGHT

Paloma

When he'd finished his story, Ramón stared at his hands for a long time before speaking again.

'I too fled to Paris after the Republic collapsed, but Celestina didn't stay in the city long. She was shunned by the Spanish émigré community, who, thanks to Evelina Montella, believed that she had betrayed Xavier and had worked as a spy for the Nationalists. All sorts of people accused my sister of denouncing their relatives. Even some of the patients she had rescued from Vallcarca Hospital turned on her, convinced that she must have used them as a cover in some way.

'My sister tried many times to contact Evelina Montella to explain what had happened, but in the end she saw it was easier for everybody if she left France for the United States. You see, Celestina believed that she had caused Xavier Montella's death and she loathed herself for it, even though she had revealed his whereabouts in order to save his family and their child.

'It was only in Paris that I learned that el senyor Pinto and Xavier Montella were the same man; and that my sister had loved one of the greatest heroes of the Republican cause.'

'The benefits of hindsight,' I said sympathetically. 'I've learned a lot about that myself lately.'

Ramón looked at me sympathetically. 'You're lucky you've learned that lesson so young,' he said. 'Self-righteousness is the greatest squanderer of time . . . time you will never get back.'

His words gave me an insight into a deep sense of regret that was belied by Ramón's loud clothes and flashy apartment.

'What did your sister do in the United States?' I asked him.

'She danced in flamenco bars and gave private lessons to movie stars. She made herself into a new person—but she kept to herself and lived alone. She never saw her gypsy clan again, although she set up a trust fund for them. She wrote to me prolifically, which enabled me to piece together what had happened during the years we were separated. I hated myself for being so stupidly stubborn. She was still my sister and I had always loved her, but I'd let my pride cloud my judgement about her.'

'Yes, I know that mistake too,' I told him.

'In one letter she mentioned that she was experiencing pain in her lower abdomen. *A wound I received in the war playing up*, she wrote. After that, I didn't hear from her for months. Then one night she turned up on my doorstep. "I've come back to Paris," she announced. Her eyes had retained their hypnotic beauty and she still held herself proudly, like a dancer, but her legendary energy was no longer there. I knew straight away that something was wrong. She told me that the pain in her side wasn't an old war wound at all; it was caused by the kidney disease she had contracted due to the deprivations she had suffered as a child. Kidney disease was common among the gypsies and the poor of Barcelona.'

My heart pinched. La Rusa must have been the most misunderstood woman in the world.

'"The doctors can't help me," Celestina told me matter-of-factly. "So I've come to a city where I was once happy in order to die."

'The money Xavier had moved to a Paris bank account for her had all gone into the trust fund for her clan, but she was under the impression that she still had millions of dollars. In truth, all her funds in Spanish banks had been seized. There was only her apartment in Paris left. So I let her believe she was still a rich woman while I took care of the bills.'

Ramón sucked in a breath. The antagonism he had initially shown towards me had dissipated. I knew he was telling me what was in his heart.

'My sister did not bother anyone in the Spanish émigré community. Thirteen years had passed since the end of the war; those who saw her in the street either no longer recognised her or decided to ignore her. She did not attempt to contact Evelina Montella again either, but she had one dying wish . . . She showed me an article from a dance magazine about the ballerina Julieta Olivero, her daughter. She was one of the youngest students ever to be accepted as a *quadrille* in the Paris Opera Ballet.'

Ramón's face turned dark as a painful memory came back to him. 'Although she was weak, Celestina dressed beautifully for the opening of *Swan Lake* in a satin ball gown with a tulle scarf over her hair. "You look like an Indian princess," I told her as I led her to the box I had chosen especially to stay out of sight of Evelina and her husband Gaspar, whom I knew would be there. What a delight it was to see the glow on Celestina's face as she watched her daughter dance. She almost became young and well again before my eyes. After the performance, my sister seemed at peace. "Now I've seen her, I can die without sadness," she told me. "I was right to try to save her. Xavier would have been so proud. She is beautiful."

'In the foyer, as we were leaving, Celestina caught sight of Evelina and Gaspar. Julieta came out to greet them. Celestina hesitated, and for a moment it seemed to me that she wanted to approach them. But then her face clouded and she turned to me with tears in her eyes. "Come on, Ramón," she said. "Let's go."

'When Celestina began to seriously deteriorate, I moved her from her apartment to mine, and brought all her clothes and furniture with her so that she would be surrounded by things she had once loved. The disease and pain made her mind fragile. With nothing ahead of her but suffering that morphia would not be able to completely deaden, she decided to take her life so as not to be a burden to me.' Ramón shook his head and covered his eyes. 'The stupid thing is . . . she seemed much better that week. She didn't show any signs of pain. I didn't realise she was rallying her strength to end her life.

'On the day she had decided to leave this world, I woke to find that she had prepared for me an elegant breakfast of croissants, fruit and coffee on her finest china. She hadn't been well enough to do anything like that in a while. "I wish I'd had a lifetime to spoil you, dear brother, as you used to spoil me," she told me. "But these last few months have been the most wonderful of my life. Don't worry about anything; everything has been taken care of."

'I thought that she was talking about the fortune she thought she had in the bank and willed to me after her death. I had no inkling she was referring to her decision to die that day. I left her with kisses and a promise to cook her *paella* that evening. But when I returned to the apartment, it was dark and she wasn't in her room. Then two policemen arrived to tell me about the "accident". But it wasn't an accident, of course . . . She chose a method she knew there would be no coming back from—no stomach pumping, no resuscitation. And a spot where the trains travel too quickly for even the alertest driver to stop.'

Ramón fell quiet. Then he placed his hand to his face and began to cry. It was terrible to watch his bitter tears. I wanted to cry with him, but I couldn't. I had to explain that he'd been as wrong about Mamie as he'd once been about his sister. He'd judged her too quickly.

'Ramón,' I said, 'Mamie didn't know. *She didn't know*. She truly believed that Celestina had denounced Xavier maliciously. Why didn't you tell her—even after your sister's death? Why didn't you settle the record then? Mamie would have been devastated that she had falsely accused your sister, but at least she wouldn't have gone through her life cursing the woman who had once been her friend, who had loved her brother, who had . . . borne her child.'

Ramón looked at me with red-rimmed eyes. 'I was angry and full of hate,' he said. 'Yes, I could have told Evelina Montella the truth, but I wanted revenge.'

I shook my head. 'Why was it revenge *not* to tell her? Imagine how she would have felt to know that the woman she had accused of murder had actually saved her life? And the life of her family?'

Ramón sat back and closed his eyes. 'It was because of what I had learned after Celestina's death from a former Spanish criminal that made me decide to keep it a secret.'

I waited for Ramón to explain. Then he uttered something that rattled me completely.

'I thought it a fitting revenge that the person who had really betrayed Xavier . . . was the woman Evelina Montella sheltered under her roof.'

I paced the courtyard for some time before I found the courage to knock on Conchita's door. I wasn't sure if I could go through with this conversation. But I decided that responsibility didn't diminish with age, especially when I considered the enormity of what Conchita had done to my family.

When Ramón had explained Conchita's betrayal, my initial urge was to go straight to Mamie to tell her the truth about her 'delicate' sister-in-law. But once my anger and excitement wore off, I knew that Mamie was too fragile to cope with such a revelation. Her heart was still weak, and the shock of the truth could be fatal. I had to protect Mamie at all costs.

Conchita must have sensed a change in my manner towards her. After she had invited me inside, she kept glancing at the photographs of her deceased second husband and twins, as if to warn me that she was frail and had experienced a terrible tragedy.

There was so much that was unknown about this woman. She had pushed Xavier away so they wouldn't have more children, but she had borne twins to another man. Why? To keep his love? Who knew? When I studied her, I no longer saw an eccentric old lady but the woman Margarida had described: 'A black hole . . . a drama queen who wants attention and wants everyone to be responsible for her.' This woman, whom I had always felt sorry for, had betrayed Mamie, deceived her and then used her!

'Feliu came to visit Mamie at the hospital after her surgery,' I said.

Conchita shrugged as if the news was of no consequence to her, but her face stiffened. 'He never loved me, that child. He never responded to me. Not like the twins . . .' She turned towards the photographs of her dead children and wiped a tear from her eyes.

I wasn't going to let her use that piece of manipulation on me again.

'Does he avoid contact with you because he knows that you, not la Rusa, betrayed his father?'

Ramón had explained to me that when it seemed certain that the Republic was going to lose the war in Spain, Conchita had attempted to make contact with her father through his friends in the Falange. She had hoped for a reconciliation with her family if she shunned the Montellas.

Conchita's eyes flashed at me. 'I don't know what you are talking about!' she said. 'From whom did you hear such lies? You have wounded me deeply by believing them!'

'You offered information you had overheard about Xavier's intelligence work to the Nationalists in order to get back on side with your father,' I said. 'You knew the night that la Rusa came to collect you all that you were going to be arrested. You had telephoned your father's friend, Salazar. That's why you didn't bother dressing properly for an evacuation. You and Feliu weren't even put in prison.'

Conchita cast me a look of contempt, but I knew what I was saying was correct. I could see it in her eyes.

'Salazar was grateful for your information, but your father still didn't want you back,' I went on. 'That terrified you. Not only were you a traitor to the Republic and the Montellas with no place to go, but you were also a potential target of Nationalist extremists because you were Xavier Montella's widow. Salazar could protect you against official prosecution but not against individual vendettas. You had no choice but to cling to Mamie to save you. You had already arranged with Salazar to let you escape to France. He had his own reasons for convincing la Rusa that she had betrayed Xavier, but the truth was that the information she gave made no difference to Xavier's fate—that had already been sealed by you!'

Conchita's mouth pinched into a narrow line. I thought she was going to deny my accusations, but to my surprise she stood up and shouted at me.

'So what if I did, you prissy little ballerina? How dare you sit there with your serious face and point the finger at me! What would you know about war? What would you know about survival? You know nothing!'

She walked over to the pictures of her children and second husband and placed them face down before turning back to me. It was an odd gesture: as if she didn't want them to hear what she was about to say.

'The Montellas ruined my life!' she continued. 'Do you think Xavier Montella was the only man who wanted to marry me? I was the greatest beauty in Barcelona. My parents arranged our marriage thinking I would have a privileged existence for the rest of my life. Well, that was Xavier's first deception. I despised him for his foolish talk about equality and a better life for the masses. What about *my* life? What about *my* birthright?'

I stared at her in disbelief. Everything Margarida had said about her was true. She was beautiful on the surface, but a black hole inside. And she had sucked everyone into her vortex.

'You'll never know what a great family the Montellas were . . . their wealth, their standing in society,' Conchita continued. 'Xavier threw all that away as if it were nothing. He was the family's heir! He had responsibilities. I was a fool to have married him. The Montellas brought shame on me—their stupid liberal ideas ruined my life. It's only right that Evelina Montella should have made it up to me. She *should* be responsible for taking care of me!'

When she saw that I was too lost for words to respond, Conchita sat down. 'All that happened long ago,' she said with a wave of her hand. 'It no longer concerns me.'

It shocked me even more that she felt no remorse for what she had done. Xavier had been Feliu's father! And for the first time I understood how she truly saw Mamie—not as her friend, not as her sister-in-law, but as her servant. Poor Mamie. I could never tell her what Conchita had done . . . how could Mamie ever reconcile herself to that? Ramón had been right: this was the most terrible revenge of all.

'So,' said Conchita, folding her hands in her lap, 'I suppose you intend to tell Evelina now and have me thrown out.'

I shook my head. 'I'm not going to tell her—for her sake, not for yours. But I won't let you suck her into your little tricks any more. You can pay your own way from now on. As far as I'm concerned you are no longer a part of this family.'

She sniffed and stared out the window.

I left, wishing that Ramón had never revealed the truth about Conchita. I was now her unwilling collaborator in the most vile of secrets.

THIRTY-NINE

Paloma

I didn't wake up the following morning until ten o'clock. Mamie was moving around the kitchen; I could hear her opening and shutting cupboards and talking to Diaghilev. I closed my eyes again for a moment and tried to take in my new identity: the granddaughter of the world's most famous flamenco artist. Was it possible that I had dreamed the whole thing? That Ramón Sánchez had never existed to tell me such a fantastic story? Overcome by everything I had discovered since yesterday—that Mamie wasn't my blood grandmother, that she had been wrong about la Rusa's betrayal and had been deceived for years by Conchita—I wept quietly. I was sorry for la Rusa, for Xavier and Ramón—and for Mamie too.

'Paloma, don't you have to practise today?' Mamie called from the kitchen.

I couldn't stay in bed all day unless I wanted to end up with muscle cramps. But I didn't want to face Mamie either. Knowing what I did now, I was frightened that the bond between us might have been severed.

I came to myself and wiped my eyes. I tore a brush through my hair and put on my dressing gown.

Mamie beamed at me when I entered the kitchen. 'Look at what I found,' she said, holding up a red cloth-covered scrapbook. At first I thought she had discovered something from her days in Barcelona but then I recognised the swirly patterns on the fabric. It was my scrapbook from when I was a child.

'Do you remember?' Mamie asked, her eyes shining as she turned the pages. 'You and I made this together when your parents were touring America. You were four years old. It was a special time for me. I had you all to myself.'

I looked over Mamie's shoulder at the pictures of fairies, ballerinas, birds and rainbows. The scrapbook was a collection of my childhood whimsies and dreams. I forgot my earlier doubts as we pored over the drawings and pictures.

'Look,' I said, pointing to a photograph of a cat lying on a cushion. 'There's your old cat, Tigre.' Some of the writing in the scrapbook had faded and a few of the drawings had bled, but I remembered those weeks when Mamie and I had been together as special to me too. 'It was raining,' I said. 'That's why we had to do something inside.'

I saw a photograph of Mamie and me sitting in a *bateau mouche*, one of the tourist boats on the Seine. It must have been Mama who had taken the picture. I'd pasted it in my scrapbook and written in huge letters above it: *Me and Mamie*.

Tears filled my eyes and I feigned a cough. I rushed to the sink to pour myself a glass of water. But you're not my real grandmother, I thought. So much of what we have lived has been a lie! I wondered if Mamie would have let la Rusa see Julieta if she hadn't thought her responsible for Xavier's death. Did she ever intend to tell Mama who her real mother was? Only Mamie could answer that question, and it was something I could never ask her.

Mamie held up another page for me to see. It was a drawing of my mother in a pink tutu.

'You were a talented artist,' she said. 'Even at that age you managed to capture Julieta's large eyes and expression. You got that gift from your grandfather.'

Avi! My beloved grandfather wasn't mine any more either. I wondered if he ever suspected the truth about whose child Julieta was when she grew into a dusky beauty. Even I recognised la Rusa now in Mama's exotic looks. But who was Mamie thinking of when she said 'grandfather'—Xavier or Avi? Or had they become one in her mind?

The emotional roller coaster was getting too much for me. I was about to make an excuse to leave the kitchen when Mamie opened the scrapbook to a page where I had glued the tickets for the first ballet we had seen together: a matinee session of *Cinderella*.

I watched the delighted expression on Mamie's face as she savoured the memory, and saw something that I had not noticed before. I saw myself through Mamie's eyes: how much she loved me; how precious I was to her. She was the woman who had been there for both the good and the difficult times. Whatever I thought she might have done differently, I realised that she had done her best. And when I thought of how people like Conchita had behaved, I could see that Mamie had acted much more honourably than most. It was futile blaming her for a set of circumstances that was not her fault.

I looked at the scrapbook with Mamie for a while longer. The glimpses of my four-year-old self were both beautiful and sad. Over the page there was a drawing of me, my mother and Mamie holding hands. Papa was standing in the background. Even as I child, I'd sensed their distance, I thought. I'd simply forgotten it.

'Mamie,' I said, 'I need to repair my relationship with Papa.'

'I know. I told you that you should.'

I held her gaze. Perhaps Mamie had known all along that it was Mama who'd had the affair. Perhaps it had been easier to collude with me in blaming Papa so that we could both go on believing that Mama had been perfect. Maybe Mamie's heart attack had made her realise that I might need my father one day. I sighed. My family was nothing like Jaime's, where everybody told each other everything, and nobody could keep a secret. Mamie and I certainly had our secrets. I couldn't tell her that I knew la Rusa was my blood grandmother or that I knew she wrote letters to her dead sister. But I realised that all it really meant was that we were more complicated than most people; and if we kept secrets it was to protect each other.

I put my arms around Mamie. As soon as I felt the warmth of her body I knew that everything was all right. She was still my Mamie and always would be.

'I love you, Mamie,' I told her and kissed her cheek.

I drove to Carmen's apartment to fill Jaime in on what had happened after he'd left the cemetery. Ernesto was in the living room, listening to the radio quiz program *1000 francs par jour* and shouting out the answers to the questions. Everyone else was at work. Jaime and I sat on the floor of the studio. When I told him everything Ramón had related to me, he looked shocked.

'You didn't say a word of this when you called me last night,' he said. 'You just sounded tired.'

'I had trouble making sense of it all myself.'

He reached out and brushed my cheek with his hand. 'Promise me that we won't have secrets from each other?'

'I promise,' I told him.

I unclasped the bat pendant from around my neck and handed it back to him. 'I think I've seen through enough illusions for a while,' I said.

'I think you have too,' he agreed, putting his arm around me and giving me a hug.

We both fell silent, contemplating the revelations the past day had brought.

'No kissing!' Ernesto's voice suddenly boomed from the living room.

Jaime and I both jumped with surprise at the outburst. Then we looked at each other and laughed.

'We weren't kissing!' Jaime shouted back.

'Well, I'm warning you,' said Ernesto. 'It's too quiet in there.'

Jaime cocked his eyebrow at me. 'Do you want to swap a family with secrets for a crazy one?'

I shook my head. 'No,' I said. 'I want both.'

Before heading home, I drove to avenue de l'Observatoire to see my father. I wandered around the jardin du Luxembourg for a while, gathering up courage. I remembered what Mamie had said about Conchita's relationship with Feliu: 'There are some things about the past that can never be fixed.' Was it too late to repair the relationship with my father?

I sat down on a bench and watched the people strolling past. A slim woman walking a dog caught my eye. She was wearing a rust-coloured jumpsuit with slingback shoes. Her stride was confident and she looked chic. Then I realised it was Audrey I was admiring! How differently you see a person when you no longer despise them, I thought.

'Audrey?' I called.

She turned around and took off her sunglasses. She was an attractive woman, I had to admit. She had captivating green eyes.

'Are you heading home?' I asked her.

I glanced down at the dog. I would have imagined Audrey owning a pedigree poodle or a Bichon Frisé, but this dog was a mutt. A very cute mutt with enormous brown eyes and a shaggy caramel-coloured coat, but a mutt nonetheless.

'Yes, I am going back to the apartment,' she said.

I sensed she was wary of me. I couldn't blame her.

'Is it all right for me to see Papa?'

I realised how our roles had changed. It used to be Audrey accosting me on the street. I bent down and patted the dog to hide my embarrassment. He smelled like green apple shampoo. He might have been a mutt but he was a pampered one.

'You are always welcome to see your father,' Audrey replied. 'But I don't want to be the messenger for either of you any more, is that understood? Whatever you need to sort out, you sort it out between yourselves.'

I straightened up. 'I'm sorry I treated you the way I did. I didn't understand.'

Audrey was taken aback by my apology, but then she shrugged. 'You are young, you were upset . . . it happens.'

I nodded, humbled by her graciousness. As we walked to the apartment she asked about my first performance with the Ballet and when rehearsals began.

'I have another month's break and then we'll be rehearsing for *Swan Lake*,' I told her. 'It was the first ballet my mother performed in too.'

The concierge opened the door for us.

'Come on, Pelé!' Audrey called to her dog when he strained at his leash to greet an Afghan hound passing by with its owner. I smiled to myself. *Pelé*? Audrey had named her dog after the famous Brazilian soccer player. There was so much about my stepmother that surprised me.

As we climbed the stairs to the apartment, Audrey said, 'We didn't get to celebrate your father's birthday with you. I was thinking that you and your grandmother might like to come on a holiday with us to Saint-Tropez before you start with the Ballet? Pierre will come too.'

'And Pelé?' I asked, bending down to give the dog another pat. I'd always wanted a dog.

'Of course,' she said, smiling.

Audrey told me that Papa was practising in his studio on the next floor up. 'I'll see you later,' she said, kissing my cheeks and then leading Pelé into the apartment. She gave me a wave before she shut the door.

Papa was playing 'El Corpus Christi en Sevilla' by Isaac Albéniz. It was the piece of music that he had given me on the cassette. I felt a twinge of pain when I remembered how abominably I had responded to his attempts to reach me. The piece was so evocative of Spain it was almost as if Papa had known that I needed to come to terms with that part of myself.

I waited until he had finished playing before slipping through the door into his studio. He turned when he heard me. I was struck by how much he looked like his old self in this room. His hair was shorter, of course, but that was the only real change. The cosy space was a reflection of him with its simple polished floor and lopsided bookshelves sagging under the weight of hundreds of novels and music scores. A black-and-white photograph of a ballerina above the mantelpiece caught my eye. I realised it was a picture of me performing an arabesque, taken a couple of years ago. I thought of the picture I had drawn of my family in the scrapbook: me holding hands with Mama and Mamie, and Papa standing apart. I didn't want it to be like that any more.

Another framed photograph of me caught my eye. I was four or five years old and standing in front of the clocktower of the Gare de Lyon.

My father turned to where I was looking. 'You used to be so happy to see me when I came back from touring,' he said. 'Your mother and grandmother had to hold on to you so you wouldn't tumble over in your excitement to embrace me.'

'I'm still happy to see you, Papa,' I told him. 'I've just been very confused.'

He studied me a moment before moving over on his piano stool and making a space for me to sit next to him.

'I'm sorry for the way I treated you,' I told him, sitting down. 'I've missed you.'

Papa put his arm around me. 'I never was very good with words, Paloma,' he said. 'It's why I became a musician. I've been thinking a lot since our last conversation. I really did have the best intentions . . . but I went about everything the wrong way. The last person I ever wanted to hurt was you.'

It felt good to be close to my father again. His warm grasp was comforting, especially in the aftermath of all I had learned yesterday. It was ironic that while everyone else in my life seemed to have changed, Papa was still who he had always been.

'Audrey is busy with meetings next week and Pierre has examinations,' he said. 'I was thinking you might like to come to Vienna with me . . . if you are free?'

I remembered the trip we had made there together when I was seven, getting around the city in an old Volkswagen and eating *sachertorte* in elegant cafés.

'I wouldn't miss it for anything,' I told him.

My father smiled at me and rubbed my arm. I smiled too . . . and then we both laughed. And just like with Mamie, I sensed the bond between us had been restored.

When the curtain rose for the second act of *Swan Lake* and I and the other dancers of the *corps de ballet* pranced into the silver-blue light of the Paris Opera's stage, I experienced the most magical moment of my life. Tchaikovsky's beautiful music swelled around us as we configured and reconfigured our swan maiden formations, using our wrists, elbows, arms and shoulders to convey the graceful sweep of wings. The *corps de ballet* of the Paris Opera was the most famous in the world for its precision—every arm, leg, and head had to be positioned exactly so as to create a sense of perfect unison.

When Odette—danced by the beautiful and lyrical Dominique Khalfouni—rushed onto the stage to beseech Prince Siegfried and his hunting companions not to harm the swans, I was deeply moved. There was so much in the story I could relate to everything I had heard from Mamie, Feliu and Ramón about what had happened in Spain. In the same way the swan maidens' fates were tied to the love story of Odette and Prince Siegfried, I felt that my life and my identity were inextricably linked to what had happened in the past. In the final act, when Siegfried told Odette of how he had been tricked by the evil Odile and her father, and the lovers ended their lives so they could be united in death, I saw a parallel with the tragic stories of Xavier and la Rusa.

The opening night of *Swan Lake* was special to me in another way too: I was making my mark as a unique dancer. Mademoiselle Louvet had told Arielle Marineau about my flamenco studies. Having transformed from my detractor into my champion, Mademoiselle Marineau had in turn spoken to Raymond Franchetti, who recommended that I rehearse for the part of the Spanish dancer in the ballroom scene. My mother had been younger than me when she was accepted into the *corps de ballet*, but this was a 'first' all of my own. The part usually went to a more senior dancer; in being cast for it, I was being showcased as a possible future *étoile* with the company. I may have only been half-Spanish, but I used every ounce of Andalusian blood in my veins to bring the ballet-flamenco dance to life. I performed my swooping backbends and soft *zapateados* while imagining that la Rusa was out there in the audience, watching me with the same pride she had once felt for Mama.

After the performance, I ran to the foyer to meet my family and friends. Mamie was there with Micheline. Jaime rushed towards me, grinning proudly from ear to ear. Carmen and the rest of the family were there too, along with Gaby and Marcel. But it was when I saw Papa, Audrey and Pierre that I felt most elated. Papa and I had enjoyed ourselves in Vienna together. Along with Mamie, I felt like I had a family again.

'Thank you for coming,' I told my father. 'It means a lot to me.'

Papa smiled. 'I wouldn't have missed it for anything.'

I should have been exhausted by physical exertion and overexcitement after the opening night of *Swan Lake*. Instead, I lay in bed wide awake for most of the night. About four o'clock in the morning, I was struck by an urgent desire to dance. I climbed out of bed and slipped on my leotard and leg warmers. When I opened my dresser drawer for my hairpins and headband, I noticed the Russian box in the corner. I lifted it out and examined the golden earrings again. I ran my finger around their smooth loops: I still didn't fully understand their significance. I took them with me to the studio.

For most of my life I had risen early to practise, but dancing this long before dawn was a record even for me. I turned on the lights of the studio and placed the earrings on a window ledge. As I began my warm-up stretches, I contemplated how much my life had changed. I used to be so alone. Now I had a wonderful boyfriend, who had also brought into the picture his lively Spanish family. I was reconciled with my father, and had gathered along the way a stepmother and stepbrother as well as a couple more pets. Although it was difficult for me to adjust to the knowledge that Mamie wasn't my true grandmother, hearing her history and understanding her faults and strengths had made me love her more deeply. I was now a member of one of the best ballet companies in the world, and I was becoming an accomplished flamenco dancer. I smiled when I thought about how far I'd progressed from being a perfectionist loner to someone described as 'charismatic'!

That day when I had first encountered la Rusa, I'd had no idea who she was. Now I understood the vital role she had played in my heritage. Ramón had said that the possessor of the golden earrings who dared to take them to the Otherworld could return to a loved one three times. La Rusa, my grandmother, had come to steer me in the direction of a bigger and happier life.

I wondered why she had given the golden earrings to me instead of my mother. Perhaps she had thought my mother was strong like her, and that I needed her more. As this thought went through my mind, I perceived a change in the atmosphere. Something like the tingle of an electric current passed over my skin. I knew that when I turned around, la Rusa would be there.

This time, when I contemplated her dignified face, I didn't feel afraid. I thought of what had happened to her: the injustices and tragedies she had suffered. The very idea of them made my heart heavy.

'I'm so sorry,' I told her. 'I'm sorry for everything you suffered. You deserved better.'

La Rusa tilted her head slightly and stared at me.

She can't hear me now, I thought. In whatever dimension she exists in, she can't hear my voice. I decided I would communicate with her in a way I knew she would understand.

I began with *palmas*, clapping out a rhythm for a *soleá*, the dance of loneliness, solitude and estrangement. I had felt all those things after Mama's death, but how much more had la Rusa experienced them! With the marking of my feet, the rhythmic movement of my arms and my melancholy turns, I tried to express to her my sorrow and sympathy. She had known the extremes of life: abject poverty and vast wealth; great love and great loss. She had been gravely misunderstood and falsely accused by those she had loved and for whom she had made so many sacrifices. I used my *escobilla*, my rhythmic footwork, to show her how much my heart ached for her. She was my blood grandmother and I had never known her.

I performed a slow turn, but when I came face to face with la Rusa again she sent me a mocking smile. I was confused when she performed a *llamada* of her own, lifting her leg, turning and then throwing down her arm proudly before clapping out another rhythm. She was making a call to commence an entirely different flamenco rhythm. I recognised it immediately: an *alegrías*—the dance of joy.

My puzzlement turned to amazement when I witnessed the fire and passion that burst from la Rusa's slight frame. She was elegant and proud with a defiant spark in her eyes. Then I understood: la Rusa was not going to allow anyone to feel sorry for her. She was telling me that she had made her choices and she stood by them.

My pity was replaced by admiration. La Rusa was every bit the extraordinary dancer that Mamie had described. She was precise, wild, intense and flirtatious all at the same time. She danced playfully and touched her arms to her chest before extending them to me, inviting me to join her. I matched the rhythm of her *zapateados* and was soon lost in our dance of celebration. Waves of happiness rushed between us, and I felt the power of her celebrated energy.

She brought the dance to a sudden stop, before gracefully placing her hands on her hips and lifting her chin proudly. It was then I noticed she was wearing the golden earrings.

'*Olé!*' she said, and vanished.

I stood where I was for a few minutes, catching my breath and realising that I had experienced what was most likely my last encounter with la Rusa's ghost. She didn't want me to think of her with sorrow but with joy. I remembered the inscription she had requested for her tombstone: *All honourable causes eventually succeed even if at first they fail.* Ramón had told me that la Rusa had wanted to honour Xavier, who had taught her that the spirits of good people, even if they die in defeat, return in future generations to continue moving the human race forwards to higher and better things. I thought of la Rusa and Xavier, Avi, Margarida and my great-grandparents—how all of their spirits lived on in me.

Perhaps that was the message of the golden earrings: out of darkness and suffering can come hope, joy and progress.

I went to the window ledge and saw that the earrings had gone. The circle was now complete.

I placed my hand where the earrings had been. 'Thank you,' I said, looking around me. A gentle warmth brushed my skin. I sensed that while la Rusa and the earrings had disappeared, her love would always remain.

'Thank you,' I said again.

The studio was still and silent, but I knew that my gratitude had been heard.

AUTHOR'S NOTE

The causes and effects of the Spanish Civil War are complex. *Golden Earrings*, as a work of fiction, does not attempt to explain all aspects of the war from all perspectives. Readers who would like to know more about the Spanish Civil War might enjoy starting with Helen Graham's *The Spanish Civil War: A Very Short Introduction* and proceed to further reading from there.

The Paris Opera Ballet is considered one of the finest companies in the world. In the examination scene I use the names of the real-life director of the ballet school in 1976, Claude Bessy, and the director of dance, Raymond Franchetti, to create a sense of time and place. However, Arielle Marineau is a fictional character created for dramatic purposes and is not based on any actual person associated with the ballet or its school at any time.

Likewise, while Sir Arthur Conan Doyle and Helena Petrovna Blavatsky are historical figures who wrote about the supernatural, the 'contemporary French psychic' mentioned in this story, Mireille Fourest, is fictional.

AUTHOR'S NOTE

Golden Earrings is set partly in Barcelona, which is situated in the region of Catalonia. The area has its own language and character. Catalans largely think of their region as separate to the rest of Spain and to discourage this tendency to separatism the use of the Catalan language in public life, as well as other cultural markers, have been banned by dominating powers at various times in history. The two instances mentioned in this book are the period of Miguel Primo de Rivera's dictatorship (1923–1930) and during the rule of Francisco Franco (1939–1975). I have used both Catalan and Spanish phrases and terms in the novel, depending on the background of the character who is speaking, to give the novel a sense of place and a certain atmosphere true to the country overall as well as this unique region. In order not to confuse readers unfamiliar with Spanish or Catalan, I've taken some liberties with the use of punctuation; for example, *Hola!* instead of *¡Hola!* I've also used capitals for words such as Pare, Mama and Avi when they are used as character's names.

A brief guide to the Spanish and Catalan honorifics is given below:

don	*don*
doña	*donya*
señor	*senyor*
señora	*senyora*
señorita	*senyoreta*

A SPECIAL NOTE
TO MY READERS

I would like to take this opportunity at the end of my fifth novel to say a special thank you to my readers. It is thinking of you all and your enjoyment of a good story that keeps me at my desk, day after day, determined to give the very best of myself to each book.

Thank you so much for the letters and cards that you send me. I keep every one, and when I find myself stuck, exhausted or discouraged in some way, I often take a letter or two out and re-read them to get me moving again.

The relationship between author and reader is a special one. While I use my words to create characters and plots, my readers use their own imaginations and life experiences to re-create my original intentions in their own unique ways. This means there are as many versions of *Golden Earrings* as there are readers. I truly enjoy this sense of collaboration.

It is always a pleasure to hear from you, so please feel free to write to me if you wish:

C/O HarperCollins Publishers Australia
PO Box A565
Sydney NSW 2000

With love and gratitude,
Belinda Alexandra

ACKNOWLEDGMENTS

Although it is my name—'Belinda Alexandra'—on the cover of my books, I sometimes think that should read 'Belinda Alexandra & Company' because there are so many wonderful people behind the scenes who work very hard to make each book the best it can be.

I would like to start by thanking my energetic and passionate literary agent, Selwa Anthony, who championed *Golden Earrings* from the beginning and gave me invaluable feedback during the writing process.

I would also like to thank the team at HarperCollins Publishers Australia for their enthusiasm for *Golden Earrings* and all they do to support me. In particular I would like to thank my wonderful publishers, Anna Valdinger and Sue Brockhoff, along with Amanda O'Connell, Jane Finemore, and the dynamic sales and marketing team.

I was privileged again to have Nicola O'Shea as the editor for this book. Her sympathetic and insightful style always makes working with her a great pleasure. Thank you also to my proofreaders, Kate O'Donnell and Chrysoula Georgopoulos.

ACKNOWLEDGMENTS

I'd also like to extend my gratitude to the experts and scholars who kindly gave me their time and shared their specialist knowledge to help me with the research for the novel: Marina Vidal, who checked the use of Spanish and Catalan and gave me advice on culture issues; Doctor Francisco J. Romero Salvadó of the University of Bristol and Professor Sebastian Balfour of the London School of Economics and Political Science for helping me with historical details regarding the Spanish Civil War; Nathalie Meier who kindly wrote correspondence for me in French and helped with cultural questions; and Kari Hanet who shared some wonderful anecdotes and other details about life in Paris in the 1970s.

I was touched by the enthusiastic help I received from the dance world while researching this book. In particular I would like to thank: Laurie Lubeck-Yeames and her mother, Nicole Alderguer, for the invaluable feedback they gave me on the ballet scenarios; Elizabeth Platel, the director of the School of the Paris Opera Ballet for her information on how the school and examinations were run in the 1970s; Lisa Howell and Catherine Jenneke for putting me in contact with various ballet specialists; and to Kate Sirvins for helping me with ballet terms. I would also like to thank Lucy Vernon for her feedback on the flamenco dance scenes.

Special thanks also goes to Pauline O'Kane of Ku-ring-gai library for the help she gave in organising my interlibrary loans (of which there were nearly 50 for this book) and her cheerful willingness to track down even the most obscure titles.

Finally, but not least I would like to thank my friends, family and animals for keeping me sane and grounded. Thank you in particular to my treasured husband, Mauro, for his patience with the long hours it took to write a book set in two countries with three different languages, two time periods and three main characters. I'd also like to thank my wonderful father, Stan, for the practical help he gave me in collecting and returning library books on my behalf so I wouldn't have to leave my desk!

The energy and good will of all the above mentioned people made writing *Golden Earrings* a pleasure I will always remember.

GOLDEN EARRINGS

BELINDA ALEXANDRA

INTRODUCTION

Paloma Batton led a relatively normal life before encountering her first ghost. A dedicated ballet dancer and aspiring member of the *corps de ballet* of the Paris Opera, Paloma lived with her grandmother in France and practiced her craft fiercely and meticulously. But when La Rusa, a famous flamenco dancer from Barcelona, appears to her with a pair of golden hoop earrings, Paloma's reality shifts as she begins to explore the roots of her Spanish heritage and discovers who her ghost is—and what it's trying to tell her. Author Belinda Alexandra tells Paloma's story in *Golden Earrings* using the voices of two extraordinary women growing up in Spain during the Spanish Civil War, and how their lives wracked with loss and passion eventually intertwine.

QUESTIONS AND TOPICS FOR DISCUSSION

1. How would you characterize the landscape of Spain in the early 1900s? How does it differ from Paris in the 1970s? In what ways do their differences color the stories of the narrators?

2. What are your initial suspicions as to why Evelina (Mamie) refuses to discuss her Spanish past with Paloma?

3. Paloma deeply resents her father for his affair with another woman while her mother was ill and dying. What details might she not know about her parents' marriage? Can you think of other explanations to the circumstances?

4. Evelina and Celestina experience their worlds very differently, despite living in the same city in the same period. How do poverty and wealth impact the girls' day-to-day lives? What knowledge or experiences are they isolated from in their respective situations?

5. Author Belinda Alexandra employs the theme of rebellion in *Golden Earrings* both as a literal and figurative story-telling device. How are they used most powerfully? Which character is most defined by his or her rebellion?

6. Describe Conchita. What does her dress and behavior tell you about her character? How does she seem to fit in with the Montella family and lifestyle?

7. In chapter 24, Celestina compares her father's death to a bull dying in a matador fight, meaning both of them were destined to lose no matter what. What else does this metaphor represent within the context of the entire story?

How did each of the main characters overcome or succumb to their respective destinies?

8. Do you think Celestina needed the tragedies in her life to happen in order to be able to dance as well as she did? Are certain experiences required to develop passion, or can a person simply be born with it?

9. Despite their upbringing, Xavier and Margarida believe in and fight for equality among classes. What kind of experiences may have influenced their altruistic personalities? Do you think good or bad can exist in people regardless of upbringing?

10. How were Paloma's and Evelina's perceived betrayals similar? How would Evelina's life been different if she had known the truth about La Rusa and Conchita?

11. Knowing the purpose for why La Rusa visited Paloma beyond the grave, why do you think her ghost appeared to Paloma during that time of her life? Why not years before, or years later?

12. Why do you think Evelina never tells Julieta or Paloma about their real mother/heritage? Do you think there were reasons beyond her shame and anger toward La Rusa?

13. In *Golden Earrings*, infidelity is never exactly as it seems to those on the outside. When have you made assumptions about a person or persons and been wrong? Is it better to always give people the benefit of the doubt?

14. Do you agree with the inscription on La Rusa's tombstone, "All honorable causes eventually succeed even if at first they fail"? Why or why not? If La Rusa's family hadn't

suffered such tragic deaths for fighting for their beliefs, what honorable causes do you think she would have fought for?

15. If you had been faced with the choice La Rusa was forced to make with Salazar, what would you have done? What do you think La Rusa's life would have been like if she had chosen to protect Xavier?

16. Belinda Alexandra uses first-person narration from three perspectives to tell her story. How is this better (or worse) than third-person omniscient? How different would your experience have been with the characters within a different narrative style?

ENHANCE YOUR BOOK CLUB

1. In *Golden Earrings*, dancing is both a form of expression and a carefully honed art. How does your reading group contribute to or participate in the fine arts? Have members bring a drawing, a short story, ticket stubs to an opera, or even a dance routine to your next book club meeting. Take turns discussing how those interests bloomed and how family or familial traditions influenced them.

2. Ramon and Celestina judged the entire Montella family based on the actions of a few. Can you think of a time when someone made assumptions about you based on your last name or who you were related to? Try describing yourself through a stranger's eyes who's meeting you for the first time, and has only ever known your parents or your siblings. What beliefs might they have about your character or personality? How would they be wrong . . . and how would they be right?

3. Evelina writes letters to her sister Margarida for years and years after her death—either as a way to cope or to express her grief. Write a letter to a passed relative or friend. What would you tell him or her about your life? What would you want him or her to know?

4. Organize a ballet or theater night with your book club— bonus points if you can get tickets to flamenco!

5. Do you have a *duende*, or demon? What would it look like, and how would you express it? Sketch or describe your demon on a piece of paper and take turns comparing and contrasting your *duende* with La Rusa's.